In the past three years, New York Times ~~~~~ ~~~~ ~~~~ ~~nor **Sherrilyn** ~~~~~ ~~~ ~~~~~~~ the ~ ~~~~~~~~~ seventeen times. This ~~~~~~~~~~~ ~~~ ~~~~ continues to top every genre she writes. With more than 25 million copies of her books in print in over one hundred countries, her current series include: The Dark-Hunters, The League, Chronicles of Nick, and Belador. Since 2004, she has placed more than sixty novels on the *New York Times* list in all formats including manga. The preeminent voice in paranormal fiction, with more than twenty years of publishing credits in all genres, Kenyon not only helped to pioneer, but define the current paranormal trend that has captivated the world.

Visit Sherrilyn Kenyon's websites:
www.darkhunter.com | www.sherrilynkenyon.co.uk

www.facebook.com/AuthorSherrilynKenyon | www.twitter.com/
KenyonSherrilyn

Praise for Sherrilyn Kenyon:

'A publishing phenomenon... [Sherrilyn Kenyon] is the reigning queen of the wildly successful paranormal scene'
Publishers Weekly

'Kenyon's writing is brisk, ironic and relentlessly imaginative. These are not your mother's vampire novels'
Boston Globe

'Whether writing as Sherrilyn Kenyon or Kinley MacGregor, this author delivers great romantic fantasy!'
New York Times bestselling author Elizabeth Lowell

Born of silence

SHERRILYN KENYON

piatkus

PIATKUS

First published in the US in 2012 by Grand Central Publishing,
a division of Hachette Book Group, Inc
First published in Great Britain as a paperback original in 2012 by Piatkus

A CIP catalogue record for this book
is available from the British Library.

ISBN 978-0-7499-5493-2

Printed and bound by CPI Group (UK) Ltd, Croydon, CR0 4YY

Papers used by Piatkus are from well-managed forests
and other responsible sources.

MIX
Paper from
responsible sources
FSC
www.fsc.org   FSC® C104740

Piatkus
An imprint of
Little, Brown Book Group
100 Victoria Embankment
London EC4Y 0DY

An Hachette UK Company
www.hachette.co.uk

www.piatkus.co.uk

For my friends who keep me sane in the midst of utter insanity, and to all of those intrepid warriors who don't live their lives by the standards of others. Those fearless souls who know the price of independent thought and individuality, and who are willing to pay it. Vive la différence!

For those who have walked through the fires of hell and rather than fall to its flames, have emerged battered, but victorious. In the immortal words of Ovid: Quin nunc quoque frigidus artus, dum loquor, horror habet, parsque est meminisse doloris—Even now while I tell it, cold horror envelops me and my pains return the minute I think of it. We can never escape the pain of our pasts, or the flashbacks that assault us when we dare to let our thoughts drift unattended, but we can choose to not let it ruin the future we, alone, can build for ourselves.

And for those who are currently trapped in a bad situation. May you find the resolute strength it takes to free yourself, and to finally see the beauty that lives inside you. You are resplendent, and you deserve respect and love. Don't let the minions of hatred or cruelty define you, or steal away your own humanity. When our compassion and ability to love and appreciate others go, then our bullies and opressors have truly won, for it is not they who are harmed, but rather we who lose our souls and hearts to the same miserable bitterness that caused them to lash out against us. The cycle can be broken—it must be broken, even though the path is never easy or without cost. Yet victory is made sweeter when you know it came from within you, without violent retribution. The best revenge is to leave them mired in their hateful misery while you learn to bask in the warmth of self-esteem and happiness. Never forget that broken wings can and do heal in time, and that those scarred wings can carry the eagle to the top of the highest mountain.

Most of all, for my wonderful boys who have filled me with more love than I ever imagined possible. You are the greatest gift I have ever known. And for my husband who dared to fight my demons with me and prove to me that there really are people out there who can find the lotus even when it's drowning in mud. Thank you for being the man I only thought existed in fairytales and dreams. I love you all! May the best day in your past be the worst day in your future.

Born of silence

"You have got to be the biggest manwhore in the entire universe. What are you trying to do? Tie Caillen for the record on how many people you can sleep with in a single month? And just so you know, his is twenty-two."

Maris Sulle, Darling's oldest and dearest friend, laughed at his dry tone. "You're only jealous *you* didn't get the waiter's digies."

Leaning back in his ornately padded chair, Darling snorted in response. He swirled the wine in his crystal glass while they finished eating lunch in one of the most exclusive restaurants in Perona—the capital city of the southern part of the Caronese Empire where Darling's family had ruthlessly ruled for more than three thousand years.

After the brutal suck-ass morning he'd already had, he really wanted something much stronger than this weak shit to drink, but his public persona kept him from ordering the hard liquor he craved.

He could only drink that whenever he was alone. Even then, he had to be careful no one found out lest they discover who and what he really was.

"I thought you were still involved with…" Darling paused as

he mentally sorted through the lengthy roll of men his best friend had been with over the last year. "I can't even remember his name now."

"Gregor?"

Darling shook his head as he finally recalled the last boy-friend's name, and it wasn't Gregor. He'd fear senility had already set in, but it was more he had a lot of other things on his mind. Besides, no one could keep up with Maris's ever revolving list of boy toys. "I'm behind apparently. The last one I remember was named Destin."

"Drustan," Maris corrected. "And yes, you are. You really should try to keep up. That was a good two months ago, and I've had three since then." He looked down at the number on his mobile and smiled as he stored it. "Soon to be four."

"Does Gregor know he's being replaced?"

"Oh don't get me started on that repulsive ape. I caught him in flagrante delicto with his personal secretary. His secretary... really? If you're going to be such a slut, the least you could do is not be a common, clichéd one. Right?"

Darling laughed, then took a deep drink of wine before he spoke again. "I'll keep that in mind for future reference. The last thing I'd ever want to be accused of is being a clichéd slut."

"Oh please. You're such a monk. I'm not even sure you've lost your virginity." With a deep, horrified expression, Maris looked up from his mobile and slapped his hand over his mouth as he realized what he'd said and the land mine of pain he'd unintentionally exploded all over Darling. "I'm so incredibly sorry, Dar. That was so insensitive of me. I didn't mean it. Gah, I can't believe I said that to *you*, of all people. I wasn't thinking, sweetie. You know I would *never*, ever hurt you. Not for anything... You can punch me if it'll make you feel better." He clenched his eyes shut and tensed, waiting to be hit.

It took Darling several more seconds before he could club the monster from his past back into the closet, slam the door on it, and then speak over the surge of barbed emotions that gutted him.

"It's all right, Mari," he said finally, his voice deceptively calm as he stroked the crystal decanter on the table. "I know you didn't mean anything by it."

Still, that didn't stop it from cutting all the way to the marrow of his bones.

Darling set the glass on the table and wished he could rip some of his memories straight out of his brain. Most pathetic part? As horrifying as *that* had been, it wasn't at the top of the list of things he'd kill to forget.

Opening his eyes, Maris reached out and covered Darling's hand with his own. "You're the strongest person I've ever known. You know that, right?"

Strange, he didn't feel that way. Most days he felt even more battered inside than he was outside. And here lately those feelings of rage and resentment, of unrelenting hatred and vengeance, were forcing him into a place of darkness he wasn't sure he could come back from.

Before Darling could stop himself, he pulled away from Maris's touch and brushed his hand over the latest bruise on his cheek. Luckily the long hair he wore covering the left side of his face concealed it and the deep, rancid scar no amount of plastic surgery could get rid of.

Another pugnacious memory he could do without, and a perpetual reminder that he really was in this world alone. Friends were friends, but at the end of the day, they all went home. Not even Maris could be with him 24/7. And though he might have tiny slices of freedom for a while, sooner or later, Arturo got nervous and had him hauled back to hell.

His mobile alarm chimed.

That's what you get for thinking about the bastard. Nothing like summoning the dybbuk up from his stygian hole.

Maris scowled. "What's that for?"

Darling cut the alarm off, then slid his mobile back into his pocket. "My uncle's activated my chip." A lovely nano tracking device that was so microscopic it couldn't be located, removed, or jammed. But the one thing Arturo hadn't counted on was Darling's ingenuity in writing a program that would intercept his uncle's access to the chip. "I set the alarm to notify me whenever he sends his goons out to drag me home." A constant in his life that always firebombed his temper.

How the hell could he still be deemed a minor when he was twenty-eight years old?

Only by something as backward as Caronese law...

A law originally designed to protect his people from the reign of an immature monarch. Instead, it'd proven to be a prison sentence that had hung around his neck like a perpetual noose.

And honestly, he was getting really sick of all this shit. Kere, his Sentella alter ego, wanted blood. Any day now, he expected that darkest part of himself to take over, forget all consequences, and lash out against the world. May the gods help whoever was in the line of fire when that happened.

In the past, he'd been able to quell his outrage with cold rationale, but every day his fury was getting harder and harder to harness. No amount of logic soothed him anymore. If anything, the attempts to rationalize his situation and the injustice of his life only provoked him more.

He felt like he was starting to go insane from it all.

Daintily, Maris wiped his mouth with his linen napkin. "We should get going, then. I don't want you in trouble."

It didn't matter. The fact he breathed got him in to trouble.

I can't take this much longer...

But he had to. It wasn't just his life on the line. It was his mother's, brother's, and sister's. And unlike his older brother Ryn, he wasn't about to turn his back on his family. Ever. Even if he hated his mother more than he loved her, he couldn't sacrifice her to his uncle.

He would never spit on his father's memory that way.

But he was getting really tired of holding that line. Sixteen years of utter bullshit had taken its toll on him. Not just physically, but mentally.

C'mon, Dar. Just eighteen more months. You can do it.

Then he'd inherit his father's empire and finally be in control of his own destiny.

You don't really think that'll happen, do you?

He had to. Even though his gut told him that he'd most likely be murdered between then and now, it was all that kept him sane these days. That and the one person he couldn't talk about to anyone.

Not even Maris.

That secret was currently the only lifeline he had.

Darling lifted his hand to signal the waiter that they were ready for the check. If his uncle's men followed their usual routine, he only had about fifteen minutes before he was dragged out of here by royal guards.

That was the last degredation he needed, especially after this morning's round of Humiliate Darling in Front of the Ruling Gerents.

Don't think about it. He would be governor soon and then they'd all learn just how not weak he was.

He pulled his card out and laid it on the table. He didn't need to look at their bill. It didn't matter to him if it was right or wrong. Time meant more to him than money.

The waiter came by, flashed a dimpled smile at Maris, and took the check and card.

He was back in record time...with a small container of the cake Maris had started to order, then changed his mind about. There was something to be said for Maris's outrageous flirting. They always received the best service in the United Systems.

Darling pressed his thumb against the scanner, then signed his name on the electronic ledger. As soon as the payment was accepted, he got up and followed Maris toward the entrance.

"Where are you heading after this?" Maris asked as he held the door open for him.

What Maris really meant was where would Darling try to hide to keep from being dragged home like a felon, and beaten because he'd dared to have an afternoon of peace out of his uncle's sight.

"I'll grab my fighter and head over to Caillen's for a while. I haven't had a chance to see his daughter since she started walking. What about you?"

Maris glanced back into the restaurant. "I want to grab something, all right. But it's not a fighter...Or maybe he is. With that tight body, it is possible."

In spite of his disgust at having to leave so abruptly, Darling smiled. It was what he loved most about Maris. No matter how bad he felt, Maris could always amuse him. "Seriously, you want to come with?"

"Sure. I can always stare at Caillen. That man..." Maris bit his knuckle with lustful glee.

Darling laughed as they joined the huge crowd on the street and had to push their way through the sea of shuffling bodies. "Better be careful, his wife might get jealous."

"True. And I'm not dumb enough to upset a woman who knows how to use a blaster and a blade. I like my body parts attached."

Darling didn't respond. Damn, the crowd was always thick this time of day, but this was ridiculous. He could barely move.

Then again, he should be grateful. It would slow down his uncle's men and help conceal him from them.

His alarm buzzed again.

"Bastard," he snarled under his breath before he looked down and reached to silence it.

"Dar! Forward front! Point one!"

With reflexes honed by the best assassins in the business who'd taught him to protect his vital areas, Darling turned at Maris's military command that warned him of an imminent attack. The instant he moved, he felt the sting of a knife sliding into his flesh, just below his shoulder blade.

A knife that had been aimed at his heart.

Cursing, he reached around to catch the assassin's wrist. For several seconds, Darling's blue eyes glared into those deadly gray ones that were too stupid to realize their owner had just made a fatal mistake.

The assassin yanked at the knife.

Grinding his teeth against the pain that rushed through him, Darling let the assassin pull it free of his flesh. But the moment the blade was out, he tightened his grip on the man's wrist and head-butted him. Wrenching the assassin's arm, he heard the bone snap before the knife fell from his broken hand. The assassin came at him with another knife he'd pulled from a sheath on his leg.

Bring it…

Darling jumped back, out of his reach. Stomping his left heel on the pavement, Darling ejected the blade in the toe of his boot and used its sharp point to catapult the fallen knife on the street up so that he could catch it with his hand.

The people surrounding them realized what was going on and began to scatter, screaming in fear of being accidentally injured or killed in the fight.

His attacker charged again.

That cold, repressed demonic part of Darling salivated for retaliatory blood. He gave the assassin an insidious smile as he twirled out of the assassin's reach. He rolled around the man's back, then turned and stabbed him in the shoulder.

His attacker screamed out and whirled to lunge at Darling. Smiling, Darling motioned at him with both hands, daring him to come closer. The assassin scowled at the knife Darling had cradled in his palm—the way he held it let the bastard know that he was as proficient with a blade as the assassin was.

Probably more so. Had Darling made a bill-kill attack, his victim would have already been dead and not fighting him.

For the first time, fear darkened the assassin's gray eyes as he finally realized he was in over his head. He dropped his knife and reached for his blaster.

His mistake.

Not wanting to chance an innocent getting shot and killed by a moron's incompetence, Darling grabbed the assassin's arm and twisted until he was at the assassin's back. Before the assassin could recover, Darling grabbed his chin, lifted it up, and made one hard slash across his throat.

Darling shoved him forward.

Choking, the assassin fell to his knees on the sidewalk. He clutched at the gaping wound, trying to block the blood that flowed between his fingers.

His anger boiling, Darling stood back to watch. The decent part of him wanted to finish the assassin off and end his suffering. But the part of him that was slowly devouring his conscience, enjoyed seeing the paid assassin's struggle to live.

Let him die in utter agony. It was what he deserved.

Better him than me.

Darling quickly glanced around to make sure there was no

other threat coming for him. His gaze met Maris's and he saw the horror in his friend's eyes. He thought it was over what he'd done, until Maris stepped forward.

"You're bleeding really badly on your back. Are you okay?"

Only then did Darling feel the pain again. "Yeah. It hurts like hell, but I'll live." He'd had far worse wounds than this. And those given to him by people who supposedly loved him.

The assassin continued to writhe on the ground, begging for mercy in a black jacket that held over three dozen hash marks on its sleeve—a sick accounting that bragged about how many people he'd murdered. And the killer had intended to add another for Darling's life.

But the marks that truly enraged him were the seven that had dots over them.

Murdered children.

Darling curled his lip at the repugnant bastard as his blind fury took him over.

His handful of friends who ran the Sentella with him had dubbed him "Kere" as a joke. The Caronese god of death and caliginosity who ruled in their version of hell, Kere was said to pull all of his sustenance from the blood of his enemies. The darkest of gods lived to fight and drew vim from those who begged him for clemency. Since Darling was normally even keeled and easygoing, his Sentella partner Hauk had thought it funny to label him that.

But now...

There was no pity or compassion as he stared at the killer who was dying from the vicious wound Darling had given him. In fact, he only felt one thing...

Would you die already, and shut the fuck up while you do it?

Before he even realized what he was doing, Darling grabbed the man's blaster from his holster and shot him with it.

A single shot through the back of his head.

Darling stood there on the street with the blaster smoking and his hand as steady as it could be. Worst of all, he felt nothing about his actions. No regret. No remorse.

Total emptiness.

He wasn't sure when it'd happened, but he'd become as callous and numb as any assassin he'd ever known. His emotions were now strangers to him.

There was only one person who could still reach past it and make him feel something other than his own bitter pain and rage.

Please God, help me...

This time, he knew the horror in Maris's dark eyes was definitely over his actions.

"You're really beginning to scare me, Dar."

Yeah...I'm beginning to scare me, too.

1

There's an intruder here…

Zarya Starska froze in her living room as she felt the subtle shift in the air around her. Most would ignore it, but after she'd spent her entire life on alert for those out to attack or kill her, she instinctively knew whenever someone had invaded her home without an invitation.

Flinging her hand down, she felt the throwing knife she hid in a spring-loaded sheath inside her sleeve slide into her palm. Whoever was in her house was about to learn an important lesson in manners.

Bring it, punk.

Prepared to tear the intruder apart, she tilted her head down and listened carefully.

It was barely a whisper of fabric. But it was enough for her to locate the interloper. With the skills honed from a thousand battles, she lunged at the shadow in the corner.

The moment she did, he sidestepped her and disarmed her so fast, it left her breathless. The knife hit the floor with a sickening thud.

Her intruder pulled her against his chest and held her fast against a body that was rock hard and toned.

A body she knew as well as she knew her own.

"Sh, Zarya," he whispered in her ear. "I didn't mean to startle you."

She let out a relieved breath as she recognized the electronically distorted voice that kept anyone from identifying him. His entire head was covered by a black crash helmet that gave no indication of his race or species. Not that it mattered. She didn't care what he looked like.

She only cared about his heart.

And that was the part of him she craved most.

Smiling, she reached up to lay her hand on the side of his slick helmet. "Kere. What are you doing here? I thought I wouldn't see you for at least two weeks."

His arm and hand brushed over her breast making her even more breathless as he released her. "I had to see you before I left."

She felt the same way about him. Every minute they were apart was agonizing.

And speaking of, he was gone again from the room.

Zarya searched the shadows for some trace of her illusive phantom. "I swear I'm going to tie a bell to you." There was absolutely no sound of any kind to betray his movements or current location in her home. Never had she known anyone stealthier.

Not even an assassin.

The lights went out, bathing the room in utter darkness. She didn't know how he did it, but he could override any system or computer. Sadly, her own security, as high tech as it was, posed no challenge to him whatsoever. She took comfort in knowing that he'd breeched far better systems than hers with even less effort.

Still...

Her mysterious shadow was amazing.

Unable to see anything at all, Zarya smiled at his usual precaution to maintain his anonymity. This time, she heard him drop his helmet on the floor by the wall switch. "You know, my sister thinks I'm insane."

"Sisters usually do." Oh yeah, there was the sound she coveted above all others... That deep, rich baritone of his true voice that never failed to bring a smile to her lips.

He was right behind her now.

How had he gotten there so fast?

Kere turned her around and captured her lips with his. Zarya groaned at the way he kissed her. Like he wanted total possession of her entire being and she was more than willing to give it to him. No one had ever kissed her the way he did.

Like she was the air he breathed, the nourishment he needed to feed his starving soul. Like he would die if he wasn't touching her.

He nipped her lips, then pulled back. "You were telling me about Sorche."

It took her a minute to catch up to him after a kiss that hot. Her whole being was already on fire and she couldn't think past wanting to lick every inch of his lush body.

"Wha... oh, yeah. She thinks I'm crazy for having a relationship with a man when I don't even know what his hair color is."

He buried his lips at the base of her throat where his breath scorched her skin. "So what did you say to her?"

She cradled his head and slid her fingers through his straight shoulder-length hair. She always imagined it black, but to be honest, she had no way of really knowing since she'd never seen any part of his body in the light. He just seemed like he'd have black hair for some reason. It would match his ruthless battle skills and his near suicidal antics.

"When you've seen someone's soul, you don't need to know his hair color."

He nuzzled her skin, raising chills all over her, before he pulled back. "You've known a lot more of me than that."

It was true. While she had no clue as to his race or physical looks, she had licked every part of him enough to know he was at least humanoid, ripped, and that he tasted divine...

He opened the front of her battlesuit and slid it slowly down her body, pausing only to nip at her hipbone—an action that made her crazy with lust.

Kneeling in front of her, he helped her step out of her clothes and weapons. She could feel his hot breath against her thigh. Something that made her wet as her heart raced even more at the prospect of what he'd be doing to her shortly.

Suddenly, his hand brushed against the center of her body, causing her to throb terribly as he removed her panties.

Then he rose slowly, dragging his hand up the inside of her calf before he brushed his fingers through the hair at the juncture of her thighs. "Have you eaten?" He cupped her between her legs.

"I...I...um..." She forgot the question as he deftly fingered her with a rhythm so perfect it left her weak and trembling.

He paused his play to whisper in her ear. "Food, Zarya. Have you eaten?"

She smiled. He always worried about her. "On the way home. I stopped by Ture's restaurant."

Kere returned to his sweet torture, his rhythm faster this time while he stroked her with his thumb and buried two fingers deep inside her body. "Good."

And before she could translate that one word, she cried out as she came for him.

Kere caught her against his chest as he continued to wring even more pleasure out of her, until she was shuddering so hard she would have fallen but for his hold on her. She never understood how he could do that to her so fast. It was like he knew exactly where and how to touch her to set her senses reeling.

He swung her up in his arms and carried her to the bedroom so that he could lay her down on her bed.

She laughed as he pulled back to undress. "The bed? How extremely atypical of you."

"I told you I could be civilized."

Only his lilting, accented speech was refined—and even that, only sometimes. The rest of him...

He was always feral. Terrifying.

Lethal.

And she loved him that way. Being with him was like lying down with a wild animal you knew could rip you to shreds if it wanted, and yet it purred only for your touch. That knowledge made being with him all the more alluring.

All the hotter.

She tried to find him in the darkness, but there was no trace. She knew he could see her though. He never had any trouble seeing in the darkest places. She'd asked him once if he was Ritadarion or Trisani—two races known for their abilities to see in the dark without light. But he'd refused to answer.

Then again, he wouldn't tell anyone anything about himself that could be used to identify him. As an outlaw herself, it was a precaution she well understood. His wasn't the only life on the line. If he were ever identified, every member of his family and all his Sentella allies and friends would be executed, too.

Not that she would ever do anything to threaten or harm him.

He meant too much to her for that.

Wanting to please him as much as he'd pleasured her, she spread her legs and bent her knees in silent invitation. "You know, I was only teasing you when I sent that text."

"You want me to leave then?" he asked in that wonderful baritone that had a way of sending chills over her. Gods, how she lived for the sound of his true voice...

Most of all, she loved to hear him laugh. It was the most infectious sound that seemed to come from some place deep within him.

"No," she said quickly. "But you didn't have to come here tonight. I wasn't trying to be clingy. I just wanted you to know that."

"I'm already away from you more than I like."

It was true. They only saw each other maybe two or three times a month, *if* they were lucky. The rest of the time, they were relegated to texting and scrying... at least *she* scried so that he could see her while they talked. He, on the other hand, was only a deep, sexy voice with no face. But she cherished every piece of contact she had with him.

Even when it was at a cloaked distance.

Reaching down, she opened herself up even more so that he could have all the access to her body that he wanted.

He sucked his breath in sharply. "Woman, you know what it does to me when you do that." The bed dipped under his weight as he crawled up from between her feet. "Now what have we here?"

She hissed as he took her into his mouth so that he could tongue her into oblivion. Biting her lip, she buried her hand in his soft hair and lifted her hips for him.

Never in her life had she been so open with or reliant on anyone, and she'd done things with him that she'd have never thought herself capable of. Things that should have shamed her to the core of her soul, but she'd learned to trust him implicitly. And it wasn't just the sex. She held a faith in him that defied explanation. For the first time, she understood what it meant to share herself with someone. To need a man by her side.

As far back as Zarya could remember, she'd always held a piece of herself away from other people. She'd only been a child when her father had been branded a traitor and her mother and sister brutally murdered. In that one instant, she'd been forced to grow up and had learned to trust no one. Ever. Not with her safety. Not with her secrets. And definitely not with her heart.

But from the moment she'd met Kere, it'd been different.

Unlike the other men in her life, he'd never once hurt or betrayed her. Never walked out on her at a critical moment. If she needed anything, he was there without fail, or complaint, or hesitation. No matter the time, day or night.

Even if it was nothing more than appearing in her home after a simple text that had said her heart would break if she had to wait two weeks to see him again.

In spite of the fact that he was one of the most wanted outlaws in the United Systems, he was the most attentive lover she'd ever known. He seemed to take as much pleasure from watching her climax as he did from experiencing his own.

And she couldn't bear the thought of living a life where he wasn't a major part of it. "Kere?"

"Mmm?"

She gasped as he slid his tongue deep inside her body, sending a shiver over her. It was hard to think whenever he touched her, but *this* she couldn't forget about. "I heard the League was stepping up their efforts to go after Sentella members, especially the High Command"—Kere was one of their five leaders—"and that the Caronese Grand Counsel has tripled the reward he's offering for your capture in particular, and quadrupled the one for your death. He's ruthlessly determined to end our Resistance and assassinate all of us in leadership roles. You are being extra careful, aren't you?"

"Always."

Good, because she knew she couldn't live without him. The thought of his being hurt...

She choked on a sob.

"Hey," he breathed, sliding up her body to cup her cheek. "Shh…no tears, Zarya." He brushed his lips against her cheek to kiss away the tear that had fallen. "They're not going to get me. I swear it to you. I'm not afraid of the Grand Counsel or anyone else."

"I know. I'm being stupid. I'm so sorry." The last thing she wanted was to taint or spoil what little time she had with him.

"Never apologize for loving me."

She nodded as she struggled to stop her tears. But it was so hard. It seemed like everyone she'd ever loved had been violently ripped out of her life. Most of them right in front of her. "I've buried too many people I care about to lose you, too." She'd worn their blood on her clothes and had watched as the life drained out of their bodies…

Her own brother had died in her arms…

"You won't bury me, Z."

Yeah, because his enemies, who were too numerous to count, would probably blow him into so many pieces there wouldn't be enough left for a ceremony.

At times, she wished she could have fallen in love with some businessman or cook or anyone who didn't live in their violent world.

But fate hadn't been that kind to her.

She loved one of the three most wanted men in all the universe. The other two being his closest friends.

If one of them went down, it would most likely take all three. *Don't think about it. But it was so hard when all she could see was Kere lying dead on the ground.*

"The League raised the bounty on your head, too."

"It's okay, Z. I knew the minute they posted it. They're not going to get me, either. I promise."

18

That was what her father had told her, over and over again. And where was he?

In his grave. Ruthlessly murdered by his own best friend.

Kere rolled over onto his back and pulled her on top of him. She savored the feel of his hard body under hers as he teased her lips with his. He was nothing but a solid wall of scarred muscle. Scars that reminded her that no matter how strong he seemed, he wasn't invulnerable or invincible.

Terrified of losing him, Zarya breathed in his warm masculine scent. He always smelled delectable and that went a long way in soothing her fears and terror.

She dragged her fingers down his whiskered jaw. "You need a shave."

"I thought you liked it when I let my whiskers grow."

That was because he did things to her with those whiskers that always set her on fire.

Her smile died as she touched his back and found...

Was it a bandage?

"You're wounded?" Pulling him to his side, she ran her hand over the coarse material and found where it was wet with fresh blood. The smell and feel of it was unmistakable and undeniable.

"It's not bad. Just a flesh wound."

Was he serious? It was an awfully large bandage for a mere flesh wound. "Shot?"

"Stabbed."

"Oh my God!" She scrambled off his hips and forced him to roll over so that she could gently probe his wound with her fingers. "I wish I could see it."

"Nothing but sutures to see."

She gentled her probing so that she wouldn't hurt him, but it bothered her that she had no real idea how big or deep it was. "Was it an assassin?"

"Yeah."

"Where?"

"My back. Obviously."

She rolled her eyes at his sarcasm. He could be so damned impossible at times. "No, goofball. Where were you when he struck?"

"Coming out of a restaurant. The crowd was thick and I know better than to get distracted. It was stupid and it won't happen again."

But it'd already happened. A few more inches and it would have punctured his lung and killed him. The mere thought of it made her light-headed and shaky. "Where's the assassin now?"

"Hell's gates most likely, though I guess there's a slim chance he might be in paradise."

She flicked her fingernail at his bandage. "You're not funny."

"Zarya, it's all right." He rolled back over and pulled her into his arms. "It's why I wanted to see you. Why I'm here with you tonight when I'm supposed to be halfway across the universe. It made me start rethinking some things."

But she wasn't ready to listen to him yet. "Where was the rest of the Sentella when you were attacked?"

"No idea. We don't live together. And they're not exactly my keepers."

"They should be...Are you laughing at me?" She had the distinct impression that he was.

"No, love. Never. I'm just amused by your outrage. No woman has ever given a single shit when I've been hurt." This time, she heard the thick emotion in his voice as he brushed her hair back from her face, then laid a very tender kiss on her cheek.

She savored that touch so much. Her worst fear was having to live in a world where she felt it no more. "Don't die on me, Kere. Please."

"I don't intend to. In fact…" His voice trailed off.

She had no idea what he intended until he slid something cold onto her finger.

Her heart stopped as she covered it with her hand and felt the contours of it.

No, it couldn't be.

Could it?

No matter how she tried to rationalize it, there was no mistaking the huge stone that was set in the middle of two smaller ones. "Is this—"

"I want you to marry me, Zarya," he said, interrupting her. "I need you in my life. Every day. By my side. I know it sounds strange, but when I'm with you, I'm the man I always wanted to be. The one I feel I was born to be. And when I'm not, it's like I'm lost to someone else…and I don't like him anymore—not that I ever really did. But since I've known you, I've learned to detest that part of me with a passion. And I can't keep living the lie that was forced on me."

"What lie?"

He was silent for several seconds before he answered. "My whole life is a lie. From beginning to end. I have to be so careful with everything I say and do. I can't drop my guard for even a heartbeat, and I don't dare let anyone see the real me. Ever… except for you. You are my only truth. The only one who knows who I really am and what I really think. And I have to have you with me before I really do go insane. I can't stand being without you anymore. Please say yes."

Her heart soared until she remembered one small fact.

He refused to let her see his face or body.

Ever.

"I'm going to look really strange blindfolded at my wedding."

He laughed. "You won't be blindfolded."

"You'll look strange, standing there in your full battle gear."

Kere kissed her lips and this time, she felt his smile. "I won't be in battle gear."

Her breath caught at what he was implying...Could it be? "You're going to let me finally see you?" She reached for her lamp switch.

He caught her hand before she could turn the light on. "Not yet. I have a few things I have to put in order first. But I promise you, the next time we meet, you will see me for who and what I am. *All* of me."

"I know who and what you are."

His grip on her hand tightened ever so slightly. "No, you've only seen my soul, never my face, and I need a promise from you before you do."

"Anything."

He hesitated again as if he was afraid, something that mystified her. She'd seen him stand toe-to-toe with the baddest asses the League and Caronese government could throw at him.

Never had he flinched or faltered.

But tonight, something was bothering him in a way his enemies never had.

"When you see me, I want you to remember not to judge me by my looks."

How could he be afraid of something so incredibly trivial? "I told you that I only judge people by their hearts." And he had the most beautiful one she'd ever known.

"But I'm not just anyone, Zarya."

"I know. You're the man I love."

He cupped her face in the palms of his hands...hands that held roughened calluses—testament, along with the scars all over his body, to how hard a life he'd lived. Her Kere was anything but a spoiled rich aristo who lived off the backs of people like her and her family and those she tried to protect from the aptly named Cruels who preyed on them all.

Though he rarely spoke of his life outside of his role in her beloved Resistance and the Sentella, she felt the road map of tragedies all over him. His past had been one marred by untold brutality and battles. All she wanted was to soothe and comfort him the way he comforted her.

"I don't ever want you to forget that, Z. Promise me?"

"Of course." She laid her hand over his damaged cheek. She knew he was extremely self-conscious about the scar that bisected the left half of his face, and the ones on the rest of his body. When they'd first started sleeping together, he'd kept his hair over his face and had pulled back from her touch anytime she went near that particular scar.

Then one night, when he'd been so exhausted that he'd fallen asleep on her, she had brushed his hair back from his face and found what bothered him most. That scar was so deep, she could feel where the wound had left a deep groove in the bone underneath it. So deep that she wondered if he might not be blind in his left eye from whatever had caused that injury.

No, he couldn't be. His aim was too perfect in battle. If he only had sight in one eye, his depth perception would be off and he'd be at a serious disadvantage. Still, there was no denying the savage ferocity of the injury that had caused a scar like that.

Her heart aching for the pain it must have caused him, she'd pressed her lips to the scar he'd always hidden from her. That kiss had awakened him instantly.

He'd turned his face and pulled away. "Don't. I'm disgusting."

"You're not disgusting." She'd felt his pain in the darkness and it had broken her heart. "We all have scars, Kere. Inside and out. Wounds that go so deep, they leave a permanent mark on us. But that doesn't make them ugly or revolting. They were hard lessons learned and for better or worse, they changed us. No matter how hard you try to hide them, they will always be there. And I think your scars are beautiful because they are what have made you the man I care about."

After that, he'd allowed her complete access to his body. But only under the protection of full darkness.

He still wouldn't let her see any part of him in the light.

Could he, who stood fearless before the scariest of enemies, be afraid of her rejecting him for his looks?

Was that even possible?

"Your features don't matter to me, Kere. I'd love you even if you had three heads and a split nose."

"You say that because you don't know who and what I really am."

"And again, it doesn't matter. I will stand by you forever. How could you doubt me?"

He laughed bitterly. "Almost everyone you've ever loved has died on you. Almost everyone I've ever loved has put me in harm's way. Not one of them ever failed to throw me to the wolves to protect their own ass. Whenever it was a choice between them and me, *I* was the one who paid for it. Once I show you my face, Z, I can't go back. You will have the power to completely destroy me and everyone I hold dear. All of our lives will be in your hands."

She stared at what she hoped was his eyes so that he could see her heart. "I would *never* hurt you."

"You're the only one I've ever trusted this much with my real thoughts and beliefs. You know me better than any creature alive."

"And I am forever yours. You can trust me, Kere. I swear I will *never* betray you. Not ever."

"I believe you," he whispered in her ear before he captured her lips again. Then he slid himself deep inside her.

Zarya groaned at how good he felt there. She cradled him with her body as he thrust himself slow and easy against her hips. "I love you, Kere," she breathed.

"I love you, too. I always will."

She smiled and tightened her hold on him. It was the first time he'd ever said that back to her. In the past, he'd always remained silent or said that he was glad that she did.

But tonight . . .

There was no longer any doubt whatsoever that she was more to him than an easy lay whenever he was horny. For the first time in their two-year relationship, he finally confirmed that he loved her and that he intended to stay.

Running her hands over his scarred back, she delighted in the way his muscles played against her palms as he pleasured her. If she could, she'd stay right here, like this, forever.

She lifted her hips, bringing him even deeper inside until her entire body was rife with ecstasy. "Tell me again that you love me," she breathed.

"I love you, Zarya. And I have *never* said that to another woman."

Most of all, he never said anything he didn't mean.

Her heart singing, she threw her head back and screamed as she came again. Still he kept that steady, deep pace until she was completely sated and begging him for mercy. Only then did he join her in that one perfect moment of intense pleasure. She held him close against her entire body as he shook in her arms. Unlike her, he was always quiet whenever they made love. He would suck his breath in sharply from time to time whenever she did something unexpected, but overall, he seldom made any sound whatsoever.

Yet another strange quirk of his. One that made her wonder if he, like many assassins she knew, was keeping his guard up in expectation of an ambush. Did he, even now, fear she'd stab him in the dark?

I hope you know me better than that.

His breathing ragged, he lowered himself to cover her and to nibble her neck and ear. "What time do you have to be up in the morning?"

"Nine, why?"

He brushed his whiskers against her breast, tickling her in a way that should be illegal. "Good. I have plenty of time to play with you and still let you get a good night's sleep."

She smiled at those words and at the fact that by his hunger, she knew he didn't cheat with other women. Whenever they were together, he was a powerhouse of testosterone—like he stored it all up just waiting for a chance to be alone with her.

And as the night went by, he made good on his promise.

Hours later, Zarya tried to stay awake, knowing that he'd be gone whenever she woke up. But all too soon her exhaustion overcame her and she drifted off while lying on top of an eight-pack of rock-hard abs.

Something loud buzzed, rudely pulling her out of her happy dreams. Groaning, Zarya rolled over and slapped at her alarm. Gah, she hated that thing.

"Ow!" she groused as something caught in her hair and pulled out several strands.

She opened her eyes to see the huge griata stone in her engagement ring.

Holy gods...

The thing was worth a fortune.

She'd known Kere was loaded. As one of the five Sentella leaders, he made a killing, pardon the pun, by taking out military targets.

But this...

Whoa. It caught the light and glittered in a spectrum of rainbow colors. There were two blood-red smaller stones on each side that only made the rich, dark color more intense.

A classic-style Caronese engagement ring, the stones stood for the past, the present, and the future. The red for passion and the center stone for fidelity.

His promise to her. She couldn't wait to call her sister and tell her what had happened. Sorche wouldn't believe it. As far back as Zarya could remember, they'd spent countless hours talking about what kind of man they'd fall in love with. Who they dreamed of marrying one day.

Never had she imagined hers would be the most lethal outlaw in the universe.

One whose face she'd never seen…

Her gaze fell to the notecard he'd left on her nightstand by her clock. How very old-fashioned and sweet, and it was so vintage Kere that it made her smile. But even more endearing, on top of the note was one perfect white rose and a small round electronic something she'd never seen before. Curious, she pulled the note and black circle device toward her.

Leaving your bed was the hardest thing I've ever done. But in four days, I will be back for you. Look for the man dressed in black, wearing your mother's ring around his neck.

You know me, Zarya, better than any person ever has. My greatest prayer is that my face doesn't offend you so much that you forget your promise to me. I could never bear to be rejected by the only woman who has ever held my heart.

Four days of absence, then a lifetime of happiness. I promise you, you will never regret loving me.

Eternally yours,
K

P.S. I designed the tricom just for you and you alone. If anyone fires a blaster at you, either in kill or stun mode, it'll deflect the shot and then emit a pulse that will render them and anyone near them, paralyzed. For a few hours, they'll be conscious, but won't be able to do more than blink.

Don't take it off. It'll protect you in my absence.

The hair on the back of her neck rose as déjà vu tortured her. Her eyes filling with tears, she touched his flowing script. The last time a man had left her a note like this, it'd been her father.

Soon, we'll be free of Caron. Then you'll never have to fear again. Two days, my precious and I'll return. Have your sister packed and ready.

Her father had died on his way back for them.

She winced in pain as a bitter lump tightened her stomach. *Please, please don't let history repeat itself.*

2

"Are you out of your mind? I would slap sense into you, but you'd most likely punch me back and that would...really hurt. 'Cause the gods know, you pack one nasty left hook that you always lead with. Might even kill me. At the very least, it would wrinkle, and stain my clothes with blood, which is worse than death, if you ask me. Still, are you out of your mind?"

Darling sighed at Maris's angry tirade as they stood in the governor's office of the Winter Palace—the main political seat Darling's family had used to rule their empire for the least two hundred years. This room was one of the few electronic dead spots of the palace where they couldn't be overheard or monitored in any way.

Richly appointed and decorated with dark blues, golds, and maroons, the study was intended to overwhelm and impress visitors with the ostentatious wealth of the Cruel family—to make others feel inferior and small in comparison.

It worked on all but the stoutest egos.

His uncle also used this room to plot the deaths and downfalls of his enemies, as well as his own allies and friends.

And it was in this very room, where there was no surveillance whatsoever, that Darling's uncle had murdered his own brother...

Darling's father.

Something Darling couldn't prove so he didn't dare breathe a word of it to anyone, not even Maris. But he knew the truth from his uncle's own lips. It'd come out as a drunken boast one night eleven years ago when his uncle had been particularly brutal with him after he'd escaped and run away from the mental institution his uncle had confined him in. The royal guards had found him in hiding and brought him back to this very room—beating him almost every step of the journey home.

His face stinging from his uncle's fists, Darling had shoved Arturo away from him. *"You're not my father, you worthless bastard. And you're not a governor in full right,* Lord Grand Counsel." He'd sneered the title he knew his uncle despised as it reminded Arturo of his lesser rank and position. *"You'll never be one. But I will be governor one day, and I don't have to listen to* you."

His uncle had slammed his head into the desk that stood on their right and used his hair to pin him to it before he'd leaned over Darling to snarl in Darling's ear with his drunken breath. *"You better wise up, you little smart-mouthed faggot. I own you and I can make your life, and your family's lives, utter hell. If you don't do what I say, when I say it, I'll kill you just like I did your spineless father. You should have seen the shock on the pathetic bastard's face when I cut his throat."*

It was a night his uncle didn't remember.

A night Darling couldn't forget.

And since the moment of that slip, Darling had been plotting his uncle's downfall in this very room where the walls bled from past treacheries.

Unfortunately, it'd taken a lot longer to put an overthrow into place than he'd wanted. But then it wasn't easy to topple a government, especially when the handful of people you loved would be executed along with you should you fail.

Dragging his thoughts away from the past, Darling met Maris's irritated gaze—Maris would be the first to die if he screwed this up. And that was something he could neither allow nor contemplate. Honestly, he could barely remember a time in his life when Maris hadn't been a major part of it.

Though they were only a few weeks apart in age, Maris looked a lot younger. He'd recently cut his black hair short and wore it in spiked waves that went in all directions. For once, Maris was dressed conservatively in a light green jacket and tan pants. Something that was a stark contrast to Darling's normal jet-black attire.

But then they were ever opposites in most things. While Maris had pale skin, Darling's was deep olive. Maris had dark eyes. His were light blue. And only Darling's sister shared his dark red hair.

Maris was lean with smooth, unblemished skin, and Darling was ripped with more scars than any aristo he knew, and that included the Andarion prince, Nykyrian Quiakides, who was a former League assassin and a close friend of Darling's.

But their most polar opposite trait was their personalities. Maris lived out loud with a flamboyant, carefree style that tended to offend a lot of people. Meanwhile Darling was quiet, understated, and reserved. A demeanor of necessity he'd developed not long after his father had died. If he wasn't noticed, he wasn't attacked.

As often, anyway.

He much preferred flying below the radar while Maris preferred flying in the face of anyone who annoyed him.

And even though he knew better, Darling was still an eternal optimist who tried to see only the best in people, and who hoped everything would get better. Meanwhile, Maris only anticipated treachery from every person he met, and expected things to worsen, no matter how good they were.

Darling was the sole living being Maris trusted. Not that Darling blamed him, given his past. Trust didn't come easy to Darling either, but he tried not to let his experience with assholes defeat his innate belief that people were good at heart.

All except his uncle.

That bastard had been born chromosomally damaged.

For the whole of his life, Darling had fought to protect, and run interference for others. Whether it was his mother, his siblings, or Maris...

He'd bled for all of them.

But never happily, and not always without complaint. While he didn't mind it so much for Maris and his siblings, he resented the hell out of his mother's inability to put his life and well-being above her own selfish needs.

She couldn't even look at him anymore. Whether it was from disgust that he wasn't her willing slave or from her own guilt over sacrificing him, he didn't know. They rarely spoke to each other, and he couldn't remember the last time she'd wished him well.

That was all right. He'd long ago accepted the fact that for all intents and purposes, he was an orphan.

Now, after all these years of battling for them, he finally wanted something for himself. And no one, not even Maris, was going to talk him out of this.

He had to have Zarya. She was the only one who could save him from the madness that was quickly pulling him under. He knew it with every part of himself. Without her, Kere would consume him, and he didn't want to be the same cold-blooded, unfeeling monster his uncle and mother were.

I'd rather be dead.

Zarya was the only good thing he had, and he intended to hold on to her with both hands. Consequences be damned.

Darling met Maris's gaze, wanting his friend's blessing for

what he was about to do. "If anyone should understand this, it's you, Mari."

Maris scoffed. "Yes, but I fall in love every five minutes and within twenty I've moved on to the next. You cannot marry a *woman*. You know that. Just imagine the scandal that'll cause."

"Mari—"

"Don't Mari me...in more ways than one. Do you remember what you said when I was about to walk down the aisle and make the biggest mistake of my life?"

"Your pants were too tight?"

Maris rolled his eyes. "After that."

"That you were sweating so badly you needed another shower or else you'd drown your bride?"

Maris actually growled at him this time. "I'm being serious, Darling. Damn it! Stop being impossible."

Darling's eyes widened at the unexpected profanity. "Wow... *Damn it*. Really? I didn't know you knew how to cuss. I'm impressed."

"What can I say?" He crossed his arms in irritation. "You've ruined me. And—"

"I hear everything you're saying." Darling cut him off before he repeated the same argument he'd been making for the last thirty minutes. "I do. But my uncle has already tried to kill me. You were there. Remember?" Not wanting to completely alienate his best friend, he tempered the sarcasm. "In eighteen months, I'll be old enough to legally dethrone him and there's nothing he can do to stop it. He knows that, and it's now open season on my ass. If I don't do something fast, you'll be visiting me in the family vault, beside my father." Darling swallowed as that pain washed over him. He'd give anything to have his father back.

But that desire changed nothing. His father was dead and he didn't really want to join him there.

Not today, anyway.

"We both know Arturo's not about to go blithely into retirement. Not while I have a younger brother who can inherit the throne after me. He kills me and then he moves his guardianship to Drakari for the next six years. Or worse, the bastard locks me up in another institution and has both me and Drake permanently declared insane so that he can rule in our names without being contested."

Darling didn't even want to think about what had happened to him the last time he'd been locked away. The pain and degradation. The never-ending meds that had left him so sick, weak, and disoriented, he could barely move. It'd taken months to detox and get that shit out of his system.

Another confinement would make him crazy. He had no doubt whatsoever. He couldn't stand being strapped down and helpless, locked in a single room where he was put on display and sold like some freak of nature for the amusement of others. It didn't pay to be a high-ranking aristo in that situation. Ever.

And he couldn't even bear to think about the other things they'd done to him. Things he'd never mentioned to anyone, hoping that if he kept it to himself, then the memories would go away and leave him alone. But it didn't work that way.

Those scars ran all the way to his battered soul. And those waking nightmares were never far away. Anytime he let his guard down, they returned to torture him all over again.

The last thing he wanted was for his brother to be put in the same situation. While Drakari was strong, he'd never been tested like that, and Darling didn't want him to be. For the most part, Drake was untouched by the ruthless violence that had been Darling's life since the day they'd buried their father. And that, too, had cost Darling dearly. He'd made sure that both Drake and Annalise had been raised in foreign boarding schools.

34

His greatest accomplishment was that they were both relatively unscathed by their uncle's hatred.

But if Darling was gone...

"Who will protect my family if I'm not here? Have you forgotten what happened to my mother the last time I was locked up?"

Maris looked away, but not before Darling saw the involuntary wince over it. "I've not forgotten. How could I?"

In a vicious show of power and intimidation, his uncle had ordered his mother brutally beaten by so-called intruders within hours of Darling being admitted into a mental ward. Her assault had been his uncle's way of letting him know what happened to his family when he didn't fall in line with his uncle's wishes.

And it was one seared into his heart and mind. While he might not like his mother, he didn't want her harmed in any way. He refused to have his family hurt because of something he did.

More than that, Arturo had made it abundantly clear that next time, Annalise might be the one an intruder broke in on.

I'll kill him if he goes after her. Since the day she'd been born, his sister had held a special place in his heart. Even though she annoyed him to extreme distraction, he adored her.

But killing anyone who dared touch Lise wouldn't undo the mental damage such an attack would cause his headstrong sister. Darling knew that better than anyone.

"Are you sure your uncle hired the assassin?"

Darling gave his friend a wry stare. "No, I'm not sure. I have no idea how to track information like that down. Pure bloody speculation on my part."

"Cut the sarcasm, Lord Smart-ass. I'm just worried about you, okay? I am allowed, after all. You are the only family *I* have in this world."

Darling checked his temper as he saw the hurt in Maris's eyes. "I know, Mari. I'm sorry." The two of them had been through so much in their lives. Best friends since they'd started preschool together twenty-three years ago.

Through thick and thin, brothers to the bitter end. That had been their childhood pledge to each other. Little had they known then how many times that bond would be tested.

Never once had they disappointed each other.

He placed his hand on Maris's shoulder to reassure him. "I already have everything arranged. Arturo thinks my mother and brother retreated to the Summer Palace after Drake's last exam yesterday. Tomorrow, I want you to head to Caillen's by midday. Then I'll pick Lise up from school and get her to Nykyrian's where my mother and Drake are waiting."

"And then you're going out alone to commit suicide. How vintage Darling of you."

He ignored Maris's dire prediction and sarcasm. "The CDS"— the Caronese Delegate Symposium that served as the secondary governing body of their empire—"meets tomorrow evening. Once I have all of you secured, I can issue my challenge to Arturo. With that many witnesses, he'll have to agree to it."

"I thought you had to be twenty-nine for a challenge."

"Normally yes, but I found a loophole last night in the Unification Laws. Since Arturo isn't a fully blooded governor, and he attempted to kill the full-blooded prince and heir, I can petition the CDS on those grounds and he'll have to meet me, or be arrested. Stupid bastard. I now own his ass." But then Arturo had no idea the kinds of skills or resources that Darling had access to.

Arturo's mistake was about to cost him his life.

Maris held his hand to his temple as if his head was throbbing from their discussion. "Okay, alien life-form here. I still don't understand the nuances of how all this works." His face was a mask of frustration. "Everyone thinks you're gayer than I am.

Won't they ask how you're supposed to produce an heir when you're ostensibly homosexual?"

Darling shrugged. "If I win, it won't matter to the CDS. As a fully blooded governor, I can name Drake my heir until I produce a legal one. Even if I don't ever have a son, it's not important. I don't care about inheriting. I only care about keeping all of you safe."

And avenging my father.

That was an account that was long past due.

When Arturo had paid for and sent that assassin after him, Arturo had made the biggest mistake of his life. By coming that close to succeeding, Arturo had rammed home to Darling that if he didn't do something, now, today, his uncle would see him dead. It was no longer a possibility, but a harsh, concrete fact. And where there was one failed aassassin, there were always a dozen more willing to take over the bill-kill target and collect the credits.

Not going to happen, old man.

Darling hadn't come this far and survived so much to die at the finish line. It just didn't work that way. And after finding the contract Arturo had placed on his life, Darling wanted to bathe in Arturo's blood until he was drunk from it.

A tic worked in Maris's jaw. "And if you fail to defeat him, you're dead."

"I'm dead anyway." Or worse, his uncle would lock him up in a place that made him wish he were dead.

No one could deny that. Arturo hated him with every part of his being. But for his survival skills and strength, Darling would have been dead a long time ago. "It's just a matter of time before Arturo finds a way to assassinate or permanently imprison me."

Maris grimaced. "You should have let one of us kill him years ago."

If only it were that simple.

"Believe me, I wish." Darling clenched his teeth. "Our laws are so fucked up and backward."

Unfortunately by Caronese law, if his uncle was assassinated by anyone from any empire, all Cruels, except Arturo's male blood children, were to be executed...that included his uncle's current wife and their three legitimate daughters. That had been the first law written and passed by his uncle when he'd taken the throne. One Arturo had created to keep Darling and Drake from killing him or having him killed.

Since Darling couldn't repeal the law until he was the governor in full right, it had forced him to protect the one man he'd wanted to kill more than anything. Had any of his friends, or anyone else for that matter, assassinated Arturo, one of the other territorial princes could have seized the opportunity made by that law to block Darling's inheritance and put his family down, then replace them with his own.

Caronese policies and laws were complicated. Darling knew that better than anyone. As Hauk would say, whenever you loved someone, you allowed your enemies to hold you by the balls. And Arturo had held Darling's in a vise since the day his father had been stupid enough to believe his own brother wouldn't kill him.

Growling low in his throat, Maris finally relented. "I hate that you're doing this. But what do you need from me?"

"In case I lose, I need you to tell Zarya what happened to me and who I really was. She deserves the truth. And make sure my Sentella assets are split between you and her so that you'll both have money to live on after I'm gone."

Anger flashed in those dark eyes as Maris glared at him. "How will I find this Zarya?"

"She'll contact the Sentella looking for Kere. Syn can help you back trace her."

"Wouldn't it be easier for you to give me her information?"

Yeah right. "Easier, but not safer. I don't want to do anything to endanger *any* of you. The less all of you know about each other, the safer you are. I know you'll be able to find her. I trust you."

Maris feigned delirious joy. "Oh great. Just the job I wanted most. A job I've dreamed about having since the hour I was born. Telling the woman you're not supposed to love that you're dead, but really sorry you died. And here, hon, here's some blood money to make you feel better about it all…" Spuriously, he slapped his hand hard over his chest. "Thank you so much for thinking of me, Darling. Whatever would I do without you?" Maris sobered and narrowed his eyes on him. "For the record, you better not die on me, you worthless beast. I will *not* forgive you for it."

"If it makes you feel any better, I'll be pretty pissed off at myself, too."

"It doesn't." Maris pulled him into his arms and held him in an iron-tight hug. "You know I love you more than my life, right?"

Darling hugged him back with everything he had. Maris was the only person who'd never failed him. He was closer to him than any brother or friend could ever be. "I know, buddy. Brothers to the bitter end. I feel the same way about you."

The door slid open an instant before Arturo cursed them. "Uh…you repulsive faggots!"

Darling saw red at his uncle's snarling voice. He started to attack, but Maris tightened his hold around him, keeping him pinned in his arms.

Damn, Maris was a lot stronger than he looked. Because Mari hated conflict of any kind and profaned physical force, it was easy to forget that he was a trained soldier. And while Maris no longer had the overdeveloped build of his military days, he was still stronger than most.

"One more day," Maris whispered in Darling's ear in Phrixian—Maris's native language that Arturo couldn't understand. "You can hold on for one more day, my brother."

Kissing Darling on his scarred cheek, Maris released him and cupped his chin until Darling met his gaze. He passed a warning look to remind Darling how imperative it was that he leash his temper one more day.

Nodding, Darling fell into the role he'd been playing for so long that until Zarya he'd almost forgotten he really was heterosexual. Not that he'd ever been attracted to men. Far from it. But until Zarya, he'd been the celibate monk that Maris always called him.

His façade was the same lie Maris had been forced to live when he'd pretended to be heterosexual to keep from "dishonoring" or "embarrassing" his royal family.

For years, Maris had played the dutiful son, dating women and hating every minute of it. In those days, only Darling had known the truth of Maris's preferences.

And only Maris knew his.

Since the night of Darling's fifteenth birthday, no one, absolutely no one, had been trusted enough with the truth. It was a lie they'd both despised and unlike Maris, it was one Darling couldn't let go of.

Not so long as his uncle lived.

God, it was so easy to speak a lie in the heat of a moment. And so hard to abide by it, especially for the rest of your life.

Even now, he could see that one long ago night so clearly.

His father's former adviser, Carus, had been sneaking out the back garden when the moron had tripped an alarm. Arturo's guards had seized him and hauled him inside for questioning.

It'd been obvious from the fresh hickeys on his neck and his recently showered condition, and disheveled appearance that he'd had sex with someone. Since Annalise and Drakari were still small children, and Darling barely fifteen, the most likely culprit had been their mother.

When Arturo had ordered her taken into custody, Darling

knew the next step would be her execution. As the mother to the heir and widow of the last governor, his mother was to keep herself pristine and chaste in memory of his dead father for the rest of her life. For another man to touch her was viewed as an act of high treason on both their parts.

The guards had seized her and she'd been screaming, protesting her innocence and begging for mercy. His brother and sister had been holding on to her waist, crying and pleading for their mother's life.

Darling had been frozen by terror. His father had only been dead three years and all he could hear was the promise he'd made to him the last time they'd spoken. *"If anything should ever happen to me, Darling, swear to me that you'll make sure your mother and siblings are taken care of. They're not as strong as you. You'll make a great governor one day. I know it. It's why I trust you to do right by the three of them."*

Still, they'd all screamed and cried until Darling was deaf from it. More guards had come forward to pull his brother and sister away and to handcuff his mother for her execution while Carus had stood there, silent. No word to deny or defend the woman he'd slept with. The woman who'd risked her life and endangered her children for him.

He was useless as a protector.

And his mother would die if Darling didn't do something.

So he'd seized on Maris's personal secret to save her life. Biting his lips to make them swell, and pinching and clawing his neck to turn it red, he'd run forward to stop his mother's arrest.

"He's my boyfriend. I'm the one who slept with him." The words had flown out of Darling's mouth before he could stop himself.

Or think through the consequences.

But then, he'd stupidly assumed his mother would cut off the affair after seeing what a feckless, uncaring prick Carus was. Instead, she'd been grateful to Darling that he'd provided her with a cover story.

Little did he know then that he'd just sold his soul to his mother so that she could be happy. After that night, she'd carelessly chosen lovers and then guilted him into pretending they were his.

Lies he'd paid for with his flesh and blood.

Over the years, it'd been ironic really. To make their parents happy, Darling had pretended to be gay while Maris had pretended to be straight. It was one of many reasons why they were so close. Each had coached the other on how to carry out his ruse. What to say. How to act and dress. They'd invented code phrases to let each other know when they'd stepped out of their role. *"I'm yanking your membership card"* was the primary one. As soon as it was heard, they knew to pull back from whatever it was they were saying or doing before they exposed their true natures.

But Maris had had the luxury of coming out in his early twenties. Darling's only way out was to find a legal way to kill his uncle and then pardon his mother for her stupidity.

Arturo made a gagging sound at them.

His hatred riding him with spurs, Darling curled his lip at the smug bastard who glared at them.

In an act of utter defiance Darling knew he was about to pay for, he kissed then licked Maris's palm while staring at his uncle with a half smile.

Snarling furiously, Arturo stormed across the room and backhanded him so hard, his neck snapped and blood instantly invaded his mouth. "What have I told you, you stupid cock-licking rimmer?"

Testing his teeth with his tongue to make sure they were all still in place, Darling forced himself to play docile and not give in to the need to strike back.

Daintily—to further piss his uncle off—he wiped the blood from his lips with his forefinger.

I could snap you in two, you bastard...

It was so unfair to have the ability to rip his uncle's heart out and not be able to do it. So long as his family meant more to him than he did, he was like a toothless lion and he hated that feeling most of all.

"We're just friends."

"Sure you are." Arturo grimaced at Maris who prissed and preened, knowing it got under Arturo's skin in the worst way. The only thing that kept Arturo from striking Maris was the fact that Maris's blood was even bluer than theirs. And while Maris had been disowned by his family for his homosexuality, he was still protected by League laws. Not to mention the small fact that Maris was the Andarion ambassador to Caron. As such, he fell under the protection of their crowned prince, Nykyrian—a former League assassin who would give his eyeteeth to have one shot at Arturo's jugular.

Unless Darling committed an act of treason, or Nykyrian's grandmother declared war on the Caronese, Maris couldn't be touched without severe consequences.

Arturo sneered at them. "Get out of my sight. You repulse me."

Maris hooked his arm through Darling's. "Come on, sweetie. The air in here is suddenly chilly."

Arturo caught Darling by the hair and snatched him back. "I didn't say you, cock jockey."

Darling locked down on his primal instincts that begged him to hand Arturo his testicles.

Maris gave him a panicked stare.

"Leave," Darling said in Phrixian.

He saw the reluctance before Maris inclined his head and did what he asked. It would only go worse for Darling if Maris defied Arturo, too.

As soon as Maris was gone, Arturo shoved Darling away, but not before he'd wrenched his hair again. "I want that other shirt-lifter out of my house."

"He's the Andarion ambassador. He can't leave without a replacement." A replacement Nykyrian would make sure didn't happen. Maris's real role here was to stay and watch Darling's back. Whenever Arturo went too far, Maris would notify Nykyrian who would then do his best to pull Darling out until his uncle had time to cool down.

Arturo cursed in frustration. "I better not catch you in another display like that. You hear me?"

"I hear you."

Arturo slapped him again. "That's to remind you of your place, cockboy. You're not governor yet. I am."

"Yes, *my Lord Counselor*." He couldn't resist using the title he knew his uncle despised as it reminded Arturo of his lesser place in their world and the fact that he could never have full governorship—only a secondary regeant position.

Arturo raked him with a condemning glare. "You look just like your pathetic father. Get out!"

Darling gave a sarcastic and effeminate military salute before he obeyed.

In the hallway outside, he licked the blood away from the corner of his mouth as he imagined kicking the door in and gutting his uncle on the floor.

One more day.

Yeah, this was going to be the longest thirty-six hours of his life.

But after tomorrow...

Zarya would be his. His uncle would be dead. And he'd finally be free of the utter hell he'd been living in for more than half his life. No more torture. No more bruises, broken bones, or scars.

No more lies.

And yet, in the pit of his stomach was a bad feeling he couldn't shake. Something was going to go wrong.

He could feel it.

You're just paranoid. Arturo would never check the location of his mother or brother. He didn't care enough to do so.

Annalise was safely ensconced in her dorm room and currently guarded.

What could go wrong?

Still, he heard Hauk's voice in his head. *Never underestimate fate's ability to screw any plan to the wall.*

But fate owed him this. All he wanted was one single chance to be happy, just once in his miserable life. It really wasn't asking too much, especially given *his* past.

He slowed as he entered the hallway that led to his bedroom. As always, his uncle's guards were waiting there for him. Yet another degrading routine his uncle insisted on whenever Darling was home, and it was one Darling would die before he told anyone about.

If only I hadn't had to come home tonight to complete my plans...

Rage clouded his sight. *I hate this shit.*

As bad as it would be just in principal, the guards lived to make it as demeaning for him as possible. They loved having power over an aristo. Of being able to use Darling as their personal scapegoat. Even now, he could hear their laughter as they mocked him.

Damn them for it.

One more day...

Yeah, what was another night compared to all the ones he'd already survived?

Still his stomach churned on bitterness as he met the guards' smirking and gloating gazes, then headed into the bathroom across the hall from his room. He turned the water on to brush his teeth. Needing something to comfort him, he pulled Zarya's ring out of his pocket so that he could kiss it and think of the only person whose smile made his life worth living.

How he wished he was with her now...

He slid the ring onto his pinkie and remembered the way she'd opened herself up for him last night. In her arms, he felt like he could fly. He didn't know how she did it, but whenever he was with her, he didn't hear the voices of his past or the ones in his head that constantly derided him. She expelled every demon inside him and made him forget the past. With her, he only saw the future.

Zarya was his haven even in this miserable hell.

Staring at himself in the mirror, he despised what he saw there. He always had. All of Arturo's insults rang in his ears. But the ones that hurt most were from his own mother's lips.

"You will never be what your father was. You're just a pititful shadow of him. May the gods help us if you ever inherit."

He flinched, then pushed those ghosts out of his memory.

Please let tomorrow work out the way it's supposed to.

Don't worry, Dar. You've been on missions before that went bad and yet turned out fine. Whatever happens, you will adapt and you will *survive.*

For Zarya, he would walk through the fires of hell just to make her smile. And if everything went through tomorrow, he'd make sure she never cried again.

Look on the bright side. Either you'll succeed tomorrow or you'll die.

One way or another, he'd finally be free.

3

Darling lay on his "bed" alone, going over all the plans for tomorrow. He mentally checked and rechecked every single second of the day. There were so many details. So many things that could get royally screwed.

It won't.

He didn't believe that for a minute, which was why he was making himself insane going over every variable, planning for the unexpected. No matter how ludicrous the thought, he prepared for it.

Even the highly unlikely possibility of a mechanical failure on his fighter.

The link he'd smuggled into his room past his guards vibrated under his hand. He glanced down, then smiled as he saw Zarya's photo. Now that was enough to reverse even the worst mood. Turning the video output off, he clicked the channel open to see her looking tired, but nonetheless breathtaking. "Hi, beautiful."

"Hey, sexy. I wasn't sure you'd be able to pick up."

Yeah, he didn't want to think about what Arturo or his guards would do if they found out he had the link with him. The least would be he'd have to postpone his try for freedom by a few days as his body healed. "Only for you."

She laughed. "I'm so glad you're not taking fire and that your voice sounds relaxed. What are you doing?"

"Relaxed" was not the word he'd use for himself right now. He was wound tighter than a cat in a dog kennel.

"Wishing I was with you." Probably not the manliest admission. But then, he'd been pretending to be effeminate for so long that sometimes those lines got blurred. Although to hear Maris berate him, he was never effeminate enough.

"I swear, Darling, you're way too masculine for your own good. I don't know how anyone buys the fact that you're gay. They'd have to be blind or stupid. Both actually."

But no one had ever guessed the truth.

Except for possibly his friend Caillen's wife, Desideria. While Desideria hadn't questioned him about it, he'd caught her looking at him strangely a few times when other women were around, as if she suspected the fact he was straight.

But she was the only one.

And Desideria wasn't the woman he wanted to think about right now.

That was reserved for an amber-eyed goddess who made his blood catch fire. He traced the line of her cheek on the screen, wishing he could feel her skin under his hand. "Did you eat anything?"

"Why do you always ask me that?"

"Because I know you. You get so wrapped up in other things that you forget all the time. It's not good for you, you know."

Her eyes were filled with love. "You're the only one who's ever noticed that."

Only because she lived so deep under his skin that he noticed everything about her and her habits.

Like now. He saw the dark shadow in her eyes and it worried him. "What's wrong?"

"I just have a bad feeling that I can't shake."

"About the Resistance?"

"No. We're making good strides there. Two of our patrols were able to turn back Caronese troops from the colonists on Arhan III, and save their homes from being burned. Clarion has something planned for tomorrow. He hasn't told me what, but he swears it'll strike right at the heart of Counselor Cruel."

"The counselor doesn't have a heart. Trust me."

"Yeah, I know. It was my mother and sister he gutted in the throne room when they went to beg for clemency for my father."

Darling winced at the pain in her voice, wishing he could take it away. It was the same agony he carried whenever he thought about his uncle killing his father—in a room he'd been forced to walk past almost every day of his life.

The worst part...Zarya's father had been not only a personal friend to his own father, but one of the royal advisers back in the day. First under his father, and then under Arturo. For that matter, one of her ancestors had been instrumental in placing his family in power back during the early days of their empire. Because of that, the Starskas and the Cruels had been allies for centuries.

But when Zalan had protested Arturo's laws that would allow his uncle to seize the assets of anyone he deemed a threat to his rule, with or without proof, Arturo had declared him a traitor.

In one single heartbeat, Zarya's family had lost everything. Their money, their titles, and ultimately, their lives. Because her mother had known Darling's father and Arturo for so many years, she'd stupidly thought she could bargain with Arturo for her husband's life.

But there was no bargaining with the devil.

Zalan had escaped as soon as he heard what had become of his wife and oldest child. He'd taken Zarya and her other two sisters and brother into hiding, and there he, along with several of his friends who'd also been targeted by Arturo, had set up the Resistance that had been plaguing Arturo ever since.

Thrown into a life of crime against his will, Zalan had been instrumental in helping to limit Arturo's power through well-placed counterassaults. And he'd trained Zarya to lead and take his place should anything happen to him.

But after years of fighting Arturo and his own allies who argued inside the Resistance, and the death of his only son and another daughter, Zalan had lost his fire. He'd decided to leave politics behind and to take his two remaining daughters far away from the horror he'd raised them in. To get them to a better place where they could finally be children and not soldiers for what appeared to be a never-ending cause.

Six years ago when Zalan had been on his way to their safe house to pick up Zarya and her sister, his best friend had murdered him.

It'd been Zarya's eighteenth birthday and Zalan had planned for their new life to be his present to her.

To this day, she couldn't stand celebrating the day of birth. Something Darling had discovered the hard way last year when he'd thrown her a "surprise" party for the two of them. The surprise had been on him more than her. Instead of being happy, she'd almost taken his head off over it.

He'd felt like a total ass when she explained to him why she hated the date so much, and why the last thing she wanted to do was celebrate it.

In the end, after her tears for her family had been spent, they'd decided to move her birthday to the day they'd first met as adults. He could still see the fire in her amber eyes as she looked up at him like he was a hero for thinking of it. "I love that idea. I never had a life worth living without you, anyway."

Tomorrow, he was going to make damn sure that she never had a reason to regret her decision to marry him.

Zarya set her link in the stand on her desk, then smiled. "Clarion wanted me to ask if you'd be back in time to help us liberate the prisoners on Baltael V, on the first."

Another example of Arturo's cruelty. Those prisoners were innocent business owners whose companies had been deemed government property and their assets and revenue seized.

Darling clenched his teeth in anger, but he didn't want her to hear it in his voice since it wasn't directed at her. "If what I'm doing tomorrow works, you won't have to worry about that. They'll already be free."

"What do you mean?"

"I can't tell you, Z. It's Sentella business."

The worry in her eyes increased. "And that's what I have a bad feeling about. I can't shake it no matter what."

"I'm going to be fine, baby. I'm not your father."

"I know. I just…I need you to be all right. You know?" Tears glistened in her eyes, but she blinked them back. He had to give her credit, she rarely gave into them so he knew whenever he saw her tears just how deeply she felt. "I love you too much to lose you now. I couldn't stand to bury you."

God, her words never failed to weaken him. "Same here. It's why I have to do this tomorrow. Not just for the cause, but for you. I want to make sure no one ever threatens you again. You're wearing the tricom I left for you, right?"

Leaning back, she lifted her shirt to show that she had it clipped to her waist. "Thank you for this, by the way. I'm not sure how it works, and I haven't tested it, but I have faith in your abilities. No one makes better tech toys than you do. What caused you to think of it?"

Darling's throat went absolutely dry at the sight of her exposed skin.

She scowled. "Kere? Are you there?"

"Um, yeah. Sorry. I was momentarily distracted by the flash of your breast you just inadvertently gave me. All the blood has now left my brain and I really can't think. What did you ask again?"

Laughing, she tsked at him. "You're so bad."

"Can't help it. Have you looked in a mirror? Damn, woman, the things you do to me."

She wrinkled her nose at him before she playfully started unbuttoning her shirt.

"Ah, now that's just wrong."

"What?" Her tone was one of complete innocence as she stopped at the last button that held her shirt closed right between her breasts. "Guess I need to go then…Last thing I want to do is torture you."

"Nuh-uh. You can't leave me now. That would be cruel."

She flicked her finger back and forth over the final button, tormenting him with expectation. "You told me it was wrong."

"Wrong is what you're doing to me right now."

"Boy, you need to make up your mind. You don't want me to show you anything. Then you do…I just can't figure you out. After all, I'm not in your head."

No, she was some place much worse.

His heart.

"You know what I want, baby."

Biting her lip, she popped the last button and opened her shirt.

Darling's entire body erupted with fire at the sight of her bare breasts. If that wasn't bad enough, she lifted her legs and propped them up on the desk. Oh yeah, he was so hard now, he could barely think straight.

She ran one hand over the top of her breast, circling the nipple, which puckered instantly. "You still alive, baby?"

"No. You've killed me."

She laughed. "Have I told you today how much I love you?"

"I love you, too. And I can't wait to see you again." Darling heard his uncle's muffled voice on the other side of his door as he interrogated Darling's guards. "I have to go."

Her features sobered instantly as she leaned forward. "Please be safe."

"You, too."

She blew him a kiss before she disconnected.

Darling had barely hidden the link he wasn't supposed to have under his cover before his door crashed open.

Arturo glared at him.

Biting back a curse, Darling forced himself to appear nonchalant. "What did I do now?"

"First, you know better than to cut the feed to your room. How many times have I told you to keep it live?"

Yeah, Arturo couldn't stand it if he couldn't spy on him. Pervert. But for obvious reasons—like plotting Arturo's death—Darling had pulled the feed hours ago. "Sorry if, unlike you, I prefer to masturbate in private."

Growling in fury, his uncle closed the distance between them to shove an electronic ledger in his face. "What's this?"

"A ledger."

Arturo slapped him with it.

Darling clenched his fist, but stopped himself before he struck back.

"Were you feeding that other butt monkey with my money?"

His rage snapped into place and it took everything he had not to crush Arturo's throat . . . one hit and he could end all his problems.

Don't do it. You won't die alone . . .

So he struck back with words. "Last I checked, it was my father's money, not *yours*."

That got him a vicious punch to the jaw. Pain exploded through his head.

Damn, that hurt. Good thing he was used to it.

Arturo kicked at him. "Do you know what your father would think of you if he could see what you are? He'd be even more repulsed by you than I am. If he were still alive, you'd have been thrown out on the street years ago. Something I should have done the first time I caught one of your butt nuts coming out of your room."

But they both knew why Arturo couldn't really throw him out. Only a full-blooded, legitimate governor could disinherit a full-blooded heir. That had been one nuisance law his uncle had been unable to overturn. No matter the threat or violence, the CDS refused to budge on the original thirty-five Unification Laws that had been drafted and ratified when the Caronese Empire was first founded 3,408 years ago. Those laws were the bedrock of all others and deemed to be sacred and above contestation or revocation.

Thank the gods for that.

Not to mention, if Darling was thrown out, his uncle couldn't monitor him.

Or kill him under mysterious circumstances.

Even if Arturo did manage to toss him out, once Darling turned thirty, as a full-blooded heir, he could return and overthrow the bastard.

And all because his uncle was the by-blow of a prostitute Darling's grandfather had elevated to royal mistress status. Arturo could only rule so long as Darling and Drakari lived, and were deemed by law to be minors or incompetent.

Should both of them die as things currently stood, Arturo would lose all power, and the ruling family would be chosen by the CDS (probably after much bloodshed) from one of their primary full-blooded male cousins.

The only other way Arturo could hold his current power was if they were dead, and he could produce a son with his blue-blooded wife, but only if the CDS ratified that son's inheritance.

That being said, Arturo's rule would end the moment his son turned thirty.

It was why Darling's father had made the mistake of trusting his much older half brother. Since Arturo couldn't rule for the whole of his lifetime, his father had never conceived of the treachery it would take for Arturo to kill him and then seize control of his sons.

That had been his father's greatest act of blind stupidity.

Arturo grabbed Darling by the neck and pressed him against the floor.

Darling locked his hands around his uncle's wrist as he glared up at him. He could break his uncle's arm so easily.

A single punch to his throat or nose and he could kill him...

It would take so little pressure, and Darling had killed enough men that way to know exactly how easy it would be.

One punch. He wouldn't even feel guilty about it.

Stand down.

You can wait one more day.

Keep your temper.

Think of Maris, Lise, and Drake.

Hating himself for loving them, he loosened his grip and wheezed, forcing himself to stay limp while Arturo choked him.

"I should do your mother a favor and kill you. Then she wouldn't have to cringe every time your name is mentioned by others."

Little did Arturo know his mother didn't cringe. She was so grateful he was a protective idiot that she was more than willing to live with the shame of a gay son than to be dead from her numerous affairs.

"*Really, Darling, how dare you complain. Am I not entitled to one single moment of pleasure in this horrible life I was shoved into? I was only a child when I was forced to marry your father and only twenty-seven when I was widowed. And after all I've done for you, is it too much to ask that you do this one thing for me? I don't understand why, since you're gay anyway, you get so upset about claiming my lovers as yours. I can't believe I raised such a selfish, thoughtless brat. Your father would be as disappointed in you as I am.*"

His sight dulled as his ears buzzed. If he died right now, the only thing his mother would miss was having him cover for her.

Yeah, that would seriously fuck up her day since everyone knew Drake was straight.

Arturo finally released him.

Darling coughed as he finally drew an unrestricted breath through his bruised throat.

Arturo raked a sneer over his naked body. "I'm pulling a hundred thousand credits out of your trust to pay for this and as punishment. You charge something like that to me again, and I swear..." His uncle kicked him hard in the groin.

Cursing, Darling cupped himself as pain exploded through his entire body. Bile rose in his throat. He felt like he was about to vomit.

With one smug smile, Arturo left him to his misery.

You fucking bastard...

He couldn't wait to kill him tomorrow night. *I'm going to bathe in your blood and drink my fill of it.*

The wolf was coming home to den, and it was going to claim sixteen years of long overdue vengeance.

4

Darling opened the door to his sister's dorm room and smiled as he saw her sitting on her bed with pink earphones set deep into her ears while she studied for her finals. He could hear the bass from her music even at his distance. Unaware of his presence and completely lost to her blissful youth, she bobbed her head and kept time to the raucous beat with her stylus. She didn't appear to have a worry in the universe—a state of existence he'd fought hard to give her.

Thank the gods she was still untouched and happy. That alone was worth every degradation and beating he'd ever suffered.

With her long red hair in pigtails that fell to her waist, Lise was beautiful—an exact duplicate of their mother, except for the hazel green eyes she'd inherited from their father. She was extremely tall for a woman. Barely an inch shorter than he was, she towered over their petite mother and most other women.

Sitting on the frilly pink bed in a blue tank top and shorts, surrounded by primitive print textbooks and her e-reader and note ledger, she was all skinny arms and legs.

How he wished he'd been able to study for his exams in such peace and security.

Unlike his brother and sister, Darling had been brought home from school the moment his father had died—two days before his brother and sister had even been notified of the murder. A lovely task his mother and uncle had delegated to him. There were some things a twelve-year-old shouldn't have to do and telling your little brother and sister they wouldn't see their father again was one of them.

After the funeral, Arturo had demanded he stay at the palace to be tutored, supposedly for his own protection. But Darling knew the truth. It was another way for his uncle to keep him under control and make sure Darling didn't try to find another relative to pose as Grand Counsel until his majority.

From that day forward, he'd scarcely had a moment of freedom from his uncle's overbearing presence or fists—not unless he'd somehow managed to run away for it. But that had changed when he was seventeen, and his uncle had made the unfortunate mistake of hiring Nykyrian to guard Darling for public functions. Thinking the fierce Andarion would intimidate him into behaving, his uncle had never dreamed they would become close friends.

His uncle's second biggest mistake.

Because of his own battered past, Nykyrian had welcomed Darling in like a brother. Rather than ride herd on him as his uncle wanted, Nykyrian had given him a cover story so that Darling could finally live like he was almost normal, and have days of freedom at a stretch.

At least until his uncle got nervous about his whereabouts and sicced his dogs on him. Then Darling was dragged back to his cell and kept there until something else distracted Arturo.

When Nykyrian had founded the Sentella to protect innocent victims from the League and her allies, Darling had gladly signed on as their youngest member, and one of the five leaders.

To this day, his uncle had no idea about the other life Darling had been living for years.

But he was about to meet Kere. And there would be no mercy for him.

First though, Darling had to make sure his family was safe.

Annalise and her roommate, who was on the bed next to hers, finally looked up from their work to see him in the doorway.

Lise smiled brightly as she turned her music off. "Sashi? What are you doing here?" Her smile turned into a look of sheer astonishment as she skimmed Darling's body from the high collar of the black battlesuit he wore, all the way to the shining tips of his flight boots. She arched her brow. "And dressed like that, no less. Wow. You almost look straight, shilo."

Darling didn't respond to her term of endearment that meant "adored brother."

"I need you to come with me."

All the blood left her beautiful face as her jaw went slack. "Momair?"

He felt like a total ass as he realized what he'd done to her. The last time he'd spoken to her in a tone like that had been the night he'd told her their father was dead. "She's fine. Drake's fine. I'm fine. I just need you to come with me."

Fury darkened her hazel green eyes. "You dick! Don't you dare scare me like that. You know better. I can't believe you'd do that to me. Asshole!" Letting out an irritated breath, she gestured to the electronics and books around her. "And I can't just leave. I have exams tomorrow."

"They can wait."

Her roommate snorted. "He hasn't met your instructors, has he?"

Darling ignored her. "Lise. Move it. Now."

This time she arched both brows at his military-issued orders. "What has gotten into *you*? You been drinking testosterone from Drake's cup? No offense, but I want my sweet, gay brother back. Please go find him and take this one away. I don't like him at all."

Darling cursed in Phrixian under his breath. He hated whenever Lise dug her heels in over something. Spoiled by everyone around her, even her own guards, she'd always been the most impossible creature in the universe. Second only to their mother, anyway. "Do I have to stun you and carry you out?"

Her eyes dared him to try it. "You do and I'll tell Momair on you."

Scoffing at her threat, he'd pay money to see his mother take him to task. Ladling him with guilt, though, was another matter entirely...

"Oh wait," he said in a fearful tone, "that would mean she'd actually have to speak to me." He made a sound of utter shock. "Maybe even acknowledge my existence. Gods forbid! Kere's fire throne would freeze over from the shock of it."

Honestly, he couldn't remember the last time his mother had said anything to him at all. Even a single syllable. Must have been at least three or four years ago. Maybe more. Whenever she found herself in his presence, she'd quickly walk out the closest door. In the beginning, he'd taken it personally. Now he strangely considered it amusing.

"Forget it, sis. It'll never happen." He tapped his watch. "You have five minutes to get dressed in something a little more appropriate before I stun you and carry you out of here. Naked if I have to."

She jerked her earphones out in a royal huff. "Gah, I swear you've been hanging out with that barbarian Syn too long. You're starting to sound like him." She finally got up and began cramming her materials into a pink tote. "Where are we going and how long will I be gone?"

"A few days."

"Does Momair know?"

"I'm taking you to her and Drake."

Lise straightened up with a frown. "Do I need to pack clothes?"

"No. I don't want you to take anything too personal. I want it to look like you'll be back any second."

She glanced at her roommate before she looked back at him. "Now you are starting to scare me."

He didn't respond to that as he met her roommate's gaze. "Can you tell her instructors that we had a family emergency?"

"Sure."

"Thank you."

As soon as Lise had pulled on a pair of acceptable pants over her shorts, and a large shirt and shoes, he took her arm to guide her from her room, and down the hallway of her dorm.

She looked around with a frown. "Where are my guards?"

"Out of commission for a while." Making sure they couldn't see him, he'd stunned them unconscious and stashed them in a back room down the hallway.

She slowed her pace. "Sashi, you have to tell me what's going on. Are we running from Arturo?"

Only Lise called him sashi. It was the Caronese word for "beloved." An epithet she'd given him when she was four years old and he'd taught her to catch glow flies in their back garden.

Even though she was twenty now, he still saw her as that adorable toddler who would run to him, laughing the whole way.

Because he'd been forced to grow up so young while his siblings had been able to have a fairly normal childhood, he had a hard time thinking of them as adults. Something that seriously pissed them both off.

But he couldn't help it. He was too used to taking fire for them. Besides, he felt more like their father than their brother.

Darling eased his grip on her arm. "Yes, we're running from Arturo."

"Why didn't you say something in my room?"

"I didn't want your roommate to know. I have to make sure all of you are safe for a few days."

She scowled at him. "You're really scaring me. I know something's wrong. What is it?"

"I'm going to get us out from under his fist."

She stopped so abruptly that he lost his grip on her. "What are you going to do? Is it dangerous? It better not be dangerous...Is it dangerous?"

He had to clamp down on the urge to strangle her for holding them up. While Arturo didn't care about Drake or their mother, he did check up on Annalise from time to time—a virgin princess was worth a lot more on the marriage market than a used one. And the guards he'd knocked out would wake up soon and find her gone.

They had to be off planet before that happened or they'd never make it.

"Lise, I don't have time to explain, okay? I need you to trust me and cooperate."

"All right." She lifted her hand to touch the scarred side of his face. "But please don't get hurt, sashi. Not for me or for anything. You're the only father I've ever known, and you're the only person in this entire universe I know I can call if I need something. I can't lose you, you know? You're all I have."

Touched by her heartfelt words, Darling kissed her on the forehead. "It'll be fine. Now we need to get moving."

She nodded before she finally picked up the pace.

He led her through campus and out toward the landing bay where he'd left his unmarked fighter.

They were almost home free.

Just a few minutes more.

If they could make it to launch, no one would be able to stop them. He'd have her safely tucked away with Nykyrian, and everything would change for the better.

Tomorrow, they would be free to live the lives they should have been living all along.

C'mon, fate, don't screw me in this.

Inside the hangar, Darling glanced over at a small group of six men dressed as college engineers, but he paid them no heed as he led his sister toward his ship on the left.

Not until he overheard one of them speaking to the others in Caronese—a language that wasn't common here in the Garvon sector. Fearing assassins were after him, he listened to their conversation intently. "Hey, isn't that the princess we're after?"

Those words registered at the same time he saw the group rushing toward them, reaching for weapons.

What the hell? They weren't Caronese soldiers or guards his uncle might have sent. They were dressed as civs.

But their weapons were military grade...

Shit. It *was* an attack.

When their leader ducked out from the corner in front of them, Darling's blood ran cold.

It was Clarion Lubomir. Zarya's right hand...and *his* ally.

No, not *Darling's* ally.

Kere's.

Double shit. Clarion would never believe that Kere was also the Caronese heir they fought against and hated. None of them would. All they saw was a royal-blooded enemy who stood for everything that had ever repressed them. Every failure in their lives. Every disappointment from not having a better job to being saddled with a spouse who nagged them to distraction.

It was *all* his family's fault.

Not one of those men knew how many shots he'd taken to

protect their backs. How many times he'd fought by their side against his uncle's soldiers.

How many times he'd carried them to safety when they were wounded or under fire. And right now, even if they did, they most likely wouldn't care anyway. *You wear the uniform, you're judged by the banner on the sleeve—the same banner we'll wrap around your body for your burial.*

Fuck me...

They opened fire.

Darling moved to cover his sister. "Run, Lise! Get to my ship."

Without questioning him, she dropped her tote, and for once, obeyed. Running backward, Darling tried to protect her as best he could.

He mentally reviewed the weapons he had on him. They were all designed to kill. If he used even a single one, it'd tear his allies apart. That was the last thing he wanted. They were good men with families he knew in some cases on an intimate level. They didn't deserve to die over a stupid mistake.

Think, Darling, think. The last thing he'd anticipated was his own allies assaulting him.

Damn it! Why hadn't he even considered it?

'Cause the bastards were supposed to be in Caronese territory, not Garvon.

Oh yeah, there was that...

Not to mention, they'd never gone after *his* family before. Arturo, his wife and daughters, yes. But Darling's immediate family had always been off limits.

He growled in frustration. He'd only had the two stun blasts he'd used on Lise's guards. Why hadn't he brought more?

'Cause who would have thought of *this*?

Darling kept himself between Lise and their fire as he went with her, toward the ship. Blasts of color ricocheted everywhere.

Thank the gods they weren't better shots. Over the past years, he'd often laughed at Clarion for his lousy aim and had even tried to teach him how to shoot better.

Thank the gods Clarion was a slow learner.

One blast came within millimeters of Lise. Had she not put her head down a second earlier to run faster, she'd have lost it.

His blood boiled. So this was Clarion's great plan? To kidnap his sister and what? Hold her for ransom? Was he out of his idiotarian mind? Arturo wouldn't pay to get her back. He'd assume her raped and then she would be useless to him. The only value she had to their uncle was as a virgin bride. *Shit, shit, shit...*

Lise made it to the ship, then hesitated as she glanced at Darling and the men on their heels. If she went up the ladder, she'd be an easy target even with their limited abilities.

Turning around, Darling pulled out his blaster and opened cover fire, trying to buy her enough time to get into the cockpit. He had no intention of wounding them. All he aimed for was the space between Clarion and the man on his left.

But it didn't work that way.

The moment he pulled the trigger, his blast was absorbed as if the Resistance fighters were protected by a force field. An instant later, pulses of energy shot out in all directions.

It was a distinctive pattern he knew all too well, since it was one he'd designed and created.

No...

Surely not...

One of the blasts struck him hard in the chest, knocking him off his feet forcefully enough to skid him across the concrete floor. Had he not been wearing his armor, it would have killed him. But worse than his wound, the pulses split into a whole round of volleys that bounced through the hangar—just like he'd built them to do.

He watched in horror as one of the pulses went straight into his little sister's back. "Sashi! Help me!" she screamed before she was paralyzed by the blast. It knocked her away from the ladder to land beside his ship.

Her cry for him tore him apart. But not as much as the fact that he couldn't get to the little sister he'd sworn over and over again to protect from all harm.

Terrified, he stared at her as a pool of red spread across the concrete, bleeding out from under her body.

No...

No!

There was so much blood. It soaked her clothes and covered her outstretched hand. Darling wanted to go to her and protect her. But he couldn't move at all.

And he knew exactly why. The tricom—the weapon he'd built solely for Zarya to protect her from enemies. Instead, it'd been used against him and Lise.

I killed my baby sister...

Tears filled his eyes as the truth kicked his teeth in and struck him harder than the blast that had paralyzed him. Grief and agony shredded his conscience.

By trying to save Lise, he'd caused her death. How could he have been so stupid? How could fate have done this to him?

The Resistance members came forward with cocky strides, laughing at their success. Two went over to Lise while the rest surrounded Darling.

One of them kicked his shoulder with the toe of his boot. "Look at that. The bastard can't move at all."

Another one clapped hands with Clarion. "I can't believe it worked! Man, we need to send Kere flowers or a woman or something to say thank you for this."

Clarion smiled as he pulled the tricom off his belt and kissed it. "I can't wait to tell Zarya how well this worked. She's not going to believe it."

The rebel who'd bent over his sister stood up. "I got bad news, guys. The bitch here is dead."

Darling felt a single tear sliding from the corner of his eye as the rebel confirmed his worst fear.

His precious baby sister was dead.

Because of me.

Because of something *he'd* invented…

Over and over, he saw images of Lise reaching for him to hold or protect her. Saw the smile in her eyes and heard her laughter as she hugged him tight, and told him how much she loved her big brother. He'd been eight when she was born, and from the moment he'd first seen her bald head and those huge hazel green eyes staring at him, and she'd wrapped her tiny, baby fingers around his pinkie before gumming it, she'd owned his heart.

No matter their fights. No matter their differences. She had meant everything to him.

How could she be gone?

How could I have killed her?

The soldier closest to him cursed. "Are you sure?"

"See for yourself. The blast left a huge hole in her. What a waste, too. We could have definitely had fun with *her* while we waited for payment."

Unmitigated fury, agony, and grief tore through Darling's blackened soul.

How could he ever face his mother and brother after this?

How could he ever face himself?

Why couldn't it have killed me, too?

One of the soldiers kicked him in the ribs. "Stupid son of a whore! Damn you, for screwing this up." Aiming his blaster at Darling's head, he looked over to Clarion. "You want me to kill this one, too?"

Snarling in anger, Clarion approached Darling. With the toe of his boot, he lifted Darling's face so that he could see his features. The moment he did, a wide smile curved his lips. "Oh no, Davon. This...this is much better than even the princess."

"How so?"

Clarion laughed again as he kicked Darling's head. "What we have here, gentlemen, is the lovely cock-sucking royal fag himself. Darling Cruel. Caronese heir to the throne and future governor of our worthless empire. We just hit the mother lode of good fortune." He clapped hands with Davon. "Get him on board before someone else sees him. He'll be worth ten times what the princess was."

His heart broken by what he'd inadvertently set into motion, Darling had no choice except to lay there as they grabbed him and ruthlessly dragged him onto their ship.

It would take at least four hours before the stun would wear off and he could move again, and tell them who he really was.

If not longer. Until then, he was as helpless as an infant. Worse, he could hear, feel, and see everything they did to him. But he couldn't make a sound.

Or make a single move to protect himself.

It was just like being in the mental institutions all over again. One of the crueler regimens they'd used on him had been the paralytics that had kept him immobile and fully aware with elevated sensory drugs to heighten his senses while they "treated" him using various aversion therapies.

Nausea swelled inside him as he remembered the weeks where the doctors had tortured him for his uncle, trying to make him docile and weak.

Trying to break him.

I can't do this again.

I can't.

Raw, unmitigated panic tore him apart. Another confinement like that would make him insane. It would.

Determined to the core of his soul, he strained to move. To fight back. To do anything other than lay here as their victim.

It was useless.

He was completely at their "mercy." *Goddamn me for being so fucking stupid…*

They dumped him in the cargo hold. Clarion and one of the others went to launch the small ship while the rest stayed in the back with him.

Three more joined their group.

A rebel on his right jerked his chin toward Darling. "Hey, Timmon, how much you think those boots are worth?"

"About a year's pay from the looks of them." Timmon moved forward to snatch one off. "Oh yeah, that ain't silver on them. It's pladin and they're custom made. Anyone wear his size?" When he went to snatch the other one off, he hit the blade release in the heel and sliced open his hand.

Cursing, he kicked Darling repeatedly in the ribs and face. "Bastard! What are you doing with an assassin's trick?"

If Darling could move, he'd show him a lot more tricks than that. Including the one Nykyrian had taught him of snatching a human heart out of his target's chest before his target died.

Another rebel came forward from the front of the ship to investigate him. He pulled his helmet off and Darling wished he could curse.

It was Pip. A man whose life he'd saved just a few months back. Pip had been pinned down by Caronese troops after they'd made a medical drop to the free clinics his uncle had wanted closed because they'd refused to pay the exorbitant taxes he'd imposed on them.

Darling still had the red mark on his side where he'd been shot while protecting Pip.

Pip leaned down to jerk at the neck of his clothes. "Man, look at this. A fortune for his battlesuit, too." He backhanded Darling. "You rotten faggot. How many people starved to buy you that, huh?"

None. He'd bought the battlesuit with the money he'd made through the Sentella. An organization dedicated to protecting the very people who were now attacking him for no reason other than a birthright he couldn't help. A birthright that had been filled with lessons from his father about protecting his people.

"Remember, son, you are a servant of the Caronese. Your job isn't to rule them so much as it is to protect and provide for their well-being. The strength of your reign will be judged by the strength of our people. Their happiness is your happiness. Love flows both ways. Never abuse your power or your people. There is no glory in cruelty. Only shame." His father's words haunted him now.

That sense of noblesse oblige was why he'd joined and funded the Resistance as Kere.

Unlike his father, Arturo saw the people as tools to be used and destroyed when they no longer served his needs.

Pip kicked him again. "Get his cards and anything else he has of value. We can sell it."

"Yeah," Timmon laughed. "I have many needs."

Shocked and horrified by their ruthless animal behavior, Darling lay helpless as they stripped him completely bare. While they pilfered his belongings, they found Zarya's ring on his pinkie where he'd placed it last night so that he could keep that small part of her with him.

Don't steal it.

It was all she had left of her dead mother...Her only inheritance.

His throat tightened as he remembered her giving it to him six months ago. *"I can't take this, Zarya. I know what it means to you."*

"Please take it. My father used to say that it would protect me from harm. See..."—she'd pointed to the side of the stone—*"it has the face of Tearsa on it."* Tearsa was the goddess of healing and protection. *"I've never been wounded while wearing it. And I want her to protect you, too. Please, Kere. You're everything to me. I have to know that you're safe at all times."*

He'd allowed Zarya to put it on his pinkie and had sworn to her that he'd protect it with his life.

It was a vow he intended to keep.

Even though Darling was paralyzed, he focused the mental powers he had as hard as he could. They weren't going to take her ring without a fight. Touching the part of his mind that functioned on a higher level, he managed to clench his fist shut to keep them from removing the ring.

They tightened their grip on his hand as they attempted to pry it open.

Darling used everything he had to keep his fist tight and to protect that ring like he'd promised.

Pip cursed him for it, then pulled out a knife and sliced his finger off.

Pain ripped through him as tears dulled his sight and his head swam. He felt so sick.

Jeering in triumph, Pip danced his severed finger in front of Darling's eyes as he slid the ring off it. "Bonus round. Now we have proof to send to the governor that we have him." He tossed the bloody ring into the air and caught it. "And I have something

I can use to buy my wife a new dress and pay some bills. Thanks, Highness. Tim, stop the bleeding. We don't want His Royal Faggotry dying on us like his bitch sister did."

Appalled, disgusted, and heartbroken, Darling let the agony and horror of everything that had happened in the last few minutes wash over him. But worse than that was the fear of what would happen to his mother and Drake after they killed him.

And they would.

There was no way in hell his uncle would ever spend a single cred to get him back. Not after Arturo had already sent an assassin to kill him. And he knew that for a fact. He had given the contract that Arturo had signed listing him as the target to Hauk for safekeeping until tonight when Darling had planned to use it to call Arturo out at the CDS.

Little did the Resistance know, they'd done his uncle a huge favor today. For once, Arturo wouldn't have to fabricate a story as to why his "obstacle" had died by an assassin's hand. Arturo would dance for joy that his enemies had killed his nephew for him.

And the men around him were going to get what they deserved. Arturo as their permanent governor. An uncontested leader who hated them as much as they hated him. One who would take the same amount of pity on them as they'd shown Darling and his sister.

None whatsoever.

May the gods help them now that he wouldn't be there to protect them from Arturo's wrath.

Yeah, fate was a bitch, but she always had a wicked sense of humor. Today, he was her punch line.

Tomorrow, she'd be laughing at them.

Darling's thoughts turned to Zarya. He wanted to believe she had nothing to do with this. That she'd never sanction such cruelty from her men.

But he knew better.

Clarion had the very weapon he'd designed for her. A weapon she'd worn on her body just last night, and had promised she wouldn't take off no matter what. The only way for Clarion to have it was for her to have given it to him.

I'm such a fool.

He'd let his love for her blind him to her true nature. She was just like everyone else. Selfish. Heartless.

Cruel.

Don't doubt her. Maybe he stole it.

Darling ruthlessly held on to that single hope until they landed and the men roughly dragged him off the ship. Like his palace guards, they took pleasure in causing him as much pain as possible.

They were halfway through the hangar he knew as well as his own when he heard Zarya's voice off in the distance.

"What's going on here?" she demanded as she closed the distance between them.

Pip answered. "We captured the effing heir, Darling Cruel. Can you believe it? How lucky are we? Bastard fell right into our hands."

Darling couldn't lift his head to see Zarya, but he prayed she would recognize him and stop this madness. Surely, she would know his body.

His scars.

True she'd never seen them in any kind of light, but she'd felt every inch of his body with her hands and tongue enough that she should know it by now. Couldn't she sense it?

If nothing else, she should recognize the tattoo on his shoulder blade that marked him as a Sentella soldier and an assassin. While it was custom designed, it still bore enough semblance to the Sentella's emblem that she'd have to know it. Surely... Not to mention the wound in the middle of his tattoo that she'd castigated him over just two nights ago.

Please, Z. Please see me...

He'd never needed her more than he did right now.

"Why is he naked?" she asked.

"His clothes fell off." Pip laughed. "Don't worry, though. We'll get some beggar's best for His Highness."

She lifted Darling's head off his chest so that they stared at each other. As it always did from years of his training it, his long hair fell over the left side of his face, hiding his scar from her view.

Even so, couldn't she recognize the lips that had kissed and pleased her for countless hours?

Zarya, please help me. Please...

I love you so much.

How could she not see it in his eye?

But there was no love in her gaze. No recognition whatsoever. Only hatred and contempt.

She sneered at him. "Bastard royal scum. You're all lying hypocrites. I hope all of you get what you deserve." She spat in his face and released his head to fall forward again.

Darling swore his heart shattered. Surely that was the only thing that could explain the utter misery and agony he felt.

The total desolation. He'd been abandoned before in his life by people he loved, but never had it hurt as much as this did.

She can't stand the sight of the real me...She wasn't able to see past his birthright anymore than the others.

So much for all her brave assertions that his looks didn't matter.

Why had he ever expected better from her? Even if everything had gone as planned, she would have never accepted Darling Cruel as the man she loved. He would have sickened her as much as he did his uncle and mother.

No matter how he mapped it, all roads led to her slapping his face and leaving him out in the cold.

He heard Maris's bitter voice in his head. *"Everyone lies. Everyone betrays, Darling. The world is eat up with selfishness and cruelty. You need to learn to accept it like the rest of us have."*

Zarya stepped back. "Clarion, report to my office."

"What about our prisoner?"

"Take him to a holding cell. You and I need to talk. Now."

Pip replaced Clarion who'd been holding Darling's left arm. "You want us to wait for you?"

"Nah. Make sure *His Highness*"—Clarion sneered those words—"is well appointed. After I talk to Zarya, I'll inform his uncle of our demands."

"Will do." Pip dragged Darling down the hallway Darling had walked a hundred times while joking with him, Clarion, and dozens of others who were here now.

None of them spoke up on his behalf. Not a one tried to help him or tell the others that what they were doing to him, a fellow human being, was wrong and beneath them.

A million regrets and condemnations tore through him. Never had he felt more betrayed by anyone.

Not until Pip chained him to the wall.

Pip raked a repugnant glare over Darling's naked, exposed body that was covered with bruises, wounds, and scars. Some from his uncle's hatred, the rest from his efforts to keep the Resistance safe and viable. "I never thought an aristo would look like you." He pulled Darling's shoulder away from the wall to examine the tattoo on his back. "You're even marked. Anyone recognize this?"

One by one they shook their heads negatively.

"It kind of looks like an assassin's mark," Pip said with a frown.

"Yeah, right," one of the others laughed. "Given its location, you can tell who's been biting the pillows when he gets screwed. I'm sure he had it done to look tough for all of his boyfriends. Make them think they were drilling a real man when they were on top of him and not some limp-stick fag."

Pip joined his laugher. "No kidding, right? The only thing he ever trained was his finger to press a button so that he could order someone else to come wipe his ass for him." Pip hit him right where he was wounded.

Had Darling been able to move or speak, he would have laughed at their arrogant ignorance. That tattoo was the mark of the Sentella and an assassin's emblem. A long knife going through the center of a skull with a snake crawling out of its right eye socket. The tail of the snake came out from the mandible and coiled around the bottom part of the blade.

It was a grim promise. *Da nullam clementiam*—"Give no mercy." As his father had taught him and as the Resistance had proven to him by their actions—*"Never be afraid to kill or destroy your enemies. They would not hesitate to kill or destroy you."*

And with what they'd done today, they had just made it to the top of his kill list.

All of them.

Pip grabbed his jaw and slammed his head back into the wall as hard as he could.

Unmitigated pain exploded through his skull, blurring his vision. Gah, that hurt.

Pip tightened his hold, making sure his fingers bit deeply into Darling's cheeks. "You better be glad we need you whole for the ransom, rich boy. If we didn't..." He held Darling's severed finger up for him to see. "This would be the least of your injuries."

Darling tried to spit at him, but all it did was come out as a low burst of breath.

Pip glanced over his shoulder at another rebel. "Grab a quarter muzzle for our guest. Last thing we want is to hear his royal complaints when the stun blast wears off."

Darling's stomach shrank at his words. A quarter muzzle was an old Caronese torture device that had once been used for traitors. It had a spiked ball that was put beneath the tongue, then two thin barbed straps that were shoved down the throat. Anytime the wearer swallowed or tried to speak, the spikes sliced into their throat and the underside of their tongue.

Though brutal, it was probably some kind of karmic justice since it'd been invented by one of Darling's ancestors and coldly used to punish his enemies. It, along with many other such vicious acts, was why his family had been given the Cruel surname by their people centuries ago.

So this is how I die.

Not peacefully in old aged sleep like he'd hoped. Or under his uncle's fist or a lucky shot taken at him by his enemies as he'd expected.

No. He would die betrayed and tortured by the very people he'd risked his own life to help.

And when they shoved the muzzle into his mouth and tightened its thin strap around his head until he tasted nothing but his own blood, a new fire burned through him.

I won't let you kill me. I will survive this.

Somehow. Someway. And when he did . . .

He was going to kill every one of them.

Slowly. Painfully.

And with relish.

"Why are you so pissed?"

Stunned by the sheer stupidity of that question, Zarya stared at her second in command. Was he out of his mind? How could he not understand her anger? "We are not kidnappers. My God,

Clarion, that's a member of the royal family you just dragged in here. Have you any idea what the League would do to us if they found out?"

He scoffed derisively. "They don't care, and you know it. Relax. We're just holding him long enough to get the ransom, then we'll release him."

"He's seen our faces."

"So? We're all off grid. Even when they know who we are, they can't find us *now*. They won't find us later. Besides, he's an aristo. He can't brush his own teeth without his valet doing it for him, never mind swear vengeance and hunt us down. All he'll do is send others after us and they won't do shit but milk his trust fund until it's gone or they get bored. It's not like the Sentella or the Tavali are going to take his contract against us. They don't work for the aristos unless it's against the League, and you know it."

Still, Zarya had a bad feeling about this. She didn't like cruelty against anyone, and the last thing she wanted was to incur the wrath of any aristo.

Look on the bright side, at least they didn't kidnap Drakari Cruel. Rumor had it he was even more brutal than his uncle. And he was battle trained by some of the best instructors in the elevated circles.

Darling...

By all accounts she'd ever read, seen, or heard, he was weak, passive, and extremely effeminate. No backbone whatsoever. It was said that even his own bodyguards ignored his orders and snatched him around like a helpless child. Most of the aristocracy hated him. Unless his uncle commanded it for state functions, his own mother refused to be in his presence or even say his name.

So in that case, Clarion was right. Darling would never come after them. Once he was home, he'd go back to his cozy world and forget about this.

Born of Silence

Wishing she could really believe that, she chewed her bottom lip as fear poured through her.

Surely, Clarion had thought this matter through. The Grand Counsel would quickly pay the ransom to get his heir back, and all of this would be behind them in a few days.

"You better be right, Clarion. If you're not, I'm going to shoot you myself."

He tsked at her. "Of course, I am. Now if you're through reaming me, I have a ransom demand to make."

"Go." Before she yielded to her desire to gut him where he stood.

Still, Zarya saw red. How could Clarion have been so foolish? How could he think she'd condone this? No wonder he'd refused to elaborate on his grand scheme for bringing the counselor to his knees.

But the deed was done now. There was no way to undo it. The penalty wouldn't be any less steep if they released the prince now as opposed to after they had the ransom. A ransom they could use to buy supplies to protect and feed Arturo's innocent victims.

Sick to her stomach with fear and trepidation, she reached for her link, wanting to talk to Kere and ask him what she should do. If anyone could advise her on this matter, it would be he.

She pressed his number.

It went straight to voicemail. "You've reached subsector 8-8-4-9-0-5. I can't take your call right now, but leave a message and I'll get back with you."

She savored the rich sound of his deep, masculine voice. "Hey, baby, it's me. Can you please call me as soon as you get this? I really need to hear from you. Love you." Sighing, she hung up, then went to her ledger so that she could pull up the news.

Sure enough, they were already reporting the kidnapping.

The male journalist's eyes glowed with glee. "Yes, you heard that correctly. Darling Cruel, the heir to the Caronese Empire, was taken today from Zanderov in the Garvon Sector by a group who has yet to identify themselves. During the abduction, the Princess Annalise Cruel was shot in the hangar. We have no word on her condition and no word from the abductors..." The reporter kept talking, but Zarya couldn't hear anything else as her heart pounded in her ears.

Clarion had shot the princess? Why had the moron failed to mention that?

Because he knew I'd kill him for it.

Oh dear gods...

This would call down the League on them in addition to the Caronese. While the counselor wasn't fond of the Resistance and did make concentrated efforts to put them down, they'd never really been his priority before.

After this, that would change.

Terrified, she left her office and stormed toward Clarion's. *You flipping, stupid, mentally deficient...* She couldn't think of insults foul enough to call him. The Caronese would tear them apart over this. While Darling might be hated by everyone, the princess most certainly wasn't. Since the moment she'd kissed her father's coffin during his funeral procession and had said good-bye to him when she'd only been a tiny child, Annalise had held the very heart of their people.

They adored their princess and the people they relied on to help them would be up in arms that anyone had dared to harm her. Especially one of their own...

Everyone would turn against the Resistance now.

Her hands shaking, she opened Clarion's door without knocking and stepped inside. She froze as she heard Arturo's voice on a secured, untraceable line.

"I don't care what you do with that little bastard. Cut him

into pieces. Feed him to your sister. Flush him through an airlock. Whatever. I don't pay ransoms to terrorists. Nor do I negotiate. As far as I'm concerned, he was dead the minute you took him. So shove your ransom demand up your ass and don't waste my time again." The counselor cut the transmission.

Stunned, Clarion cursed as he sat back in his chair.

Zarya couldn't believe what she'd just heard. The cold, harsh brutality.

Kere had been right. The counselor had no heart whatsoever. How could anyone be that viciously callous about the life of their own family?

The same man who killed your mother and sister for daring to ask for mercy for your father...

But that wasn't what concerned her most. By their actions today, her men had broken numerous League laws. And that was something that carried a harsh death sentence should they ever fall into League custody.

"Why did you shoot the princess?"

Clarion swung around in his chair like he was ready for battle. His features relaxed as he saw her. "I didn't. The prince did."

"What do you mean?"

Clarion pulled her tricom off his belt and set it on the desk in front of him.

Fury tore through her as she felt her waist to find it gone. "What exactly did you do?"

"After you told me what it was this morning, I borrowed it for today. Just in case. Boy, was I right and glad we had it."

Disgust for him overwhelmed her. *That's what you get for having a thief as your second in command.* He'd sworn to her that he was reformed. Obviously, he was as much a liar as he was a thief. "Are you completely insane?"

A tic started in his jaw. "Hey, the little prick opened fire on us.

Had we not had it, one of us wouldn't have come home. Would you rather *we* be hurt?"

Reminding herself that she couldn't show her emotions or else she'd be replaced as their leader, she took it off his desk, and counted to ten. The one thing she hated about being Caronese, they were a patriarchal race and in the mind of most men, women didn't belong in the military or in politics. And as leader of the Resistance, she was neck deep in both.

Still, she wanted to beat him for what he'd done. "Of course not, but you had no right to take this from me. It wasn't designed for you."

"Sue me, then, okay? Besides we have bigger problems." Clarion sat back in his chair. "What do I do with a prince no one wants?"

"I don't know, Captain Intelligent. You were the mastermind behind this fiasco. Fix it."

Clarion rolled his eyes. "How?"

Like she had a clue? "I'll talk to Kere and see what he thinks. Maybe the Sentella has something we can use to wipe his memory and we can dump him somewhere that they can find him."

"Fine. But while we have him, maybe we can use him."

Another fear settled deep inside her. After this mess, she wasn't sure of his intentions anymore. "What do you mean?"

Clarion wagged his eyebrows as a smile split his face. "Think about it, Z. As the royal prick, Darling can give us details about security on the palace and all the government buildings. There's no telling what all he's been privy to that could prove invaluable to us. Do I have your permission to interrogate him?"

She mulled the idea over. Clarion could be on to something. If they had details about security and Arturo's plans, it could save a lot of lives.

Still…

It's only an interrogation. She'd done dozens of them herself over the years with various prisoners. It wasn't like they were going to torture him or anything. A few questions before they released the prince.

What was the harm?

"If you must."

Clarion's smile widened. "Thank you."

Inclining her head to him, Zarya left his office and pulled her link out again. She tried Kere one more time, but again all she got was his voicemail.

C'mon, baby, answer me soon.

Then, she tried calling the Sentella who refused to do anything more than take a message for him.

Why wasn't he getting back to her? It wasn't like him to go this long without at least texting her a note to say he'd call her when he had a chance.

By the time she returned to her office, the sick feeling in the pit of her stomach had bred babies. They were jumping up and down, until she was absolutely ill with nausea.

Kere was in trouble. She knew it. She could sense it with every part of her being.

But how could she find him when she didn't know who he really was?

5

Darling hung from chains by his throbbing, bleeding wrists. Both of his legs had been broken repeatedly so that his wrists supported all his weight.

Unrelenting pain coursed through him with merciless knives that shredded every part of him...

It was unbearable. He kept drifting in and out of consciousness. The horror of his time here in Resistance custody blurred with his stints in mental institutions, and the times his uncle had punished him at home. They blended together into one unending nightmare of bitter agony.

I just want it to stop.

At this point, he wasn't sure how long he'd been held. It seemed like eternity, but since he couldn't see daylight, he had no way of gauging one day from another. Unless they were coming in to hurt him, which they did at random intervals, they kept the lights off. Something they thought added to his misery.

But it didn't. Courtesy of his mother's mutated genes, he saw as well in pitch-black darkness as he did in brightest sunlight.

Right now, his head swam and his empty stomach churned so much that he feared he might vomit again—something that made the muzzle tear into his throat and choke him with blood and bile. Worse, it produced a severe drowning sensation, like being waterboarded.

The pain and deprivation, as well as the fever he'd been burning, caused him to hallucinate. Sometimes he thought he saw his father. Or his uncle.

His friends.

But the two people who haunted him most were Maris and Zarya. They drifted in and out of the room like ghosts who tormented him with memories of better days. Of the happy future he'd thought to have.

Sometimes the loss of that dream was even harder to bear than the torture.

The only truth he knew for certain was that he was starving, aching, and woefully alone.

No one had come for him. Even though he had a tracking chip encoded in his body that Arturo had used to find him over and over again when Darling hadn't wanted him to, no one came.

So what's new?

Stop it. They were looking for him. They were. This wasn't the same as when he was in a mental institution and his friends couldn't get him out without a court order or his uncle's permission. He was in a secure facility that would block his chip from transmitting to an outside source. That was the only reason they hadn't found him.

It had to be.

Nykyrian had known that he would be bringing Lise to his home. The minute Nyk caught word of her death and of Darling's kidnapping, he and the rest of the Sentella would be out scouring space for him.

So would Maris.

His friends wouldn't betray him.

Only Zarya had done that. And what cut him deepest were the times when he heard her voice through the door as she walked past it. Especially when she was laughing with the very people who tortured him.

He'd been willing to give her the universe.

She couldn't even give him the time of day. How could *she*, as the Resistance leader, not come in here and see what they were doing to their prisoner? Did she know or did she just not care what they did?

How could she not know? his mind kept asking. The rebels constantly bragged about it to others—another thing he'd heard outside his room at all hours. They thought his humiliation and torture were funny, and they mocked him for it. That was what ate at him constantly.

How could he have so misjudged the people he'd been willing to die for?

How could he have ever trusted Zarya?

All men and women lie. But never lie to yourself. That had been one of the primary rules his father had forced him to memorize as a boy. Never be deceived by others.

And never deceive yourself.

Yet his love for Zarya had blinded him to her real nature. She was every bit as apathetic to the suffering of others as Arturo. She didn't care enough about her prisoner to even open the door. Or click on the cameras that were pointed at him.

That would only take seconds of her time.

Unless she sat in her office watching what they did to him. That one thought alone was enough to drive him insane. Had she watched them as they beat him to the brink of death? Was she one of the people who laughed at him while he suffered? One of the ones who enjoyed watching his misery?

"You don't look so regal now, Highness. What? Common-ers offend you? You still think you're too good to be with us, don't you?"

But those were their insecurities. He'd never felt that way about anyone. And every time they mocked him, it made him wonder if Zarya was sitting on the other side of the camera, doing the same. Laughing at him. Telling them to hurt him more...

Had she ever loved him at all? Or had she used Kere for his money and military support? Didn't she miss him in any capacity?

From the sounds of her in the hallway whenever she spoke to the others, it didn't seem like she'd even noticed he was gone.

Was he nothing more than a means to her end? He didn't want to think that. He tried not to.

But nothing else made sense.

Not that it really mattered to him anymore.

Nothing did. The one good thing about pain and grief were that they put everything else in perspective.

Even if he survived this, he was mangled so badly at this point he'd be lucky to walk again. Never mind fight. Every day, his body shut down more and more. It no longer even felt like it was his. Rather, he seemed to be a caricature in a hazy kaleidoscope.

Just let me die. Please. He was through with trying to live for revenge.

Why should he?

Lise was dead because of him. He should have left her in school. Had he not tried to make it better, she'd be alive and he...

He'd be in pain, but not like this. As bad as his past had been, it didn't compare to what they'd done to him since his capture. None of it. His head reeled from memories of their abuse that he knew would never leave him. Those images would torture him into eternity.

And he didn't want any more memories shredding his dignity and tearing into what little self-esteem he'd managed to salvage from the brutality of his life.

I'm through. There was nothing left but the dying that refused to come and relieve him of his misery.

"I'm heading home, guys. I'll see you tomorrow."

He winced at the sound of Zarya's cheery voice outside his room. There was no grief in her tone. No sign that she was missing him, or even concerned about Kere at all. There hadn't been. Not once the whole time he'd been held.

I'm not even worth a passing thought.

She never even mentioned his name or said that she was looking for him.

"I copied you in on the report I sent over to Sirce," she continued to whomever she was talking to. "I'm not sure what they'll do with it, but I wanted to make sure they had it, just in case. Do you have any plans for the weekend?"

"Not really," Clarion said. "I'll probably stay here and work through it. What about you?"

"My sister's coming in for a visit, and Ture's meeting us for dinner tonight. It should be quiet for a few days."

"With you two? I doubt that. I can just imagine the late night slumber party with both of you dressed in lacy underwear, having pillow fights on your bed."

Zarya laughed. "You really need to stop watching those crap programs, Clair. Women don't do that."

"Sure you don't. That's just a lie you tell us guys so that it won't make us any crazier than normal."

She laughed again. "Good night, hon. I'm out of here before I'm late to dinner. See you later."

Late to dinner . . .

He could only vaguely recall what it was like to sit at a table and eat his fill. *I hope you choke on it, bitch.*

Never had Darling hated anyone more than he did her. She would go home and have a fun weekend with her sister and best friend while he would never see his again.

The image of his precious Lisie lying dead was permanently seared into his mind. Every time he closed his eyes, he saw the blood pooling around her. His guilt flogged him more than they ever could.

I'm so sorry, Lisie. Please forgive me for failing you.

The door opened to admit Clarion who wore a gas mask to protect himself from the noxious odors in the room. If only Darling could escape it.

Even for a nanosecond.

But Darling had to give his ex-ally credit. Clarion had told him when his uncle refused to pay the ransom that they were going to take all of their ills out on his hide and make him wish he'd never been born a prince.

They'd certainly delivered well on that vow.

Funny how that was the only promise someone had ever made to him that they'd kept. Not the one to love or protect him.

Just the one to make him regret every breath he took.

Clarion turned the lights on. "You asleep, Your Royal Faggotry?" He slapped Darling's face, causing the muzzle to bite into his tongue and throat.

Darling wanted to lunge at him, but all he could do was turn his head so that Clarion could slap something other than the bone deep gash on his cheek that had festered over the last few days from an infection he hoped killed him.

"Sorry about our poor hospitality. I was told that no one's fed you in the last three days. We can't have you dying on us, now can we?"

Cold, fierce panic went through Darling. Not only could he not stand them feeding him, it was *what* they usually fed him that was the worst. He did his best to resist, but it was as futile as trying to stand.

Against all his efforts, Clarion grabbed him by the throat and tilted his head back so that he could pour a cold, salted broth into his mouth.

Thank the gods, it was broth this time. Still, the spices and salt made every injury in his mouth and throat burn and ache as he choked on the blood and broth mixture. Worse came when he coughed and the barbs bit in even deeper. It was more than his weakened body could take.

Unable to tolerate the agony, he finally passed out.

A week later, Zarya called the Sentella. Again. "Can I please speak to Kere?"

"I'm sorry, he's not here."

If she heard that one more time, she was going to scream. "Why can't someone help me? Isn't there anyone I can talk to about his current location?"

Or lack thereof?

"We don't give out that kind of information. Sorry." The woman hung up on her.

Zarya wanted to kill someone. As of today, it'd been nineteen weeks since she'd last spoken to her fiancé.

Nineteen. Weeks. Tomorrow would be five months.

His voicemail had filled up over three months ago, and hadn't been cleared.

I know he's dead. He had to be. It was the only explanation that made sense. Why else had he not called her?

Kere would never leave her hanging like this. Without word. Without notice. Not by choice. He knew her better than that. Thought more of her than to hurt her this way.

He was gone.

Just like my father. She winced at the comparison. But how could she deny it another minute?

Why wouldn't someone, anyone tell her the truth about his whereabouts? She had used what little money she had to bribe every informant she could find for some clue.

No one took mercy on her. For weeks, she'd searched even though she didn't know where he'd gone or where he lived.

Why aren't you here?

The Sentella had to know he was dead. Why wouldn't they just say it already so that she could stop hoping that the next time she called his number, he'd pick up and chastise her for not eating and for being worried about him when there was no need?

Just call me, baby. Please, don't be dead...please.

The very thought of it tore through her and left her light-headed. It hurt to a level she'd never imagined was possible, and it made a mockery of the grief she'd had when her family had died.

How could anything hurt so much and not kill her?

She stared down at her beautiful engagement ring as her heart shattered all over again. Holding her link in her hand, she laid her head down on her desk and wept in utter misery.

Why couldn't I have one thing for myself? Just once?

Was that really so much to ask?

Other people were allowed to have families and spouses. People they loved and cherished without their dying on them. Why couldn't she?

But it wasn't meant to be. For whatever reason, the gods wanted to punish her. Unlike other people, she wasn't allowed to love someone.

The moment she did...

They died.

Only her younger sister, Sorche, seemed immune to that curse.

Gods, the pain of his loss was so unbearable. It was like her heart was being clawed out of her chest and swallowed whole by some unrelenting beast. Why couldn't the world explode and end her suffering?

I just want him back. She'd sell her soul for it.

Tightening her grip on the link, she stared at his name in the short list of people she trusted. *Damn you, call me!*

Someone knocked on her door.

Wiping her tears away, she drew a ragged breath and tried to get a hold of herself. Because of the way she'd been raised, she didn't share personal pain with others.

Ever. Especially not those who served beneath her. Being Caronese, the men of the Resistance were already predisposed to thinking of women as lesser beings. The only reason she'd been allowed to lead was out of respect and loyalty to her father. If they saw her crying, they would refuse to follow her.

Only Kere had ever seen her weak or vulnerable. Never had he thought less of her for it. And for that reason, he was the only man alive she'd ever trusted with her real thoughts and fears.

With her heart.

Where are you, Kere?

Taking a deep breath and forcing herself not to think about that right now, she pressed her hands to her face and put on a smile she didn't feel. "Come in."

The door slid open to show her Pip who had a disdainful twist to his lips. With furious strides, he came into the room and tossed a small plastic bag down on the desk in front of her.

"I don't get it," he said, putting his hands on his hips.

She scowled. "Get what?"

He jerked his chin toward the bag. "Out of everything we confiscated from our royal prisoner, *that* was the only thing the bastard put up a fight to keep. Only that. I figured it had to be worth a fortune given the rest of his shit and how much it cost, so I took it home and gave it to my wife. Last night, we decided we'd rather sell it and buy something we both could enjoy. So I ran it over to a jeweler to be appraised this morning, and the damn thing is as fake as it can be. He said it wasn't worth the price of the appraisal. Can you believe it?"

That *was* strange. Why would a prince have a fake piece of jewelry?

But more to the point...

"The prince is still here?"

"Uh, yeah...like we were going to free him and make all of them happy after everything we've suffered?"

That was an entirely different story than Clarion had told her. Unmitigated fury tore through her that they'd have kept the prince here all this time.

Why hadn't she checked on that?

The answer didn't make her feel any better. As preoccupied as she'd been, she still should have asked Clarion about it.

Castigating herself for the neglect, her gaze fell to the ring and then something that felt like a fist, slamming into her stomach.

No...

Her heart stopped.

It was her mother's second wedding ring. The one that her father had bought as a present when they'd been on a pilgrimage years ago and had renewed their vows...

The ring she'd placed on Kere's pinkie...

Why would the Caronese heir have the ring she'd given to Kere?

The truth slapped her hard.

No, surely not...

*   *   *

Darling was too weak to look up as he heard the door open and the harsh lights flared on again. Besides, it no longer mattered to him who his torturer was.

In the beginning, he'd been determined to remember everyone who hurt him so that he could hunt them down and kill them.

But all hope of ever tasting freedom again was gone. He'd faced the truth weeks ago. He was never going to get out of here alive. And at this point, he didn't want to.

All he wanted was to die. *C'mon, you fucking bastards, just kill me.*

Was that really so much to ask?

"Where did you get this?"

He could barely open his swollen eyes to see what someone was holding right under his nose.

What was it?

The woman slapped him hard on his festering cheek. "I asked you a question."

This time, he recognized the voice.

Zarya.

Hope tore through him. Had she finally come to set him free? His breathing ragged from the effort it took, he lifted his head to meet her gaze. Surely she would recognize him this time...

But there was still no recognition in her cold amber eyes. Only bitter, cruel hatred. "Where's Kere?"

I'm right here in front of you.

Why can't you see me?

She backhanded him so hard that the engagement ring he'd given her sliced open his cheek again. "I want you to answer me! Now! What did you bastards do to Kere? Damn you! Tell me!"

How could he answer her? Couldn't she see the muzzle straps

that wrapped around his head to hold it in place? A muzzle that pierced his throat and tongue every time she hit him?

Blood filled his mouth, choking him until it had no choice except to run from the corners of his lips. The pain of it made his eyes water. He winced as the saline in those tears burned like acid on his skin.

Burying her hand in his hair, she wrenched his head back, which caused the muzzle to cut even deeper into his throat. "You killed him, didn't you?"

No. *They'd* killed him. Her soldiers. His former allies. Her unfeeling apathy and callous disregard for what her men did to him. Their cruelty and torture had ripped the last shred of his soul out of him. He was nothing but an empty shell now.

After all the years of Arturo trying to break him, it had been his own allies who had finally succeeded.

There was no Kere left anymore. Kere had been a champion for people like her and Pip and Timmon and Clarion.

The last thing Darling desired was to help anyone now. All he wanted was for them to die slowly and painfully.

Just kill me. Please. For the love of the gods, have some compassion. A pittance of human decency. Even rabid animals were given more mercy than this.

She'd already ripped his heart out. Why wouldn't she finish him off?

Suddenly a shrill alarm rang in short, staccato bursts.

Shouting orders and questions, people ran along the hallway outside an instant before the door to his room burst open.

Clarion paused as he saw Zarya. His look of shock turned to relief—an expression that only confirmed the fact that she must have known what they'd been doing to him. "The Sentella's here."

Her face lit up. "Is Kere with them?"

"I don't know. They came in hard and shooting at us."

Her happiness died. "What?"

"Yeah. Pip said they're seriously pissed off over something. Damned if I know what."

She scowled in disbelief. "That makes no sense. We haven't done anything. Why would our allies attack us?"

Darling wasn't sure if all of this was real or if he was hallucinating again. He'd imagined his rescue so many times . . .

It's not real and you know it.

No one's ever going to release you.

Clarion pulled his blaster from its holster. "I'm going to meet Pip at the con room. He was trying to talk to Nemesis, but he said it was ugly. I'll let you know what I find out."

Zarya did her best to make sense of why the Sentella would attack them when they'd always been their best allies. But at least she'd get some answers now. "Send me word immediately when you find out what's going on."

Nodding, Clarion left.

Fear cramped her stomach. She turned back toward the prince and for the first time, she realized the horrendous condition he was in. Granted she'd been furious over Kere, but how had she failed in her anger to see what a wretched mess they'd made of him?

And the smell in his room . . .

She gagged on it.

What *was* that? It smelled like a herd of something had died and rotted.

Pressing her hand to her nose to block the foul odor, she cringed at what her soldiers had done to the poor man who hung from the ceiling by chained, raw wrists. His long red hair was matted and gnarled with blood and dirt. A thick auburn beard obscured his features and like his hair, it was matted with blood and something she thought might be vomit.

His naked body was bleeding and bruised everywhere. So

much so, that there was a pool of blood, both dried and fresh, on the floor around his ravaged feet.

She couldn't even begin to count the bruises and cuts that marred his frail body. A body that had been ripped when they'd brought him in.

Now...

He looked tiny and shriveled from malnourishment. Had they not fed him at all?

Not even once? From his ragged appearance, she'd say no.

Aching over his abuse, she dropped her gaze. All of a sudden, a scar on his right thigh caught her attention. Unique and unusual, it was more than familiar to her.

No...

Her heart hammered in panic. It couldn't be.

It couldn't.

Yet she remembered tracing a raised and puckered scar that went off in five directions like that one, on Kere's thigh.

Right. Where. That. One. Was.

She wanted to deny the obvious. But as she looked him over with new sight, she realized he was the same height as her unseen lover. When he'd been brought in, his hair had been the same length.

His build...

Oh God, no. There was no way.

It wasn't possible.

Was it?

Her entire body shaking from dread fear, she moved closer to him. There was one way to know for certain.

Please, let me be wrong. Please. She wasn't sure if she could live with herself if her suspicion was right.

She cupped his chin in her hand and carefully lifted his head. Bile rose in her throat as she saw his injuries. Through that thick, matted auburn beard, Pip had carved his name deep into the prince's right cheek. The man's eyes were swollen closed by bruises that were in various states of healing.

Her hand shook even more as she pushed his filthy hair back from the left side of his face and she saw the confirmation of her worst fear. The prince had a vertical scar that ran from hairline to chin, over his eye.

One identical to Kere's.

Tears welled in her eyes as reality slammed into her with a violent fist.

"When you see me, I want you to remember not to judge me by my looks…Promise me." She'd stupidly assumed that vertical scar that bisected his face was what Kere had feared her leaving him over.

But it wasn't.

He'd feared that when she learned he was the prince they fought against that she'd hate him for it.

Pip's words rang in her head again as he threw her mother's ring on her desk. *"Out of everything we confiscated from our royal prisoner, that was the only thing the bastard put up a fight to keep. Only that. I figured it had to be worth a fortune given the rest of his shit and how much it cost…the damn thing is as fake as it can be. He said it wasn't worth the price of the appraisal."*

Darling Cruel had fought only to keep her mother's worthless ring—a ring Kere had vowed to protect with his life.

Kere had gone missing the same day Clarion had abducted the prince.

The Sentella was here and they were pissed.

Her soul screamed with a truth that terrified her. *Please let me be wrong.*

"Kere?"

He opened his eyes as much as he could—two small slits to pin her with a look of such profound hatred that it stole her breath.

It was then she knew it for a fact.

While she'd searched everywhere she could think of, Kere had been with her the whole time. Right here. So close that all she had to do was come into the room and find him. But the worst part of all, her own people had brutalized him and, by her ignorant silence, she'd condoned it.

What have I done?

She'd been so worried about finding Kere that she hadn't even thought about the prince they'd held for months. For that matter, she'd stupidly thought they had already released him.

Why didn't I check? Why?

Because I was too busy looking for him everywhere else…

Before she could say another word, the door behind her burst open. Smoke filled the room, choking her with a bitter stench.

She reached for her blaster, then froze as three targeting lasers hovered over her heart, letting her know exactly what they'd take out if she moved.

Slowly, she held her hands up so that they wouldn't mistake her intentions.

Through the hazy smoke, three Sentella members stormed inside. And there was no mistaking the anger that was plainly evident in the way they carried themselves.

Dressed in matching black battlesuits and helmets that obscured any identifying features, the shortest one grabbed her by the arm and hauled her away from Kere, then slammed her into the wall so hard, she saw stars. The next tallest Sentella member pulled his helmet off.

He had short blue-black hair and dark eyes rimmed with black eyeliner. Eyes that filled with tears when he saw the condition the prince was in. "Darling? Oh my God…what have they done to my baby?"

Darling blinked as he heard a familiar male voice. One that was thickly accented, yet lyrical and refined.

At first he thought he was dreaming...until he saw the last face he'd ever expected to see again.

Maris.

Tears fell down Maris's cheeks. He lifted his wrist to speak to the others through the link in his cuff. "We've got him, and he's alive. But he's hurt really badly. I need Syn here immediately. Tell him to run." Tenderly, Maris cupped his face in his hands. "What, in the name of the gods, did they do to you, sweetie?"

What *hadn't* they done to him?

Darling stared at his best friend in total disbelief. *Are you real?*

But he still couldn't speak past the painful ball under his tongue.

A distorted Andarion curse rang out from the man who stood behind Maris as he came closer to inspect Darling's condition.

Hauk. Even with the voice distortion that cloaked Hauk's real identity, Darling would know that giant hulking form anywhere.

Or was it someone else? Darling wasn't sure if he could trust his blurry eyesight any longer.

It wasn't until Nykyrian, Caillen, Nero, and Syn entered the room that he finally believed this was real and not another delusion.

Even though they were swathed from head to foot by their black uniforms, he knew who they were. He'd fought beside them for too many years not to recognize the way they moved and stood.

After all this time, they'd finally come for him...

He choked on the muzzle as tears filled his eyes and stung like hell as they fell down his bloodied cheeks.

Syn let out a foul Ritadarion curse the minute he stepped in front of Darling. He repeated Maris's words. "Dear gods, what have they done to you?"

Maris moved back to give Syn room. "I don't know. Damn them for it. Bastards! Every one of them. I hope they all roast their nuts in hell's hottest fires."

Nykyrian grabbed Zarya whose eyes betrayed her terror at the giant size of him.

Almost seven feet tall with his boots on, Nemesis's lethal carriage had made grown assassins piss their pants. He completely dwarfed Zarya. "Where's the release for the prince's chains?"

"I...I don't know."

Syn snarled as he tried to break the chain around Darling's neck with his bare hands. "We've got to get him down. Fast. He's hurting so badly that his jaw's quivering and it's damaging him even more." He cupped Darling's cheek in his gloved hand and held it so that Darling couldn't move it anymore. Then he wiped some of the blood off Darling's chin. "Hang on, buddy. Just a few seconds more and we'll have you out of this."

Shoving Zarya into Jayne's custody, Nykyrian came forward. His anger was palatable as he grabbed the cuff around Darling's neck and ripped it in half with his bare hands. The snapping metal was the most glorious sound Darling had ever heard.

For the first time in months, he could breathe without it cutting into his throat.

Nykyrian moved to Darling's right wrist to break that chain, too. He froze when he saw Darling's missing finger. Cursing, Nykyrian gave Darling's hand a light squeeze before he tore the cuff open.

The moment he was free, Darling started to fall, but Maris caught him against his chest and held him in a tight hug. "I have you, baby. Don't worry. No one's going to hurt you now."

Nero snapped the cuff on his left hand with his powers.

When Nykyrian reached for the muzzle, Syn grabbed his wrist and stopped him. "I'll have to surgically remove it."

"You sure?"

"Yeah. The fucking bastards left it on him so long, it's grown into his throat. See the marks?"

Though they were currently hidden by the black crash helmet he wore, Nykyrian had scars on his face from when he'd been a child and a different kind of muzzle had been used on him. Like Darling's, his muzzle had been left in place for so long it'd grown into his skin.

Nykyrian cursed again.

His breathing ragged, Darling barely heard them as he held on to Maris with what little strength he had. Never in his life had he been more grateful for his best friend's appearance.

"I've got you, Darling," Maris whispered in his ear. "Through thick and thin, brothers to the bitter end. No one's going to hurt you again. I swear it."

Syn gently touched Darling on the shoulder. "I'm going to knock you out, okay?"

Darling nodded. *Please make the pain stop.* He didn't care if Syn's dosage killed him so long as it made his body numb.

Syn pulled out an injector from the deep pocket on his left leg, then shot it into Darling's arm.

Over Maris's shoulder, Darling locked gazes with Zarya who'd been cuffed by Jayne. He saw the horrified agony in her amber eyes that were filled with tears.

I didn't know what they did to you, she mouthed to him. *I'm so sorry.*

Did she really think that mattered to him now? After all he'd been through?

Go to hell, bitch.

The last thing he heard before the drug knocked him out was Nykyrian's angry order for the rest of the Sentella members. "Kill them. Every fucking one who breathes. I want them hunted down and ripped into pieces. Take your time and make it hurt."

Nero inclined his head to Nykyrian. "I'm going to help end a few lives." Then he left the room.

"Save some for me, boy," Hauk called, following after him.

Caillen placed his hand on Darling's head. "I plan to find a few of them to party with myself. I'll meet you guys back at the ship." He made an even quicker exit than Nero and Hauk had.

Jayne grabbed Zarya by the hair, and held her for Nykyrian's inspection. "You want to kill her, or can I do it?"

Nykyrian considered their options and the bloodlust that lay beneath Jayne's tone. The hyshian lived to kill.

But not that one.

Not yet.

"Save her for Darling. He deserves the honor of killing at least one of them. And since she was the last one in here..."

Jayne sighed in disgust. "Damn, boss. You take all my fun away." She shoved Zarya back against the wall. "Be grateful, 'ho. There's nothing I love more than a good, long skinning."

Ignoring them and swinging Darling up into his arms so that he could gently cradle him, Maris wept over what had been done to Darling's now frail body. He'd been so beautiful and strong before...

Now, he looked like a walking corpse.

What they'd done went beyond inhumane. For the first time in his life, he wanted blood from another human being. "Have you ever seen anything like this?" he asked Syn.

"Not in a long time." Syn glanced over his shoulder at Nykyrian. "Nemesis has been through worse, and for a lot longer period of time."

Maris glared at that woman as true hatred filled him. "How could you!"

"I didn't—"

Jayne backhanded her, then shot her in the chest. "Don't worry," she assured Nykyrian as he took a step toward her in protest of her actions. "I didn't kill the bitch...yet. It's just a good stunning to shut her up before I yielded to the desire I have to gut her."

Nykyrian shook his head. "I'll carry Darling," he said to Syn. "You get the woman."

Syn put the injector back into his pocket. "You won't hold it against me if I accidentally drop her a few times on her head, will you?"

"Not at all."

"I knew I loved you for a reason." Syn went to retrieve her.

Maris stopped Nykyrian before he took Darling out of his arms. "Will he be all right?"

Syn was the one who answered. "Physically, I think I can fix most of it. Mentally..." He glanced at Nykyrian and paused.

Nykyrian snorted. "Yeah, I'm still severely fucked up. I own that fact. It's not like I can hide it." He cleared his throat before he continued. "But to answer your question, Mari, there's no telling. No one comes through torture intact. You've been around us long enough to know that. After mine, I was like an animal for a long time. Some days, I still am."

Syn tossed the woman roughly over his shoulder. "Ditto. I was certifiable and alcoholic until my sister-in-law verbally kicked my ass and made me realize what I was doing to myself. I can't believe I'm going to admit this outside my head, but thank the gods for Kasen. Anyone *ever* tells her I said that and I'll deny it, then kill you."

Sick to his stomach, Maris allowed Nykyrian to take Darling from him, and lead him back toward the hangar. He wasn't as optimistic about his friend as they were. He knew Darling better than anyone, and before this had happened, Darling had been surfing the edge of paranoid insanity.

Every time he'd seen him, Darling had become more and more silent and sullen.

More unpredictable and defiant.

The ongoing hatred and rage Darling kept for his mother and uncle had blazed in his eyes like a tangible beast that wanted blood, and that repressed fury had scared Maris to the point, he'd expected Darling to lash out at them and kill them for it.

Would this push him over the edge?

It's all my fault...

"If I'd only found him sooner," he breathed.

Jayne rubbed his arm with a kind caress as she walked by his side. "Don't go there, Mari. But for you remembering the woman's name, we'd have never found him at all."

Perhaps.

Yet looking at Darling's condition, it was hard to see any kind of bright side. They'd torn him up so foully.

So cruelly...

How could anyone do this to another human being?

I wish my fighting skills were honed and up to date. Had they been, he'd hunt them down and make them regret their vicious brutality. But he'd walked away from his training years ago, and while he did work out to keep his lean muscles defined and was occasionally Darling's sparring partner, he no longer had a warrior's build.

Even when he'd possessed some of the best fighting skills in the universe, he hadn't wanted them.

Unlike his brothers, Maris had never enjoyed hurting other people, especially not for sport or practice.

However, tonight, he understood the need to taste and let blood.

Please be all right. He wouldn't be able to live if anything happened to Darling. He knew that.

Darling was his entire world. He always had been.

And as he watched Nykyrian carrying Darling on board their ship, a bad premonition went through him.

By their actions with this, the Resistance had awakened the devil himself and there would be hell to pay for it. Not from Maris. Not from the Sentella.

But from Darling.

If there was anything in this universe Darling truly hated, it was being a victim. Having his hands tied so that he couldn't fight back.

It was an unforgivable sin where Darling was concerned. And contrary to popular thought, Darling was one of the most skilled fighters out there. Maris would even run him up against Nemesis/Nykyrian.

Once Darling regained his strength from this, he would become the very god of death and retribution that Hauk had proclaimed him as a joke. No one suspected that darkest side of Darling existed, but Maris knew and it scared him to the core of his soul.

Take cover, bitches.

The right hand of retaliation was about to come calling. And it was going to be brutal.

There would be no escape or sanctuary. Not for any of them. May the gods take pity on all who came into Kere's path because he knew Darling wouldn't.

6

Darling came awake slowly to the sound of something beeping in a steady rhythm nearby. He held his breath, waiting for that familiar, rancid pain to kick in.

It didn't.

But when he tried to open his eyes and couldn't, panic tore through him immediately. Had they finally blinded him?

Am I dead?

He felt a kind, gentle touch on his shoulder. "Sh...It's okay, baby. It's me, Mari. Don't strain yourself. You're safe. No one's going to hurt you."

Darling relaxed at the sound of Maris's soothing voice in his ear. He tried to speak, but he couldn't do that either.

What was in his mouth now? Even with Maris here, panic consumed him.

Maris took his right hand, and cupped it with both of his. "You're in the Sentella's hospital. Syn's been tending you since you were freed. We have you, sweetie. It's all good now. Don't worry about anything, okay?"

Darling tightened his hand around Maris's fingers as gratitude overwhelmed him and he remembered his rescue. It hadn't been a dream after all. He was free and alive.

Thank the gods.

"Is he awake?" That was Caillen's voice from a distance.

Darling heard his heavy footsteps as he neared the bed on the opposite side of where Maris stood. Since Caillen had been trained as a smuggler and not a thief or assassin, his footsteps were very distinctive and extremely loud compared to the rest of Darling's friends.

"He just woke up."

Someone touched Darling's left arm in a roughened grip. "Boy, I ought to kick your ass for this. What kind of fool-headed lunacy were you thinking? Taking off alone? You better be glad you're on a monitor or I'd be strangling you right now." That was Hauk's gruff, accented voice, taking him to task. Something that meant the Andarion had been terrified for real. Hauk had the most screwed up way of showing his emotions.

Caillen rubbed Darling's shoulder above where Hauk had touched him. "We searched everywhere for you, for months and months. I give those bastards credit, they were slippery. But for Maris, I'm not sure we'd have ever found you."

Another thing he owed Mari.

"He's up?" Syn asked as he entered the room. Unlike Caillen, Syn's footsteps were as silent as Hauk's and Nykyrian's, something extremely impressive given their heights and Hauk's mountainous build.

Darling felt Caillen and Hauk step back as Maris released his hand so that Syn could examine him.

"If you can hear me and understand what I'm saying, Darling, tap my hand one time with your thumb." Syn slid his hand under Darling's.

Darling tapped him once.

"Good, man. Now if you want me to update you on your condition, tap again."

Darling did, even though he could tell by the catch in Syn's voice, and the fact that he couldn't move at all or see anything, that it was bad.

Real bad.

"All right. I had to do surgery on your mouth and esophagus. And you're still on a ventilator, which is one of several reasons why you can't speak. Everything has been repaired, but it'll need a few more weeks before you can use your voice again. Whatever you do, don't try to speak until I give you clearance for it."

Darling tapped Syn's hand to let him know that he understood. The last thing he wanted to do was prolong his healing.

Syn kept speaking. "I have your eyes bandaged because you had severe hyphemas and orbital blowout fractures."

Like he knew what those were. *Damn, Syn. I'm not a doctor.* And while blind, he couldn't look up a definition.

"They're from..." Syn paused for a second and when he spoke again, there was no missing the bitter rage in his voice. "Being kicked and punched repeatedly in the face and head. Because of that, I had to reconstruct your nose, both cheekbones, and part of your jaw. We also implanted teeth that had been knocked out or damaged beyond repair. You'll have lifelong problems with your sinuses because of the reconstruction, and you'll be susceptible to nosebleeds and infections, but we'll deal with those when they happen."

Darling flinched as those words reminded him of the blows he'd taken from his former allies, and the blood that had poured out of his nose, mouth, and eyes from their attacks.

He couldn't even think about the rest of the damage they'd done. Not without wanting to scream.

"Both eyes are healing fine and I should be able to take the bandage off your right eye tomorrow. The left one will take a little longer to heal. I'm not sure how badly your vision will be compromised from the injuries, but with any luck, you won't be blind. You should have most of your vision in both eyes."

Most? Darling clenched his teeth in anger.

"Hopefully all of it. We won't know for sure though until about a week after both bandages are off. I called in an old friend of mine who's a specialist to do the last surgery on your eyes, and he said you had a better than a forty percent chance of a full recovery."

Forty percent? He didn't want to even contemplate what degree of blindness comprised the other sixty. It was sad when Syn was excited by a number that made him sick to his stomach.

"I know you know that they did a lot of other damage that you're probably worried about, too." Syn paused. "Guys? Can you give us the room?"

Cold dread consumed him as he waited for the really bad news Syn was obviously about to give him.

Syn didn't speak again until they were alone. "They seriously screwed you up, little brother. But you *should* be able to have sex again. At least eventually, though there's a fifty percent chance you might have chronic and severe pain with either an erection or ejaculation. Possibly both. And you have a seventy-five percent chance that you'll have some erectile dysfunction."

Oh yeah, there was something a guy wanted to hear. *Welcome back, Darling…*

Why the hell was he still alive?

Syn took a deep breath and continued to make him feel even worse. "You'll have to use stool softeners for the rest of your life, too. Any bowel movement is going to hurt like hell, and you are not going to want to ever allow yourself to be constipated. Hopefully, some of that pain will dull over time."

He pressed his hand against Darling's shoulder as if bracing him for the next round of Let's Make Darling's Day Bright and Shiny. "As your doctor, I have to stringently advise you against any kind of anal sex ever again. It's just not going to be worth the pain you'll have from it. Never mind the risk of infection. And while we did reconstruct a lot of your intestine and rectum, there's no telling what further damage any intrusion there might do to you."

That had never been his problem, but Syn didn't know that. Only Maris did.

Syn covered his hand and gave a light squeeze. "I should probably tell you that I've had you in a chemically induced coma for a little over four months now."

Four months.

Shit...Darling's heart thumped hard in his chest as that news slammed into him. Something that caused the monitor in the background to pick up tempo and start squealing. Syn stepped away to turn the volume down.

How long had he been out of things entirely?

Horror filled him as he realized he would have had another birthday during that time. *I'm a year older.*

So was Drake.

Just how long had Lise been dead? *I missed her funeral.*

Maybe that was for the best. Yet...

Why couldn't they have killed me, too? Why the hell was he still alive?

"Your family's fine," Syn said, completely unaware of the rising panic that was shredding him. "Nyk sent them to the Summer Palace the day after you were abducted so that your uncle wouldn't suspect anything. As far as anyone knows, you were simply visiting your sister at school when the two of you were ambushed."

At the mention of Lise, he choked on a sob.

"Take it easy, Darling." Syn put his hand on his shoulder again to steady him. "Annalise isn't dead. She lived, okay? She used her powers to pretend to be dead in the hangar so that they would leave her alone. It was a bad injury, but she's recovered from it now."

Darling held his breath as that news echoed in his head.

Annalise was really alive? Could it be true? Dare he even hope?

He tried to speak, then choked again.

"Careful. Breathe slowly. Remember what I told you about speaking... And yes, I'm serious. Hold on." Syn removed his hand from Darling's shoulder.

After a few seconds, Darling heard a link buzzing.

"Hello?" It was Lise's beautiful voice.

Tears stung his eyes as he whispered a silent prayer of gratitude. She *was* alive. Never in his life had anything meant more to him.

His precious Lisie lived...

"Hey, Annalise, it's Syn. I have Darling with me. He's finally awake. He can hear you, but he can't speak. I need you to say something to him so that he knows you're all right." Syn moved the link closer to Darling's ear.

"Sashi?" Lise sounded thrilled. "Hey, big shilo. I'm so glad you're back, you had us worried sick, and you made me flunk *all* of my exams. I had to repeat the entire semester. Thanks a lot. I still love you though, and I'm so glad you're still with me. Don't *ever* scare me like this again. You hear me? I have to have my good brother around. The other two really suck."

In spite of her chastising him, her voice was the sweetest sound he'd ever heard.

"I'm so sorry I wasn't there when you woke up. I stayed with you for over a month."

"I'm the one who told her to go back to school," Syn said, interrupting her. "There was nothing she could do to help and once school started back, I knew you'd want her in class."

He was right. Had he been conscious, Darling would have insisted on it.

"I'm on semester break right now," Lise continued, "so I'll come see you first thing in the morning. I promise. Even if I have to hijack something. I love you, Darling. Please get better soon."

"Thanks, Lise," Syn said. "Is your mother or brother around?"

"Drake isn't. He left a little while ago for a date, but let me check on Momair."

Unfortunately, Lise forgot to put the link on mute. He heard her walk from her room to their mother's.

"Hey, Momair? Darling's finally awake and he's on the link. You want to say hi to him?"

His mother let out a long breath of frustration. "Can't you see I'm busy, child? Really? He's been unconscious for months now, I don't think I need to rush to speak to him right this second, do you?"

"But—"

"Don't interrupt me. Tell him that we're all right, no thanks to him. Does he have any idea what he's put you through? How much damage he caused you to suffer? The scars you now have on your back? It's awful. Because of his puerile selfishness, you'll be disfigured for the rest of your life. And for what? So that he could pretend to play hero and get abducted? He's useless. I can't believe I thought for one instant that he might actually be able to help us. I guess we'll have to wait for Drake to get older. Maybe then things will get better."

"Momair...please. We almost lost him. I think he's suffered enough, okay?"

"Trust me, he doesn't know what suffering is. He should have to live my life for five minutes. Then he'd learn a thing or two about pain. Now go. I just want a few seconds of peace. Thank you both so much for interrupting what little time I take for myself. Gah! Just when I'd found my tranquility. I swear, that boy can't live unless he's causing problems for other people."

He heard Lise shut the door before she returned to speaking into the link. "Syn? Sorry that took so long. Momair can't talk right now. She's having a facial. She said to tell Darling that she hopes he gets better soon and to not worry about us. Just focus on getting back on his feet."

How nice of her to lie...

"All right, Lise. Thanks." Syn cut the channel.

Darling felt that stab from his mother all the way to his soul. But why was he surprised? Of course his mother couldn't be interrupted to talk to him. A facial was a lot more important than her oldest son. What kind of fool was he to think otherwise?

Nothing had changed while he'd been out of commission. How nice of the gods to put his insignificance on display and highlight it so.

Except he now knew the truth of Zarya and her cold apathy. She was just like his mother, thinking only of herself.

Thank the gods I didn't marry her. That was the only blessing to come out of this hell. Had the Resistance not taken him prisoner, he'd have tied his life to that whore.

Still, it hurt. Her betrayal. Their torture. His mother's condemnation. Lise's disfigurement.

All of it.

He wished Syn had left him in a coma. Anything would have been better than this agony that ripped him apart when there was nothing he could do except remember what he'd been through and hate himself for it. He'd lost everything that was important to him. His dignity. His body. His heart.

His soul.

All he had left inside was hatred and rage. Deeper and nastier than it'd ever been. The only thing to live for now was the day that Syn healed him enough that he could exact the revenge he'd sworn himself to.

*   *   *

Tired, defeated, and soul sick, Zarya sat in the same tiny spartan cell she'd occupied for countless months now. It had four tan walls, a small sink, a toilet, and one pallet on the floor with no blanket or pillow. She had no idea what had happened to her Resistance members or to her sister—something that panicked her every time she thought about it.

Please let Sorche be okay…

She didn't know what was going to happen to her, either. Not that it really mattered. She only wanted Sorche to be safe. Whatever happened to her, she'd deal with. She always had.

Over and over, she'd begged for someone to tell her something, anything, but no one would take mercy on her.

Not that she blamed them. Not after what she'd done.

While she hadn't participated in Darling's kidnapping or torture, she hadn't stopped it. And that made her every bit as guilty as the others. She wasn't about to sugarcoat the bitter truth. It wasn't in her to shirk responsibility. *"We are all the masters of our own decisions. Right or wrong, Stupid or intelligent. Only we are to blame for our missteps and mistakes."* Her father's words haunted her. She'd turned a blind eye to Clarion while she'd searched relentlessly for the very man they'd held.

How stupid could one person be? How cruel were the fates?

Part of her wanted to blame Darling for it. Why hadn't he told her his identity just one day sooner?

But she knew why. His fear the last time they'd been together had said it all.

"My greatest prayer is that my face doesn't offend you so much that you forget your promise to me. I could never bear to be rejected by the only woman who has ever held my heart."

And what had she done?

She'd spit on him. Literally and figuratively. When he'd needed her the most, she'd been right there and done nothing to help save him from...

Her own people.

His people.

Every time she thought about it, she wanted to vomit.

After all of her promises to him, she'd done the very thing he'd feared. Not because he was scarred.

Because he was a prince.

Sickeningly ironic. Most women dreamed of a prince to come and sweep them off their feet. She'd had one and she'd spurned him. He had promised her the world and she'd slapped him in the face.

She was ill from it all. Even more so because as a child, Darling had been her hero. Before the death of her mother and sister, before his father had been murdered, they had played together. Not often. But from time to time, whenever his father had visited hers, Darling would come with him. It was something she'd forgotten about completely over the years.

Until a dream a few weeks ago.

Somehow those long buried memories of a happy childhood had come back to haunt her with a vicious vegeance. Her first memory of Darling was when she'd been five and he nine. Her cat had climbed out of her room, onto the roof after her sister had left their window open. Terrified it would die or get hurt, she'd asked her older brother Geritt for help, but the rotten little beast had refused, saying he hoped her cat jumped to its death so that it wouldn't bite or claw him anymore.

Without hesitation and after chiding her brother for his cruelty, Darling had bravely climbed out after it, onto her steep roof. Twice he'd almost slipped off. But instead of saving himself and returning inside where he'd be safe, he'd gone the whole way to the gutter and then brought her beloved pet back to her. Even now, she could see the way he'd looked as he came back through the window with her cat cradled in his bloodied hand—her cat had clawed and bitten him the whole time he'd been rescuing it.

His short red hair had been tousled from the wind. His sleeve torn from where he'd almost fallen and his arm was scuffed and bleeding through the material. Still, his blue eyes had been shining with concern for her and her beloved pet as he handed it back to her with a smile that had only increased his boyish handsomeness and charm.

He hadn't said a single word about his injuries. Rather, he'd closed the window and then wrapped her cat in a blanket so that it wouldn't scratch her.

Worse, his father had loudly and very publicly castigated him when he'd seen Darling's condition. "You're a prince, boy, not some lowborn hooligan who can't control himself. You have to live and breathe decorum at all times. Do you understand? When you look like this and roll around on the ground like some recumbent barbarian, you not only embarrass yourself, you embarrass me. What were you thinking? You're too old to behave like this. I swear, Darling, it's ridiculous that I can't depend on you for something as simple as staying clean for an hour. What was so important to you that you had to get filthy for it, huh?"

She'd held her breath in fear that Darling would tell their fathers that she was to blame for his dishabille. While his father's setdown had been bad, hers would have been much worse. To have endangered their heir...

That was a crime punishable by death, and while Arturo wouldn't enforce that law to protect Darling, his father would have.

Not to mention, her father would have killed her for letting Darling take the blame for something that was her fault, and not speaking up to defend him.

But she'd been too petrified of the consequences to say a single word.

To Darling's credit, he'd kept his spine straight as he stoically took his father's berating. He didn't speak until his father had asked him what he had to say for himself.

Her eyes filled with tears, Zarya had held her breath, waiting for Darling to denounce her like her brother would have done in a heartbeat.

Instead, Darling had met his father's gaze without flinching. "I'm sorry, Your Majesty. I shall endeavor to do better and not shame you again." He'd inclined his head to her father. "Please forgive me, my lord. I meant no disrespect to you or your family by being unkempt in your home. I hope I haven't offended you overmuch."

His father had sighed heavily, then looked at her. "I swear, Zalan, he is a good boy. I hope you won't hold it against him."

"No harm done, Your Majesty."

Still, the fury on the governor's face said that Darling would be punished later for saving her cat.

But rather than being angry at her for getting him into trouble, Darling had looked up to where she was peeping through the staircase spindles on the landing above him and winked at her. Then, after making sure his father wasn't watching, he'd smiled and given her a military salute.

He'd been her hero that day.

More than that, he'd kept her brother from mocking her anytime Darling was around. Darling had a problem with anyone picking on or belittling another. It was something that had gone against his grain as a child...

And as an adult. Kere had zero tolerance for cruelty of any kind. Physical or verbal.

On another visit, when she'd been seven and he was eleven...

just months before his father had died, she'd wanted to play ball with them, but Geritt had adamantly refused to have her join them. So she'd followed behind them in what she thought was stealth mode. Geritt had caught her and shoved her away, telling her that girls had no business playing boy games.

Darling had stepped between her and her older brother. "She's your sister, Geritt. You're supposed to protect her, not hurt her." He'd picked her up from the ground, then taken her back to the house. Instead of playing ball with her brother, he'd spent the entire afternoon drinking imaginary tea with her and her dolls.

How could she have let her blind hatred for his uncle rob her of those wonderful memories of his kindness when they'd been kids?

Darling had never been anything but gentle with her. And the worst part of it all was the knowledge that he, being older, would have remembered those childhood visits even better than she did.

Yet he'd never once mentioned them.

Her door slid up.

She froze, wanting it to be Darling there so that she could finally apologize and beg him to forgive her.

It wasn't. Rather a very tall, athletic woman and a short, round man. The woman stayed in the doorway with her arms crossed over her chest while the man came forward to examine Zarya.

"Open your mouth."

She arched a brow at his sharp order. "Excuse me?"

He grabbed her jaw and forced her to obey.

Zarya tried to fight him, but he appeared to be used to that. It was like trying to swat away a combat fighter with a shoe.

"So what do you think?" the woman asked as he stepped back.

Grimacing at Zarya, he shrugged. "She's not the most beautiful, but she's not hideous. Teeth are good. She's mid-twenties, which isn't quite too old yet, though she's getting there. You said she's not a virgin, correct?"

"Yeah."

"Too bad...Unused women always go for more. Still, we might get a decent profit on her, if I hold her back and put her with slim pickings. But it won't make us rich."

Were they discussing what she thought they were?

Surely not.

"What's going on?" she asked them.

The woman looked at her coldly. "Darling wants nothing to do with you. Said he never wants to lay eyes on you again. Since he doesn't care what we do with you, I decided to sell you off to a concubine dealer. After all, it's what a whore like you deserves."

Horrified, Zarya started to speak, but before she could, the man clapped a choker around her neck.

An instant later, she was fully aware of everything surrounding her, but incapable of responding in any way. Not a single sound came out of her mouth. She couldn't even open it.

The man pushed a button and she stood up as if he controlled her completely.

No! She'd heard of things like this, but she'd always thought they were lying about them.

Why would Darling do this to her?

Why do you think? Could he really hate her so much that he'd let *this* become her fate?

Her heart shattered as the truth stared her straight in the eyes. In the end, he was an aristo. Buying and selling people like her came naturally to him.

With a satisfied smirk, the man forced her to walk out of the cell. "I'll send your credits to you after the auction."

"Thanks."

Once they were alone, the man stopped Zarya so that he could touch her hair and smell it. "Too bad the prince is gay. Sometimes

I can get a lot more money for a prince's whore. Male plebs like to take possession of something they know was used by a blue blood. It makes them feel important."

If she'd been able to, she'd have laughed at his words. Darling wasn't gay. Not by a long shot.

But who would ever believe *her*?

The man's eyes softened as he released her hair. "Don't worry. We'll find you a worthy master."

You're not going to find me anything. She'd kill herself before she allowed him to sell her.

And as he forced her to walk in front of him, she realized that death was the only outcome she could have.

It's all right. At least in death, she'd be with her family again.

Darling stared at the scars on his face. After all the surgeries and pain...

He looked even more like a twisted freak than he had before.

It'd been bad enough when only half his face was scarred. But this was revolting. They had literally butchered him. There wasn't an unmarked inch left anywhere on his face or neck.

"You're going to remember us. Every time you look in a mirror, Your Putrid Highness, you're going to think back and know that your family is the one to blame for your deformity. They wouldn't pay two creds to save you. You're going to wear their cruelty on your face the way we wear it in our hearts." Pip's voice rang in his ears. His only wish was that his friends had saved Pip for him. That heartless bastard was the one he'd wanted to rip to shreds the most.

Then again, he had a long list. Not everyone who'd attacked him had been there when the Sentella had freed him.

But soon they would meet again. And this time, he wasn't chained...

He looked down at his hand where Syn had attached a cybernetic finger to replace the one Pip had cut off. At least it looked natural.

Unlike his face.

But what did it matter, really?

After what the Resistance had repeatedly done to him, he had no intention of ever touching or being touched by another human being again. He was sick of it.

Then again, he was sick. Period.

And now that his physical therapy was done and he could use his body again, he had an appointment to keep. One that was a long time past due.

This is going to hurt you a lot more than it's going to hurt me.

It wouldn't bother him at all. Not even a little.

No, it wouldn't give him peace, but he was going to clean the gene pool—one dreg at a time. And this way, he knew they'd never victimize another helpless being.

It was part vengeance. Part housekeeping.

But mostly it was justice. If they would do it to him, they would do it to anyone.

Darling picked the mask up that he'd made for himself, and covered his face with it. Shaped from solid gold, it held a blank expression—justice took neither pleasure nor pain from punishment. It just was. Frigid, unfeeling, and swift.

The only part of him the mask didn't conceal was his scarred mouth and his eyes. Eyes that were now as cold as the rest of him.

I am retribution.

For the first time in well over a year, he headed home to his father's Winter Palace. The palace where Darling had been born.

The one where his father had died.

It took him several hours to get there. Time enough for his temper to ignite to an even higher level. His link buzzed almost constantly as Maris, Syn, Nyk, Nero, Caillen, Hauk, and the others tried to reach him.

He ignored them all.

They weren't going to stop him. This wasn't the time for reason or rationale.

It was time for ruthless action. A time to bathe in blood.

Payback's a bitch...

And today her name was his.

As soon as he was docked at the palace, Darling made his way inside and walked straight to his uncle's study.

Unfortunately, the bastard wasn't there.

Figures. With his luck, his uncle might have known he was coming for him and had gone into hiding.

But just in case, Darling methodically searched the rooms.

He was about to give up when he finally found Arturo in the back courtyard where he was pawing some poor servant he'd trapped there. No older than fifteen, the girl was whimpering and crying, begging him not to dishonor her.

Darling saw red as old memories tore through him, and the beast inside him roared to life at the prospect of being set loose.

He could already smell the blood.

"Let her go."

His uncle turned, then frowned at the mask on his face. "Darling? Is that you?"

Without responding, Darling pulled the girl off Arturo's lap. "Run."

She didn't hesitate to obey.

Indignant, Arturo came to his feet with a feral snarl.

When he went to hit Darling, Darling dodged and then punched him with seventeen years of repressed fury. He felt his uncle's cheekbone shatter underneath his fist. The blow twisted Arturo around and sent him straight to the ground.

Arturo went pale as the night fog as he stared in horror at the blood pouring from his lips and nose. His face a mask of utter disbelief, he gaped at Darling.

"That's right, you bastard. I don't just take a punch. I *can* give one." He pulled Arturo up like a rag doll and held his uncle in front of him. "And more than that, I can kill."

The old familiar smug contempt returned to his uncle's eyes. "You can't kill me and you know it. If you do, you and your family die with me."

Darling let out an evil laugh. "There, you're wrong, old man. I finally thought of another way out. Too bad you won't be around to see it." He drove his blade straight into Arturo's heart where it would keep him alive, but in pain for a few minutes longer. *Let's hear it for all the years you forced me to study human anatomy.* It'd made him a much more proficient killer. "That's for my father." He pulled the knife out and then cut Arturo's throat, again with a wound that wouldn't kill him immediately.

Rather, suffering in pain, he'd bleed out at Darling's feet before help could arrive. "And that was for me."

Guards came running from all directions as Arturo reached for them, trying to get to help.

But it was too late for that.

Kicking his uncle back, Darling dropped his long coat to the ground to let the guards see that his entire body was wired with enough explosives to take out them, the palace, and everything that was within three miles of it. One shot anywhere near him with a blaster's charge, and they'd all go to hell together.

The guards hesitated, forming a circle around him.

"Who wants to die with me tonight?" Darling taunted them.

As expected, there were no volunteers.

No heroes.

Like the coward they'd served, the guards shrank back to protect their own asses. However, it was too late for most of them...

I should have thought of this years ago.

But that was the problem with being sane. Sane people played by the rules. They looked for rational explanations and solutions in an insane universe.

Now, he *was* one of the animals. And never had a more vicious one been born.

The one thing the Resistance had taught him was who his friends were. Who cared about him.

Who didn't.

It was a lesson Darling would never forget.

He glared at the imperial guards and made note of the faces of the ones who'd dragged him home under his uncle's orders. The ones who'd taken pleasure in assaulting and mocking him over the years when he'd been under their "care" and "protection."

They were going to pay later.

For now...

"Notify the other aristos, there's a new Caronese governor. And if any of you think you can overpower me later, think again. I was trained by Nemesis himself and I learned well. You come for me, you *will* die. *All* of you. There's no one alive who can stop me."

He gestured toward Arturo's body. "And I promise you, I won't be nearly as merciful. If you think Arturo ruled you with an iron fist, you ain't seen nothing yet, bitches. Before I'm done, you will fear me as you've never feared anyone."

Wanting one of them to try something, he pushed his way through them and made his way into the master suite of the palace.

It reeked of Arturo's stench.

Even though it was almost midnight, he pressed the link for the housekeeping staff. "I want the sheets and covers in here dragged out and burned, and new ones brought in." Tomorrow he'd have the staff throw out everything that had belonged to Arturo.

In the meantime...

He had more people to visit and kill.

7

"Darling has gone bat-shit crazy."

Maris gave Caillen a "duh" stare through the vid screen. He was in his bedroom at the Caronese Winter Palace while Caillen sat in Nykyrian's office at the Sentella's headquarters with Nero and the rest of the Sentella High Command—Nykyrian, Syn, Jayne, and Hauk. And all of them were worried about Darling and what he'd become over the last few weeks.

Every day, Darling slipped farther down the insanity chain. At the rate he was going, if they didn't stop him soon, he would be lost to them forever.

"You think *I* don't know that, Cai?" Maris asked. "I live with him. He jumps at any sudden sound. Pulls a blaster on you if you so much as sneeze unexpectedly. And if that's not bad enough, he's walking around wired with enough explosives to take out half the capital city."

Maris's stomach tightened as he saw an image of Darling's current sorry state in his mind. "Swear to the gods. I think he even bathes with it on...although, to be honest, I don't think he's had a bath in weeks. He looks like utter hell. Smells even worse. He's planted dirty bombs all over the place, but he won't tell anyone where they are. He has all of us held hostage by fear. If he dies and can't reset the timers every few hours at random intervals that he alone knows the schedule to, they'll go off, and we all go bye-bye in a nasty way. No one knows how he has them wired or timed or anything. He *has* lost his mind. Completely. Totally. Fully. I can't even talk to him anymore. He just stares at me with these beady, creepy eyes through that garish mask that gives me the jumping heebies."

Caillen arched his brow. "Damn, Mari, that's some rapid-fire dissertation there, buddy. You practice that much or did it naturally roll off your tongue like that?"

"You're not funny." Maris glowered at him. "What are we going to do?" he asked Nykyrian. "He's quickly ascending to the top of every hit list known and probably those unknown, too. At this point, everyone *is* gunning for him." Literally. "And that's just making him even more paranoid and insane. You should see the grisly monument he's building in front of the palace of the idiots who've tried to kill him—he has Arturo's decaying head mounted on a spike out there, along with those of the guards who beat him in the past. It's like he's some ancient barbarian warlord showing off his power and daring someone to come after him so he can add them to the pile. It's as if he wants to die, and he plans to take as many of us with him as he can."

Their eyes mirrored the same horror Maris felt.

Caillen bit his lip in frustration. "I don't know how to help him. I don't. You're the only one of us he'll let in the same room with him. He won't take any of *our* calls. We can't get the time of day out of him."

That was true. Every time Caillen, Syn, Nero, Hauk, Nykyrian, Jayne, or Darling's family tried to see him, he emphatically refused.

Darling had only spent ten minutes with Lise—long enough to assure himself that she really was all right, then the instant he saw the leftover limp she had from her injury, he was done. She hadn't been allowed near him since.

Maris raked his hand through his unstyled hair and cringed at his own sorry appearance. Gah, he was a mess, too. But he was more worried about Darling than his own vanity, and that concern kept him up all hours of the night as he tried to reach Darling through the potent rage his best friend had cloaked himself with.

"For the record," Maris said to the others, "he won't *talk* to me either. I'm serious about the beady-eyed stare thing. That's all I can get out of him. That or a growl. Meanwhile, he doesn't sleep. Doesn't eat. He just drinks things that double as rust removers, and pops pain meds like candy. He walks the halls, day and night. I'm telling you right now, he terrifies me."

All of them knew that Darling was spinning out of control and none of them could stop it.

Since Syn had given him leave to travel, Darling had been on a vicious killing spree, taking out every member of the Resistance he could find. He'd brutally killed every doctor who'd ever treated him under his uncle's orders, and half the staffs of the mental wards where he'd been confined over the years. Two of the buildings, he'd blown into rubble. The third he'd burned to the ground and toasted marshmallows over its smoldering embers. Then, he'd laughed as he ate them.

For that matter, he'd offered one to Maris.

Worse, he'd slaughtered several dozen members of his own royal guard, which hadn't gone over well with the ones he'd spared. Okay, so the guards he'd killed had deserved it. They'd been the men his uncle had sent after him over the years who had done unspeakable things to him, but still...

It was scary.

And there was no end in sight. Each kill fueled him to the next.

The League had sent more than three dozen of their best assassins after him, and Darling had plowed through them like they were rookies. If that wasn't bad enough, he'd sent them back to the League in pieces.

Now even the League was reticent to send anyone else to the slaughter party.

But that kind of fear wouldn't last. Sooner or later, the League and the rest of the United Systems would band together to kill Darling if he didn't stop his homicidal rampage.

Syn sat back in his chair. "C'mon, Maris, can't you reach him?"

"I've tried. Believe me. He won't listen to me any more than he'll let you operate on him. The last time I suggested he let you finish with his surgeries, he tore my head off. In fact, the last words I got out of him were that he was fine with looking like a twisted, monster freak. He said it was time the world saw what they'd made of him, or something creepy like that."

Hauk frowned. "You think maybe his mother could talk—"

"Don't even go there, bud," Syn said, cutting him off.

Maris agreed. "I wouldn't put it past him to gut her at this point. He hates her almost as much as he hated Arturo. When Lise forced her to come visit a few weeks ago, I had to stop him from shooting her in the reception room. Seriously."

Guilt stabbed Maris at the memory. He'd been the one who'd stupidly talked Darling into meeting with her instead of sending her back into exile at the Summer Palace.

Maris had cornered Darling in his office. *"Look, Darling, my mother won't even acknowledge the fact that I was ever born. I'm told she was the one who burned my birth registration on my wedding night. I know you two have had a bad past, but still…she made the effort to be here. The least you could do is spend five minutes with her. You can't repair the relationship unless you're both willing to give something. C'mon, Dar. I'd do anything if my mother would visit me. Allow yours a chance to redeem herself."*

Darling was right. He was a naïve asshole.

As soon as Darling had entered the reception room where his mother had waited, she'd curled her lip in revulsion of his appearance. Her first words to the son she hadn't spoken directly to in more than four years? The same son who'd been lost to them for half a year and who'd almost died?

"You should consider abdicating in favor of Drakari. I know he's still too young to rule, but with your support the CDS might be swayed to accept him early. And make sure when you speak to them that you cover up that face so that it doesn't sicken anyone."

She'd actually shuddered as she held her hand up in front of her face so that she wouldn't have to look directly at Darling. "You're so hideous. Even if you were straight, there would be no chance of marriage or children now. No one in their right mind would touch you. So, for once in your selfish life, be decent and let your brother have the inheritance he deserves. Maybe he can finally redeem the family name before you destroy it even more than Arturo did. The people need a hero to follow, not some grotesque, effete egotist."

Bellowing in rage, Darling had pulled his blaster out to shoot her. Luckily, Maris had stopped him, but in the scuffle, Darling had almost shot *him.*

Not an event or mistake Maris was eager to repeat. He'd learned his lesson. For whatever reason, Darling's mother really didn't care about her eldest child.

But Maris did.

He sighed regrettably at the only other people in the universe who loved Darling as much as he did. "I've seen him bad off before, but never have I seen him like this. He has absolutely snapped. He's gunning for any and everyone. *I'm* an idiot for being here."

Nykyrian's features sharpened. "Do we need to evac you?"

Maris shook his head. "No. Darling's in consummate turmoil and agony, and like Cai said, I'm the only one he'll let in a room with him right now. If I have to die for his friendship, so be it. I won't leave him alone when he's hurting this much."

But it broke his heart to see Darling like this. Darling had always been so strong, so resolute. Maris wasn't used to being the strength in their friendship. He was used to being able to lean on Darling.

How do I reach him before it's too late?

Maris frowned as an idea came to him. "Nykyrian...when we rescued him, you said that you'd been where he is. What saved you from your madness?"

"My wife."

"Excuse me?" Syn asked in a highly offended tone. "I think I was there for you a *little* longer than she was, by a couple of decades as I recall. No offense."

Nykyrian rolled his eyes. "Syn helped, too."

Syn snorted at that. "'Helped' my ass, you psycho son of a bitch. How many times have I been shot protecting your hulking ass? Yeah, I'm going to remember this the next time you're in the dog house 'cause you left a sock on the floor or didn't lower the seat, or an assassin comes at your back."

Nykyrian gave him a feral grimace. But when he spoke, his soft, lilting tone belied his fierce expression. "Syn...what can I say? I love you, man. I can't live without you. *You* are the air I breathe."

Syn scooted his chair farther away. "Man, don't say shit like that. Other people are listening."

Jayne handed Syn a small pill container.

Syn frowned at it. "What's this?"

"My period medication. I think you could use some."

Hauk, Nero, and Caillen burst out laughing.

Grimacing, Syn gave it back to her, then glared at the three men who were still cracked up. "I hate you people."

"I'm not people," Hauk reminded him. "I only eat them."

Ignoring them, Nykyrian returned his attention to Maris. "All idiocy aside, I was never as far gone as Darling is right now. I always had control of myself. As badly as I wanted to, I never gave in to my need for human extermination. Aside from, you know, assassination contracts. But that was business and not pleasure."

Caillen nodded as he sobered. "Which is why we think you're the only hope he has. He loves you, Maris. He always has. Can't you seduce him or something? Give him one really good, mood-altering lay or blow, and make him see reason?"

Hauk scoffed at Caillen. "Sex isn't always the answer, you know."

"Bullshit," Caillen said with a laugh. "You obviously ain't never had a really good lay or you'd know better. Nothing clears the head faster or changes a man's direction about where he wants to stay."

Syn concurred. "I'm siding with Caillen on this one."

"Me, too," Jayne said.

Nero nodded. "Add me to that list."

Hauk rolled his eyes. "You're all morons." He looked at Nykyrian. "You're with me on this one, aren't you, Nyk?"

"No. I'm definitely with them. There's no one in this universe who can defeat or weaken me. But Kiara can bring me to my knees with one single pout, and when she takes me into the bedroom, nothing can pull me back out. I have absolutely no will where she's concerned, other than to make her deliriously happy."

"Well, that explains all the kids," Hauk said under his breath. "Since I've obviously been doing something wrong—"

"Yeah," Jayne raked him with a sneer, "lay off the cheap 'hos, and try finding a decent woman for once."

Hauk started to respond, then he must have realized he was about to bring a knife to a blaster fight. "Fine. Maris, can you seduce him?"

That might work if Darling were gay. But . . .

It did get him thinking.

"Give me a couple of days to work on something, okay?" Maris cut the transmission as he drummed his fingers against his thigh while he thought through the one thing that might save Darling's soul.

Zarya was the only woman Darling had ever loved. Before all of this had blown up, he'd been willing to die for her. To risk everything he had, even his beloved family, to claim her as his wife.

"Jayne, I couldn't care less what you do with her so long as I don't ever have to see her face again."

That had been a harsh sentence Darling had handed down, but Zarya was the only member of the Resistance Darling had spared from death. He had torn the rest of them apart as soon as he located them.

Was it possible that Darling might still love her?

C'mon, Mari . . . he's in enough pain. The last thing you want to do is add to it.

Don't even consider what it is you're thinking.

But what choice did he have? Maris knew no other way to reach Darling.

You're a friggin' imbecile. If Darling truly hates her now, he will never forgive you for returning her to his life.

It'll end badly . . .

For all of them.

But it was all they had. *I've tried everything else.* Nothing had worked.

If anyone could seduce him, surely it was the woman who'd claimed his heart when no one else had.

Would Darling ever forgive her though?

Was it possible?

Maris had never taken a lover back after they'd broken up. But then he'd never been in love. Not really. Not the way Darling had been with Zarya.

It's worth a try.

Worst thing would be that Darling killed her. *And then he'll probably shoot me and add me to his monument in the yard.*

But if he was right about Darling's feelings...

Zarya could save him from his suicidal path. She alone might be able to get past his rage and touch the human part of him again and bring him back to all of them.

With no other recourse, he called Jayne to find out who'd bought Darling's girlfriend.

As soon as he had that information, he headed for the dealer, praying he could bribe Zarya's owner's name from the man and then buy her back.

Please let this work.

Zarya held her spoon tight, trying to pry open the door of her cell so that she could escape. Yeah, okay, so she'd been trying to do this for weeks, but...

It was better than blithely accepting a fate she didn't want. So long as there was breath inside her, she would fight.

C'mon, Z. You can do this...

In only a few hours, she was going to be stripped naked and then marched outside to be bid on like a piece of merchandise. Because she wasn't a virgin, strange men and women would be able to grope and examine every private inch of her body at their leisure. She couldn't imagine anything more humiliating.

C'mon, fate, work with me here. Don't let me go to auction.

She'd rather die than be put through that.

As she ground her teeth and strained to get more torque without bending her spoon, she heard footsteps in the hallway.

They were headed toward her cell.

She jumped away from the door, and hid her spoon under her pallet. The last thing she needed was to have it confiscated. Not that it was all that much. Still, it was the only thing she had.

The door opened slowly to show her dealer. He stood there with a harsh glower on his face as if he wanted to hurt her.

What had she done now?

"Come here."

Panic ripped through her. Had he moved up her auction time? The thought made her sick.

She shook her head no.

Cursing at her, he pressed a button on her controller and forced her to obey him.

Gah, how she hated that device. If she could have three seconds of freedom, she'd rip it off his arm and shove it somewhere really uncomfortable.

As soon as she reached him, he stepped aside for a man to examine her. A man whose face she remembered clearly from the worst day of her life.

He was the one who'd pulled his helmet off to help Darling...

Maris, that had been his name. And by his ornate orange and yellow robes, she could tell he was an aristo with a lot of money and power. One who was used to having people bow and scrape before him.

The kind of aristo she loathed with every molecule of her being.

Narrowing his eyes on her, Maris nodded. "She's the one I'm looking for. I'll have the funds transferred to you immediately."

The slaver handed him the bracelet. "Trust me, you're going to need it. If you want to activate her sex drive, it's the red button. The blue stalls her. Green makes her obey whatever your last command was. Yellow releases her to her own power... Yeah, that's not really something you want to do. She's a lot stronger than she

136

looks. The black button will knock her unconscious. You might want to keep a finger near that one until you break her in. She's a handful even with the collar on."

Maris passed a haughty look at the slaver to let him know he'd been summarily dismissed. It was the type of smug insolence that made Zarya despise the ruling class.

The slaver smirked at her before he left the room. "Enjoy her, my lord. You certainly paid more for her than anyone else would have."

As soon as they were alone, Maris placed the bracelet on his wrist, then pressed the yellow button.

Zarya was grateful that she had control of herself again, but... "I'm not about to be your sex slave, buddy. You can forget it."

Maris laughed at her angry indignation. "My bracelet says otherwise."

She glared at him. "If you think—"

"Stop with the threats and relax," he said with a purely feminine wave of his hand. "Trust me, hon, you fully lack the anatomy I need to be attracted to you."

"How so?"

He arched that regal brow again. "What are you? Blind? I'm as gay as they come, sweetie. Your body holds no appeal for me whatsoever. At least not sexually."

"Then why did you buy me?"

His gaze burned into her with a malice that actually scared her. "You're the one who was sleeping with Kere, correct?"

Zarya didn't dare answer. Even now, after everything she'd suffered because of him, she refused to betray his trust. Why? She had no idea.

Actually that wasn't true. She knew why. If nothing else in her life, she was loyal. Even when it was stupid.

Maris tsked at her. "Oh, that look says it all. You are definitely the one I need." He took her arm and started forward. "Come with me."

Zarya refused to blindly follow him or anyone else until she had more information. She stopped dead in her tracks. "Where are you taking me?"

"To save my best friend's life."

She felt as if they were speaking two entirely different languages. So much for having learned Universal. "I don't understand."

He pinned her with a warning glower as he let go of her arm. "You and your little rebel friends have destroyed the best man I have ever known. You took a noble, kind hero and turned him into a self-serving beast who is bent on total annihilation of everyone around him, including himself. So it only stands to reason that ye who broke him, might be the one to fix him."

Those words made her see red. "If you mean Darling, he's the one who sold *me*. I don't ever want to see him again. I'm done. You hear me? No one treats me the way he has. No one." What she wanted to do was beat him until he hurt as much as she did.

"And I'm the one who bought you, which means you will do what *I* say." He tried to pull her forward.

Shaking her head, she refused to be budged. "You send me to him and I will kill him for this."

"I seriously doubt that, sweetheart. Over the last month, I've seen him take down six League High Commanders without breaking a sweat. Three of them attacked him at once. And you don't want to know how many of their assassins he's killed in total. It's actually kind of scary when you think about it."

That she didn't doubt. She'd seen with her own eyes just how skilled Kere was in a fight.

And Maris was right. In spite of her skills that were superlative, she was no match for him... which brought out a whole new fear. "He'll kill me."

Maris shrugged nonchalantly. "So he kills you. So what? If he gets five seconds of pleasure from either screwing you or killing you, then I'm happy."

Yes, but *she* wouldn't be.

Disbelief over his attitude flooded her. "Are you out of your mind?"

"No, but Darling is." Maris glared at her as if he wanted to beat her as much as she wanted to strangle his friend. "Did you ever really love him? Tell me the truth."

She started not to answer, but for some reason, she couldn't keep it in. "More than my life."

"And now?"

Zarya tried to stamp down her tears, but against her will, they swam in her eyes as she thought about Kere and everything they'd had.

Everything she'd lost.

There were so many tender memories. So many nights of laughter over their links. Sharing their dreams and hopes.

Their deepest fears...

No matter how bad she felt, he'd always made her smile. Just the sound of his voice, the smallest whiff of his skin, set her on fire.

She'd never felt for anyone what she felt for him.

But he'd betrayed her. He'd thrown her away like she was nothing, condemned her to this hole without a single regret or thought.

That was unforgivable. She wasn't trash to be discarded the moment it became unpleasant.

Still, her emotions were tangled where he was concerned, and they weren't simple. How could she love and hate someone as much as she did him? And all at the same time. It didn't make sense.

Despising herself, hating her situation, and none too pleased with Darling or Maris, she sighed. "I honestly don't know. Yes, I still love him. I hurt for him and I'm so mad, I could stomp him into the ground, and laugh while I do it. He's hurt me worse than anyone ever has."

One black brow shot north as if he couldn't believe her words. "You? *You* were hurt?"

"Yes."

He looked at her as if she repulsed him. "Are you in total denial or are you really that stupid? Or are you just that selfish? Please tell me. I have to know."

Anger pierced her over his condemnation when he didn't know anything about her. "Excuse me?"

"My God, woman, how can you talk to me about *your* hurt after what *you* put Darling through? Really?" He paused before he added another, "Really?"

A bad feeling washed over her. He wouldn't be this angry without a good reason. Would he?

What did he know that she didn't?

"They were wrong to interrogate him so harshly, but—"

"Lady," he said, interrupting her, "they didn't interrogate him at all. They had a muzzle buried so deep in his throat that it caused permanent damage to his esophagus and voice box. Darling said it was the first thing they did to him when they took him into custody and before he'd regained his ability to move, never mind speak. There was no way for him to answer anyone's questions once that was in place. And I know he's not lying. It took the surgeon four hours to dig it out of the tissue it'd cut and grown into because he'd had it in his mouth for so long."

Her stomach hit the floor at what he described.

No...she refused to believe it. Her men wouldn't have done something so awful. Not to mention, she didn't remember seeing a muzzle on Darling.

Could she really have missed it?

She tried her best to think back to her few minutes with Darling before they'd rescued him. But all she could remember was the feral hatred in his eyes and her own absolute lack of judgment. "Was he really muzzled?"

The moment those words left her lips, and even before Maris spoke, she flashed on the men who'd freed Darling.

The angry conversation between themselves. Darling *had* been muzzled. She remembered them talking about it now. So much had happened so fast, that it hadn't made an impression on her at the time, and since then, her thoughts had been on other things.

I am the biggest dolt who was ever born.

"You truly don't know what was done to him, do you?" Maris pushed her back into her cell and sat her on the floor while he pulled out his mobile device.

Oblivious to the fact that he was wrinkling what had to be an extremely expensive outfit, he sat down beside her and handed her the file he'd just pulled up.

"What's this?"

His dark eyes blistered her. "Just read."

Irritated, Zarya let out a breath of frustration. But as she began reviewing Darling's medical report, her stomach shrank into a painful knot. No wonder Maris had sat her down first. Had she been standing, she might have fallen. "Is this for real?"

"Yes. It's why I pulled it. I knew if I told you, you wouldn't believe me." He reached over her to scroll to photos of Darling that were also in the file. There, she saw for herself the damage done to his mouth by the muzzle. It had worn permanent holes under his tongue and had pierced it through.

But that wasn't the worst damage. Not by far.

Oh my God…

Her "friends" had brutalized him in a way that defied belief or imagination. And like Maris had said, with a muzzle in place, it wasn't done for information.

He'd been tortured for entertainment.

Maris clicked to another page of the report. "They fed him his own vomit, along with urine and excrement."

Zarya couldn't see past the tears in her eyes as her stomach lurched over the viciousness. "I knew them. They...they weren't animals. They were fathers and sons, daughters and mothers. Loving spouses and parents. How could they do that to anyone?"

Yet there was no denying the proof in her hands. She saw it with brutal clarity.

They had torn Darling apart. No wonder he was insane. Who wouldn't be?

"Darling wasn't a person to them," Maris said in a strained voice. "He was an effigy. He stood for everything in their lives that they despised and hated—for every person they felt had it better or easier than them, anyone who had ever done them wrong or ever used them—and they took their own anger at the world out on him. They didn't see him as a human being. Only as an enemy they wanted to feel every pain, real or imagined, they'd suffered in their own lives." Maris went to yet another page. "They even cut off his finger and fed that to him, too."

She rushed to the toilet and barely made it before she was sick.

Still, Maris took no pity on her. "They brutally and repeatedly sodomized him with objects we have yet to identify, and beat him to the brink of death. They attached electrodes to his genitals and muzzle, and ran enough electricity to him to leave burn scars all over his body, including his face. Anyone would be broken by that. But you have to remember, these weren't strangers to him. These were people he'd protected. People he'd risked his own life, and that of his family, to help."

People he'd been wounded for...

Zarya's stomach heaved again under the true horror of what she'd allowed her men to do to him. Why hadn't she checked on their prisoner?

Just once...

Her head swam from the horror of it all. "I didn't know. I swear I didn't. I wouldn't have allowed them to do that to my worst enemy...not even Arturo."

"You were in the room with him when we arrived."

She sputtered in guilt and remorse. "I had just found out that we still had him in our custody. Literally right before your arrival. It was the first time I'd gone in. I swear." But like the others, she hadn't seen Darling as a person either. He'd been nothing to her but...

Dear gods, I slapped him while he wore a muzzle...

Her stomach heaved again as she realized just how much that would have hurt him. *How could I have done something like that?* She'd always prided herself on being fair and impartial. Compassionate.

Yes, she'd thought that he'd harmed Kere. Still...

I should have seen him. Should have seen the condition he was in instead of latching on to my own pain and being oblivious to the one right before my eyes. Someone who was hurting so much worse.

She'd always prided herself on being kind and sympathetic to others. The reality that she could be as cold and indifferent as those who'd wrong her, was a harsh slap in her face.

Pressing her hands to her eyes, she tried to blot out the image of Darling in those photos. The sight of him in that awful room when she'd finally become aware of his condition.

She couldn't stop herself from seeing every minute detail. And the worst was the guilt that ate at her. She, who had promised to love and protect him from all enemies, had failed him horribly.

Maris flushed the toilet, then brought her a cool cloth and

pressed it to the back of her neck to soothe her. "Until this moment, I didn't believe that about you."

"And now?"

He brushed the hair back from her face. "I see the truth in your eyes. You do love him, and I believe you when you tell me that you didn't know what they'd done." He narrowed his gaze at her. "Now I'm asking you to help me save him before it's too late. Please, Zarya. I love Darling. I always have. You've no idea how many times he took up for me when no one else would. How many fights he fought for me. How many times he held me when I cried because I was afraid of other people's prejudice and cruelty, and you know what he always said to me?"

She shook her head.

"Life sucks, Mari. It's never fair to anyone. But I'll always keep you safe from it. As long as I breathe, I won't let them hurt you. Night or day, you call and I will drop everything to come running to you."

That sounded like Kere.

"Now that he needs me to be there for him, how can I turn my back on the only true friend I've ever had?"

She felt the same way and yet…

"He hates me, and given that"—she gestured at his mobile—"he has every right to."

Maris sighed. "You know, that's the sickest thing about love. When it's real, you'll forgive anything."

"How do you know?"

"Because I've seen the way Darling's family has treated him over the years. The thoughtless things they've said and done, and all the fights they've had. And I've seen him not only forgive them for it, but risk his life and health to keep them safe. Over and over. If he can forgive them, I know he can forgive you, too."

She wasn't so sure. "What about the Resistance? What's happened to them while I've been imprisoned?"

"They're...gone."

She cringed at the news. Not that she hadn't suspected it given the way the Sentella had attacked them to get Darling back, but hearing the confirmation was another matter. "Did Darling kill any of them?"

Maris dropped his gaze to the mobile, then showed her the burn scars on Darling's nipples and groin where he'd been electrocuted...and that done while he wore a muzzle...

She flinched at the sight of such wanton brutality.

"What would you have done?" he asked her.

The same. If not worse. There was no doubt whatsoever. In fact, she wanted to kill them herself for what they'd done to him.

It was so wrong. The Resistance hadn't been founded on cruelty. They were supposed to be a humanitarian organization that protected people from those who wrongfully hurt others.

How had the oppressed become the oppressor?

But she knew that answer, too. Like Maris said, they'd felt justified in their violence. Arturo had hurt them and their families. Why not hurt his?

They hadn't bothered to find out that Darling was innocent. That he was one of them.

They hadn't cared. In war, the innocent died and were punished along with the guilty. That was the one thing her father had drilled into her most.

In a fight, no one walked away unscathed.

Zarya drew a ragged breath and asked the most important question of all, even though she dreaded the answer. "What about my sister, Sorche? What has become of her?"

Had Darling killed her, too? If he had...

That she would *never* forgive. And she would kill Darling herself if he'd hurt Sorche.

Maris paused until she thought she'd be sick again. How bad was the news that he couldn't even speak of it?

"Sorche Starska?"

She nodded as the knot in her stomach tightened with dread.

Please, don't be dead. She could handle and maybe forgive anything, except that.

Maris sat back in thought. "So that's who that was...Weird."

"What?" Why wouldn't he answer her already?

"Nothing bad," Maris said quickly, as if he'd finally realized he was being cruel. "Darling has her enrolled in the same academy his sister attends."

It took several seconds for that to fully register over the wave of disbelief that crashed through her. "I don't understand."

Why would Darling have helped her sister after he sent *her* here to this hell?

Maris pulled up her sister's private transcript. "I've been wondering who she was and why he cared what happened to her. Der to me, I should have paid attention to the last name. But what can I say? I have great moments of epic stupid like everyone else." He bit his lip. "No wonder Darling had such a strange reaction."

"To what?"

"Well, I saw the bill for her tuition a few weeks ago in his office and when I asked him about it, he got highly testy at me and refused to answer. He actually tossed me out of his office and told me to quit snooping through his things. I thought for the merest instant, she might be his mistress or something. I knew it was an odd reaction to something that didn't require that degree of hostility. But you can see for yourself that she's in the best classes and has a private tutor three times a week...All paid for by Darling."

Zarya held his mobile like a lifeline as she saw her sister's record.

Guernelle Academy had been both their dreams as far back as she could remember. It was the same school where their parents had met, and then graduated.

For Zarya, the dream had ended on her eighteenth birthday when her father had been murdered. She'd been forced to leave school before graduation to take over her father's position in the Resistance. But she'd refused to allow Sorche to join her cause. Unlike her, her sister had stayed in school and kept her grades up.

Two years ago, Sorche had graduated with honors and scored so high on her entrance exams that the academy had actually courted her for admission.

However, the exorbitant cost was prohibitive. Since their father had been branded a traitor and Zarya was currently a wanted outlaw, Sorche wasn't able to apply for scholarships or grants. Something that had torn Zarya up since she blamed herself for impeding her sister's dream.

Relentlessly over the last two years, they'd been trying to save up enough for Sorche to attend, but they hadn't been able to even scrape together the down payment.

Kere...

No, Darling had known that. He'd offered to pay Sorche's board and tuition on several occasions.

"I don't mind, Z. I swear it won't take anything away from me to do this. Please, let me help you."

Afraid he'd think she was using him for his money, Zarya had refused to accept his offer.

Now...

It didn't make sense that he would still help out her sister. Especially if he blamed Zarya for what had been done to him.

She handed Maris the mobile. "I was so afraid he'd killed her or sold her off like he did me."

Maris turned his device off. "Was she part of the Resistance?"

"No. Never. I wouldn't allow it."

"Then there's your answer. She was innocent."

Like Darling had been. Only her people hadn't cared about that. They'd hurt him regardless.

Damn them.

"Darling lives his entire life by the Code of Twenty his father taught him. Number nineteen... *Love all, regardless of what they do. Trust only those you have to. And harm none until they harm you.* He would never punish someone without reason. No matter what, unlike his uncle and even in this insanity that currently has possession of him, he's always been fair and just."

And for that, she'd never been more grateful.

Maris tilted his head down and pinned her with a probing stare. "So I'm asking you one last time, Zarya. Will you please, *please* help me save a good man who is in a really bad place?"

8

Maris spent hours prepping her on what to expect from Darling as they'd traveled to the Winter Palace.

Once they were there, he smuggled her through the servant entrance and into his private suite so that he could meticulously dress her in a long white, sleeveless gown that was trimmed in silver and lace, and apply her makeup. It was sad when a man knew more about being a woman than she did. But she'd never had the money to waste on something as frivolous as vanity, clothes, and cosmetics.

Maris stepped back so that she could see herself in the mirror.

Zarya's jaw went slack at a face she barely recognized. Her eyelids felt heavy from the eye shadow and mascara, but the color made her amber eyes glow, especially the way he'd ringed her eyes with a thick band of black and swept it out at the sides. Her skin appeared smoother and more radiant than it ever had before. He'd pulled her mahogany hair back from her face to show off her deep widow's peak, and laced white and silver ribbons through it.

She felt like a mythical princess.

One about to be fed to a dragon...

"You are beautiful," Maris said as he fussed with the back of her hair, fluffing out the fat curls he'd made.

"I've never felt beautiful." And she definitely wasn't the kind of woman who turned men's heads when she entered a room. Their stomachs, she'd been told, was another matter.

Other than Darling, she could count her number of boyfriends on two fingers. And neither of them had stayed around for very long. One had left as soon as she refused to pay his rent. The other after he realized she had a much prettier younger sister. Sorche had sent him packing immediately, but the damage to Zarya's ego had already been done.

Maris smiled at her in the mirror. "Don't listen to the haters. Trust me. I'm not the kind of guy who notices women, but I can see why Darling loves you. Aside from being a sweetheart, you have hair to die for. Your eyes are unusual, but stunning, and your skin...perfection. I envy you so much."

The last part surprised her. "Why?"

"You've done things with Darling that I've only dreamed about. I would give absolutely anything to have one night in his arms."

The painful regret in his voice touched her. "You really do love him, don't you?"

His dark gaze was so sad as he closed the lid on her blush and set it back on the table. "Yes, I do. You've no idea how many times I've wished that I'd been born a woman...or that he really was gay."

"He never experimented?" From what she'd heard about the men of the ruling class, they were indiscriminate about their lovers' genders.

A shadow of inner turmoil darkened his eyes.

Even though she hadn't known Maris long, she'd learned to fear that expression and what it usually signified. "What?"

Maris moved away from her.

Zarya got up and went to him. She knew from his reaction that it had to be bad. Still, if it was about Darling, she needed to know before she went in there to face him. "What aren't you telling me?"

Tears glistened in his eyes. His lips quivered.

A knot formed in her stomach. How awful could it be, given what her people had done to Darling?

Maris touched a trembling hand to his lips. "I promised Darling I would never tell anyone. Sorry."

"Did you and he . . ."

"No!" he said emphatically, slinging his hand downward. "Never."

"Then please tell me, Maris. I swear I'll never speak a word of it to another living soul. I'll take it to my grave."

A muscle worked in his jaw as he debated with himself. After a few heartbeats, he pinned her with a warning glower. "If you do, I swear I *will* kill you. I mean it. And don't think that I can't. I assure you, for Darling's sake, I can and *will* be brutal."

She nodded. "You have my word, and in spite of what you might think of me, I don't break it."

Even so, it took him several more minutes before he spoke again. "Darling was fifteen when he confessed to being gay."

Which was all she'd ever heard about the eldest prince and his gender preferences. To her knowledge, he'd always been very open about it. "So he's bisexual?"

Maris let out a bitter laugh. "No. Not even a little."

"Then why would he say he was homosexual?"

By the expression on his face, she could tell he was having to force himself to continue. That rare loyalty caused her to respect him even more than she already did. Most people didn't hesitate to betray a secret.

The majority of people she'd known in her life ran fast to be the first to reveal it. It was as if they took perverse pleasure in betraying someone's confidence.

Maris was a rare man, and one of the best friends anyone could have. "He did it to protect his mother. You have to remember,

Natale was only a baby when Darling was born. Widowed in her mid-twenties, she was extremely lonely. Because of her beauty, she was used to men paying a lot of attention to her, and she loved it. Lived on it, point of fact."

Zarya sucked her breath in sharply as she saw where this was going. "She took lovers."

Talk about a no-no in their society.

What had his mother been thinking? It was an automatic death sentence for the governor's widow. But then that was something Zarya complained about all the time with most women her age. Way too many of them lacked good sense, especially where men were concerned.

Maris nodded. "Foolishly, she got caught...or rather her lover was found on his way out of the palace. To save her life and to keep Natale from being arrested, Darling said her boyfriend was his, and that her lover had been leaving *his* room."

"But he wasn't."

"No, and thankfully there weren't any surveillance cameras on the inside of the private wing at that time to refute Darling's confession. And once Darling started the ruse, his mother seized on it. She used him to cover all her lovers from that point on, and he had no choice except to claim them or watch her die."

Zarya winced at the cruelty of forcing someone to live a lie over something so ridiculous. The woman should have never put him in that position. How could *any* mother do such a thing?

She couldn't imagine the horror of being trapped in his situation. But it went a long way in explaining many idiosyncrasies about Darling that she'd noted while they dated. His knowledge of fashion. His excessive cleaniness, especially compared to her brother who'd lived his life like he'd learned hygiene from bears. "No one ever suspected the truth?"

He shook his head glumly. "They didn't care. People love

dirt and rather than judge for themselves, they prefer to believe the trash spewed by others. From the moment word got out that he was homosexual, and it flew fast, Darling was ostracized over it. Whenever we had state functions and events we had to attend, the other boys refused to dress in the same room with him. They treated him like he was diseased and contagious. Threw things at him as he passed by, and insulted him constantly. No one wanted to talk to him or be near him for fear of being accused of homosexuality, too. I remember the first time he sat down in a prince's dining hall after word had spread. Everyone at the table, including those he'd considered his friends, got up and moved away. I'll never forget the look on his face as he sat there, alone, his head held high and his jaw locked to keep from showing any emotion while he ate as they mocked him."

"What did you do?"

Tears glistened in his eyes as he looked away from her. "To my eternal shame, nothing whatsoever." He flinched and squeezed his eyes shut as if trying to banish an even worse memory.

When he met her gaze again, the bitterness there stung her. "Because I *am* gay, and others had long suspected it, I was even more terrified of having that allegation thrown at me. I saw how they treated Darling and I didn't want any part of that abuse. So like everyone else, I avoided him in public. He told me that he understood, and that he didn't want me to talk to him anywhere others might see us. He said it was safer that way for me. But even so, I could tell it hurt him that I avoided him like they did. That I'd be standing or sitting with those who mocked him while he stood alone in the crowd." A single tear slid down his cheek. "You have no idea how much I hate myself for that cowardice. I abandoned him to their hatred when I should have stood by his side, regardless. What kind of friend am I to ignore him while others cursed and mocked him?"

"He understood, Maris."

"But that doesn't make it right, does it?"

No, it didn't. Zarya patted his arm in sympathy. She couldn't imagine how awful it must have been for Darling to face that at his age. Puberty was hard enough when you fit in. To have something like that make you a target to your peers...

It was hell.

And for it to be a lie...

No wonder he hated his mother. He was more than justified.

"Didn't any of the adults do anything to help him?"

Maris shook his head. "They were even worse than the kids. And they turned a blind eye to how he was treated, even when it was right under their noses. Every time he moved, Darling had to fight someone over it. And his uncle was the most brutal of all. Anytime Arturo saw a man in the palace he didn't recognize or one anywhere near Darling, he accused Darling of sleeping with him. And when Darling was sixteen..." He flinched as if someone had hit him.

Her own stomach tightened in reflex. "What?"

His breathing ragged, Maris's eyes blazed with fury. "Arturo sent him to a mental institution for it."

She gaped at his disclosure. A mental institution? She'd ask him if he was serious, but she could see that answer clearly enough. "How could he do that?"

"He was the acting governor," Maris said simply. "Absolute power and authority. He demanded the doctors use aversion therapy to cure Darling of his homosexuality."

"I don't understand. What's aversion therapy?"

Maris couldn't even meet her gaze.

When he finally spoke, his voice was thick and constrained. "It's where they inflict severe pain, and use negative reinforcement to cause someone to alter their behavior."

"Like putting pepper sauce on a child's thumb to keep them from sucking it?" Her father had done that to her when she was six. To this day, she couldn't look at a pepper without cringing.

Maris toyed with the edge of his sleeve, but he still refused to meet her gaze. "General idea, but much worse. The point is to make the activity so repugnant and horrifying that the patient never wants to do it again."

Biting her lip, she wasn't sure she wanted to hear anything more.

Unfortunately, he didn't stop there. "That was how Darling lost his virginity...and it wasn't to a woman."

She choked on a sob.

Maris swallowed hard. "He was brutally raped, Zarya. Repeatedly. It was so bad, that for weeks after his release, he sat huddled in a corner, with his back against the wall. Like now, he wouldn't speak to anyone, and he had violent nightmares from it for years. Sometimes I think he still does."

His gaze haunted, he wiped a hand over his face. "When I finally saw him for the first time after he'd been released, I stupidly asked what they'd done to him...tears welled up in his eyes and then flowed down his face—and Darling doesn't cry, Zarya. Ever. Not for anything. He refused to look at me or to speak about it at all. By that, I knew what he wouldn't say."

"Did he ever tell you for sure?"

"Years later, when he was extremely drunk and ranting about his uncle, but he's never gone into any details. Other than to say he wanted to kill them all...and now he has."

Sighing, Maris returned to the counter to finish putting away her makeup. "For over a year after his release, he wouldn't let anyone touch him at all. Not even his own sister, and Darling has always adored Lise. If a man came anywhere near him, he literally ran away, and he refused to be alone with anyone. Even me. It was two full years before he'd even look another person in the eye, male or female. So no, he's never experimented. Until you, I've never known him to voluntarily be naked with anyone."

Her heart ached for Darling and what his uncle had put him through. It was *so* wrong.

But it left her with one question. "How did Darling pull off being gay if he was so repulsed by men?"

Maris smiled sheepishly. "I taught him how to use men he knew were safe to keep up the ruse—like I did with the women I dated. Men who wouldn't touch him or beat him over it. It took a lot of patience, but I got him to the point that he'd let me hug him again. He knew I wasn't going to make a move on him. And once he was used to me, we took smaller steps. First with his friend Caillen, who is rabidly heterosexual, and yet completely at ease with homosexuals. I taught Darling how to stand close to Caillen, and lean in to him so that other people would misinterpret his actions. If anyone asked him if he had a crush on someone, we chose Nykyrian because we knew Nyk would never hurt Darling for it. And once I came out, it was a lot easier. I was the one person he could be openly affectionate with who wouldn't be offended or expect anything else from him."

It was actually a brilliant plan. "So you've protected him all this time?"

"More he protected me. Until I came out, he took the heat for a lot of things I had."

"Such as?"

He gave her a duh stare. "I'm gay, Zarya. I've been that way as far back as I have memories. Obviously, I like to look at men, and read about men being together. I didn't dare do that at home where my brothers or parents might find it. So Darling kept...items for me, and I kept things for him."

That made sense, but it also made her feel stupid that he had to be so explicit. "Sorry. I didn't mean to be dense."

"It's okay. We're all dense from time to time." He let out a bitter laugh. "I still can't get over the shock on my parents' faces when I told them the truth about me. And all I could think was, *Are you people totally blind? Did none of you ever really look at me?* Even though I'd tried to hide it, I don't see how they missed it. Any more than I've ever understood how someone couldn't tell Darling was straight."

"I have to say I never had any doubts." But then she'd never seen the "Darling Cruel" side of him. As Kere, with a tiny handful of exceptions, he'd been all testosterone, all the time.

That thought made her flash back to one of their first missions together. They'd been ambushed by Caronese troops. When the blaster volley had started, he'd caught her about the waist and pulled her out of the line of fire. With one arm only, Darling had lifted her and held her against him with so much ease that his strength had temporarily stunned her. He'd wrapped himself around her body so that they shot his armor and left her unscathed.

When their attackers had paused to recharge their weapons, he'd literally skated across the slick floor to dump her into an access hallway before he turned. His head low and lethal, he'd stalked down the smoke-filled hallway like the fiercest predator she'd ever seen, and opened fire on them.

She still got chills whenever she thought about the tough vision he'd made in that dimly lit hallway, surrounded by smoke and blasts, as he returned their fire, and set their enemies into retreat.

Single-handedly.

Yeah...

No one messed with Kere, or her, without feeling his wrath.

Now she understood a lot more about why Darling had always been so hungry for her whenever they'd been alone. If he'd been keeping all of the real him bottled up around everyone else, it made sense that he'd savor their time together.

And savor her.

There was nothing she loved more than the way he buried his face in the curve of her neck and breathed her in like she was a drug he craved with every part of his being. He could make love to her for hours without tiring. Whenever they were together, he was focused only on her and nothing else.

Always attentive. Always gentle.

Always feral.

Gods, how she'd missed those moments. Missed the sound of his deep, lyrical voice, talking to her for hours on end. No one pronounced her name the way he did.

And his laughter...

It never failed to make her smile. He had the most wicked sense of humor imaginable. Dark and sarcastic, he found amusement in the bleakest and most bizarre things.

Maris cleared his throat, bringing her back to the present.

And to the pain of the fact that she might never have those moments with Darling again.

Tormented agony glowed deep in his eyes. "You've no idea how many times I've wondered if Darling would have been better off had he not been my friend."

She frowned. "Why would you say that?"

"Had we not become friends when we were so young...had he not known and accepted the fact that I was homosexual, he would have never thought to claim his mother's boyfriend as his. It wouldn't have even occurred to him to do it—all of that was totally my fault and I know it."

His words stunned her. "They would have killed his mother, Maris. How could that be better?"

"Honestly?" Maris asked in a deadly serious tone. "I don't think that would have been as bad as what's happened to him since. Yes, he would have had grief from losing her. But I don't think her loss would have been nearly as awful as his stints in the asylums, and what they did to him every time he was confined for it. The unrelenting hell he's had to endure all these years over pretending to be something he's not."

The saddest part? She had a sick feeling in her stomach that Maris might be right. To be punished and humiliated for a lie you were forced to live...

It had to have been brutal.

And it made her curious about something else. "How long have you two been friends?"

Maris grinned as if the memory was one of the best of his life. "Since preschool. I met him the first day there when we were five."

Zarya smiled at the love she saw in his eyes. How she wished she could have found a friend like Maris so young. But most of her friends had turned on her over the years, for one reason or another. One, wanting the bounty on her head, had even told the League where she lived. It was why she was so skittish and suspicious of people now.

She hadn't met her best friend, Ture, until a couple of years ago—he was a cook in the restaurant she'd started patronizing on her way home to keep Darling from fussing at her for not eating.

And thinking of Ture, who had only confessed his sexual preference to her a few weeks before she'd been taken prisoner, made her wonder how long Maris had waited with Darling. "When did you tell Darling you were gay?"

"I didn't have to. He always knew." Maris shook his head. "We were twelve before I knew he knew. Things were starting to get really awkward for me then. When we were younger, it didn't matter so much. But once puberty kicked in...it was extremely hard as I realized just how different I was from the other boys I knew. Being Phrixian, didn't help. We're a warrior culture where men are men, and you better be testosterone driven every nanosecond of the day or you're going to get your ass kicked. For years, I didn't know *anyone* else who was gay—I really thought I was defective. I was born number seven in a total of nine boys, and my brothers are all you'd expect from a Phrixian family. Fierce, tough, and brutal. I'm actually lucky they didn't kill me for it."

He laughed all of a sudden. "Ironically, Darling was the one who introduced me to my first boyfriend when I was nineteen. But for him, I'm not sure I would have ever found a community that accepted me."

She rubbed his arm in sympathy. "I can only imagine how many women must have thrown themselves at you, given how handsome you are. And the fact you're a high-ranking prince...bonus."

Maris nodded grimly. "Yes, they did. Anyone who thinks men are more sexually predacious than a woman hasn't been around any. I've never had a man come on to me as strongly as some of the women I met both before I came out, and since. You'd be amazed how many of them have offered to try and convert me. Like that's all it would take, right?" He rolled his eyes. "And they don't like to take no for an answer either. I had this one who...Never mind." He waved his hand in front of his face as if to cool it down. "Girl, the stories I could tell you about some of them."

Zarya felt her own face flame. Now that he mentioned it, she'd been the one who made the first move on Darling.

Yeah, let's not go there...

She still couldn't believe how forward she'd been with Darling in the early days of their relationship. But like Maris said, she'd seen what she wanted and she'd gone after him.

"So how did you find out he knew?" she asked, trying to get Maris back on the original topic and not a segue that mortified her.

"One night, not long before his father died, I was sleeping over. Darling had gone out to see Ryn who was training with the guard." Maris paused to give her a wicked smile behind his hand as if he were imparting a secret to her. "Did you know most of them train without their shirts on?" He wrinkled his nose and bit his lip playfully. "I didn't, and Phrixians don't. I'd never been around men built like they were who were that close to naked and not related to me. No matter how hard I tried, I couldn't stop my eyes from betraying my interest. I absolutely licked them with my gaze."

He fanned his face again. "Anyway, I suddenly realized Darling had stopped talking to Ryn and was watching me with an evil smirk. I was sick from it. All I could think was that he'd send me home and never speak to me again. Or worse, be like everyone else I knew and beat the mess out of me for it. Instead, he came over and clapped me on the back. Then he leaned to whisper in my ear so that no one else would overhear him, and said, 'I don't care what your tastes are, Mari. I never have, and I've known about them for a long time. So don't ever be afraid of me because of it. You're still my brother, and you always will be. If we were all made the same, the universe would be a boring place. And while my tastes are much more traditional, I will never judge you for yours. Just don't ever grab my junk, and I won't kill you for it.' "

She had to bite back a laugh at his unexpected anecdote. "Did he really say that?"

"Yes, yes he did. And he meant it. So I promised him he would always be safe from my groping…unless he begged me for it. And unfortunately, he never has." His gaze turned sad again. "I miss my best friend, Zarya. I really want him back."

"I feel the same way. I miss him, too." And she did.

Under the guise of Kere, Darling had been everything to her.

Maris cupped her face in his hands. "I should warn you, when he came back after his first assault, he was angry like he is now."

First? There had been more than one? She wanted to cry over that disclosure.

But Maris didn't pause to elaborate. "Think of him like an

animal in the wild. You have to move slow around him, and let him know you're not going to hurt him. He's in raw survival mode. It's not that he wants to hurt others as much as he wants to protect himself from harm. So he's liable to strike out verbally. Pay it no attention. He will be sorry for it later. Right now, he's just in pain, and he's acting out. Take nothing he says or does personally."

"Okay."

His gaze intensified. "Remember, he's not really attacking you. It's the world he wants to punch. You have to be strong and don't back down from him."

Instead of making her feel better, this "pep talk" was beginning to make her want to run for cover.

Maris kissed her cheek. "You ready?"

"I'm scared."

"Me, too. Now don't forget that he's not what he was. He's changed a lot. But if we stand together, I think we can still get him back."

She hoped so. It'd been well over a year since she'd last held him, or heard him ask if she'd eaten anything.

No man had ever treated her the way he did.

Like she mattered.

Come back to me, Darling.

Maris tucked her hand into the crook of his elbow and led her from his room.

With every step they took closer to Darling's office, the more nervous she became. Her hands were clammy and her heart pounded in trepidation. It was so loud, she was amazed Maris couldn't hear it.

How would Darling react to her presence? She saw various scenarios in her mind, but none of them were particularly favorable to her.

I can't believe I slapped him.

162

Twice...

She wanted to cry every time she remembered that. *I didn't know who he was.* But that was only an excuse, and she knew it. Did it really matter who had been held in chains? What kind of person would hit someone who'd been so damaged while in their custody?

The fact that she hadn't even seen him enough to register his ragged condition before she'd attacked him bothered her most of all.

Deep inside, she was as disappointed in herself as he'd been. Yes, she could make excuses. She'd been worried about Kere. She'd been focused on her pain and not his...

But in the end, wasn't that the very thing she and her allies accused the ruling class of? The thing the Resistance had condemned them for? Being numb to others who were suffering right before their eyes? Not caring about their pain?

And what had she done?

The same damn thing.

Truth scalded her throat, and the bitter taste of it hung heavy on her tongue.

Would she be able to forgive Darling if she was in his place?

No, she wouldn't. So what made her think for even a nanosecond that he'd be a better person than she was?

Because he'd always been a better person.

Guilt, dread, and raw fear tormented her with more scenarios.

And all of them ended with him killing her...

Maris left her alone in the hallway so that he could enter Darling's study first.

Tempted to run for cover, she listened intently. If Darling spoke, she couldn't hear him through the door. But Maris's voice was plain.

"I think I might have found something to finally brighten your foul mood." Maris opened the door and motioned her forward.

163

For a full minute, she couldn't move as terror overwhelmed her. *I can't do this*. Fear had her absolutely paralyzed.

"I won't let him hurt you," Maris whispered. He held his hand out for her.

Summoning her courage, she allowed him to pull her inside. She'd barely entered the room when her gaze locked with Darling's.

Time hung still as they stared at each other.

She wasn't sure what she'd expected, but it wasn't the man in front of her. First, she couldn't see anything of his face. He wore a gold mask that had no expression whatsoever.

Only a pair of furious blue eyes showed his emotions, and the hatred there was a living, tangible entity that held her immobile.

Like some menacing demon, he wore a black hood pulled up over his head with tendrils of long, greasy red hair peeking out around its edges. Not a single millimeter of skin showed other than his scarred lips and bearded chin. He was swathed from head to toe in black and his hands were covered with leather gloves. But what held her attention hard and fast was the explosive device he wore around his chest.

Maris was right. Darling was deranged. She could feel the violent undercurrent in him with every instinct she possessed.

Run!

But her limbs wouldn't obey her...

Darling didn't move as he stared at the last human being he'd ever thought to see again. For a full minute, he couldn't breathe as he gazed into the amber eyes that had haunted him for months now. At first he thought his drunken mind had conjured her, but one look at Maris and he knew the truth.

The treacherous bastard had betrayed him.

Even worse, Maris must have dressed her. Darling had never known Zarya to wear makeup of any kind before. Nor curl her hair.

Tonight, she was exquisitely perfect in his office. Not that she hadn't always been exquisite. From the first time he'd met her as an adult, and she'd been covered in grease and blood from a mission she'd been on, he'd thought she was the most beautiful woman in the universe.

You're all I ever wanted…

In spite of everything her soldiers had done to him, a part of him wanted to run to her and hold her. To have her soothe the blackened misery that consumed every last molecule of his soul.

He hated that part of himself.

She betrayed you. She spit on you like you were dirt beneath her feet. When he'd been helpless and torn apart by her friends, she'd slapped him.

He still bore the scar on his cheek from the ring he'd given her. It bisected the one his brother had given him.

But worse was the agony deep inside. The part of him she'd kicked the hardest.

His heart.

All of his volatile, competing emotions slammed into him with resounding violence. In that one heartbeat, he wanted only to kill her. He could already feel her last breath. Smell her blood on his hands.

"What is she doing here?" he snarled.

Zarya swallowed as she heard what Maris had warned her about. That wasn't the lyrical, refined voice that used to whisper in her ear. It was a gruff, raspy growl that sounded like it caused him pain to speak. One that told her just how badly the muzzle had damaged his throat.

Her poor Darling…

Maris faced him bravely. But for his reassuring hand on her arm, she'd be running for the door.

"I thought she'd make you happy."

Darling came out of his chair with a feral snarl. "Get her out of my sight."

"But—"

Before Maris could utter another syllable, Darling let out a fierce roar and overturned his ornately carved desk. Everything that had been on top of it went flying.

The air was charged with Darling's fury as he stormed toward them.

Fearless, Maris released her and put himself in Darling's path. "If you want to hit someone, hit me. I'm the one who bought her for you."

"You're going to tempt me one time too many to hit you, Maris. One day, I'm not going to pull back."

"And I'll still love you, even if you knock my teeth out."

Those words seemed to calm Darling a degree. At least that's what Zarya thought until he looked at her. Then the bitter, insane rage returned to his eyes.

He stepped around Maris to grab her by the arm.

"Darling? I—"

The frigid look he gave her froze her vocal cords. "*I* am the Caronese governor, with one of the purest aristocratic bloodlines in the United Systems. You will refer to me as 'Your Majesty' or 'my lord.' Do you understand?" He literally spat every syllable at her.

She nodded.

His grip tightened on her elbow as he pulled her from the room.

She looked back to see Maris following after them. She considered fighting Darling, but her sanity kept her from it. In the mood he was in, he might kill her if she tried.

Without slowing his determined stride, Darling hauled her through the palace and into a huge, industrial kitchen. There he flung her toward an older, portly woman who appeared to be in charge of the area.

The woman and her all female staff bowed low to Darling.

When he spoke, that raspy growl chilled every part of her. "You have a new slave for your staff. Do with her what you will." He turned and glared at Maris before he left her there like a discarded toy he'd grown bored with.

Her sight blurred as she saw the relief on Maris's face that Darling hadn't hurt her. At least not physically.

Emotionally, however, she felt kicked and bruised by his rejection.

What were you expecting?

In all honesty, she should be grateful he hadn't beat or killed her. This was far kinder than all but one of the things she'd imagined for their reunion.

In that one, Darling had actually welcomed her.

You're an idiot.

He would never welcome her again. Why should he?

And this finalized it. Darling hated her. He had every right to.

"Maris!"

Maris jumped at Darling's gruff bellow. He gave her one last look of sympathy before he went to see what Darling needed.

Zarya swallowed. There had been a time when Darling had needed *her*.

But never again.

By her own actions, she had destroyed his love for her. The worst part was that she couldn't even blame him for it. She'd done this to herself.

"Here." The kitchen warden shoved a filthy trash bin into her hands. "Dump that in the receptacle out back...*my lady*," she sneered, then broke off into mocking laughter. "And try not to muss your hair or get shit on your dress."

The others laughed, too, as Zarya headed for the door. Yeah, she could just imagine how pathetic she looked dressed like this while she went about household chores. Every one of them knew exactly what had happened.

Their governor had rejected her.

Even so, she kept her chin up and her spine stiff. Let them mock her. She didn't need their approval or their friendship.

All she needed was a man who hated her guts.

Darling glared at his oldest friend as he toyed with the idea of gutting Maris where he stood. "What the fuck was that?"

"I thought she'd cheer you up."

He curled his lip. "Don't lie to me. You thought you could weaken me with her. Admit it."

A tic started in Maris's jaw—something that didn't happen often. It took a lot to make Maris lose his temper, especially with Darling. "I'm not trying to weaken you. I'm trying to *help* you."

Yeah, right. "Help me what? Get killed?"

Maris sighed. "You know better than that. But what am I supposed to do?" His tone sharpened as the fire returned to his dark eyes. "Stand by and watch as you drink yourself into another coma? Really? And when was the last time you bathed or shaved? You look awful and you smell like the back end of a dead, rotting yaksen's ass."

Darling wanted to kill him as those words cut to the core of his battered soul. The impulse was so strong, he wasn't sure how he kept from it.

How could Maris say *that* to him?

Maris had always been so intuitive, but in this...

The bastard was wrong.

Dead wrong.

"You want to know why I don't bathe?" Darling snarled at him. "Because I have to look at *this*." He jerked his mask off and threw it at Maris. It was the first time since he'd been rescued that he'd allowed anyone other than Syn to see what was left of him.

And it was truly repulsive.

His expression unreadable, Maris caught the mask to his chest. Tears welled up in his friend's eyes as he finally saw the true horror of what had been done to Darling.

And *that* was just on the surface.

Darling turned away as agony washed through his entire being. It was the internal damage that tore him up the most. Every time he saw his face or his skin, it took him right back to that room where they'd hung him up, naked, like a piece of meat to be butchered. All of it hit him again as if it were still happening—as if he'd wake up and be right back there at their mercy. He felt every stinging emotion of being abandoned and alone and hopeless.

Helpless.

He, who had the power, speed, and skills to kill a man with the ease of a League assassin, had been completely unable to stop them from violating him.

Over and over.

With every glimpse of his skin, Darling smelled the blood, the shit, and the urine. The vomit. Every vicious thing they'd said to him while they'd carved him up—the laughter and joy they'd taken in their cruelty rang in his ears until he was deaf from it.

Nothing could silence it.

Nothing.

And above it all, was the sound of Zarya on the other side of the door, going about her daily routine while they viciously brutalized him, day after day, month after month.

Even then, he'd prayed that she, the woman who'd sworn she would never betray or hurt him, would just open the door and help him.

Instead, when she'd finally come inside, she'd slapped and cursed him like all the others.

That was what he couldn't face.

And now Maris dared to bring the bitch back into his life...

Maris *was* lucky he hadn't punched him.

Sick to his stomach and battered to the core of his soul, Darling fished through the mess he'd made in his office and pulled his bottle of Tondarion whisky up from the floor where it'd rolled after he'd overturned his desk.

This had been the only comfort he'd had since they'd rescued him. Nothing else eased the bitterness in his dead heart. While the whisky didn't get rid of the voices entirely, it at least dulled them enough that he could function around the memories.

He took a deep swig straight from the bottle and let the liquor burn down his damaged throat. The one thing he'd learned in his useless life was how to find pleasure in pain. It was all the gods had left him with. "You'll have to excuse me if I'm not feeling up to a shower or shave right now."

Maris closed the distance between them. He set the mask down on the shelves to Darling's left, then pulled the bottle out of Darling's hand and placed it beside the mask. "I don't care what you look like, Darling. I never have. It's your heart that's beautiful."

Darling cursed him for a liar as he reached for the bottle again.

Maris caught his hand to keep him from touching it. "You don't need that."

Yes, he did. He had nothing else in his life. "There's no beauty left in me, Mari. People are nothing but rabid animals who attack friend and foe for no reason whatsoever. They don't care. They don't feel. All they want to do is crush others and make them bleed as if that will somehow miraculously aleviate their putrid misery. There's nothing left but hatred, contempt, and disgust in my heart. I finally understand what drove Arturo and why I was attacked."

Wanting only to comfort him, Maris wrapped his arms around Darling's waist and held him close.

To his surprise, Darling actually leaned back against his chest and closed his eyes. Then, he reached up to curl his arm around Maris's neck. Darling hadn't allowed him to hold him like this since before his first rape. If nothing else, that told him just how much pain Darling was in.

"How flagged are you, Darling?"

"Very." His breathing ragged, he swallowed hard as he surrendered his weight to Maris. "I'm so fucked up, Mari," he whispered. "All I feel now is unending pain and utter misery. I just want to sleep and I can't even do that. I'm so tired of it all..."

Maris tightened his arms around him, wishing there was something, anything, he could do to make it better. He held Darling tight as a thousand regrets ripped him apart. "I know, sweetie. I've got you. I won't let you fall, I promise."

Swaying with Darling in his arms, Maris brushed the hair back from Darling's scarred face and kissed his bearded cheek before he spoke the words that broke his heart into pieces. "But we both know that I'm not what you need or want. No matter how much I love you, I can't heal you."

Tears swam in Darling's eyes, but not a single one fell. Darling's strength had always amazed him. No matter the firestorm, he'd always stood so proud and defiant in the midst of it.

Leaning his head back onto Maris's shoulder, Darling cupped his cheek in his gloved hand. "Why couldn't I be gay? It would be so easy to love you if I were. You've always been here for me, Mari. You've never hurt me. Not once."

The truth stung him as Maris thought back to all the times

Darling had been ostracized, in need of a friend, and he'd been too afraid to publicly acknowledge him. But Darling never seemed to remember that part of their friendship. It didn't tear him apart the way it did Maris.

"You know that's not true, Dar. I got your ass kicked the first day we met."

Darling let out an unexpected tiny laugh at the memory. "But I won the fight."

"Yes, you did." Maris smiled as he saw that day so clearly in his mind. He'd been pinned to the school wall by a bully who'd been pounding on him. Out of nowhere, this tiny little red-haired boy had come charging in like a hurricane. Barely five years old, Darling had been short for his age. But what he lacked in height, he made up for in ferocity.

In no time at all, he'd beat the bully back and had him on the ground, crying for his mother. After making him swear he'd never even look at Maris again, Darling had stood up and come over to him. Forever proud and fierce, Darling had wiped the blood from his lips, then offered Maris his other hand. "Hi, I'm Darling Cruel. We should be friends."

Maris had fallen in love instantly.

And he'd been in love with Darling every day since.

"You have always been my champion," Maris whispered to him.

Darling closed his eyes as he clenched his fist in Maris's hair. "Why couldn't they have killed me, Mari? My mother's right. I have no reason to be here. I shouldn't be alive. The empire would be better off with Drake as governor and not a freak like me."

"Don't you *dare* talk like that!" Maris didn't want to think about a life without Darling in it. He couldn't face the pain of even the thought, never mind the reality. Not knowing where Darling was had been the worst time of his life.

He didn't care what condition Darling was in. He just needed him to be here.

"It's true and you know it," Darling said, his speech slurred as his hand fell away from Maris's hair. "I'm sick of hurting all the time, Mari. I just want the pain to stop. But it doesn't. It only worsens. I can't even dull it anymore." His words were really slurred now. "I just want..."

Maris tightened his arms around Darling as he finally passed out. "My poor baby." But at least Darling would have a few hours of rest now.

Maybe by tomorrow he'd feel a little better. Not likely, but he could hope.

Swinging Darling up in his arms, Maris carried him upstairs, to the governor's bedroom.

He lay Darling down on the large bed and removed his boots, hood, and gloves. His heart broke as he saw the damage they'd wrought on Darling's face, hands, and feet.

It was so wrong. Damn them for their cruelty.

Darling had been so beautiful in his youth. So flawlessly handsome. But first his own brother had given him the vertical scar on the left side of his face, and now this...

Bastards.

Maris started to remove the explosives that were woven around Darling's tunic, then caught himself. Knowing Darling, they were trip wired. It was extreme, but he understood that insanity, too. Every Cruel governor for the last three thousand years had been assassinated.

All of them.

It was one of the reasons why Darling had been so fascinated by electronics and explosives as a kid. As far back as Maris could remember, Darling had been obsessed with protecting himself from would-be assassins.

Ironically, it had been an assassin who finally quelled Darling's fear of them. Nykyrian had taught Darling every trick a trained assassin had. Even some that no one knew.

And Darling had learned well. He forgot nothing. If any member of his line stood a chance of making it to old age, it was he.

Maris covered him with a blanket.

At least he's talking to me again. That was something. But as he watched Darling finally sleep, he had the worst feeling that it was too late to bring him back from the insanity that had sunk its hooks into him. After all the things Darling had been through, Maris had never seen him like this.

His anger and rage were tangible.

"I just want the pain to stop." Darling's heartfelt words haunted him.

Maris's gaze fell to the scars on Darling's wrists that hadn't come from his attackers or Arturo. Those had been Darling's attempts to stop his pain when he was just a boy. Three times he'd tried to kill himself—once with drugs and twice by slashing his wrists. Three times they'd brought him back against his will. The only thing that had kept him from a fourth attempt had been Arturo's threat to kill Lise if Darling tried again.

Darling's entire life had been a study in trying to find shelter in the middle of an unrelenting storm that was determined to bring him to his knees.

Wishing he could help his best friend, Maris picked up Darling's hand from the bed and studied the scar on his finger that showed where Syn had added the cybernetic replacement for the one they'd cut off.

He laced his fingers with Darling's scarred ones. *Why couldn't I be what you need?*

It was why he'd never been serious about anyone else. How

could he? He was in love with his best friend and no one else measured up.

But Maris had long ago accepted the fact that they could never be lovers. Darling couldn't help being straight any more than he could help being gay. Having tried to live in each other's worlds, they knew that for a fact.

Even so, they were closer than most couples he'd known, straight or homosexual. Closer than any siblings. Maris took pride and pleasure in knowing that. He held a part of Darling that no one ever had. A special place that was reserved exclusively for him.

Still, it wasn't Darling's heart.

Only Zarya had ever held that. *How could she have been so stupid?*

She'd had Darling wrapped around her finger. He'd been his happiest when she was a part of his life. Maris could still see the light that had been in Darling's eyes when he spoke of her in ways he'd sell his soul to have Darling speak about him.

It wasn't meant to be.

It could never be.

But Zarya could heal him. He knew it.

And deep down, he suspected Darling knew it, too. Why else would he have kept her here tonight? He could have easily ordered one of his soldiers to take her away. Or he could have killed her.

Instead, he'd taken her to the kitchen to work where the entire staff was female.

That said it all.

Even in his drunken rage, Darling had made sure she went untouched by another man and that she'd been put some place safe. That wasn't the action of someone who didn't care.

In time, Darling would forgive her for being stupid, and Maris would do everything in his power to make sure that happened sooner rather than later.

Zarya sat in her new room, completely mortified. *So this is how Darling felt in our hands...*

After the kitchen staff had finished dinner and then cleaned up, they had turned on her with a passion.

Everything on her body had been stripped off and stolen while they'd laughed about it. Even the pins from her hair. They'd left her with nothing, not even her undergarments.

Take that back. She still wore her damnable slave collar. Who in their right mind would want *that*?

Then they'd locked her in a spartan, closet-size room with the promise that they'd bring her new clothes in the morning—something Clarion had failed to do for Darling when he'd been in their custody.

There was no window, not that it mattered. She wasn't about to try and escape with no clothes on. And while she sat on the floor with no light or blanket, all she could see was the way Darling had looked when Clarion and crew had been callously dragging him naked through the landing bay like some prized stag they'd shot in the wild.

Because of the tricom he'd made to protect her, Darling had been paralyzed. Completely unable to defend himself from them.

I spit in his face.

Tears blurred her vision. She was no better than the bitches who'd attacked her. True, his uncle had murdered her parents and sister. That her other sister and brother had been killed in the fight against his uncle.

But Darling had done nothing to deserve it. Over and over, she saw the images Maris had shown her of Darling's wounds. Heard him telling her about Darling's brutal past.

And that mask...

As scary as it was, it'd been nothing compared to the unreasoning hatred she'd seen in his eyes.

Eyes that were steel blue. All these years, she'd wondered what color Kere's eyes were. She'd imagined everything from exotic humanoid species to dark like Maris's.

Tonight that knowledge gave her no comfort at all.

It was a wonder Darling hadn't killed her on sight. She wasn't sure she could have held herself back if she'd been in his place.

"I'm so sorry," she breathed. No one deserved the indignity they'd put her through. Never mind what had been done to him. At least the women hadn't dragged her naked through public grounds.

Yet.

There's always tomorrow.

But that wasn't what she wanted to think about. Instead, she closed her eyes and remembered what it felt like to be held in the arms of someone who loved her.

"I want you to marry me, Zarya. I need you in my life. I know it sounds weird, but when I'm with you, I'm the man I always wanted to be. And when I'm not, it's like I'm lost to someone else, and I don't like him anymore. I can't keep living the lie that was forced on me."

Now she knew the lie.

And it broke her heart.

But tomorrow, no matter what it took or how hard it was, she was going to try and find that man he'd spoken about.

She'd found him once.

Now it was time to bring him home...

9

Darling came awake to the worst pain in his skull imaginable. His head felt like it weighed five hundred pounds and that his uncle had bounced it off the marble floor a few dozen times.

Damn, it hurt.

He pressed his hand to his forehead and went cold as he felt skin on skin. What the hell? He hadn't removed his gloves since Syn had released him from the hospital.

Panic tore through him. How could he be in his bed without his mask and gloves?

What happened to me? He couldn't remember anything from the night before.

Who'd undressed him?

"It's all right, Darling." Maris came out of the shadows to stand next to him. "You passed out last night. I carried you in here and put you to bed."

Thank the gods for that.

But his relief was short lived. Frowning, which made his head throb even worse, Darling did his best to recall something from last night.

Everything was a fog. It was like trying to chase down a phantom wind.

How flagged had he gotten?

Yeah, okay so he'd started drinking on a stomach filled with nothing but painkillers around lunch, and hadn't stopped until he must have passed out. Still…

"I don't remember anything."

Maris snorted. "I believe it. You were pretty wasted. I haven't seen you like that in a very long time."

"How long was I out?"

Maris turned the clock to face him.

Darling cursed as he noted the time. "It's the middle of the afternoon?"

"You haven't slept in days, probably weeks," Maris said simply. "You were exhausted."

He'd lived his whole life exhausted. Sleep had always been a stranger to him. Peaceful sleep even more so.

Squinting against the faint light in the room that pierced his brain, he grimaced at Maris. "What about you? You look like shit, buddy."

"You keep sweet talking a girl like that and you're liable to get lucky."

Darling didn't comment on that. "You haven't slept, have you?"

"No. I kept watch for you while you slept."

Of course he did. Maris was the only one who fully understood his lunatic idiosyncrasies and paranoia…

And the fact that a sleeping governor was usually a dead one.

"I appreciate it. Thank you."

Maris inclined his head. "You know, you might want to think about showering at some point today."

"Why?"

He rolled his eyes. "You really don't remember anything from last night, do you?"

Darling tried to think through the throbbing haze. He saw images, but he wasn't sure if they were real or imagined or dreamed. One thing that he did vaguely recall was Maris holding and rocking him...at least he thought he might remember it. "Did you kiss me?"

"Only on the cheek."

Darling wasn't so sure about that given the evil light in Maris's dark eyes. It was a look he knew all too well. Maris had a secret he was hiding from him.

Something that would make him mad when he found out.

Gods, I hope I didn't respond to any official e-mails...

If he had, he might be on the brink of war today. *Better check on that soon.* If there was an armada coming, he might want to rally some troops before they arrived.

Then again, in his current mood, a war might not be such a bad thing. Yeah, he wouldn't mind tearing into a few of his enemies.

His thoughts drifted to the night before when he'd been in his office. Someone had been there dressed in white. It was a color Maris despised on himself for several reasons.

Maris would only wear it if he were dead...

Closing his eyes, Darling wasn't sure what his mind was trying to tell him. But one thing tugged at his memory...

The smell of a woman's skin. Something he hadn't been near in a long time. And then, he saw an image of someone standing behind Maris in his office.

He looked at Maris and scowled. "Did you bring me a woman?"

"I did." Now his expression and demeanor were completely unreadable.

Suddenly, Darling caught the scent that was still on his clothes from the night before. One that seemed to have permanently attached itself to his very skin. Unforgettable and as individual as the woman who bore it, he knew that scent better than any.

It hit like a kick in the crotch.

Still, he didn't want to believe it was what he thought. Surely, Maris had more sense than that.

"Zarya. She's here?"

Maris nodded.

Raw, unmitigated fury exploded through his entire being. Never had he wanted to kill anyone more than he wanted to kill Maris in that instant. "Goddamn you! How could you do that to me!" He winced as the pain in his head sharply intensified, but right now he had more important things that hurt him.

Things that cut a lot deeper.

Maris gave him a droll stare as if he couldn't care less that he stood one wrong answer away from death. "I've been up for more than forty hours, and I'm too tired to fight with you right now. I'm going to bed. You dumped her in the kitchen, and abandoned her there for the others to humiliate. Just so you know." And with that, he left the room.

Darling lay completely still as his emotions ripped him apart. Rage. Hatred. Revulsion. And an effing headache that rode him with spurs.

But underneath all that was a need so deep and compelling, he wanted to claw it out of his heart.

Zarya was in his home. She was *here*. Close enough to touch…

Don't be stupid. She's a lying whore who slapped you. Twice.

Just like your mother. Throwing you to the wolves to save her own ass. Hauk's right. All women do is take and forget every-thing you did for them. Every sacrifice you made. You were never anything to her.

Nothing.

Just a means to an end. A tool to be used. Dirt beneath her feet.

And he kept coming back to the reality that she was in his home. Just down the stairs and one long hallway...

His stomach heaved. Darling rolled from the bed and stumbled to his bathroom. He barely made it to the toilet in time.

His body was really not happy with him.

Gah, he'd drank himself stupid last night. He felt like complete crap.

Maybe Maris was right.

It was time for him to finally shower.

"What is taking so long? Are you an idiot retard or just lazy?"

Zarya counted to ten so that she didn't grab one of the knives on the nearby table and cut the cook's throat with it. She was getting really tired of the offensive insults and abuse dealt to her. Not just from the cook, but by all of them.

She was a trained soldier, not a domestic. Since they'd eaten mostly table scraps since her father had been branded a traitor, cooking had never been a skill she'd had an opportunity to pick up.

The ability to kill bitches...

That was something she was more than proficient at.

Calm down, Z, calm down. They're not worth a death sentence.

But if they didn't lay off her, she might reconsider.

And now that she had clothes again, she'd be able to escape tonight. One way or another, she wasn't about to spend a single second longer as a slave than she had to. Collar or no collar, she was out of here. And damn anyone who came after her because they wouldn't live long enough to regret it.

Part of her wanted to stay for Darling and keep the promise she'd made last night, but at this point, she was done. He didn't want her and she wasn't going to put up with this kind of abuse, waiting for him to come to senses he most likely didn't have anymore.

Screw him. If he didn't want her, she didn't want him—plain and simple.

His life might not mean anything to him, but hers meant something to her and she'd be damned if she would spend it waiting on a man. Any man. She might be a lot of things. Stupid wasn't one of them.

The kitchen bitches had been riding her since they'd dragged her out of her closet at dawn. Nothing she did was right and she was done with the pinches, slaps, and insults.

No man was worth this.

She tightened her grip on the extremely heavy tray of vegetables that the head cow wanted on the cook's prep table. There was no reason in it being piled so high...

Suddenly, she hit a really slick spot on the floor. Before she could catch her balance, her feet came out from under her.

No!

But the gods weren't listening to her right now. Apparently they needed entertainment and lucky her, she was their chosen buffoon. The vegetables flew everywhere as she slammed down on the hard floor. Her elbow hit first, then her head bounced off the tile.

For a minute, the unexpected pain stunned her as stars dimmed her vision.

"Get up, you lazy, worthless whore." The cook viciously kicked her in the ribs. "Clean this mess up. Now!"

Zarya clamped down tight on the desire to physically retaliate for that. The cook was a freewoman. She was a slave.

If Zarya attacked her...

She's not worth your life.

Tell that to her base anger that didn't want to listen to her brain. It wanted blood...

Rolling over, Zarya pushed herself up, then hissed as she realized she'd sprained her ankle in the fall. Yeah, that was just what she needed. *Let's make running from here as hard as possible on me, shall we?*

"Crap," she breathed, trying to put weight on it in spite of the pain. By the gods, she wasn't going to give these cows the satisfaction of knowing she was hurt.

"What now?" The cook slapped her. "I've never seen anyone so worthless. No wonder the governor threw you to me." She grabbed Zarya by the hair and started pulling her across the room.

"Let her go." Those growled words came out in a deep staccato beat that emphasized the fury and unspoken threat beneath them.

The cook freed her instantly and bowed low. "Yes, Your Majesty."

Everyone in the kitchen immediately stopped what they were doing to follow suit.

Stunned, but refusing to bow down to anyone, Zarya straightened to see Darling just inside the kitchen doorway. From behind his gold mask, those merciless blue eyes cut her to the bone. It was obvious he wanted blood, too.

Her blood.

Without another word, he closed the distance between them with long, furious strides.

Zarya held her breath and tensed her entire body, waiting for him to attack her.

Instead, he swept her up in his arms and carried her from the room as if she weighed nothing at all. She couldn't have been more shocked had he slapped her. At least that she'd expected.

This...

She couldn't comprehend his kindness given the way he glared at her. He didn't speak a single word as he carried her through the palace, back to his study where someone had cleaned up the mess from the night before. His desk looked as if it'd never been upturned.

Still silent, he set her down on his burgundy leather sofa and knelt in front of her.

Then to her complete amazement, he picked her foot up to examine it.

"Your Majesty—"

"Don't speak to me," he ground out between his clenched teeth. But the tenderness in his touch as he felt her foot for broken bones belied the hostility in that sharp command.

Without meeting her gaze, he got up and went to his desk where he buzzed his staff. "I need a medic in my office immediately."

"Ke—"

He held his hand up in a sharp gesture that instantly silenced her. He turned his head to pin her with a furious glower that was evident even with that featureless mask covering his face. "What did I tell you?"

"Not to speak."

"Then I suggest you obey me."

Zarya arched a brow at that imperious command.

Oh no, he didn't…

"Obey? Obey!" she repeated as her own anger ignited. No one said *that* to her. Not even if he owned the galaxy! Which Darling actually did, but that didn't matter. "I know you did not just use that word with *me*."

He growled at her. "Woman, if you have an ounce of self-preservation, you will heed my orders to be silent. Right. Now."

She glared at him. That arrogant, imperial tone destroyed every last piece of common sense she possessed. "Fine. Shove it straight where the sun doesn't shine, buddy. You don't talk to me like that. No one does. I'm done with this and with you!" She got up and limped for the door.

Before she could take more than four steps, he was there,

sweeping her feet out from under her again. He cradled her against his chest.

It took everything she had not to punch him. "Put me down!"

Darling wanted to choke her. His breathing ragged, all he could think about was hurting her until she begged him for mercy.

That thought took him straight back to Clarion and Pip, and his days under their "tender" care.

"I've had to eat shit from the aristocracy my whole life. It's time you choke on it, too, you rich prick. You and your kind gave us nothing as you ate your fine, overpriced dinners and lounged around while we worked until our hands bled. So we're not going to give you any mercy either. For once, you can choke on our shit."

He ground his teeth as he fought against the pain of that memory and countless others that refused to give him any peace or quarter.

But as Zarya's scent filled his head and she glared at him with high color in her cheeks, he remembered something so much better. Nights of being held and loved. Nights when they'd been together and she'd breathed a life and warmth into him that he'd never known before.

Gods, how he missed those times. The sound of her sweet voice in his ear while he was deep inside her. Of her lips buried against his throat . . .

Suddenly another urge rose up inside him to quell the others as he remembered how good it felt to slide into her body.

At least he finally knew *that* part of him still worked properly, and thankfully there was no pain with it. Well, nothing more than what was normal when a man went this long without sex.

And that didn't help his resistance toward her either . . .

His gaze dropped down to the low cut of the cheap dress she wore. One that didn't fit her at all. The entire top swell of her breasts hung out of it, making his mouth water for a taste of her. Even now, he could taste her skin as he imagined her sliding her fingers through his hair.

He hadn't touched a woman in over a year. Not since the night he'd asked her to marry him.

Those buried emotions rose up to play even more havoc with him, especially as her breath tickled his ear.

In that moment, he forgot his bitter rage as he went right back to that time and place when he'd lived for no other reason than to be in her arms. She was all he'd ever had...

All he'd ever wanted.

And she was here, in his arms.

So close he really could taste her...

Zarya froze as she saw the heated look in his eyes. It wasn't anger anymore.

It was desire. He stared at her as if he could eat her up and relish every bite.

This was the man she remembered so well. The one who had made her so happy. The only one she'd ever lived for.

The only man she'd been willing to die for.

Licking her lips, she could already taste his kiss. *Come back to me, baby.* It'd been way too long.

He dipped his head toward hers...

A knock sounded on the door.

Instantly, his entire body went rigid. She silently cursed and condemned whoever was on the other side of that door as the moment was broken and he pulled back. The anger returned to his gaze full force.

Darling returned her to the sofa. "Enter," he growled, stepping away from her.

The medic hesitated in the doorway. Tall, slender, and blond, she was extremely attractive in her dark blue uniform. Something that made Zarya feel like a ragamuffin Darling had dragged in from the trash bin.

The medic bowed low to Darling. "You summoned me, Your Majesty?"

He gestured toward Zarya. "She injured her ankle."

The medic came forward to tend her foot while he left them alone.

The minute he was out of the room, the medic let out a long breath in relief. She looked up at Zarya. "What did he do to you, hon?"

The question confused her. "He carried me in here."

The medic indicated her foot. "What did he do to sprain your ankle? Did he beat you?"

Why on earth would the woman think that? "I slipped on the floor."

Zarya could tell the medic didn't believe her as she pulled out a scanner and ran it over her foot and calf. "If he hurts you again, call for Senna, or Dr. Yerzan. That's me, and I'll document his abuse. If you want, I can even tell him that we need to transfer you to the hospital for observation. That should get you out of his hands for at least a day. Maybe longer, if we're lucky."

The woman was serious…

Not sure if she should be appalled or amused by the medic's erroneous assumptions, Zarya stared at her. "Governor Cruel did *not* hurt me. I fell in the kitchen."

Senna set her scanner aside. "Look, I know you're afraid of him. We all are, but—"

"I'm not afraid."

Her green eyes glittered with disbelief. "I suppose you're going to tell me that he didn't hit you either?"

There was no amusement now. The woman's stubborn insistence and inability to hear what Zarya was saying was beginning to really piss her off. "What are you talking about?"

"The contusion on your cheek. I see the outline of his entire hand where he slapped you. Not to mention the contusion on your elbow and the handprint bruise on your upper arm."

"He didn't do that. The cook did."

"Yeah, right."

Zarya was appalled by her accusations. Why would she assume Darling had beat her? "Would you listen to me? Governor Cruel has *not* hurt me."

Senna rolled her eyes dismissively. "At least you don't have to worry about him raping you. I guess that's one blessing. Though I've heard he has other perversions for women."

Oh this she had to hear. "Such as?"

"He likes to kill them, then dress in their clothes... especially their panties."

Zarya would have burst into laughter had that not been so ludicrous.

Could they honestly think Darling did that? Really?

Maris was right. They were all blind. Brainless. And ridiculous. Inconceivable...

Senna leaned forward as if she were imparting a grave secret to her. "It's why his mother and sister refuse to visit him, you know. They are even more terrified of him than they were the Grand Counsel. As soon as the governor took power and murdered his uncle, all the women—his aunt, and her daughters, his mother and sister moved out... Literally, the very next day." She glanced toward the door before she lowered her voice. "You know, the governor's been confined to mental wards six times since his teens."

They'd even twisted that. How disgusting.

"Yes. His uncle did it to torture him. It wasn't because there was anything wrong with Darling."

"Wow..." Senna sat back on her legs to gape at her. "What has he done to you? Some kind of mind control? I'll have to add that

189

to the list. We knew he made weapons...It only makes sense he could create something to also mess with the brain, too."

Zarya's jaw went slack.

But before she could say anything more to contradict the medic, Darling returned to the room.

Her hands shaking, the medic quickly wrapped Zarya's ankle. "It's not bad at all, Your Majesty. She barely twisted it." Senna met Zarya's gaze. "Keep it iced and don't put any weight on it for about a week and it should be back to normal, very quickly. I sent a prescription for painkillers and a speed healer to the pharm tech. They will have it delivered as soon as possible." She stood and bowed to Darling. "Is there anything else you need, Your Majesty?"

He barely glanced at her as he walked to his desk. "You're dismissed."

Senna hurried from the room as if she was terrified Darling might shoot her before she could clear the doors.

Never had Zarya seen the like. It absolutely blew her mind apart that anyone would say such horrible things about a man who'd lived his entire life fighting to give all of them a better life.

"They are terrified of you."

Darling opened the bottle of whisky on his desk, then reached inside a drawer to pull out a small shot glass. "Good." He poured the glass full.

How could he be so blasé? Did he not know about the rumors? Or did he just not care?

"Not really." He needed to understand how dangerous these things could be. "I mean, they are...Words fail me to describe their skewed beliefs. They really think you're worse than your uncle."

He knocked back the shot glass, then poured another. "I *am* worse than my uncle. Unlike him, I'm trained to kill with my bare hands."

190

"So it doesn't bother you to have people tremble in fear around you?"

He still refused to look at her. "Should it? As long as they're scared, they won't attack."

Yeah, right. He had to know better. Was he being obstinate to annoy her? "I wouldn't bet on it."

"Then let them try," he said in a low, deadly tone. "I could use the target practice."

He definitely had the skills to warrant that bragging right, but she'd seen a lot of good soldiers fall over the years. Nothing took them down faster than the misconstrued belief that no one could get the drop on them, or outgun them.

"Arrogance comes before the fall."

He knocked back another drink and laughed bitterly. "I'm already in the gutter. There's not much farther down I can go." He poured yet another shot, then brought it over and offered it to her.

She cringed as she realized he was drinking Tondarion Fire—a hard liquor so potent it was banned by most civilized govern-ments. It was a miracle he still had a stomach lining left after drinking it. "No, thank you, Your Majesty. I don't drink *that*."

"Get assaulted enough and you'll learn to." He spoke those words in a tone so low, she wasn't sure she heard them correctly as he walked back to his desk.

"Why did you bring me here?" she asked.

He drank her whisky, too. Then he finally set the glass down. "Were you unconscious or inhaling fumes? Maris brought you here. Not me."

She scoffed at him. "Obviously something's wrong with me, 'cause I could have sworn it was *you*, and not Maris, who carried me into this room a few minutes ago."

"Consider it a momentary lack of sanity. Something I've had a lot of lately." He raked a sneer over her dress. "Wherever did you find those rags?"

His question cut what little vanity she possessed, but she would die before she allowed him to know that.

Still, there was poetic justice in what had been done to her. That should lighten his dour mood somewhat. "You'll be happy to know they stripped all my clothes off me last night and stole them. This is what they threw at me to wear this morning."

He went completely still. "Why should I be happy about that?"

"I figured you'd think it karmic retribution for what was done to you."

Those furious blue eyes bored into her. "You never really knew me at all, did you?"

"I knew you. I knew every thought in your head."

"Then what am I thinking now?" His tone held a fierce challenge it.

But there was no need in that. "I don't know anymore. You never showed me this side of you."

"And what side is that?"

"The aristo who treats everyone around him like they're beneath him."

He laughed bitterly. "Then we're even."

"How so?"

"You never showed me the ruthless bitch side of you."

Now that set her temper on fire. How dare he! "That's not fair."

"Not fair?" He snarled those two words. "Not fair is watching my baby sister get shot in the back by a weapon *I* made for *you*." He stormed across the room to tower over where she sat on his sofa. "Not fair is hearing a man *I* fought beside, tell other people I'd put my ass on the line for, that '*the bitch*' is dead. That bitch is the same age as *your* sister, and I feel the same way about her that you do for Sorche. So don't you *dare* talk to me about fairness."

Her throat tightened at every angry word he spat at her. She heard and she understood. If that had been done to Sorche, she'd be out for blood, too.

But she had to put at least part of the record straight. "*I did not give that to Clarion. He stole it from me.*"

He scoffed at her. "Do you really think that inconsequential detail mattered to me while I hung for months in that room, thinking I'd killed the sister I swore to protect?"

No. The guilt and grief had to be horrifying. She couldn't imagine thinking that something she'd created had been used to kill her sister.

There couldn't be any worse hell. If he was insane, that alone was reason enough for it.

Wanting to comfort him, she reached up to cup his face.

He pulled back with a snarl. "Don't touch me."

Those words hit her like blows, and once more, they brought home the fact that he hated her.

"What do you want me to say? I'm sorry? I am, just so you know. But I'm also aware that words cannot undo what was done to you. They can't fix those wounds. I would give anything if they could. But I know better." She looked up at him, wishing there was some way to reach him and make him see the truth inside her.

But there wasn't.

And that hurt most of all.

Licking her lips, she kept coming back to the one thing she couldn't deny no matter how hard she tried. "Gods spare me the agony, but I still love you."

He raked her with a repugnant glare. "And I hate you in a way I've never hated anyone. Not even my uncle."

The acrimony in his tone tore into her like knives and shredded her heart. "Why would you say something so mean?"

"Because it's true. I always knew where I stood with him. He hated me from the moment I was born. But you…" His scarred voice carried the full weight of his disgust. "You made me believe a lie. And then you kicked me in my teeth and rammed it down my throat. When I needed you most, when I was being brutalized by the people I stupidly thought were my friends, I heard you laughing on the other side of the door every day with the same people who were torturing me. Every moment of that horror, I kept hoping and praying you would come in and help me. And every day you disappointed me until the only thing I could think about was ripping your callous heart out of your chest and eating it whole."

Zarya wept at what he described.

But what hurt the most was what he hadn't thrown in her face…

When she'd finally gone into that room, she'd slapped him. "I'm so sorry."

"Don't you dare cry."

"Fuck you, you sanctimonious bastard! At least I didn't throw you away…twice!" She got up to leave again.

Once more, he cut her path off and stood between her and the door. "Aren't you full of surprises? I've never heard you use profanity like that."

He was lucky she wasn't spewing even more at him. 'Cause right now, she wanted to verbally strike him as much as he'd struck her. And honestly, she wasn't sure how she was keeping it all in. "What do you want from me?"

"I don't know. I…"

Darling forgot what he was going to say as his gaze dropped to see the deep cleft between her breasts. She was so much shorter than him that he had a direct view all the way down to the fact that she didn't have on any underwear.

His throat went dry.

He wanted to hate her. He needed to hate her and yet...

Memories of the past tortured him. In all of his life, she had been his only refuge. Her voice had guided him through hell and led him out the other side of it. No matter how bad things had been, she'd always made it better.

In her arms, he'd never known pain. Only comfort.

Pleasure...

She betrayed you.

He couldn't allow himself to lose sight of that brutal fact. Yet right now, he felt himself slipping under her spell.

He was so confused. It was so easy to hate her when she wasn't around.

But one whiff of her scent. One glimpse of her body. The sound of his name on her lips...

He was weakened and undone.

Don't you dare think about forgiving her. He wanted to hang on to his anger and hatred with both hands. To wrap himself up in its protective coat so that no one could ever hurt him again.

And yet as he looked into her amber eyes...

He saw what no one else had ever given him.

Her heart.

God, help me. Please...

Zarya froze at the sight of his hunger for her. This was the man she knew. The one she wanted back at any cost.

But underneath that was a pain so profound it stole her breath. He was wounded so badly that it made her own heart ache for him. She couldn't stand to see him like this. He looked lost and tormented.

Please come back to me. She needed what they'd had. Needed him to tell her everything would be okay and that he still loved her, no matter what.

Before he withdrew from her again, she rose up and captured his lips.

He wrapped his arms around her, fisting his hands behind her back as he kissed her senseless. Closing her eyes, she breathed him in. All of her emotions slammed into her. Her fear that he'd been killed. Her guilt over what they'd done to him. Her anger over the way he'd treated her.

But most of all was the love she despised feeling for him. Only he could destroy her.

Darling burned with a need to kill her. He did. The darkness inside wanted nothing from her except to feel her blood on his hands. But the man in him only wanted to lie in her arms until she drove the demons inside him straight back to hell where they belonged.

He needed the peace she alone gave him. Just for one moment, he wanted to feel secure again. Feel something other than this bitterness that ate at him until it drove him to murder the ones who caused it.

For so long now, he'd been lost. But as he tasted her, he remembered what it was like to be home. To feel welcomed...

And in this instant, that was what his battered soul craved most.

Growling, he picked her up and carried her over to his desk. With one arm, he sent everything on top of it to the floor. Then he set her down. His heart hammering, he stared at her, torn between the two things he wanted most.

To kill her and to love her...

She pulled the gown off, over her head.

His thoughts scattered as he saw the body that had haunted him since the moment he'd first touched her. She had the most beautiful breasts of any woman ever born. And as she arched her back, all the blood drained from his head and went straight to his groin.

He'd be mad at her later.

Right now, all he could think about was being inside her. Of tasting her until he was drunk from her rather than the alcohol that had sustained him for months. Desperate for her, he dipped his head down to take her right breast into his mouth. He sucked his breath in sharply at how good she tasted, at how much he'd missed this.

Closing his eyes, he savored the sweet scent of her skin. It made him light-headed.

He rolled his tongue around her puckered nipple while she cradled his head against her. With her right hand, she reached down between them, into his pants to cup him in her hand. Darling saw stars as pleasure tore through his entire body. The only thing that felt better than her hand there was when she went down on him. Little did she know, whenever she did that to him, she owned him, body and soul. There was nothing he wouldn't do for her or give her whenever she tasted him

That memory alone almost caused him to come.

She wrapped her legs around his waist and leaned back on the desk to stare up at him and cup her breasts in her hands. Damn, the sight of her there...like that...

Zarya was beautiful. Nothing was better than when she looked up at him like he was hers and she wanted him as much as he wanted her. He pulled his gloves off so that he could run his scarred hands over her smooth breasts.

Taking his hand into hers as he cupped her breast, she ground the center of her body against his swollen cock. "I need you inside me, Darling. Please..." She guided his hand down over her flat stomach to where she was already wet for him.

He ground in his teeth as he fingered her and she murmured in pleasure. In that moment, he forgot everything except them.

There was no pain now. No past. Nothing else in existence

except his hunger to have her. He needed her like he needed air to breathe.

Zarya opened his pants so that she could guide him into her body. For the first time in their relationship, she saw his blue eyes staring into hers as he filled her. Her breath caught at how good he felt like this. And when he started thrusting against her hips, she groaned out loud.

This was what she'd craved for so long. To hold him again in her arms. No one loved her the way he did. No one. Happy to have him back, even for only a moment, she lifted his hand so that she could nip his fingers and suck on them as he made love to her.

Darling let her cries of pleasure wash over him while she held him close and ran her hands over his back. He'd forgotten the fact that she was an outrageous screamer whenever they made love. And there was nothing he liked more than hearing his name on her lips when he was inside her.

"Say my name," he panted in her ear. "My real name."

"Darling!"

He thrust harder and deeper while she punctuated each stroke with her voice. She came an instant later with a cry of pleasure so loud, it echoed in the room and his ears.

Smiling in triumph as he watched the ecstasy on her face, Darling waited until she was completely finished before he let himself go.

Oh yeah...that was what he'd needed. Thank the gods, he didn't have any of the pain Syn had feared would come with an orgasm. At least the most important part of his body still worked the way it was supposed to.

Spent, weak, and finally sated after all these months, Darling lay himself down on top of her while she ran her hands under his shirt, over his scarred back. Her touch felt like heaven.

But as his senses returned, he realized where they were.

Not in her house.

They were in his office…

And he was a soulless, hideous monster. One who hated her.

He lifted himself up to look down at her as his anger renewed itself.

Her eyes smiled at him as she reached for his mask. "You told me that the next time we were together, you'd let me see all of you."

Yes, but things had been different then. As ugly as he'd thought himself before, it was nothing compared to what he was now. They had utterly destroyed what little he'd had, and left him completely disfigured and foul.

Bracing himself for the horror and rejection he'd see in her amber eyes, he didn't move as she released the strap on the mask and pulled it free.

She didn't disappoint him in the least. He saw just what he'd expected. She was as repulsed by his looks as he was.

Who could blame her? He looked like a total hideous freak. How could anyone ever love someone so ugly?

Zarya gasped at what they'd done to him. Even with the thick auburn beard that covered most of his face, she could see the deep, awful scars all over it. From the depth and number, it was obvious that each one had been intentional. Done for no other reason than to ruin his looks and make him suffer. There was a scar along the length of his left nostril where someone had sliced it open. The one on his right was even longer. Two more jagged scars ran from the corner of his right eye, causing it to droop. Another thick one ran over his upper lip, causing it to arch up at a peculiar angle. Both corners of his mouth held definitive scars from the muzzle they'd forced on him.

And there, in his right cheek, through the beard, she saw where Pip had carved his name in giant letters.

How could they have done this to him?

She wanted to cry over the cold brutality that had disfigured his face. Damn them all for it!

Darling took the mask from her hand and gave her a harsh, condemning stare. "Just so you know, this changes nothing between us." He withdrew from her and fastened his pants. The coldness of that action made her eyes water.

Then he returned the mask to his face and left her there.

Her heart shattering, she scooted off his desk and retrieved her gown from the floor. Normally, she would have insulted him back for the verbal slap he'd given her, but not this time.

He'd been put through a far worse hell.

What would you do? She couldn't imagine having her face destroyed the way his was.

Yes, Darling was part of the ruling class they'd all hated, but he wasn't evil. He didn't hurt other people. Not unless they came at him first.

Sick about it, she'd just pulled her gown back on when three guards entered the study in military formation. Her heart stopped beating.

They looked like they'd come to arrest her.

Without a single word, the largest of them crossed the room to stand beside her before he picked her up in his arms.

"What are you doing?" she asked.

His features impassive, he spoke in a low, unemotional tone. "What the governor told me to do."

Terror consumed her. Was this really what Darling wanted done? "I'm being arrested?"

He didn't answer as he carried her out of the study. But instead of taking her outside to where she would assume the jail to be, he turned and headed up the elegant staircase while the other two guards followed closely behind them.

Completely baffled, she didn't say a word until he took her into the largest, most elaborate bedroom she'd ever seen. There was a heavily carved canopy bed against the far wall. To her left was a huge marble hearth with chairs and a fur rug set before it. A small dining table and two chairs were set on her right. The table was topped with two ornate silver candelabras and an impressive bouquet of freshly cut flowers.

The top of the extremely high walls had carved and gilded crown molding. But the strangest part was the ceiling, which appeared to be a dark brown smoked mirror. One that clearly reflected whatever was going on in the room.

Was this Darling's bedroom? With all the lace and pastels, it seemed more feminine than masculine. But it was a pale blue...

The guard carried her to one of the white chairs in front of the hearth and placed her in it.

An older woman came forward with a frown. Tiny and frail, she had her light gray hair pulled up in an elegant chignon and she was dressed in a somber brown dress. "This is the royal mistress?" she asked the guard.

"Yes, ma'am."

His answer only seemed to confuse her more. "But she's a woman." She turned her scowl to Zarya. "You are a woman, correct?"

"Last time I checked."

The guard shrugged, then went to the door where the other two guards waited. He stepped back and held it open for Maris before he took his leave.

Sweeping into the room with a flourish, Maris grinned like a criminal who'd just made a record score. He laughed giddily. "I knew he'd go back for you. I knew it."

"Do you mind, my lord?" the older woman snapped. "I have duties to attend."

Maris waved a hand at her. "Relax, Gera. I'm here to help."

He frowned as he saw the bandage on Zarya's ankle. "What happened?"

"I fell in the kitchen and I'm supposed to..." Her words broke off as the door opened and a servant came in with a cold pack. Without pausing, the servant came straight to Zarya and lifted her foot to the ottoman, then placed the cold pack over her ankle.

"Let me guess," Maris said with a proud smile. "Keep it iced?"

"Yes."

Gera excused the other servant before she approached Zarya's chair. "Then I take it you're not supposed to be walking on it, either?"

"Not for a week."

Gera sighed wearily. "How am I supposed to get you into the tub then?"

Maris made a strange noise before he picked Zarya up. "Just show me where you want her."

Ramrod stiff, Gera sputtered in indignation. "No men are allowed in here, except for the governor. You should know that, Lord Maris."

He tsked at her. "And Gera, you should know by now that I'm just one of the girls. Darling will understand and I'm sure he'd much rather I carry her than one of the guards. Now where's that tub?"

Without another word of protest, Gera led them through the doorway next to the bed.

Zarya's face flamed red as she saw the mirrors that covered every wall. How could anyone bathe in this place? It was horrifying!

The ceiling was painted with people in all kinds of sexual positions, some of which she wasn't sure would be feasible for anyone with a spine. "Oh my..."

Maris laughed. "Tawdry, isn't it?"

"Not the word I was thinking, but it'll do."

He kissed her on the cheek, then set her on the wide tiled edge of the tub where someone had already drawn a warm, sudsy bath. "Before I scandalize Gera any further, I shall take my leave. But I'll be back."

Scowling even more, Gera came forward with the cold pack. "I'm so confused. When the governor told me to make preparations for a mistress, I assumed it would be Lord Maris, or another man. Are you sure it's you?"

Well that wasn't something a woman wanted to hear. Especially since Zarya wasn't exactly sure of her position here or what Darling intended for her. "I...guess."

"Very well then, we should get started."

Started with what?

Gera set the cold pack down, then helped Zarya pull her ugly gown off. But the moment Zarya was naked, the older woman hesitated. Her features pinched, she reached down to touch Zarya's inner thigh where Darling had left visible proof of what they'd done a few minutes ago.

Zarya's face exploded with heat.

Eyes wide, Gera pinned her with a condemning look that actually scared her. "You've already been with a man today?"

"Relax, Gera. It's mine."

Her skin turning as red as Zarya's, Gera faced the door where Darling stood, and bowed low. "Forgive me, Your Majesty. I meant no disrespect to your mistress."

Zarya would have covered herself with the gown, but Gera had tossed it out of her reach. She had no choice except to sit there completely naked while Darling's gaze burned into her with a powerful hold she couldn't break. How she wished she could hear his thoughts.

That look felt like hatred, and yet...

Why bring her here and declare her his mistress if he hated her guts? Was it to humiliate her? Or did he honestly want her here with him?

Nothing he did made sense.

Finally, he blinked and looked at Gera. "I forgot to tell you that she'll need an entire wardrobe purchased. Not just boudoir, but clothing for inside and out. Formal, business, and casual."

"Yes, Your Majesty. Is there anything else?"

"If you have any questions, confer with Lord Maris. He knows my tastes intimately." He gave a curt nod to his servant and before Zarya could speak a word, he was gone again.

Darling paused outside the room that had been reserved for the governor's mistress for hundreds of years, and tried to sort through his ragged feelings that assaulted him with conflicting emotions. He felt so lost and confused, and at the same time...

He finally felt like he was home.

It didn't make a bit of sense. Even though he'd been born here, this particular palace had never felt that way to him before. No place had. For most of his life, the Winter Palace had served as his prison. So much so that he couldn't bear to walk past his old bedroom or the ones his family used whenever they were in residence—he wouldn't even go near those wings. The memories there were just too brutal to face.

But being here didn't bother him as much as it had before. Something inside him was different now. It seemed ludicrous that it would be from the presence of a single person.

I'm just getting used to the fact that Arturo's dead.

Darling was assuming more and more of his duties, and becoming the emperor his father had trained him to be.

That was it. It had to be. His mind was finally accepting the reality that he was safe, and that his life was finally his own.

It has nothing to do with Zarya.

This was about him. His was transitioning on his own. This was who he was always meant to become.

I'm the governor…

Stepping away from Zarya's room, he headed for the stairs.

Before he could take more than three steps, Maris met him from the opposite hallway. Maris beamed a smile of smug satisfaction as he pranced and preened a circle around Darling like a child who was overly pleased with himself.

Refusing to be charmed or amused, Darling narrowed his gaze at him. "I'm still mad at you."

As usual, Maris completely ignored his angry tone. "You'll get over it. You always do."

"Highly doubtful."

Maris shrugged nonchalantly. "You've been wrong before. Many times, point of fact. I have most of them documented."

Yeah, but this was different. *He* was different. The Resistance had turned on him and that wasn't something he'd ever forget or forgive.

As for Zarya…

I'm losing faith in humanity one person at a time.

He glared at Maris. "Why are you doing this to me?"

Maris tsked at him. "It's such a shame you have no recollection of last night."

"Why?"

Wrinkling his nose in a playful gesture, Maris draped his arm around Darling's shoulders and whispered in his ear. "You proposed to me, my precious. Told me that you loved me and had dreamed of me naked in your arms for years. You even begged me to ravish you right in your own bed."

That actually amused the hell out of him. Ravish him…right. Darling smiled in spite of his agitation. "You're such a liar."

Maris blinked innocently. "How do you know?"

"You have absolutely no self-control, Mari. Had I begged you to ravish me, I'm positive you would have. And we were both fully clothed when I woke up this morning."

"But you don't know that for sure…" Maris's gaze was bright with his teasing. He squeezed Darling, then moved ahead to reach the stairs first. He flounced around and raked a lustful gaze over Darling's body. "I can see the doubt in your eyes. Admit it, Dar. You secretly want me. You dream about having me naked in your bed. You know you do."

Darling laughed until he caught a glimpse of himself in the smoked mirror wall. His humor died instantly. There for a minute, he'd completely forgotten what had been done to him.

The horror that had become his existence.

Maris sobered. "It's all right, sweetie."

But it wasn't. They both knew that. Darling wasn't sure if it, or he, would ever be all right again. "Have you ever felt lost, Mari?"

He folded his hands in front of him in a somber pose that was out of character for him. "Yes, I have. And I know that place of crazy where you asphyxiate every time reality crashes down and you see the nightmare that has become your life. The darkness that swallows you whole until you fear you'll never see light again."

Darling paused by his side. "How did you find your way home?"

"I didn't." Maris reached out and brushed a strand of Darling's hair back from his mask. "My best friend found me wandering in the darkness and carried me back to the light."

Darling fell silent as he remembered finding Maris in a Ladorian whorehouse after his parents had thrown him out. He'd been too proud and ashamed to tell Darling what they'd done to him. Instead, Maris had lied and said that his parents had forgiven him and that Darling had nothing to worry about.

Until the Resistance had tortured him, that had been the worst three months of his life. He'd had no idea where Maris had gone. No one knew anything about what had happened to him.

No one in Maris's family had even cared. Darling would never forget the words Maris's father had growled at him when he'd asked if Maris's father knew where he was. *"Hopefully, he's in a grave somewhere. At least then he can't shame us anymore."*

By the time Darling had tracked him down, Maris had become addicted to drugs and was selling himself for food and shelter. He'd looked so terrible. Gaunt and pale.

His entire body covered in sweat, Maris had been lying naked on a flea-infested bed that had been crusted over with stains. He'd been so out of it that he hadn't recognized Darling at first.

Once Maris realized who he was, he'd thrown up all over him.

Darling had carried him out of there and then stayed with him for weeks as he sobered up. Maris hadn't touched anything stronger than sweet wine since.

To this day, Darling had no idea what he would have done had he not found Maris that day. Maris was the one person he could always confide in without fear of being judged or hated. The only person who'd kept his most guarded secret and held it close.

Darling sighed. "We're a pair, aren't we?"

"Through thick and thin, brothers to the bitter end." Maris tucked his hand into the crook of Darling's elbow before he leaned over and whispered in Darling's ear. "And you did offer yourself to me last night. I'm just too much of a lady to take advantage of you when you're drunk."

Darling smiled at Maris's old joke. Then he sobered as his thoughts turned to a more somber topic, and a new fear. "Did you, um…did you bring Zarya in through the front last night?"

Maris scoffed. "I am not *that* stupid. My goal was to get you laid, not bitch-slapped. I daresay had she seen your little tribute to all the failed assassination attempts, especially from the Resistance members she might recognize, she would have probably run screaming straight into traffic."

Darling was extremely grateful for Mari's common sense. "Would you mind having the groundskeepers disassemble my... tribute, as you call it?"

"Oh thank the gods. I'm really sick of seeing and smelling that."

Yeah, it was pretty grisly. But it had made the point Darling wanted to make with his enemies.

Mess with him and it would be the last mistake of your life. "Have them return the bodies to their families."

"And your uncle?"

"Burn whatever's left. There's no one to mourn him. I sent my aunt and cousins to the Summer Palace to stay with my mother. Drake said that they're happy now that they finally believe I have no intention of killing them or selling them off. I don't want to do anything to taint that for them. They deserve to be happy after all they've been through."

Maris squeezed his arm affectionately. "I'll take care of it."

Good.

Feeling calmer than he had in a long time, Darling headed down the stairs. "Is Syn at home?"

"Should be. Why?"

Darling wasn't completely sure if he wanted to go through with what he knew he should. Thanks to his mother's mutated genes, he'd never tolerated anesthesia very well. It left him sick and out of it much longer than it did most people.

And he ran a much higher risk of death anytime he went under. Still...

His reflection in the wall screamed at him. For the last few months, vengeance had reigned supreme and driven out everything else in his life.

Maybe now that his anger was spent and the ones who'd hurt him most were gone, maybe it was time to start healing.

It had nothing to do with Zarya. It didn't. He was doing this for him. Like moving out of his old room.

If he removed himself from the reminders, it was easier to let go of the past.

Arturo was dead now.

And this was the reign of Darling Cruel—the 139th governor of the Caronese. It was his empire now, and he was the one his people would look to for protection and leadership. That cloak of responsibility was heavy, but it was one that had been worn by generations of his family.

The only way to serve his people was to be whole again. They would accept nothing less. And they deserved only his best.

He paused at the foot of the stairs. "Do you remember how many more surgeries Syn said he'd need to finish me?"

"Three or four, depending on how well your body accepts the procedures."

Inwardly, he cringed at the number. But he'd never been a coward.

And he couldn't keep living this way anymore. It was time he made some changes for the better.

Time he took control of his life.

Checking his watch, he realized that he had no reprieve. Syn would still be up for a few more hours. "I need to talk to him."

"He's even more sadistic than his uncle." Senna looked around nervously as she sent her text over the secured line to her superiors. One could never be too careful, especially with an aristo as paranoid and skilled as the current governor. He had cut his teeth on technology and knew it better than anyone.

The last thing she wanted was to be added to the bodies that had been hung in front of the palace as a warning to those who opposed the new governor.

She typed her next message. "You should have seen Zarya. She was so scared of him, she wouldn't even speak against him when he was out of the room."

Hector responded immediately. "Believe me, we know. He's all but destroyed us."

It was true. There were barely a handful of Resistance members left. Governor Cruel had been merciless with his slaughter.

And damn the bastard, he was good at hunting people down. Now he had their beloved leader in custody, and had brainwashed her.

"What do you want me to do?" she typed back to Hector.

"Keep sending reports. We have a plan in formation. Within two weeks, we'll be able to assassinate him."

That thrilled her to no end. "Are you sure?"

"Yes. We have agents already in place. It's just a matter of finding the right opportunity."

And then Darling Cruel would join the rest of his sick family in hell.

10

By the time Zarya was through with her "prep," she was ready to hunt Darling down and make him pay with blood. A herd of so-called grooming women had descended on her like locusts. They had plucked, shaved, and "honed" areas of her body that no one other than Darling, her, and one other boyfriend had ever touched.

It was absolutely awful.

One woman had even rouged and flavored her nipples, and Zarya was trying real hard to forget what they'd done to another part of her.

Gah, was that ever going to itch when it grew back...

If that wasn't bad enough, she was going to be "schooled" on how to pleasure Darling, and how to perform erotic dances for him.

Her classes would start tomorrow.

Could they offend me any more? Probably. But she hoped to not find out for sure anytime soon.

At least they'd finally left her alone in the bathroom with Gera. Now she sat at the ornately carved vanity table while the older woman brought over a mirrored tray littered with beautiful bottles, and set it in front of her.

Zarya frowned at the collection. The perfume bottles strangely reminded her of jewels, and some of them were encrusted with stones she was pretty sure were real. "What's all of this?"

"Scents the governor has approved."

Oh no, Gera didn't say that...

Did she?

"Excuse me?"

Gera held up a tiny blue bottle and removed the glass stopper. "This one should blend well with your natural scent. Care to smell it?" She waved the stopper near Zarya's nose.

Zarya started to protest until she caught a whiff of it. Yeah, okay, it did smell great. She couldn't even begin to describe it. While she'd smelled perfumes before, none of them could compare to this one. "What is that?"

"It's called Kiss."

Well that explained it. "The really expensive perfume?"

"Yes."

No wonder they charged so much. Normally, Zarya despised perfumes of any kind. They made her sneeze and gave her headaches. But this one was very subtle and...

Yummy.

Gera smiled in satisfaction. "The trick to wearing perfume correctly is to only apply enough that if someone else can smell it, they'd better be intimate with you. A fragrance should never linger without you in an area after you've left it. Rather it should be a subtle reminder that only stays on your pillow or clothes, and only when your lover's face is buried in them."

That was an interesting philosophy and one Zarya could agree with. Nothing bothered her more than to step into a room and be assaulted by oversprayed scents.

Gera dabbed the stopper on Zarya's neck and then her wrists and elbows. When Gera went to put it between her breasts, Zarya protested again. She was a little tired of being groped by other women.

Tsking, Gera gave Zarya a chiding, but patient stare. "Mistress, please, we've already gone through this. Either you allow me to prep you or I'll be forced to have the guards hold you down for it. Either way, you will submit to this."

They'd be bloody and blue from it if they tried... While she might not be able to expertly groom herself to Gera's satisfaction, she did know how to fight.

Zarya started to tell the older woman that she wasn't Darling's property, but legally she was. Something the slave collar around her neck testified to.

Damn you, Maris.

Couldn't someone have removed the stupid thing?

No doubt Darling intentionally kept it there to remind her of her new position in his world. No longer the love of his life...

She was now his piece of property to do with as he wished, regardless of her own thoughts.

A knot formed in her stomach as she remembered his words from last night. The words he'd growled to her downstairs after they'd made love.

"This changes nothing between us..."

He hated her.

Her stomach cramped with pain. "Fine," she said irritably. After all, none of this was Gera's fault. The older woman was just following orders and the last thing Zarya wanted was to get her into trouble.

But...

Darling had better duck when he came in the door.

Gera slid the stopper down Zarya's chest, then underneath her breasts.

She tried not to cringe. "I don't think you're paid enough for your job."

Gera smiled. "It's not so bad. The other mistresses I've tended haven't minded my attention. Most enjoyed it immensely."

The thought of Darling having a mistress really stung, even more so if he'd had one while he was seeing her. "How many have you served?"

"Between the four rulers I've worked under, it's probably somewhere around seventy total."

That was a lot of women cycling through this room, especially for only four men. "Why so many?"

Gera returned the bottle to the tray. "There were fourteen under Governor Ehrun Cruel."

Ehrun...That would have been Darling's grandfather.

"He was very kind and giving to his mistresses, but he never kept one for more than three years."

A bad feeling went through her as she remembered what Senna had accused Darling of. Could his grandfather have been that twisted?

"Why not?"

Gera picked up a brush to style her hair. "He would choose women from the stews who were already selling themselves, and then have us educate them. After two or three years, their choice not his, he'd set them up with a new home and a stipend for them so that they could move on with their lives. They were allowed to take all of their clothes and any gifts or jewelry he purchased for them while they were here. He considered it an even exchange. They would provide him with temporary companionship and he would take care of them for the rest of their lives. Many of their children and grandchildren still live on the trusts he set up for them."

While that was extremely generous of him, she couldn't help but wonder about Darling's grandmother. 'Cause she knew what she'd do to her husband if he set a woman up in this room and she found out about it. "His wife didn't mind?"

Curling Zarya's hair around her face, Gera shook her head. "It wasn't for her to say. But no, she didn't mind. She never spent much time with him. Rather, she stayed with her family on her home planet and only visited a few times a year until she birthed Lord Drux. Then she didn't come back at all."

Drux had been Darling's father.

"Why? Did they not get along?"

Gera shrugged. "Political marriages don't always match up those most compatible. Her ladyship didn't have much of a sense of humor and she was very fastidious. His lordship was much more fun loving and free spirited. Very much like Lord Drakari and Lady Annalise. He lived for intelligent debate, and she didn't like thinking that hard about anything. She found him tiring, and he found her tedious."

How sad for the two of them. They both must have been terribly lonely.

"What about his lordship's father? How many mistresses did Lord Drux have?"

"Only one. A beautiful, fiery woman he met in a club he shouldn't have ventured into." Gera tucked the curls she'd made around a small white band on Zarya's head. "Kirren was something very special."

She paused to meet Zarya's gaze in the mirror. For the first time, she had a feeling the older woman might actually like her. "You remind me a lot of Mistress Kirren—you have the same defiant and fearless look in your eyes."

"I hope that's not a bad thing."

Gera's smile widened as she went back to styling Zarya's hair. "Not at all. I honestly had a lot of fun while she was here. She taught me some rather interesting things."

"Such as?"

Gera blushed.

Wow, that was a first.

"C'mon, Gera, dish…What did she teach you?"

"Things about men that you will now be learning."

Oh great. She'd learn tricks from someone her mother's age. That was…

Creepy.

"So what happened to her?" Zarya asked.

"His lordship asked her to leave when his father betrothed him to her ladyship."

That was stunning. Rarely to her knowledge did the rich give up their mistresses for a wife. "Really?"

Gera nodded. "Lady Natale was so young and uncertain of herself at the time their parents contracted their marriage that Lord Drux feared hurting her feelings. Because of his parents, he didn't want to start their relationship off badly. He also felt that it wouldn't be fair to Kirren to keep her while he was married to another woman. He really did love her, and they remained friends to the day he died."

That said a lot about Darling's father. He must have been an incredible man. She only had a handful of memories of his visits to her home. He'd been tall and usually smiling, but other than that, she remembered very little about him really.

The one thing she did remember though was that her father had never once spoken out against Drux Cruel. Not about anything.

He'd railed solely against Arturo.

Gera sighed. "Oh you should have seen how happy they were together while he lived. They loved each other so much. His lordship even moved her ladyship into this room to have her near him at all times—something no governor had ever done before. Lord

Darling and his siblings were all conceived and born right here in this very room."

That was an interesting tidbit, and Zarya wasn't sure how she felt about it. On the one hand it was sweet. On the other...

Ew!

Zarya looked up at the pornographic illustrations on the ceiling over her head. "Was it always decorated like this?"

Gera giggled as she glanced up, too. "No, Mistress. Her ladyship has much more modest tastes and would have been horrified to bathe here." Her gaze turned sad. "Lord Arturo had it redecorated to his tastes after he became Grand Counsel."

"So where did Lady Natale go for a room?"

"The governor's family quarters are on another wing entirely. Far enough away that none of the ladies ever ventured here. Rather the governors would go to them when they wanted to father children."

That seemed odd to her. "Lord Arturo kept Lady Natale at this palace even after her mourning period ended?" Normally the widows were set up in their own households on other planets, or they returned to their families and home planets.

Zarya couldn't miss the way Gera's hands started trembling. "He...he used her ladyship to control Lord Darling, and he used Lord Darling to control her ladyship."

"How so?"

Gera flinched. "I'd rather not say, Mistress. I promised her ladyship that I'd never betray her. Sorry."

Those words gave her a sick feeling of dread. What exactly had gone on here?

It made her wonder if that was why Darling and his mother seldom spoke to each other. She remembered asking him once about his parents when he'd been Kere to her.

"My father died when I was young."

"And your mother?"

"We don't talk much."

"Why not?"

"It's complicated. Whenever we're together, I disappoint her, and she disappoints me. It's easier on both of us if we just avoid each other."

Since both of her parents were dead, she'd never understood how he could avoid his mother who was still alive.

What could make a mother hate her son so much?

The light returned to Gera's eyes. "It did my heart good to see the governor's parents together. The only blight they ever had on their happiness was his lordship's illegitimate son who lived here with their children for a time. Her ladyship tried not to let it bother her, but she couldn't seem to help resenting him."

Zarya frowned. Darling had an older brother? She'd never heard that before and the Resistance had done a thorough background screening on the ruling family.

How had they missed *that*?

Frowning, she couldn't remember another son ever coming in with Lord Drux on his visits to her childhood home. Nor had Kere ever mentioned it.

Of course, Kere had never mentioned his younger brother, either. And very seldom had he spoken of his sister.

"What son?" she asked Gera.

"Lord Ryn. He was conceived during Lord Drux's short affair with Kirren. After his lordship married, Lord Ryn would spend the school year here and then his breaks with his mother."

Ryn...that was who Darling had been visiting when Maris had found out that Darling knew he was gay. Finally, things were starting to make sense.

Sort of.

But Zarya wondered what had become of Darling's brother. "Where is Lord Ryn now?"

"He was an ambassador, last I heard. But I don't think it's for us. He and Lord Darling were extremely close when they were young, but regretfully they grew apart after Lord Drux died."

"Do you know why?"

"No, Mistress. Sorry."

Fascinating. It made her curious which of them had caused the tear in their relationship.

Darling or Ryn…

"So all the other mistresses belonged to Lord Arturo, then?" she asked Gera.

Unless Darling had someone in his past that neither she nor Maris knew about. That thought stabbed her.

A troubled frown creased Gera's brow. "Yes. They were all his. You're the first of Lord Darling's."

She didn't like the way Gera phrased that. She didn't want to think about Darling with other women. Men, either, for that matter, especially given what Maris had told her…*I don't want to be his first.*

She wanted to be his last.

Not wanting to think about a time when she might not be with him, she returned to their discussion. That was a lot of women for only one man, especially one who'd been married before he became Grand Counsel. "Why so many?"

Gera set the brush aside. "He kept four and five at a time."

Zarya was aghast at that. "In this room?"

She nodded. There was a troubled cloud in her eyes. Something else had happened here.

A chill went down her spine as she looked around with new eyes. There was no way to describe the uneasy feeling she had. "What, Gera?"

She stepped away, but not before Zarya noted her sudden nervousness. "I shouldn't say anything more. It's not my place to judge or gossip. Suffice it to say, I hope Lord Darling doesn't follow in his uncle's footsteps. Though it's not looking good given the way he's been since he took power...and especially given the way he seized it."

Since Zarya had been locked in a hole with no access to the outside world, she knew nothing about Darling's ascension to the throne. "What did he do?"

Gera swallowed hard. "He murdered his uncle, Mistress. With his bare hands. Right outside in the gardens. I assumed you knew given that it's all anyone talks about."

Zarya shook her head. "When? How?"

"A few months back. For reasons unknown, Lord Darling stormed into the palace at midnight, hunted Lord Arturo down and butchered him, right in front of his own guards. Then he dared them to attack him. Begged them, point of fact. The guards have been terrified of him ever since. They believe his lordship is completely deranged."

A chill went down her spine. What had made Darling do that after all these years of tolerating Arturo's reign? Something inside him had snapped, but what?

"It was so brutal," Gera whispered. "After that, his lordship went on a bloody killing spree against his enemies and anyone else who crossed his path. At least a hundred, probably more, have lost their lives to his bloodlust."

Zarya was flabbergasted by the number. "Darling?"

"Yes, Mistress. Did you not see the pile of bodies at the front gate? His lordship threatened the life of anyone who dared remove them."

Was that the real reason Maris had brought her in through the back?

"No. I didn't see it." A shiver ran down her spine at the very thought. Why hadn't Maris mentioned *that*?

"It's dreadful, Mistress. I've never seen anyone do something so horrible," Gera whispered as if she was terrified of being over-heard. "So my advice to you is to make his lordship happy and to not upset him in any way. There's no telling what he might do to you." Her eyes troubled, she leaned forward and patted Zarya on the side of her arms. "Now if you're ready, Mistress, I'll have you carried back into the boudoir."

Zarya cringed at the thought of another stranger touching her. She was really over it. Especially given the way Gera had forced her to dress. "May I please walk? I really don't want anyone I'm not *well* acquainted with to see me in this…" She searched for a word that wouldn't offend the older woman. "Outfit."

Glancing around nervously as if she expected someone to be watching them, Gera hesitated. "I don't know, Mistress. I could get into a lot of trouble for not following his lordship's exact orders, and he was insistent that you rest and not hurt your ankle again. The last thing I want to do is be added to the mass grave outside."

Zarya was definitely going to have to find out more about that. Like Gera, she didn't want to be its next acquisition.

"I promise Lord Darling won't be angry at you if he catches me. He knows exactly how stubborn I am, and I'll be glad to tell him it was me who did it."

The friendly light returned to Gera's eyes. However, there was still a bit of doubt behind it. "Very well, but at least let me help you."

Zarya stood up slowly and leaned against Gera as she limped her way back to the bedroom. She did her best not to see herself in the mirrors. While she had no problem with her makeup, the rest of her was…

Scary.

Gera had dressed her in a white lace gown that revealed more of her body than it covered, especially since her nipples had been darkened by the flavored rouge. The gown was tied together with only one ribbon between her breasts and while standing, it was closed, but whenever she sat, it would open to reveal her entire lower body that was as naked as the day she'd come into the world.

Yeah...a man had definitely designed this for easy access.

Gera led her to an ornate white and blue striped sofa near the bed that was wide enough to allow for things other than sitting. In fact the entire room was nothing more than a glorified sex dungeon.

I really hope this place has been sanitized. The thought of Darling's uncle in here with other women he'd probably tortured turned her stomach.

But there was nothing she could do about it at present. While Gera might be older, Zarya had a distinct impression that Gera could take her in a fight. And if not, the older woman would definitely call for backup.

Either way, she didn't want to chance it.

Zarya sat down slowly, then propped her foot on top of a pillow that Gera brought over to her. Gera adjusted the gown to give her some degree of modesty.

"Thank you, Gera. I'm sorry that I was so irritable earlier."

The apology seemed to perplex her. "You're welcome, Mistress. Is there anything else I can get for you?"

My freedom would be nice. But only Darling could do that.

Zarya looked around the room that really didn't have anything other than sex toys and other items she didn't want to think about. For that matter, there was a wall display of things she couldn't identify. *And here I thought I knew about sex.* Apparently, there was a whole subculture she'd never even heard of.

"Is there any kind of entertainment here?"

Gera gestured to the entertainment armoire. "There are a number of sex programs designed to stimulate you."

Of course, there was. "Not exactly what I was thinking. Anything else I can do?"

"Unfortunately, no."

Great.

She just might die of boredom.

Gera brought over a light blanket and tucked it around her. One advantage to being virtually naked, Gera must have deduced she was cold in here. Not like she could hide that fact given her state of undress.

"Don't fear, Mistress. You'll have a full schedule starting tomorrow."

Of new sex positions and other things Zarya really didn't want to be schooled in by strangers.

"Looking forward to it." She was proud of herself for keeping the sarcasm out of her voice.

Gera handed her a small white remote. "The button on the right is to summon me and the one on the left is for the kitchen staff should you become hungry. If you need anything at all, just call me."

"Thank you."

Gera curtsied, then left.

The remote in Zarya's hand started buzzing so suddenly, that she jumped and dropped it. It took her a couple of seconds to fish it out from under the sofa and answer it.

"Hello?"

"Z? Is that really you?"

The sound of that unexpected voice brought tears to her eyes. "Sorchie?"

Sorche let out a screeching shriek. "Hey big sis! Oh I can't believe you're all right. I was so afraid you were dead."

Tears welled in her eyes as she heard the one person in this universe who loved her as much as she loved them.

Don't cry...don't cry. If she did, Gera might make her redo her face and that had been hard enough to endure the first time. "Me, too, baby sis. I mean.that you were dead. Where are you? How did you get this number?"

"I don't know. Some guy with this really weird, creepy voice called earlier and left it as a message. He said that he had a way to contact you, and for me to call this number as soon as I could. And you'll never believe where I am!"

Zarya had never before heard such excitement in Sorche's voice. Gods, she sounded so happy.

"I got a full scholarship to Guernelle Academy!"

That news stunned her almost as much as hearing Sorche's voice. "A scholarship? How?"

Maris had told her Darling was paying for...

Oh wait. It suddenly made complete sense. That must be how Darling was doing it. Like her, Sorche would never have taken money from a man to pay for her school, especially not from an aristo.

Her sister had no idea she had an individual backer.

"It's a special deal set up by a company called the Dagan Investment Group. I have to major in mechanics, which is what I wanted to do anyway, and so long as I keep my grades up, they'll keep paying for everything. I even get a monthly stipend for living expenses so that I don't have to work and can focus all my attention on my classes. Every year I maintain my grades, it'll go up. And if I graduate with honors, I'll get...brace yourself...a fifty *thousand* cred bonus! Is that not stunning?"

In that moment, Zarya had never loved Darling more. What he'd done went beyond kind, and the fact that he'd done it in such a way that it built up Sorche's confidence and made her strive to do her best was incredible.

"How did you find out about the scholarship?"

"The school called me about it the week before I had to register for classes. They said that the board at DIG had reviewed all the applicants for their incoming class, and that I was the only one out of all the others they thought had real potential. Can you believe it? Me? Me!"

"It's not that amazing. I always told you, you were the best."

"Yeah, but someone who isn't related to me thinks I don't suck, too. Sorry, that counts more."

Zarya laughed. Sorche had no more belief in herself than she did. Too many years of them struggling, of Sorche trying her best and then being slapped down by things like getting into a prestigious school and then not having the money to attend it had clubbed them both so many times that it was hard to have any confidence in anything, except the universe's willingness to bitch-slap them.

"So where are you?" Sorche asked. "Why haven't you returned any of my calls? Do you know how long it's been? I *really* thought you were dead."

Yeah...that was one question Zarya had no intention of answering. The last thing she'd ever do was bring down her sister's rare excitement.

But at least, because of Zarya's less than legal occupation, Sorche was used to her disappearing suddenly and being gone for a long period of time without communication.

However she'd never been gone *this* long before.

"I've, um...I've been really busy. After what happened with... the fall of the Resistance, I had to go into hiding. I honestly had no way of getting in touch with you. I swear."

"You suck, Z! You shouldn't scare me like that. But it's what I'd hoped and figured. Still, you should have found *some* way to get word to me. It's been over a year, sis. A year!"

"I know. I'm sorry."

"Hey, Sorch? Are you coming to eat?" It was another girl's voice that sounded like it came from a doorway or somewhere at a distance.

"Just a sec."

"Who was that?" Zarya asked.

"Oh, that's my roommate. Annalise Cruel. You wouldn't believe how sweet she's been to me." She lowered her voice to a whisper. "I know how you feel about her family, but I'm telling you she's really decent. She's my age and a little over a year from graduating—she started on time, lucky thing…Gods love her, she's taken time to show me how everything here works and where to go. How to pick classes and where to get the best study guides. She even bought me a school jersey for my birthday, and lets me borrow her makeup anytime I want. She has some really nice stuff, too. It's almost like having another sister. I hope you can meet her soon."

"I would love to."

"Hey, Lise?" Sorche called out so loud and unexpectedly that Zarya almost dropped the remote again. "Can you say hi to my sister?"

"Hi, Sorche's sister. I'm glad she finally found you. She's been worried sick, and talks about you all the time. She says you're the best sister ever. I wouldn't know since I only have smelly brothers. Well, two of them stink. Darling always smells nice."

Zarya couldn't argue with that. Even when he was sweaty, he smelled divine. And the sound of Darling's sister's sweet voice made her smile. The way she spoke and her accent reminded her a lot of Darling's voice before they'd destroyed it. Though his had been a lot deeper, they were still similar. "Hi, Lise. Nice to meet you."

"You, too. And I hate to be rude, but do you mind if I borrow Sorche? If we don't leave for the meal hall now, they'll close it on us, and I'm not really able to walk all the way into town yet."

"Yeah, Lise was shot in the back by some bastards who kidnapped her brother last year. I'm sure you heard about it. And she really hates to inconvenience her bodyguards, especially in the evenings. Anyway, I have to run. You take care. Love you!"

"Love you, too." Zarya wasn't sure if Sorche heard that last bit or not. She'd hung up, laughing with Lise.

Her heart light, Zarya studied the remote, trying to find a way to use it to call Darling and thank him for what he'd done.

But it seemed to only receive calls, not make them.

She pressed the button for Gera who answered right away. "Yes, Mistress?"

"I'm sorry to disturb you, Gera. How do I contact Lord Darling?"

"You don't, Mistress. It's forbidden. He will come to you when he has time."

Well that instantly sucked all the warm tender feelings out of her. How rude! Call her when *he* was ready? The very thought flew all over her.

Making sure to keep the ire out of her tone, she tightened her grip on the remote. "Thank you, Gera." She cut the feed, then got up to go find him.

But as soon as she limped her way to the door, she had another rude surprise.

"You've got to be kidding me…"

None of the doors opened. She was locked in like a well-kept pet.

Darling's head ached from all the shit he was supposed to go through and answer. For hours, he'd been listening to reports from the other gerents and administrators, whining about everything imaginable. Most of it absolute crap.

How had his father stood it? No wonder the man had migraines all the time.

It was like refereeing a hundred spoiled toddlers with ADHD.

You know, Dar, there's no problem so big that an adequate supply of explosives can't cure it.

There was that. But people tended to protest being blown up.

Bunch of krikken weirdos.

He glanced at the half-empty bottle of whisky on his desk. It was tempting, especially given the throbbing pain in his head and back. A pain that wasn't helped by his eyesight dancing against his will.

But he didn't want to be numb right now.

He'd rather see a pair of amber eyes set in the face of the most beautiful woman he'd ever known. Even though he was still angry at her. Even though she'd betrayed him.

He still wanted to be with her.

I'm an effing idiot…

But before he could stop himself, he was headed out of his office and up the stairs to her room.

His body already on fire at just the thought of seeing her, he opened her door.

In the next instant, a fluffy slipper flew at his head. He dodged it, but not before another followed so close behind that it hit him in the arm. "What the hell?"

"You rotten bastard!"

Other things came flying at him so quickly that he couldn't even identify them. They slammed against the door and walls, many shattering while others made loud thuds before crashing to the floor.

Damn, she could aim. In fact, she was deadlier with a blaster at a distance than he was.

And with his limited vision, he wasn't as good at dodging projectiles as he used to be. Darling took cover behind the end table. "Zarya, what's gotten into you?"

Shrieking in outrage, she responded by throwing more things in his direction. Glass shattered all around him. It'd been a long time since anyone had ambushed him and all he could do was be grateful she wasn't armed with anything more than household objects.

Thankfully, she finally ran out of ammunition.

When she limped to find more, he bolted across the room toward her. He caught her arm as she seized a heavy lead vase. Yeah, that would *really* hurt if she hit him with it.

He gently twisted it out of her grip. "What's wrong?"

"You!" she snarled. "How dare you!"

Her anger baffled him. "How dare I what?"

"Lock me in here like I'm a criminal!"

It was probably a stupid idea, but he couldn't resist laughing at her. "Technically, you *are* a criminal."

Yeah, not the brightest comeback he'd ever made.

She raked him with a scathing glare. "Oh wait, Lord Sentella. My bounty is nothing compared to *yours*. You want to talk criminals? How many governments want *you* dead? I'm only wanted by one. And it happens to be *yours*."

He had to give her that, and it reminded him that he needed to put through a pardon for her.

You hate her, remember?

Yeah, but she'd been outlawed for no reason whatsoever, and he wasn't about to hold her accountable for her rebellion against his uncle's reign when he'd been the one who'd helped her pull off her most damaging attacks. His personal feelings for her shouldn't prevent him from doing what was right...

Her expression fuming she gestured toward the door behind him. "In spite of what you might think...*man*...I am *not* your pet or your toy. Why did you lock me in here, you bastard!"

He ignored her insult, which was mild compared to what others routinely called him. "I didn't know you were locked in."

Her gaze turned suspicious as if she didn't believe him. "What?"

"You heard me. I didn't do it. I knew nothing about it. Are you sure it's locked and not jammed or something?"

Zarya hated how reasonable he was being. It was beginning to make her feel like a hysterical child. "No, I'm too stupid to tell the difference between a locked door and a stuck one. Thanks." She pushed him toward it. "Go, try to open a door. *Any* door."

He went to the one in the middle of the wall and opened it with an ease that made her ill. "See. It's fine."

Zarya limped toward him to try it herself. But she'd only taken two steps before Darling recrossed the room and picked her up, then carried her to the door. She wanted to maintain her anger at him, but it was hard when he was being so nice.

Damn him for it!

She reached for the door. Once again, it refused to open. "See," she said triumphantly.

He scowled as he tried it again and once more, it opened easily for him. "It must have a bio sensor on it. Since they always open for me, I didn't think to check. Sorry. All you had to do was tell me calmly, and I'd have gotten it fixed. You didn't have to throw things at me."

She narrowed her gaze at him, still not quite ready to believe his easy explanation. "You didn't order me locked in?"

"Why would I? You're injured. Not like you're going to run. At least not for a week. I think I could have heard your limping gait across the floor and caught up to you before you made it down the stairs to the drive. Right now, an arthritic snail could catch you."

She suddenly felt like an idiot. But he'd brought up the first thing that had ticked her off at him. "How was I supposed to tell you I was locked in when I can't call you? Hmmm?"

He appeared completely perplexed by her question. "You can call me anytime you want. Hell, a call from you I'd actually welcome as opposed to the other assholes I've been dealing with all day."

She gestured around the room. "Please notice, Lord Governor, the lack of IT equipment in this room. All I have is that stupid pastel remote and I can't use that to call anyone, except the kitchen and Gera. She told me that I'd have to wait on you to call me at *your* leisure. When *you* felt like it."

He actually had the gall to look amused by that. The man really had no sense of self-preservation. "Gera's nine hundred years old. She can't conceive of a mistress being anything more than a play toy for the governor."

"Isn't that what I am to you?"

"It depends." The teasing light in his blue eyes charmed her against her will. "If I give you the wrong answer, are you going to hit me again?"

"Not while you're holding me. How stupid do you think I am?"

Darling heard her speaking, but he couldn't really focus on her words as he caught a whiff of something delectable. Without thinking, he nuzzled her neck where it was strongest and inhaled.

Ah yeah, that smelled good, and it set him on fire again.

Zarya's eyes widened as she felt Darling run his tongue along her collarbone, beneath her slave collar. "I'm still mad at you."

"It's okay," he breathed against her skin. "I'm still mad at you, too."

But she didn't hate him.

He hated her.

That made her ache all over again, especially deep in her heart. *I really want you back.* She missed them as a couple. The nights where they'd stayed up until dawn talking about nothing important. The sound of his refined voice in the dark, soothing her with compliments, endearments, and support. The feel of his breath on the back of her neck as he held her until she fell asleep in his arms. The warmth of his body on hers, and the sound of his laughter in her ear. That had never failed to cheer her even during the worst moments of her life.

He'd been her best friend.

In many ways, even better than Ture or Sorche.

Desperate to find what she'd lost, she reached for his mask.

He pulled back and turned his head away from her. "Don't." The agony in that one single word made her eyes water.

"I want to see you."

"Why? There's nothing worth seeing that won't turn your stomach."

She blinked back her tears. The agony in his gruff voice made her heart pound. "You don't turn my stomach, Darling. I love to nibble your jaw and earlobe. I can't do that with the mask on. It covers them both."

Utter misery darkened his eyes and it caused guilt to scorch her. "They're not the same anymore. All you can feel are the scars under my beard. It's revolting."

She brushed the hair back from his mask and sank her hand in the soft dark auburn strands at the nape of his neck. "They're still you, Darling. That's all that matters to me."

This time when she reached for the mask, he allowed her to remove it.

His entire demeanor changed instantly. Instead of being the fierce, steadfast soldier she'd always known, whose confidence bled out through his pores, he was now bashful and quiet. Like he was embarrassed or afraid she'd shun or curse him for his looks. But what hurt her most was the self-loathing in his gaze.

No one should ever feel that way when they were alone with someone who loved them.

She dropped the mask to the floor, then laid her hand over his scarred cheek where Pip had carved his name. Damn those bastards. Someone had crosshatched lines all over Darling's face. The scars ran so deep that even with his thick auburn beard covering them, they showed through.

And they were nothing compared to the ones that marred his beautiful soul.

Please let me help you. She couldn't bear the thought of his suffering any longer.

Keeping her eyes wide open, she pulled his scarred lips to hers so that she could kiss him.

Darling's entire world shattered as he watched her watch him kiss her. How could she not be repulsed by him? He couldn't stand to look at himself. There wasn't enough whisky in the universe to blind him to his appearance.

"Your face is so hideous. Even if you were straight, there would be no chance of marriage or children now." His mother's first condemnation when she'd seen what had been done to him still stung.

Yet Zarya didn't seem to mind his hideousness in the least. And when she left his lips to kiss her way across his cheek so that she could breathe in his ear and tease his earlobe with her tongue, he forgot all about his damaged body.

Nothing mattered to him except the woman in his arms.

Sighing in peace, he sank down on the floor with her. Her transparent gown spread open, exposing her entire body to his hungry gaze. He skimmed his hand over the soft skin of her stomach, through the dark hair at the juncture of her thighs until he touched the wet part of her he craved most.

She cried out the moment he slid his fingers into her body.

A smile curled his lips. "Come for me, baby," he whispered to her as he quickened his rhythm. "I want to hear you scream from it." Dipping his head, he pulled open the tie between her breasts with his teeth, then nuzzled the silk aside so that he could taste her puckered nipple.

He jerked back at the unexpected taste. "Is that—"

Her laughter interrupted his question. "Gera said that red berries were your favorite fruit."

"And you're my favorite meat." Smiling at her, he returned to lave her breast.

Zarya rubbed herself against his hand and cupped his head to her while her senses reeled. She'd missed him so much. Her heart hammering, she stared down at his red hair while he played with her.

She finally knew his hair color. And how beautiful it was. While his looks were new to her, his touch wasn't. Biting her lip, she cried out as her pleasure overwhelmed her.

Darling gave her breast one long, savoring lick before he lifted his head to watch her climax.

Screaming from the sheer intensity of it, she wrapped her arms around his shoulders and threw herself back, arching her body against his.

"That's my girl," he said proudly. He always took so much pride and pleasure whenever she came, especially when it was quick. His smile turning wicked with that thought, he slowly kissed his way down her body until his mouth replaced his hand.

Zarya cried out again as he did the most amazing things with his tongue. There was no way to describe it. It was as if he lived for no other reason than to taste her.

And she loved it.

She buried her hand in his hair, then realized that the ceiling above them was mirrored so that she could watch him as he tasted her.

But as her gaze dropped to his back, she frowned at the Sentella tattoo on his left shoulder.

It, like the rest of his body, bore those deep ugly scars.

She wanted to ask him why her soldiers had continued to torture him given that tattoo, but she didn't want him to stop what he was doing.

Later...

She cried out again as he plunged his tongue deep inside her.

Yeah, much later.

Darling laughed as he heard her screaming in the throes of another orgasm. In that moment, all he wanted was to be as deep inside her as he could get.

Rolling her over on the floor, he pulled a pillow off the chair next to them and elevated her hips with it. He snatched his shoes, shirt, and pants off as fast as he could, then nipped her buttocks gently before he laid himself over her and entered her from behind.

She growled out loud as he buried himself deep inside her body, then thrust himself against her hips. His heart pounding, he reached his hand around so that he could stroke both sides of her.

Bucking wildly against him, she screamed out again and again.

"Careful, sweet," he whispered in her ear. "You're going to throw me out."

"Not possible as large as you are."

It was more than possible as she'd done it to him before, and he knew from experience that it hurt her when she did. Which right now was the last thing he wanted.

So he held himself still and let her take control of their pleasure. He wanted to wait on her to come again, but it wasn't possible. She felt too good under him.

Before he could stop himself, he came.

Zarya laughed in triumph as she felt him finally shuddering from his own orgasm. That, and a subtle intake of breath in her ear was her only clue that she'd sated him. He was always so quiet whenever he made love to her that in the beginning of their relationship, she'd feared he wasn't enjoying it. Rarely did he make even the slightest sound.

But she had no doubts about his pleasure tonight as he buried his hand gently in her curls, then kissed the nape of her neck. "I think I've died and gone to paradise."

She was still getting used to his new voice. How odd to know his touch so well and to have all the rest of him be a stranger to her.

He lay himself over her body so that she could feel his heart pounding against her shoulder in a frantic rhythm.

"Are you all right, back there?" she teased, wanting to keep him in his current playful mood.

"Never better." He brushed her hair across her shoulders before he nuzzled her neck and breathed her in. "I didn't hurt your ankle, did I?"

"No."

Grateful for that, Darling pulled away enough so that he could admire her beautiful skin. But he frowned as he saw the marks on her that his beard had left behind. Her skin looked so irritated from it. He brushed his hand over the rash as guilt stabbed him.

Damn...

"I'll be right back."

Zarya rolled over with a contented sigh to watch him walk naked toward the bathroom. Though he still wasn't as muscular as he'd been before his torture, his lean muscles were well defined and prominent.

Even scarred, he was gorgeous, and that predacious walk...

It made her hot all over again.

Smiling, she lay there lost in thought until she heard a loud, resounding curse ring out from the bathroom. It was followed by the sounds of things crashing to the floor and breaking.

What in the known universe?

Worried that an assassin might be attacking Darling, she

pushed herself up and went to see what was happening. As she opened the door, her worry turned to horror. There was blood everywhere. On the counter, the towels, and all over the sink.

Darling sat on the floor with his legs pulled tight against his chest, his forehead resting on his knees and his head covered by his muscular arms. He was so still that she wasn't sure he was breathing.

Blood covered his hands and ran down his legs to drip onto the tile.

Had an assassin broken in and hurt him? That thought terrified her.

Ignoring her ankle, she rushed to him. "Darling?"

He tightened his hands over his head, but refused to look at her.

That only scared her more. "Honey, what's wrong? Where are you wounded?"

"I'm not wounded," he snarled in rabid anger.

She touched the hands he had laced on top of his bent head. "I don't understand. What happened?"

When he finally lifted his head, her breath caught in her throat. But it was the bitter rage in his eyes that tore through her.

His left cheek was bleeding profusely.

He curled his lip. "I can't even shave for the fucking scars. I keep nicking them."

Completely confused, she tried to understand. "Why were you trying to shave?"

He reached out and touched her shoulder. "I didn't want to irritate your beautiful skin."

Her heart wrenched at those sincere words, at the tenderness in his voice. He'd hurt himself attempting to protect her. That, and for many, many other reasons, was why she loved him so.

She picked his hand up from her shoulder and kissed it. "You didn't have to shave for me."

Rage flared in his eyes before he banged his head against the wall so hard, she was surprised he didn't break through the slate tiles. "I'm so fucking useless. What kind of man can't even shave his own face?"

The agony in his damaged voice made her eyes water as her heart broke even more. She cupped his face in her hands. "You're not useless. Damn it! Grow a beard to your knees for all I care. It doesn't hurt me."

But the problem was, it hurt him and that was unbearable to her.

He scowled. "How can you even stand to look at me like this? I'm revolting."

"No, you're not. And it's not a hardship by any means. I think you're gorgeous."

He scoffed. "Bullshit. You think I don't know what'll happen if I show this"—he scraped his hand angrily against his bleeding cheek—"in public? I already went through this once. The cringing and grimacing, and the whispering. The sighs and looks of gratitude that they're not the ones who are scarred. The glares of distaste as people step away from me, or refuse to look at me at all because it turns their stomachs. Having people ask what happened so I can relive it over and over again until I want to scream. I couldn't stand it the first time, but at least it was only on one side of my face then. So long as my hair stayed in place, no one saw it. This shit"—he gestured at both sides of his face—"I can't hide."

Except with the mask that covered everything . . .

She set her chin down on his knee and looked up at him, wanting desperately to make him feel better. "You know I'd do you."

The corners of his mouth twitched. "You're a fool."

She trailed her hand over the muscles of his chest to his ripped eight-pack and then lower still. "What's that say about you since you're the one keeping me around?"

Darling didn't really hear those words. Not while she stroked his cock with her hand and he stared into those amber eyes that soothed him in a way nothing else did. He could almost believe he wasn't disgusting when she treated him like this and looked at him as if he were worth something.

Like he was human and still desirable.

She slid herself closer, then went down on him.

His breathing ragged, he ground his teeth at how good she felt tonguing his body. All his thoughts scattered and he forgot where he was and how he looked. The only thing he felt now was how much he loved the way her long hair fanned out across his legs. Sighing, he leaned his head back and savored her sweet mouth on him until there was nothing else in existence except the two of them.

After a few minutes, she lifted her head to smile at him. "Come on, sweetie. Let's get you cleaned up and I can continue, okay?"

Right then, he'd have followed her into hell, smiling the whole way.

Zarya stood, hoping she'd helped his mood. In a strange way, his current bashfulness and reserve toward her reminded her a lot of how he'd been after the first time she'd touched him. For weeks afterward, he'd been bashful and awkward whenever she was near. Finally, she'd cornered him one afternoon in the kitchen of the Resistance's HQ.

Even though she couldn't see anything other than his black battlesuit and helmet, he was still the most beautiful man she'd ever known.

"Kere, nothing has changed between us." She'd taken his gloved hand into hers and kissed it. "I don't ask or expect anything of you. I'm here if you need me, that's all. The last thing I want to do is to make you uncomfortable."

"It's not that."

"Then what?"

He'd led her hand down his body, to his crotch so that she could feel how swollen he was. "Every time I see you now, all I can think about is how good you felt. How much I want you."

Grateful for that, she'd smiled up at him. "I'm here for you anytime you want me. No strings. No demands." She'd locked the door and then turned the lights off for him. Because there were no windows in the room, it had been so dark she couldn't see anything at all.

That was how she'd learned that Darling had perfect vision in the dark. How she'd learned that he could make her come within minutes of touching her...

Now, after all they'd shared, he was bashful with her again.

Unable to look at her, he stood, then picked her up and carried her to his room that connected to hers through the door in the center of the far wall. While her room was pastel blue and white, his was decorated in dark blues, maroon, and gold. The royal Cruel seal was carved into a headboard that went all the way up to the ornately gilded ceiling.

Even bigger than her room, it was one of the largest rooms in the palace. Only the throne room, dining hall, and ballroom were larger.

Darling closed the door to her room and headed for his bed. As gently as he could, he set her down on the mattress.

"Where are you going?" she asked as he stepped away from her.

"I'm not completely helpless, Z."

"I didn't say you were, Captain Defensive."

He paused before he opened the door. "Stay there. I'll be right back. Have no fear. If I use a razor again, it'll be to cut my throat."

Zarya cringed at his warped humor. "That's not funny, you know."

He didn't respond. Instead, he vanished into what must be his bathroom.

A few seconds later, she heard water running.

After a handful of minutes he was back with two warm, damp cloths. He handed one to her to clean herself while he called house-keeping to clean her room next door.

Then he laid back on the bed, and covered his face with the other cloth.

As she leaned against him, she saw a frame on his nightstand. Curious about its contents, she reached over him and pulled it closer, then turned it on.

It was a photo of Darling as a boy, probably around the age of ten. He stood beside his tall, lean father, and behind his mother who sat holding a female toddler with curling red hair. A dark-haired boy a few years younger than Darling stood next to Natale's knees.

"Is this your family?"

He pulled one corner of the cloth back so that he could see what she was looking at. "Yeah. That's them."

They looked so happy together. But that made her wonder something…

"Why isn't your family here at the palace?"

Shouldn't they be the ones helping him to heal instead of Maris? Granted Lise was in school, but still…

If Darling was her brother, she wouldn't have left him alone in the mental condition he was in. He needed people around him who loved him and could reassure and help him while he healed. People who didn't mind his physical appearance or limitations.

He sighed irritably. "My sister's at school, mad that I caused her to flunk her classes, and that she's going to have a permanent limp because of the attack she survived."

"That wasn't your fault."

"Wasn't it? If I hadn't pulled her out of school, she would have been fine. Not still going to physical therapy twice a week and living on painkillers that make it hard for her to maintain her course load and grades. But for my interference, she'd have graduated with honors this year. Now, because of me, she'll be lucky to graduate at all."

That was twisted logic. "I doubt she thinks that."

"I don't. I hear her rant about it every time I call."

Zarya started to tell him that she'd had an entirely different impression from her earlier conversation with Lise, but she wasn't sure he wanted her talking to his sister.

"What about your brother?"

"Poor bastard's taking care of his mother."

She noted the fact that he didn't refer to Natale as his mother. "And she is...?"

"At the Summer Palace."

Zarya frowned at that. It didn't make sense. His brother and sister...Okay, there were times when she couldn't be there for Sorche.

But a mother?

"Why isn't she here? Is she ill?"

When he spoke, the raw anger in his voice chilled her. "No. I don't want her here."

"Whyever not?"

"I don't want to see the way she refuses to look at me, okay?"

"I don't understand."

He sighed wearily. "Be glad you don't. My mother doesn't mean to be selfish. She just always had a man to protect and care for her, a staff of servants to cater to her every whim, and a nurse or tutor to care for us. She doesn't know what to do when she's supposed to be the caregiver—other than delegate it to someone else. It's hard for her to think about other people."

"But you're her son."

"I know. I love my mother and I hate her guts. I guess that's my curse. To only want women who put me through hell."

That stung her like a slap in the face, but she forced her own anger down. "I didn't hurt you intentionally."

"My mother doesn't believe she does either. She thinks she's a great, loving mother who has done nothing but sacrifice her life for us. One who does her best and only tells us what we need to hear." Sliding the cloth to his neck, he returned the frame to his nightstand. His eyes were empty as he turned the power off and lay back against the pillows.

Zarya glanced around the elegant room that held no other personal items of his in it. Nothing. No childhood mementos of any kind. No other pictures.

Not even a hairbrush.

She scowled at that realization. Did he not have them or did he not want them?

Her gaze went to the scars that marred him from head to toe. While many were new, a lot of them weren't. Never in her wildest imaginings would she have thought an aristo would be damaged like this. Her parents had been nothing but kind and protective of them. They'd have killed anyone who dared raise a hand to her or any of her siblings.

Yet Darling's own uncle had caused many of those scars. Meanwhile, his mother had allowed the abuse to go on for years without stopping it. "Have you ever had anyone protect you?"

His eyes closed, he brushed the cloth against his ravaged cheek. "Nero. Nykyrian. Caillen. Hauk. Maris. Jayne and Syn."

She paused as she realized that list corresponded to the number of people who'd come into the room after she'd discovered Darling's presence. "They're the ones who rescued you?"

He nodded.

"How long have you known them?"

"Nero all my life. He swears he's the reason I was named Darling, and if he really was, I'd like to kick his ass for it. Gah, what a stupid name. I can't believe my parents couldn't find something better...like Dogshit or Dumbass."

She snorted. "Could be worse. They could have named you after a girl."

"Might as well have. A name like Darling sucks all the testosterone right out of you. Of course, it also made it easy for me to pretend to be gay, so I shouldn't complain. What self-respecting man would use something so god-awful and stupid?"

Propping her head on her arm, she traced the burn scar on his nipple where he'd been electrocuted. Not wanting to think about that and the bitter agony it caused both of them, she tried to distract him. "What about the others? How did you meet them?"

"They were friends of Nykyrian's."

When he didn't continue the explanation, she prodded him. "And...how did you two become friends?"

He took a long breath before he answered. "When I was finally skilled enough to breech the palace security system and evade Caronese guards, my uncle hired Nykyrian to *protect* me."

"From whom?"

"Anyone I might run to for help. Arturo lived in fear that I'd find another aristo willing to be my guardian, and thereby usurp him."

"Why didn't you go to someone else?"

He laughed bitterly. "I tried twice, and all I did was get slapped back to him so fast that my ears rang from it. In the end, my situation was made worse by attempting to make it better. So I stopped trying to find someone to help, and concentrated on just getting away from here for as long as I could as often as I could before Arturo had me dragged back."

The bitterness in his tone said it all. She couldn't believe no one would help him. "I take it you and Nykyrian hit it off then?"

He arched a brow at her. "Have you ever seen Nykyrian Quiakides?"

That was a name she knew well, and to her knowledge there was only one man who bore it. But the universe was vast, so she wanted to make sure they were talking about the same person. "The Andarion prince?"

"Yeah."

Zarya conjured a perfect mental image of Nykyrian. A former League assassin who'd left their ranks when they ordered him to kill a mother and small child, the man was huge and lethal in a way very few were. So much so, that the League had actually pardoned him for deserting—something they had never, ever done before. He was the only assassin to leave them and survive.

"He's a little scary."

"No," Darling corrected. "He's a lot scary. I shit my pants the first time I saw him, which was what my uncle wanted. Even with opaque sunglasses over his eyes, Nyk has a way of looking at you that can freeze your blood in your veins. Back then, he never spoke a word to me. He just followed me everywhere I went, and would grab me by the scruff of my neck and pull me back if I so much as took one step in a direction he didn't want me to."

"That must have been awful."

"It definitely wasn't fun. And I hated him for it. It was bad enough everyone else mocked and emasculated me. The last thing I needed was some League asshole jerking me around like I was his backseat bitch."

Her stomach sank as she considered the underlying venom in his voice. "Did he hit you?"

"No. He didn't have to. He could literally lift me off my feet with one hand. For that matter, he still can. That son of a bitch is huge and ungodly strong."

"Then how did you become friends?"

He wiped carefully at his face with the cloth. "One night after my uncle had *counseled* me for a couple of hours, I slipped Nyk's custody and blew up his prized fighter during my escape."

Her jaw went slack. She was as impressed with his skills as she was with his stupidity. "No, you didn't."

"Yeah. He was really unhappy about it, and I had no idea how rare a ship it was, or how much he loved it. But after he tracked me down, I figured it out real quick. It was the first time I'd seen him lose his temper. Not something you *ever* want to experience, believe me. I honestly thought he was going to rip out my spine and beat me with it."

That had to be terrifying. She'd rather go up against Nemesis again than to face the Andarion prince. Darling was right, Nykyrian was extremely off-putting. "So what did he do to you?"

Darling fell silent as her question took him right back to that stygian alley on the backside of hell where he'd hidden, thinking he was safe from his uncle's reach. After three days where he didn't dare spend a single cred lest it be used to locate him, he'd been starving. Half dead from that and a severe cold he'd contracted while sleeping out in the frigid winter weather with no jacket or cover, he'd left his filth hole long enough to try and scrounge food.

There had been a restaurant around the corner from where he'd set up a temporary home on the street. He was hoping to find something to eat in the trash. Since he'd been so careful to cover his tracks and not use anything that could trace back to his location, he'd foolishly thought himself safe.

Especially in the middle of the night.

He'd just found a bag of outdated bread when he'd heard a faint scraping sound behind him in the shadows. Thinking it was one of the restaurant's late night cleaning crew, he'd broken out into a sweat, terrified that they'd call the authorities on him.

But it had been something much worse.

Nykyrian had snatched him down from the dumpster and slammed him on the ground so hard he'd seen stars from it. Cursing him, Nyk had pinned him with one massive forearm across his throat. "No one fucks with my ship, you little bastard," he'd growled. "Believe me, it's worth more than your putrid life. I don't care what your uncle pays for your protection or what the League does to me. You're going to die for defiling it."

Darling had tried to push Nykyrian's arm off so that he could breathe, but it was useless. Nyk was too strong. All he could do was cough and wheeze.

Until Nykyrian saw the original scar Ryn had given him that covered the entire left half of his face, and the bruises on his cheek and black eye from his uncle that still, three days later, looked like shit.

Before Darling could regain his senses and to his eternal shame, Nyk had yanked his shirt up to see the other bruises and scars that covered his torso. Then, he'd grabbed Darling's wrists to examine the scars that Darling had made on his own body when he'd been unable to take his uncle's bullshit anymore...

"They beat you?" Nyk had asked.

Darling had shoved him away and scooted out from under him. "Why do you think I run? Do you really think I enjoy eating garbage out of dumpsters in the middle of the night when I could be warm at home in a palace?"

Little had he known then that Nyk had endured a childhood that made his seem like paradise in comparison.

Instead of killing him, which would have been preferable all things considered, Nyk had shrugged his coat off and wrapped it around Darling's shoulders. There was so much difference in their height and build back then that his coat had swallowed Darling whole.

"C'mon, kid, let's get you fed and cleaned up."

Darling had stood his ground. "I don't want to go back."

"I know...I do. But we both know that you have no choice. If I don't take you back, someone else will, and they won't feed you first."

Disgusted by the fact that Nyk was right, he'd lowered his head and nodded glumly.

"Don't worry, kid. Now that I know what you're running from, I'll give you as much protection as I can."

"Why would you do that?"

"Because no one deserves to be afraid to go home."

From that night on, Nyk had done his damnedest to keep him safe. Sometimes it'd worked.

Others...

Darling sighed as he ran his fingers through Zarya's hair. "After Nyk saw the condition I was in, he told me he would do his best to keep me out of the line of fire, and that he would teach me how to protect myself."

"He trained you as an assassin?"

Darling nodded.

"Is that where your tattoo came from?"

"Yeah. After I'd completed my training, Hauk, who is an old childhood friend of Nyk's, designed it for me and his brother Fain was the one who did it." Darling wouldn't have trusted anyone else to touch him that intimately. But the Hauks had always been good friends to him and he treasured them both.

"Has no one ever realized what it is, and the kind of training you've had?"

Bitterness choked him as he thought back to his stints in various asylums over the years. Like Pip, they'd assumed the tattoo was done as a joke or a way for Darling to attract men, and had mocked him for it.

Because of the embarrassing scars and bruises he went out of his way to conceal, no one else had ever seen his bare back.

Not even Maris.

He swallowed before he told her something he probably should keep to himself. "You're the only woman I've ever been with, Z."

Zarya froze as she heard those words. Was that even possible? "What?"

"I was always too afraid of being outed either as a heterosexual or a member of the Sentella to take the chance. It was why it took me so long to touch you, even though I wanted you from the first time I saw you."

Her head swam as she thought back to the early days of their relationship. Even though she'd craved him from the moment he'd first saved her, she'd had no idea that he found her even remotely attractive. Kere had started out as a liaison from the Sentella and he'd turned into an ally who helped them fight against Arturo's tyranny.

Yes, he'd spent a lot of time with her, but she'd foolishly assumed it was for Resistance or Sentella business.

Until they'd been on the run from Caronese soldiers. To keep from hurting the soldiers, they'd hidden in a tight closet where there had been no room for them to even breathe. As she was forced to press tight to his body, she'd felt him swelling against her hip.

Neither had moved for countless minutes, but she could tell by his rigidness how much he desired her.

When the coast was clear, she'd swallowed hard, unsure of what to do.

"Sorry," he'd whispered to her. "I—um...I hope I didn't offend you."

It was the first uncertainty she'd ever heard in his voice. "You didn't offend me, Kere. I feel the same way about you."

Without a word, he'd opened the door and checked to make sure it was safe to leave.

They had made their way out of the closet and back to the hangar bay where his fighter had been docked. After they launched and once they were sure no one was trailing them, she'd turned around in her seat to face him.

With a boldness she'd never had before with any man, she'd reached down to undo his pants.

"Zarya—"

"Sh," she'd breathed, cutting off his protest. "I don't expect anything from you, Kere. I more than understand why you can't let anyone know who you are—that you have to stay in the shadows. I accept and respect that. But after everything you've done for me and the Resistance, I just want to give something back to you. I really do want to do this for you."

She'd waited for him to protest again.

When he didn't, she'd opened his pants and stroked him until her fingertips were wet from his desire. There in the darkness of space, he'd cupped her face with his gloved hand.

Already in love with him, she'd leaned down and taken him into her mouth to taste him for the first time. She could still hear his heavy breathing as he'd leaned back in the seat and let her lick and suck on him to her heart's content.

Hear his expelled breath when he'd climaxed a few minutes later.

It stunned her to find out now that he'd never been with any woman except her.

She rested her chin on his chest to stare into his incredibly blue eyes. "Given how skilled you've always been in bed, I would have never guessed that I was your first."

"That's because I spend a lot of time thinking about what I want to do to you."

She smiled as she remembered all the little things he'd done over the years that had made him such an important, vital part of her life. "Thank you, by the way."

"For what?" he asked with a scowl.

"I assume you're the reason my sister called me earlier."

He stroked her hair tenderly. "I figured you'd want to talk to her. I know how close you two are and I'm sorry I didn't get you in touch with her sooner."

She should probably hold that against him, but for some reason she didn't. "I also assume you're...whatever that group is that's sponsoring her scholarship?"

"DIG."

"Yes, that was it."

He shook his head. "It's actually the company owned by Syn and his wife. They do all kinds of charitable deeds under it."

Now she was confused. "So are they the ones funding her?"

"No, they just loaned their company name to me so that I could do it without her knowing."

She would never fully understand him. But then he'd always been a contradiction. "Why did you do that?"

"I was afraid if she knew a Cruel or the Sentella was financing her degree, she'd refuse to take the money."

Sorche would have. Zarya had raised her better than to take charity from anyone. "I still don't understand why you would do something so kind for her when you hate me."

He shrugged. "No one should work that hard and not be able to go because of something as trivial as money. I know how much it meant to her and I wanted her to have it. She deserves it after all she's done to get in."

"You've made her very happy. Thank you." Zarya laid her head on his thigh as she watched him. He was such a contradiction. He hated her, but he protected her. He'd sold her, and yet paid for her sister to have her dream.

Nothing about him made sense.

He could be so frustrating.

But as they lay in the silence, one thing became clear to her. He wasn't his uncle. She'd spent her entire life trying to bring down his family, but the real villain was dead.

Darling would be as good for their empire as his father had been.

Better if the truth was known.

As Maris had said, above all, Darling was always fair. He hadn't punished Sorche for Zarya's actions. He hadn't even lashed out at Zarya herself. Not really.

And as a member of the Sentella, he'd been a hero for the working class even though he'd been born to one of the oldest and richest families in existence.

But how could she convince people like Senna and Clarion that he was a different man? Most people hated without cause. Without reason. It was irrational jealousy, and if she knew anything about people like that, it was that they couldn't be reasoned with.

Their hatred was blind, and all consuming.

Even if Darling did something good, they would twist it to make it seem evil or wrong or self-serving.

Words wouldn't convince them. Only actions would. And she'd have to move fast to keep the Resistance from building up again and coming after him, night and day. Since she wasn't there to lead it, she didn't know who was left. But someone would come forward. They always did. And Senna had told her that she was documenting Darling's "crimes." Which meant the Resistance was still there. Still plotting the downfall of the House of Cruel.

Fear for Darling consumed her. How could she protect him from his own people?

And that irony wasn't lost on her. Here she was, the former leader of the Resistance that had done its best to destroy the Cruel line and all its members, and all she wanted to do was ensure *his* safety. That he had a long reign.

Her father was most likely rolling in his grave.

But as she traced Darling's scars, she made a silent vow. No one would ever again hurt him on her watch. Even if he never loved her again, she would die to protect him.

And as that thought finished, a bad feeling came over her. It was just like the one she'd gotten right before her father had died. The one she'd had that last night she'd spent with Kere.

Something evil was coming for them, and it was going to be out for their blood.

11

Four days later

Her thoughts drifting, Zarya idly brushed her hand through the tangles of Darling's auburn hair. Not long after daybreak, he'd finally fallen asleep with his body between her legs and his head on her stomach. She was exhausted too, but she'd promised him that she wouldn't sleep while he did.

He was so paranoid about attacks...

Not that she blamed him given his family and personal history—what she'd learned from Maris during a small break yesterday was that Arturo would often have someone storm into Darling's room at odd hours of the night or early morning to make sure he was alone in his bed. Sometimes they'd allow him to go back to sleep, and others...

They'd cuff his hands behind his back and drag him out of his room for his uncle to beat while in the throes of a drunken rage. Arturo had taken issue with not only Darling's confessed homosexuality, but also because he looked, moved, and sounded like his father, whom Arturo had always hated. And then there was the small matter that both Darling and his younger brother were a constant reminder that Drux had been able to father sons while Arturo had only daughters.

Something Arturo took out on those daughters as well as his wife—as if it were somehow their fault and not his.

To protect them, Darling had done his best to keep his uncle's anger directed at him as much as possible. He'd go out of his way to provoke his uncle so that his cousins would be left alone. And true to his nature Darling had considered it a moral imperative to make the man spin out of control as often as possible. He'd admitted to her that he'd been hoping to cause Arturo to have a stroke from the stress of dealing with him.

Only Darling would think of that...

But his incendiary actions had kept Arturo in a perpetual state of fury where Darling was concerned. And Arturo had made it his life's ambition to take everything out on the nephew who didn't dare physically retaliate for fear of what would happen to his family if he did.

Because of that, Darling didn't like to sleep at all. And it was why he'd been wearing explosives on her arrival. Before Maris had brought her here, Darling had walked the palace halls, wrapped in them, refusing to rest until utter exhaustion forced him to it. Since his own guards had been the ones who'd thrown him to his uncle, and had done their own share of abuse to him over the years, he didn't trust them to protect him now that he was governor.

It disgusted her whenever she thought about it, and the one thing she truly didn't understand was why Darling had ever fought *for* the Resistance. Yes, his uncle was a bastard who needed to be put down, but Darling had been attacked even more viciously by the working class such as his guards who resented his royal blood, and who enjoyed having power over an aristo. She really couldn't understand why he'd want to help them. If any aristo had ever possessed a reason to absolutely hate the pleb class, it was Darling.

Yet he didn't.

"Some people need a reason to hate in order to live. It's easy to despise someone you think has it better than you. Or who has more than you, especially when you think they don't deserve it and you do. But at the end of the day, life sucks for us all. You do what you have to to get through it.

"Personally, I'd rather they hate me for who I am, rather than for the lies spewed by others. But either way, I can't change their opinions. And I refuse to be like them and to hate them for something they can't help any more than I can help being born a prince.

"The hatred has to stop somewhere. I'm not going to let resentment for someone else, especially someone I don't know who has never harmed me, ruin what little time I have in this existence. I'd much rather focus on trying to be happy, than looking for a reason to be miserable."

Darling's words haunted her. He really did have a beautiful soul even as battered as it was.

But he couldn't change the world alone and she knew it as well as he did. Still, it didn't stop him from trying, and that was what made him so special.

While he would risk his own life to save a complete stranger, Darling trusted very few.

Yet even with their less than perfect past, he trusted her to watch over him while he slept. Something Maris had assured her was nothing short of a miracle.

That being said, she was positively starving this morning. She'd call for food, but since she didn't want to disturb Darling while he slept so soundly, here she lay, her stomach grumbling so loud, she was surprised it didn't wake him.

It was okay though. She really didn't mind. Hunger had been a part of her life for as long as she could remember. It was why she forgot to eat and why Darling nagged her about it. There wasn't a lot of money to be made as a Resistance fighter and since her father had been an outlaw, he'd been relegated to menial jobs that didn't require a background check or any form of government reporting. Unfortunately, those jobs didn't pay enough for a family of five.

Anytime they'd start to piece together savings, either someone got terribly sick or they died and wiped out whatever they'd managed to put away, and then some.

And since she'd been forced to leave school before graduation, she'd been relegated to the same kinds of jobs as her father. It was why she'd been so adamant that Sorche stay in school and finish. She didn't want her baby sister living a life this hard.

At times, she was bitter about it. Before Arturo had turned on her father, they'd been extremely wealthy. And it was why she'd wanted Arturo's head so badly. Vengeance was an ugly thing and she'd wanted to ram her family crest down the bastard's throat.

Now that he was gone, she didn't know what would become of her. While Darling had been kind over the last few days, she hated being dependent on him. It wasn't in her nature to rely on anyone for anything. And Darling had already thrown her away twice. What would keep him from selling her off the next time she did something that displeased him?

Yeah, that stuck in her craw. No longer his fiancée, no longer the leader of the Resistance, she wasn't sure what her current role was.

Part of her still wanted to run away and start over. But her heart wouldn't let her leave Darling while he was like this. Other than Maris, he had no one in this world who seemed to care about him. No one to watch his back.

No one to hold him while he slept, and unless he was wrapped around her or on her like now, he woke up all throughout the night in a panic and cold sweat, his eyes feral and his breathing ragged as he looked around for an attacker. But as soon as he saw her in his bed, he'd calm down and relax again. So how could she abandon him to his pain?

He never told her what those dreams were about. He didn't need to. In his sleep, he mumbled the names of those who'd hurt him the worst. Arturo's was the most common. But Ryn, Clarion, Pip, and Timmon were there, too. Along with other names she didn't recognize.

And if any of them were still alive, she hoped she never met them. If she did, she'd kill them without hesitation. Whatever they'd done to him had been horrific enough to torture him even when they were in a place where they could no longer reach him.

Her heart aching for the anguish that robbed him of something as simple as peaceful sleep, she played with his hair while his breath and beard tickled her skin.

His link buzzed on the nightstand. Frowning, she started to ignore it until she saw it was Maris. He never bothered them unless it was something important.

"Darling?"

"Mmmm." With his eyes still closed, he nuzzled against her thigh.

"Maris is calling. You want to take it?"

He scratched at his ear, then sighed before he seemed to go back to sleep.

She smiled. "Are you awake, baby?"

"No," he groused. "I don't want to get up. I like it here."

Tsking at him, she reached past the computer pad he'd been using to work in bed during the past few days, and leaned over to grab the link. She placed it in his hand and tried not to think about the eyeglasses that she'd almost knocked off the nightstand in the process.

Yet another injury her men had caused him.

Their torture had given him spontaneous nystagmus, which

caused his eyes to jerk unexpectedly for no reason, leaving him blind until they stopped and focused again. And he was partially blind in his left eye and near-sighted in his right, something that seriously compromised his depth perception and aim.

In a fight, either condition could prove fatal.

Together, they were a bonus round of vulnerability for any enemy or assassin to exploit. God help him if anyone ever found out. It was why his doctor had refused to document those conditions.

But Darling had trusted *her* with the secret that could kill him.

She winced as the thought of his ongoing physical pain hit her anew. He would never again be the warrior he once was. While his skills were still better than most, he was now at a massive disadvantage in a fight. And because of the nystagmus and structural damage her men had wrought, he couldn't wear contacts or have surgery to correct his vision.

He clicked the link on, then placed it against his ear. "Mmmm...Maris? Yeah...no, I'm not awake." He lifted his head to squint at the clock. "What day is it?"

She laughed at his shocked expression after Maris must have answered.

"Yeah, okay. I need a quick shower. Give me fifteen minutes, then bring them up." He clicked the link off.

"Who's here?"

Yawning, he set the link back on the nightstand before he slid his eyeglasses into the drawer where he kept them. "My doctor."

That news surprised her. She glanced at the makeshift bandage on his left hand from the night before—an injury she was sure needed stitches, but he'd adamantly refused to call a medic. "I thought you hated them."

"Not *all* of them." He nudged her thighs farther apart so that he could finger her.

Zarya sucked her breath in sharply as he found the place and the rhythm that never failed to go straight to the core of her pleasure zone. "What are you doing, sweetie?"

"Having breakfast."

She groaned as he started tonguing her. Her body erupted with fire, but she had to stay focused. "What about your shower?"

He made her crazy with lust as he licked and teased her until she couldn't think straight. "You really want me to stop now?"

When she didn't answer, he laughed. "Didn't think so."

Smiling, Maris greeted Syn and Hauk in the palace foyer and excused the butler who seemed more than relieved to flee their fierce presence. Something highly entertaining since, for once, they were dressed like decent citizens and not the infamous outlaws who were wanted dead by most governments.

Still, their collective ferocity was hard to disguise no matter their wardrobe choices.

Syn had even gone so far as to not line his black eyes or wear his earrings. Rather he had his long dark hair pulled back into a proper queue and was dressed all in white, which made his tawny complexion a deeper shade of olive.

Even though Syn had been raised alternately in prison and on the streets, and was the son of one of the most notorious serial killers in history, he held an air of poised refinement that would rival any aristo. An upper-crust demeanor Syn had refined after Nykyrian had helped him get off the streets and financed him through med school.

A renowned tech thief and trained assassin, that man was truly one of the most intelligent creatures Maris had ever met. And the only clue Syn gave this afternoon to his real lethal nature was the small lump at his hip, underneath his jacket, that betrayed a concealed blaster.

All of that combined to make Syn one of the most lickably delectable men in the universe.

Too bad he was straight...

Hauk was no exception to the lickable list himself. Indeed, he tied all the Sentella men for the number one slot.

Unlike Maris and Syn, Hauk was an Andarion—a lethal humanoid warrior race that valued physical perfection above all things. As a result, they were truly bred for size, speed, stamina, and beauty.

It was also rumored that their warrior spirit, that-live-for-now-and-damn-tomorrow attitude, made them some of the best lovers in the universe. But unfortunately for the other species in existence, they very seldom slept with non-Andarions.

Such a fetid shame...

Not that that was Maris's only roadblock to having a taste of Hauk...

There were far too many men who played on the other team for Maris's tastes.

Like the Sentella leader Nykyrian, who was half Andarion and half human, Hauk was as beautiful as a woman. But the rugged cut of his jaw, and that overwhelming aura of feral testosterone kept him from appearing even the least bit feminine.

He absolutely oozed raw, sexy masculinity.

Standing almost seven feet in height with a body full of rippling, taut muscles, Hauk towered over both of them. And he always looked like he was ready to break someone in half. Another lickable trait if ever one existed.

The only thing that detracted from Hauk's looks was those Andarion eyes that were extremely disconcerting, if not downright off-putting. White irises rimmed in red, they never failed to send a shiver over Maris. Thankfully, Nykyrian had green human eyes. Not that he showed them often, but...

The few glimpses Maris had been lucky enough to catch had left a lasting impression.

Unlike Syn, Hauk's two blasters were strapped to his lean hips in plain sight. As if he needed *that* to look intimidating. More likely, they were there for his ease of use—the other bad thing about Andarions... they were notoriously short of temper.

Dressed all in black, Hauk stood with his weight on one leg, and his muscular arms crossed over his chest, his hands tucked under his biceps.

What was it about that pose that made men so delectable?

Maris would have purred at them, but he wasn't sure what their reactions might be. While the two of them had always been ambivalent to his sexual preferences and outrageous mannerisms, they were both hardcore heterosexuals and trained killers with vicious tempers.

Only a fool would risk their wrath.

And he wasn't feeling particularly stupid or adventurous today.

Syn arched his brow into a curious expression as he glanced around the entryway. "So where's Darling?"

Maris gestured up the stairs. "He said he needed a quick shower. Give him fifteen minutes and I'll take you up to see him."

Hauk smirked. "Well isn't he Lord Hoity-Toity all of a sudden." He waved his hand in a grand dismissive gesture at Maris and Syn. It was always so funny to watch a straight man pretend to be gay, especially one so steeped in masculinity. "You plebs need to stay downstairs with the riffraff while I leisurely prepare myself to stomach your repugnacious presence."

Syn rolled his eyes at Hauk's made-up word and affectation. "Give him a break, Hauk. You know Darling would never do that to us."

"I know, but it's fun to bust on him for it." Hauk grinned good naturedly, showing off his set of fangs in the process.

Ignoring him, Syn turned back toward Maris. "So does this mean he's sleeping finally?"

That was an interesting question...

"I don't know how much sleep he's been getting, but he hasn't left his bedroom in over four days."

Worry creased Syn's brow. "Is he all right? Has he been having trouble moving?"

Maris had to force himself to keep a solemn expression—something that really wasn't in his nature. "From what I've been hearing, day and night, I would say that's a resounding yes that he's fine and definitely able to move without any trouble whatsoever."

Now it was Hauk's turn to frown. "What do you mean?"

Okay, there was no way to keep a straight face as Maris recalled his earlier conversation with the Sentella about Darling's mental state. "I think it's safe to say that all of us were right, and *you*, my dear Hauk, were most definitely wrong about what it would take to settle Darling down and make him quasi-human again."

Hauk laughed as he caught Maris's meaning. "So you finally nailed him, huh?"

"In a manner of speaking."

Before they could say anything else, a loud throaty scream echoed from upstairs.

Hauk and Syn pulled out their weapons, ready for battle.

"Whoa"—Maris gestured at them—"down lethal killers. It's okay."

"Bullshit," Hauk growled. "Sounds like someone's being murdered."

Maris laughed. "Yes it does, and no they're not. I promise you. Not unless one can die by orgasm, and if that were the case, I think both of them would have died days ago." He put his hand on Syn's blaster and pointed it toward the floor. "But I do believe Darling's going to need a little longer than fifteen minutes before he's ready to see us. Shall we go to the reception room and wait?"

They exchanged perplexed grimaces before they finally holstered their blasters.

Maris turned around and led them deeper into the palace to the large room that was reserved for those waiting to have an audience with the governor. It was always kept stocked with a variety of beverages and snacks for unexpected visitors.

"Would either of you care for something?"

They shook their heads.

"So what exactly's going on?" Concern was thick in Syn's voice. "I'm still reeling over Darling calling me the other night. What made him change his mind so suddenly about having more surgery? Last time I broached the subject, he damn near took my head off. He told me he wasn't about to put himself through it again."

Maris poured a cup of tea for himself. He wasn't about to spoil *this* surprise.

Not for anything. He lived to see people knocked off keel by the unexpected. And he wanted to savor their reactions when they saw Zarya in Darling's room. "You'll have to ask him. As I said, I haven't seen him in days now."

Hauk let out a low, sympathetic breath. "Man, given how tight the two of you have always been, I thought you'd be the one to screw him blind."

"Yeah," Syn agreed. "You two always seemed to have a lot of chemistry together."

How he wished. But that was all right. He was happy Darling had someone he desired to the degree he did Zarya. If he couldn't have Darling's heart himself, he wanted it to belong to someone who would appreciate it, and who would treat Darling the way Maris would treat him if he'd been lucky enough to have him.

Maris sipped his tea. "What can I say? I found him someone much more suited to his particular tastes."

Syn appeared impressed by his words. "That was extremely generous of you, Mari. I don't think I could hook up the love of my life with someone else."

Those words stung, but Maris didn't let it show. If Syn only knew how much he really did love Darling.

But if wishes were cake, no one would starve.

And Maris had never made the mistake of thinking he could change Darling. Nor did he want to. He loved Darling just as he was.

Syn patted him sympathetically on the back. "This new guy must be special indeed for you to be so altruistic. I can't wait to meet him."

Maris smiled mischievously. "I can't wait to introduce you."

Knocking on Darling's bedroom door, Maris stood back so that he could watch Syn's and Hauk's expressions.

As he expected, Zarya opened the door. Her cheeks flushed bright, she was still breathing heavily. Dressed in one of Darling's black shirts that fell all the way to her knees, she was stunning with her dark mahogany hair tousled. And from the depth of her exposed cleavage, it was obvious that she was naked beneath that shirt. "Please come in, Darling will be out in just a second."

Now there was a look Maris would have paid money for. Hauk and Syn stood completely slack jawed as their gazes went up and down her body, trying to make sense of what they saw.

Unaware of the havoc she caused, Zarya opened the door wider, then went deeper into the room to pick up some of the mess the two of them had made.

Laughing at their continued shock, Maris reached up and closed Hauk's mouth.

Hauk blinked twice. "Is that...?"

"...a he or she?" Syn finished for him.

"She," Maris said with a wicked grin. "Definitely a she." He headed inside and arched a brow at what he found there.

Oh yeah, this was...

Pretty much what he'd assumed from all the things he'd heard coming out of this room for the last few days. But still, it was impressive. The room was a disaster from the unmade bed to the paintings on the walls that had been knocked askew...if not completely off the wall, to the stacks of pillows all over the place.

No wonder the housekeeping staff had been complaining.

Over the last four days, Maris had visited with Zarya several times while Darling attended business. But he'd only been in her room. This was the first time he'd ventured into Darling's. And while he'd spent time with Zarya, Darling's duties and strange hours had conspired to keep them from seeing each other.

Zarya returned some of the pillows to the bed, then paused to frown up at Hauk's giant size. "Are you the doctor's bodyguard?"

His brow still furrowed, Hauk ran his thumb along his jaw as his lips quirked with amusement. "Yeah...no. Pretty sure he can handle himself. Most days anyway."

Syn snorted at him as he stepped forward to offer her his hand. "I'm Dr. Syn Dagan-Wade."

"Dagan as in the Dagan Group?"

That too appeared to take him by surprise. "You've heard of us?"

Zarya smiled happily as she realized exactly who these men were. So, Darling's friend was also his doctor...interesting. It also explained why he was finally willing to see a doctor, and why he'd chosen DIG as his shadow company.

"I have indeed. Thank you so much for allowing Darling to

finance my sister's education through your company. I can't tell you how much that means to us."

Syn looked as confused as she felt. "Sorche's your sister?"

She paused, unsure if it was a good thing or bad that he knew Sorche's name so quickly. "She is."

He instantly relaxed. "Well, I'm glad we can help. I owe my education to someone who did a similar act for me, and I'm more than happy to pay that forward. I always say that nothing will improve your life quicker than a good education."

"And nothing can destroy it faster than one bad decision," the Andarion said drily.

Syn rolled his eyes at him. "You're such a pessimist."

"I'm practical. It's true and you know it." The Andarion offered his hand to her. "I'm Hauk, by the way."

Now that was a name she knew well from some of Darling's stories.

She shook his hand. "Ah, the one who doesn't like explosives. Is it really true that you once hid in a shielded closet for eighteen hours because you thought there was a bomb in your kitchen?" A bomb that turned out to be a plastic kid's toy.

Hauk growled. "I'm going to kill that little bastard for telling you that... and it didn't look plastic."

Syn broke out into a round of evil laughter. "My favorite part was when Darling threw it at him and he screamed like a woman. Hell, I had no idea you could jump that high, Hauk. You should have played sports, buddy."

Hauk narrowed a dangerous glower at the much shorter man. "Shut the fuck up, Syn, before Darling has to find a new doctor. Be a shame for you to lose that head of yours."

"Ah now, you know you're not going to hurt me. Another bomb might run your fat ass up a tree and who would help you then?"

Hauk cut a feral grimace toward Maris. "You'd help a brother out, wouldn't you, Mari?"

"Not with a bomb. Sorry. I was raised with Darling. I know how volatile they are. Kind of like Nyk on a bad day."

"Darling's not still sleeping in one, is he?" Syn asked her.

Zarya gaped. "He wasn't really sleeping in it, too, was he?"

Maris shrugged. "What can I say? When Darling makes a binkie, he doesn't joke around with it." He glanced over to the men. "Fortunately, she was able to get him out of the bomb."

"I'd say she got him out of a lot more than that," Hauk said under his breath as he looked around the room, and more pointedly at the clothes strewn about the floor, then trained those spooky eyes on her.

Maris laughed.

"What about the dirty bombs?" Syn asked.

Sobering a degree, Maris folded his hands in front of him. "I'm going to hazard a guess that he's deactivated them since he's been rather…"—he cut a meaningful glance toward Zarya—"preoccupied lately and we haven't died yet. I'm rather sure he's found something he'd rather tinker with than bomb timers."

Dying to distract them from this entire line of thought, Zarya faced Syn. "I wanted to mention that Darling cut his hand rather badly last night, and I think he might have bruised a couple of ribs. He wouldn't let me call the medics to check him out. I field dressed his hand as best I could, but it was still bleeding a little this morning and I don't want it to get infected. Would you mind taking a look at it?"

"Sure. How did he…uh, hurt it?"

Her face turned even redder as she rubbed the back of her neck nervously. So much for getting them away from this line of thought… "He fell in the shower."

Hauk let out a low, evil laugh. "How'd he fall in the shower?" he asked playfully.

She couldn't meet any of their gazes as she remembered the extremely intimate moment that hadn't ended well for either of them. "He accidentally slipped."

It was Syn's turn to laugh at her until he paused next to a bloody hand towel that Darling had tossed at the door leading to her room last night. His humor died instantly as he bent over to pick up and examine the saturated cloth. "How bad was he hurt?"

Fury darkened her brow, but it wasn't at them. Her anger was reserved for the members of her team. "*That's* from a nosebleed."

Syn cursed. "Are they getting worse?"

"It's hard to say," she answered honestly. "Sometimes it's just a little blood for a few minutes, and others…" She gestured toward the towel in his hand. "That one was severe."

"Any idea what triggered it?"

"No. They're random. That one started right after he'd dozed off."

Syn dropped the towel in the trash. "What about pain? Does his head hurt with them?"

"Sometimes. But it's not too bad, so I'm not sure if it's from the nosebleeds or…" She caught herself before she mentioned his eyesight. Syn obviously knew about it, but she wasn't sure if Hauk knew. "Something else."

Syn nodded. "Anything else I should know about?"

Zarya hesitated as she remembered the nasty incident Darling had the day before. "I probably shouldn't say anything, but I don't know if he will, and it is something that concerns me."

"What?"

She bit her lip as she glanced to Hauk.

Hauk winked at her. "You can speak freely, little sister. Don't worry. I'm well aware of his current injuries and limitations. He's been my wingman for a long time, and when you put your life into the hands of others, you don't keep secrets. We know everything about each other."

Not entirely true. Darling had never told them he was heterosexual, but she didn't want to remind them of that.

She glanced back at Syn. "He has a lot of pain in the bathroom. He won't let me check on him and he keeps the door locked whenever he goes. But I know it's bad. It takes him a long time, and when he comes out, he's always shaking and pale. Usually clammy, too. And very weak. It takes him at least half an hour before he's moving freely again."

Sadness darkened Syn's eyes. "That unfortunately isn't going to change. They messed him up really good internally. We're damn lucky to still have him with us." He swept his gaze around the tattered room, then flashed a wicked, lopsided grin at her. "But at least the front plumbing seems to be in excellent working condition. I'm sure that's a relief to him."

Those words mortified her. She wanted to crawl under something and hide.

Fortunately, Darling finally came out of the bathroom, wearing nothing but a towel around his lean hips. He rubbed a second one against his damp hair. "I see you two met Zarya. Did they introduce themselves to you, love?"

"They did, indeed." She looked up at Darling as he paused by her side. "I'll leave you alone to talk in private. Do you want me to order you something to eat?"

His eyes glowing with warmth, Darling gave her an evil grin that rivaled Syn's. "I had my breakfast already." Wrapping one possessive arm around her, he leaned down and gave her a kiss that instantly set her on fire.

Maris cleared his throat. "Should we come back at a later time?"

Ignoring the question, Darling pulled away and met Maris's

arched brow. "Sweetie, will you please make sure she gets something to eat for me? I know her stomach was growling earlier."

"Absolutely. We'll be next door if you need us." When Maris went to pick her up to carry her, she stopped him.

"My ankle's better. I'm not even wrapping it now."

He looked to Darling for a confirmation.

"You can argue with her if you want. I always lose. Maybe you'll have better luck. I'm pretty sure she likes you better anyway."

Maris laughed, then offered her his arm. "Come, my lady. Let's go gossip."

Darling waited until Maris had closed the door to Zarya's room before he faced his friends. He draped his towel over his shoulder.

Hauk kept opening and closing his mouth like a fish out of water. "I am so confused. *That* was a woman, right?"

"Yes."

Syn scratched at his ear. "The same woman who was in the room with you when we rescued you? The leader of the Resistance that tortured the hell out of you? And you're paying for her sister to be educated?"

"Again, yes, yes, and yes."

Hauk turned around slowly, looking at the mess in the room. "But... you're gay."

Darling snorted. "Apparently, I'm not."

"Since when?" Syn asked.

"Birth."

Grimacing, Hauk pressed his hand against his temple as if trying to make sense out of it all was giving him a vicious headache. "You are totally screwing with my head, and you're doing it on purpose, aren't you?"

"No," Darling said, sobering. "It's really a long story, and I don't feel like getting into it right now." He had something much more important to think about.

He faced Syn. "What I want to know is if you can fix this," he gestured at his face. "And how long will it take to make me look human again?"

Syn let out a slow breath. "You want the bad news or the worse news?"

12

Finishing up her breakfast, Zarya kept glancing back at Maris who watched her closely as if she was some kind of experiment that had gone horribly awry. Dressed in an elegant gold jacquard jacket, he stood with one foot toward the door, ready to bolt for some reason. "What's wrong?"

He widened his eyes innocently. "Not a thing."

Yeah, right. She wasn't about to believe that given his strange behavior. Quirking a brow at him, she placed her napkin next to her plate. "Then what's with that look?"

Blinking with feigned innocence, he postured behind the padded chair next to hers. "What look?"

She waited until he did it again. "*That* one."

He visibly cringed, then made an exaggerated twist of his hand. "Uh...well...I'm trying to think of a way to broach an uncomfortable topic with you."

She would much rather have the truth, plain and simple. "Just spit it out, Mari. I can't stand games. Whatever it is, I assure you, I can handle it."

He chewed his bottom lip. Something that made her even more trepidatious. How bad could it be?

"You sure you're ready for this?" he asked hesitantly.

Not really, but... "Absolutely. Hit me."

"All right then." He spoke in a tone that made the knot in her stomach tighten even more. He pulled the chair out from the table and finally sat down. Still, he hesitated as he toyed with a bit of lace that fell from his gold sleeve. "I'm sure you're aware of the fact that when you're having sex you're a screamer, right?"

Now it was her turn to cringe as a nasty suspicion went through her.

Please, please let me be wrong...

"You heard us?" she whispered in horror.

"Oh honey..." He placed his hand over hers comfortingly. "With the acoustics in this place...*every*one has heard you. Even Syn and Hauk. That's how I knew to wait almost an hour before I brought them up."

She felt suddenly ill over that news. "What?"

Patting her hand, he nodded. "Three quarters of the staff is convinced he's torturing you up here. None are willing to believe any man can have that kind of stamina or that any woman can have that many orgasms in a week, never mind a single day."

She wanted to crawl into a hole and die over that. "Why didn't you tell me this earlier?"

"Didn't want to embarrass you. As you saw, I had to force myself to bring it up even now. I knew you'd feel awful about it." He screwed his face up sympathetically. "But look on the bright side. I'm both jealous and impressed with Darling's skills. I had no idea he had all that in him. Girl, you are so lucky. Trust me, for I have a lot of experience in this area, most men cannot do what he does to you for as long as he does it. If we could figure out what he's eating or doing to cause that, we'd be even richer."

Mortified to the core of her soul, she leaned forward on the table and covered her face with her hands. "I am so humiliated."

"Don't be. We should all be so *lucky*."

"Could you please stop using that word?" Lucky kept ramming home how much she'd been screaming the last few days.

She was even hoarse from it.

Maris laughed. "Sorry, sweetie. Couldn't resist. So, now that it's just the two of us, how did Darling cut his hand last night?" He wagged his brows wickedly at her.

Of course, he'd ask her *that*. Could this day get any more mortifying?

But for some reason, she really didn't mind talking to Maris about such intimate things. Somehow, he made the most embarrassing moment funny. "You know the tawdry murals in my bathroom?"

"Yes."

"Some of those positions should come with warning labels."

Maris laughed. "I would have paid to see that."

"And I feel terrible about it," she said, covering her plate with the silver dome, and pushing it aside. "I'm the one who slipped first. Darling got hurt because I'm a klutz."

"Well, from where I was standing in there, he didn't seem to mind."

"That's because he's insane."

"He is indeed." Maris shooed her from her seat. "You go on and get your bath. I'll take care of this for you."

"Thank you, Mari."

He squeezed her hand before she got up and made her way into the bathroom. Thank goodness someone had cleaned up the mess from last night's "accident." Aside from the broken glass, there had been blood everywhere—even on the walls.

Between cutting his hand and three nosebleeds, it was a miracle he hadn't bled out.

But that wasn't the most disconcerting part.

Gah, someone…a complete stranger…had come in here last night and seen what all we'd done…

And they'd most likely heard us in Darling's room while they cleaned in here. Zarya covered her face with her hands as she realized what an insatiable slut she must look like to everyone. Never in her life had she been more horrified.

Well, you are legally his sex slave…

His very public mistress as the collar on her neck attested to. Still, that didn't make her feel any better. In fact, it stung what little dignity she had left.

Why was it whenever Darling was around, all she could think about was touching him? Having him inside her? Of course, it didn't help that whenever he was around her, he was a complete and utter horndog.

An exceptionally *skilled* horndog who knew how to set her on fire with nothing more than a quirk of his lips and a hot look that scorched her all the way through.

Even so, she'd had a life before this. Granted it was one focused on destroying his family, but she had been a well-respected military leader.

Now…

I'm a nobleman's plaything.

No, not just a nobleman.

Darling's. If it were anyone else, she wouldn't stomach it.

But the very thought of him wrung her heart. His life had been so unnecessarily tragic and it shouldn't have been like that for him. Any more than she should have had the tragedies that marked her past—the loss of her sisters, brother, and parents.

She couldn't even think of them without wanting blood. Especially Gerrit. While they had fought every day of their lives together, he'd died protecting her from their enemies. She winced at the involuntary image of him expelling his last breath before he went limp in her arms while she begged him not to die on her.

Or the look on her father's face when she'd told him how Geritt died…

A part of her had always wondered if he hadn't wished it'd been she who'd died that day.

To this day, the guilt of surviving an attack that had killed her brother haunted her unmercifully.

Yeah, life sucks for us all.

The tragedy of her own past was what allowed her to understand Darling so well. And it was what made her recognize the saddest truth of all—those events, as horrific as they were, were what had forged the man she loved. Without them, he'd be like the rest of the spoiled aristocracy she and the Resistance had been trying to overthrow. Obnoxious. Selfish.

Revolting.

Instead, he was a man worth dying for.

Pulling his shirt over her head, she paused as she caught his scent on her skin. It sent a rush through her body. There was nothing she loved more than that warm, masculine scent.

All he had to do was look at her and she was his.

Strange how she seldom saw his scars now. It was only when he slept in her arms that they were apparent to her. While he was awake, she was more focused on his eyes and quirky expressions and personality. So much so, that she barely noticed his physical appearance.

She turned the water on and regulated it. A smile curved her lips as she remembered Darling pinning her to the wall last night while the water poured over them.

Maris was right. He did have more stamina than anyone she'd ever heard of. Even after he'd fallen and bled all over this shower, he'd been unwilling to stop long enough to bandage his hand. Instead, he'd laughed about it and told her not to fret.

"I can't feel pain and pleasure at the same time. So I'd rather focus on the latter and deal with the former when I have to."

The man was nuts.

Trying not to think about Darling's lunacy, she stepped inside to bathe.

Zarya lost track of time while she savored the warmth of the water, and washed her hair. She was just about to finish when the door opened behind her.

Ready to fight, she turned to confront her intruder.

Darling stood there, ogling her.

"Oh gods..."—she covered her heart with her hand—"you scared me. You need to make some noise when you move."

"Sorry." He leaned down to kiss her bare shoulder.

"So what did the doctor say?" she asked him.

Darling straightened, his features deadly earnest. "I'm going in for surgery day after tomorrow."

Her heart clenched at those words and the fear they gave her. Why would he choose to do it so soon? "Are you sure you want to do this?"

"Yes."

Worry ran rampant through her. Maris had told her that Darling didn't do well under anesthesia. His body barely tolerated it.

"Are you doing this for you or for me? Because you know I don't care about it at all. I think you're wonderful just like you are."

His features stern, he pulled the washcloth from the bar, then turned her around so that he could wash her back. She didn't know why he liked doing that, but it always felt really good.

He made small circles over her back, then trailed the cloth down her spine. "It's not for you, Z. I mean...some of it is. I hate that this is what you have to look at when you hold me. I know how awful I appear and I applaud you for not cringing every time you see me. But honestly, *I* can't take it anymore. I can't stand to look at myself. Every time I catch my reflection against anything, I get severely sucker-punched over what I see there."

Darling swallowed. "Believe me, I know removing the scars won't fix the rest. I know they're superficial. My voice and vision will still be screwed up. And the memories will always be there, stabbing me." He flinched as if one of them hit him just from mentioning it. "But the scars bring it home and kick it down my throat. I'm ready to move forward, and I can't do that when all I see is a victim every time I look in the mirror."

She wanted to tell him he wasn't a victim. That he'd never been a victim, but that wasn't true and she knew it. The worst tragedy of all was when someone this strong, this capable, was held down and unable to protect himself while others abused and violated him. Like her with this damnable collar on. To know that you were fully capable of protecting yourself and to be unable to do so...

That was its own special kind of hell and it did untold damage to the psyche.

In her mind, she saw the photos Maris had shown her from Darling's medical report.

Saw the way Darling had looked hanging in front of her that day when she'd thought he'd killed Kere. What had been done to him disgusted her. And she was an outsider to it. He'd been the one who had to endure the true, unvarnished degradation and horror of his torture.

The one who couldn't even sleep for it.

All she wanted was to heal him.

His breathing ragged from the pain of those memories, he returned the cloth to her hand. He glared at her throat with so much animosity and fury that it actually scared her. She wanted to say something to soothe him, but fear froze her vocal cords.

This wasn't the man who made love to her for hours on end.

This was the feral warrior, Kere, and by the look on his face, it was obvious he wanted blood.

Her blood.

With a twist to his lips that was truly terrifying, he reached for her throat.

He's going to kill you...

Just as she started to punch him to protect herself, he broke her slave's collar in half. Her jaw went slack as he stepped away and angrily tore the collar into pieces, then tossed it into the trash can next to the tub.

"What are you doing?" she asked, confused by his actions.

Those blue eyes scorched her with his repressed insanity. "I spent too many years imprisoned here. I refuse to do that to someone else, especially you. I don't want you to stay with me because you have no choice. I want you here because you want to be with me." A tic worked furiously in his jaw. "I told Gera not to prep you anymore unless you requested it."

His gaze dropped to her breast before his features softened to the teasing countenance she'd come to cherish most. "Although I did like the flavored body paint."

She smiled at him. "As long as you're the one who applies it and not some strange woman I've never met before, I have no objection to using it."

He gave her a lopsided grin. "Gera's having your clothes sent up, and she assured me that you would have things appropriate for public wear. You're free to come and go as you please. Your apartment's just as you left it. I've been paying the bills for it, and they're all up to date. But I did have the door rekeyed for you as a safety precaution since I didn't know who might have access to it. I left the new keys and a link for you on the table by your bed. The link's yours to keep. I went ahead and programmed my number so that you can call if you get locked in here again, and I set Sorche's as your first contact and Ture's as your second."

She didn't miss the fact that he hadn't set himself in as a contact. Was that a presumption that she didn't want him there or did he not want to be listed?

"Lastly, there's a transport in the hangar for you to use as you wish. It's in your name, so don't be afraid that someone will report it stolen if you take it. Or you can use a public transport. Your cards are with the keys and link if you need money."

Unsure of his mood and the source of his sudden charity toward her, she stepped out of the shower and turned the water off. She reached for a towel, then wrapped it around her body. She moved to stand in front of him.

Zarya bit her lip in uncertainty. "Are we good?"

Darling ran the back of his hand along her jaw. There was a haunted shadow in his gaze that concerned her. "You want the truth?"

No. Not if it was bad.

But she wasn't a coward either. "Always."

His brows furrowed as that angry insanity flashed across his features. And as quickly as it flared, it settled down into a pained expression that showed how much anguish he still carried inside him. "You are my heaven...And you will always be my eternal hell."

Those words stabbed her straight through the heart. "Darling—"

He put his finger over her lips to silence her. "When it's just the two of us and we're alone, I can forget what happened, and I'm better. Then just as I think I'm all right, it all comes barreling back and kicks me in the crotch again. I can hear you laughing out in the hallway when I needed you most. And honestly, it ravages me so deep inside that I feel like I'm going crazy from the anger and hurt. I feel so betrayed, Zarya. I know you didn't do it on purpose, I know you didn't know, but my feelings don't have ears and they don't listen to my head. No matter what I do, I can't reason it away. It just hurts and I don't know if it'll ever stop."

Those words brought tears to her eyes. God, if she could only go back and change what had happened...

Like Hauk had said...Nothing ruined a life faster than one bad decision.

Darling swallowed. "I would give everything I have, even my soul, to let it go. I would. But no matter how hard I try, Zarya, it just keeps coming. And it lights a fury so deep inside me that all I can think about is hurting you in retaliation. It's so demanding that it scares me. And it takes everything I have to stop from lashing out at you. I can't keep those feelings or memories from returning. But I am trying to. I am."

Those words made her heart ache. For all of his confessed rage, he'd kept it bottled inside to the point that she'd never suspected he had any inclination except to be kind to her.

It said a lot about him that he hadn't once said or done anything mean.

He stroked her cheek with his thumb. "What about you? Do you still hate me?"

She shook her head. "I never really hated you, Darling. I was hurt by your rejection. Bitterly. But what I went through was nothing compared to you."

"Are you sure?" His tone was strained and searching. "I get sick every time I think about the fact that I caused you to be thrown to a slaver. And when I consider all the things that probably happened to you there..." He clenched his teeth so violently that it made the muscles in his jaw protrude. "You've no idea how much I hate myself for it. How much it worries me that I abandoned you when I had no right to do that. I swear to the gods that I didn't want you harmed. I didn't. It was a stupid, selfish thing I did and I'm so sorry."

Her throat tightened as she heard the agony inside him. He'd had every right to strike out after what she'd done to him. Slapping him when he'd been tied up had been wrong on so many levels. "Baby, don't take that onto your shoulders. You've been tortured enough. I wasn't physically hurt at all."

He narrowed his gaze at her. "Are you lying to me?"

She covered his hand with hers and held it tight. "No. I swear. No one touched me the entire time. I was too old for the slaver's tastes. And he thought I was too skinny to get top credit so he didn't want me to do anything or for anyone to bother me. He kept me isolated in a less-than-pleasant room, but I was alone there and it wasn't so bad. Boring, but not bad. It's why I was still there when Maris came to find me. The slaver was trying to fatten me before the auction."

Darling saw the truth in her eyes. Relief poured through him. He'd mentally flogged himself with the fear of someone raping her because of his thoughtless words to Jayne. When he'd said them, he had no idea that Jayne would give her over to a slaver. At worst he'd thought jail. At best, he'd assumed Jayne would let her go. Never had the concept of slavery for Zarya entered his mind.

And even though Zarya hadn't shown any signs of having been violated, he knew from experience that the aftereffects and emotions didn't always manifest the same way. Sometimes there was shame that made you lock yourself away from the world. Other times it was anger that caused you to lash out at everyone. And sometimes it was a mixture of both, or nothing more than a cold emptiness that left the soul sick and numb for weeks on end.

Grateful that the gods hadn't punished her for his stupidity, he pressed his forehead against hers and cupped her face in his hands. "I'm so sorry I did that to you, Zarya. It was wrong and I had no right to treat anyone like that, least of all you. I was such a stupid dick for it. I was just—"

This time, she covered his lips with her fingers to keep him from speaking. "I know, sweetie. I do."

But she didn't know how much he hated himself for what he'd done. Not really. Out of nothing more than sheer selfishness, he'd put her in harm's way. Twice.

How could I have done that?

To her.

He, who knew exactly what it felt like to have someone shove him aside while they wallowed in their own grief and pain, had done that to the one person in his life he'd sworn to love and protect.

I am my mother.

Even worse, he felt like his uncle. And that was what stung the deepest.

How could she forgive him when he couldn't forgive himself?

"No, Z, you don't know. There's so much darkness inside me that sometimes I feel like it's going to swallow me whole. It makes me want to lash out, and explode all over everyone around me."

"But you don't."

"I have. And worse, I did it with you. I wouldn't have been able to live with myself had you been hurt. I swear to you I will never, ever do something like that again no matter how mad I get."

She hugged him close and he savored his body against hers. "Had I been physically assaulted, I probably wouldn't be so forgiving." She nuzzled his neck. "It was extremely humiliating to be told how worthless and undesirable I am. I'm not going to downplay it. But I've had worse."

"Yeah, well, he was a fucking idiot. I think you're more beautiful than any woman I've ever seen."

Zarya trembled as he took her hand into his and led it to his cock that was already hard again. It was so erotic to have him hold her palm against his erection while he stared down at her with a hunger that was hot and tangible. "Believe me, no one has ever done this to me like you do. Every time I look at you, hear your voice, or smell your scent, I want to be inside you so badly it hurts."

And he had definitely proven that. A lot over the last few days. It was a wonder the man could walk.

Her either.

She smiled up at him. "Thank you." Then she pulled his lips down to hers so that she could kiss him.

He growled low in his throat as he hardened even more underneath her hand. As he deepened their kiss and went to remove her towel, she stopped him.

"You haven't eaten."

"I—"

She covered his lips before he could contradict her. "You need something more to nibble on than me."

"Fine," he groused with an uncharacteristic pout. "I need to get some real work done anyway. I'm not sure how the gerents are going to deal with that e-mail I sent out last night."

"You're going to eat first, right?"

"Yes, my lady."

She smiled. "By the way, did you really fine and fire the cook?"

He actually turned sheepish over her question. "Well, yeah. I wasn't going to let her near my food out of my eyesight after I fined her. What kind of stupid would that be?"

She laughed. "You know what I mean."

"I do, and yes." He sobered. "She had no right to treat you like that. I won't have that kind of abuse in my home. If you tell me who stole your clothes, I'll—"

"It's all right," she said, interrupting him. "I don't care about something so trivial."

"I do. Stealing from others isn't trivial to me."

He was right, but given everything else, she just wanted to forget it'd happened.

"Go and eat, my lord. The sooner you take care of your business, the sooner you can come back up here and take care of me."

His eyes darkened playfully before he picked her hand up and kissed it. "Very well, my lady. I shall obey. But only because I need to make sure I still have an empire."

"You have been a little neglectful," she teased. Then she paused as another thought occurred to her. "Out of curiosity, who runs things when you're gone? Maris?"

"No, since he's an offworlder, Mari can't. My brother, Ryn, is actually the pro tem in my absence."

The half brother he'd once been close to . . .

That made the hair at the nape of her neck rise. "You trust him not to backstab you for your throne?"

"I do. He wants nothing to do with the throne, or the empire for that matter. So he officiates when he has to, and then steps down happily when I return."

That was a lot of trust for someone he'd grown distant with. "Are you sure he has no designs on replacing you?"

"I have the scar to prove it." She didn't miss the underlying bitterness in those words.

And that concerned her most of all. "What do you mean?"

"Nothing." He offered her a smile that didn't reach his shadowed eyes. "I should go. If I don't, we'll be on the floor, or the counter, or—"

She playfully pushed him away from her and laughed. "Go."

He kissed her again, then left.

Pulling on a robe, she went to her room, hoping to find some decent clothing.

She paused as she saw Maris putting her new clothes away

in the tall armoire beside her bed. "Were you here when Darling was?"

He shook his head "I left the minute he came in, and didn't return until after he was on the stairs. Voyeurism is not my sin."

She loved the way he phrased things. "Thank you, Mari. For everything."

He inclined his head to her. "Gera wanted me to tell you that she rescheduled your first lesson for four."

She cringed at the mere thought. "Great."

"If it makes you feel better, I told her I didn't think you needed any help. Obviously from what we've been hearing, we all know you're quite capable of pleasing his lordship."

"Are you going to keep torturing me with that?"

"Probably." He handed her a sedate dark green dress. "This will be lovely with your coloring."

Taking it from him, she ignored his comment as she returned to their previous conversation. "Darling said that he'd told Gera I didn't have to be prepped anymore."

"He did tell her that. She didn't listen. She said that this was one lesson you really didn't want to miss."

Zarya quirked her brow at that. "I think I'm afraid."

"I definitely would be," he whispered. "But it could be good... Maybe. And if it is as good as she says, you'll have to share with me later."

"You're terrible." She went back to the bathroom to put her dress on.

As soon as she finished, she rejoined him in the bedroom where he waited patiently. "Maris? Can I ask you something?"

"Sure, just as long as you understand I'm not obligated to answer."

She also loved Maris's disclaimers. He almost always had one for every occasion. "Darling said that he trusts Ryn to run things for him and that he knew his brother didn't want the throne. He said he had the scar to prove it. But he wouldn't elaborate. What was he talking about?"

The humor drained from his face. "Are you sure you want me to answer that? It's not very pleasant."

It seemed nothing about Darling's past was. "Yes, please."

Maris paused as if he was considering something. After a few seconds, he narrowed his eyes on her. "Come with me."

She followed him out of the room and down a long, winding hallway. Ornate and gilded, it was breathtaking. For all the brutality members of the Cruel family had committed, the palace itself showed nothing but beauty. They passed countless portraits of Darling's numerous ancestors who had ruled before him.

"Where are we going?"

Maris slowed. "The family wing." He opened a set of heavy doors that led to another ornate, marbled hallway that stretched out for what seemed to be a mile at least. Each side of it was lined with doors. "This is where the governor's wife and children stay whenever they're in residence."

So this was where Darling's room had been before he killed his uncle.

As if he heard her thoughts, Maris led her down to the next to the last set of doors on the left side of the hall. She wasn't sure what to expect as he opened the room and stood back for her to enter first.

Large and airy, it was definitely a boy's room. Decorated in maroon, dark blue and gold—the national Caronese colors—the room held a large canopy bed with a seal on the headboard that matched the seal in Darling's current chambers. There was an old computer on a huge desk that was littered with chemistry sets and spaceships.

The wall on her right was covered with intricate drawings and sketches pinned over each other. "Are those…chemical compounds and bombs?"

Maris laughed. "Darling was always a little strange. But yes, they are components to different devices and explosives he was working on."

But as she looked around more, she was nonplussed by what she saw. The room was like a time capsule. Covered in dust and obvious signs of neglect, it appeared as if Darling had been ripped out of it as a boy and never allowed to return. There were even toys left scattered across the floor.

It didn't make sense. "This was his room before Arturo died?"

Grief and sadness lined Maris's features before he spoke. "We were at school, laughing during study hall about something innocuous. Suddenly, there was a shadow falling over us. Thinking it was a teacher there to yell at us to lower our voices, we looked up to see three Caronese guards. Without any compassion or decency, their captain glared at Darling and said coldly, 'Your father's been assassinated. You must come with us.'"

Bile rose in her throat at the cruelty. How could anyone be that cold to a child when telling him his father was dead? "Are you serious?"

He nodded. "I'll never forget the look on his face when he heard those words. They didn't give him even a second to recover or pack so much as a toothbrush before he was hauled back here. He was only twelve. A scared little boy who had no idea what had happened. When he tried to see his mother, she refused."

"Why?"

"I don't know. Grief does strange things to people, and everyone copes differently. I won't pass judgment on her for it. But it devastated Darling. After the funeral, we came back here to his

SHERRILYN KENYON

room. His mother wouldn't even look at him. She retired to her chambers with Drake and Lise, and Darling wasn't allowed near them."

He jerked his chin toward the desk. "Darling sat there looking shell-shocked for hours. He didn't speak. He didn't cry. Just stared at nothing, except the floor, while I sat on the bed, waiting for him to say something. Ryn was the one who finally came to check on him. He told Darling that he couldn't stay, but that if he needed anything at all to call him."

Zarya tried to make sense of that. "Ryn abandoned him, too?"

"In his defense, there wasn't much Ryn could do. Both Arturo and Natale hated him. Natale had driven him out not long before Drux died. And at the funeral, Arturo made it abundantly clear that Ryn would never be welcomed here in any capacity. But Ryn tried to keep in touch with Darling. Three days after the funeral, Drake and Lise were allowed to return to school. Arturo withdrew Darling and kept him here."

"Why?"

"The Grand Counsel isn't a blood position. It's anyone the governor appoints. As the future governor, Darling could have chosen another."

She'd never heard that before, and it didn't make sense that Darling would live under his uncle's vicious rule if he didn't have to. "Why didn't Darling choose someone else?"

"It's not quite as simple as it sounds. First, the replacement has to agree to it and show cause as to why he would be a better counselor than the one picked by the former governor. And Darling had to be sixteen to make the declaration."

"Was that the only way?"

Maris nodded. "It was why Arturo wanted to keep Darling close by so that he could watch him. And I'm sure it's why he didn't tolerate Ryn's presence here. He knew how close Darling and Ryn were." He motioned her to follow him again. He went down the hallway, back toward the main part of the palace.

They turned a corner into a smaller corridor that was far less ornate.

Maris stopped at the first door on the right. "Three weeks after Darling turned fifteen, this became his room." He opened the door and stepped back for her to see it.

Horrified, Zarya covered her mouth with her hand at the tiny room that had no windows. It was completely empty except for a single blanket on the floor and a flat pillow.

Maris jerked his chin to the door across the hall. "That's his bathroom and dressing chamber. Every night, he had to go in there, get ready for bed and remove all of his clothes. Then naked, he'd come here so that his guards could cavity search him."

Her stomach heaved. "Why?"

"Darling kept running away from home. Arturo wanted them to make sure he didn't have anything he could use to escape or to call anyone with. Once he was searched, and they were never gentle about it, he'd be locked in here until morning."

Or until they dragged him out for his uncle's amusement.

She wanted to hurt someone over it. "How long was he kept here?"

"Till the night he killed Arturo."

"No..."

He nodded.

Her senses reeled as she thought back to the times when she'd been speaking to Kere...

Had Darling really been in this room during those times?

Was that even possible? "I don't understand. If he was kept here, like that, how did he ever have any freedom?"

"He's cunning and resilient. Plus Nyk, Ryn, and friends helped him to escape from time to time under various ruses for a few days or weeks at a stretch. And once Nyk was crowned prince, he appointed me as an ambassador so that I could watch out for Darling and use my political ties to get him out of here whenever it got too bad for him. But this was always what he was dragged back to."

Her mind boggled over all the things she'd never known about the man she loved. All the secrets he'd kept and things she would have never, ever guessed at.

All of it made her angrier at the world on his behalf.

Damn them!

She swallowed against the painful knot in her throat. "Please tell me that there was at least some brightness to his existence."

"How so?"

"His brother and sister? Did Arturo treat them like this, too?"

Maris closed the door to that awful room. "No. As long as they stayed out of his sight, he left them alone."

"Meaning?"

"Lise never pushed it. She would hit the door running to her mother's chambers and stay there until she could return to school. Drake's a little more...offensive. As he got older, he became cocky, and he had no respect for Darling back then."

"Why not?"

"Like everyone else, he bought into the rumors that Darling was a crazed degenerate who earned his punishments. Since Arturo didn't beat on him or confine him, Drake figured there had to be a reason for Arturo to beat Darling. Obviously it was all Darling's fault."

Obviously, indeed.

Zarya was beginning to really not like Darling's brother. The more she learned about Drake, the more he seemed like a selfish ass.

"I'm surprised Darling has any use for his brothers."

Maris shrugged. "Darling doesn't forgive easily and he never forgets. But at his heart, he is a peacemaker. His father used to have a saying. *The world isn't fair. And no matter how good and decent you are, no matter how much you give to others, someone is always going to hate you for no other reason than the fact that you breathe. You can't help that. You can't change people or their minds once they've allowed them to get twisted by hatred. But you can change how you deal with them. Never back down, but walk away when you can, fight when you must. Whatever you do don't give them the power to hurt you. Don't let them inside you. They're not worth it. Live your life for yourself. Stay true to yourself and if they can't see the beauty that is you, it's their loss. Let the bitterness take them to their graves. Spend your time on what matters most. Being you and appreciating the people who see you for who and what you are. The people who love you, and the ones that you love. They are all that matter. Let the rest go to hell.*"

Those words touched her. "His father sounds like he was a great man."

"He was, indeed. Very much like Darling."

But those words also made her stop and think. Most of all, they made her wonder if there could ever be a real future for them after everything that had happened to divide them. Maris had said that Darling didn't forgive easily, or forget. So where did that leave her? "Do you think he can ever forgive me, Maris?"

"Honestly, I don't know. I think he wants to. But he's been hurt so badly by so many. You're just going to have to give him time to learn to trust you again. Have faith that his love for you will erase the rest."

Something that was much easier said than done. Broken trust was the hardest thing to repair. But she wouldn't give up on Darling. She couldn't.

But what if he gives up on you?

*   *   *

Darling wiped at the sweat underneath his mask as he sat at his desk, reviewing his mail. Strange how quickly he'd gotten used to not wearing the stupid thing with Zarya. But it was easy when she didn't seem to notice his grotesque scars.

Unfortunately, he knew the rest of the world didn't view him through her eyes.

Don't think about it.

How could he not when he was forced to stare at the mask while he worked? A mask that made him remember the scars it covered. And there were so many of them. Scars that twisted his lips and made his eye droop. Scars that ran down the side of his nose and across his cheeks.

And the one of Pip's name showing through his beard as plain as the writing on his monitor.

His head throbbed from the eyestrain of trying to catch up. And then it started...

That irritating jerk.

Closing his eyes, he pressed his finger against his eyelid, trying to will them to stop. Still they spasmed and twitched. The motion made him queasy. But most of all, it made him blind.

Damn it! It was the most irritating thing and it wasn't helped by the addition of a sudden nosebleed.

Great. Just great. What next?

Just don't let me have to go to the bathroom. He couldn't take any more of his broken body. He was tired of being in pain all the time. Of having to fear the next round of What's Going To Piss Me Off Now.

As he reached for another tissue to replace the one that was already saturated, something crashed through the window on his right and exploded.

Trying to focus his jerking gaze, it took him a second to figure out what it was. Faster than he could move, fire spread up the wall, setting off alarms and sprinklers.

Crap! It was an attack and he'd left his blaster upstairs.

Darling held his breath as he tried to get to the door. Something easier said than done while his eyes kept jerking. Everything shifted and moved which disoriented him even more. Worse, his eyes and skin burned from the fumes.

In that moment, he realized what had been shot into his office. Fledon. A nasty little chemical that was lethal when inhaled.

He pushed the controls for the door.

It didn't move.

What the hell?

As part of the fire system, the doors were supposed to spring open automatically whenever the room was occupied to keep from trapping anyone inside the office.

Panic set in as he realized that someone had intentionally blocked them and reset the sensors. He reached for his link only to remember that he'd left it in the bedroom this morning. He'd been so preoccupied with setting up Zarya's link that he'd forgotten all about his own.

His eyes burning even worse, he pressed the alarm for his guards.

Why weren't they coming?

Because they want you to die...

For all he knew, one of them could have locked the doors and sent the Fledon in.

Coughing, he pulled his knife out to try and pry the doors apart.

The blade snapped in half.

His head swam as he felt the poison invading his body. Unable to fight it and his dancing eyesight, he pounded against the door, trying to call out for help. But his damaged voice wasn't loud enough to be heard over the fire.

Maris and Zarya were upstairs. They'd never make it down here in time.

I'm going to die.

And there was nothing he could do to stop it.

Look on the bright side. At least she's not outside your doors, laughing this time.

It was sad when that thought actually did comfort him.

Coughing and choking, he hit the floor a moment before everything went dark.

13

Maris finally had Zarya laughing again as he told her stories about his older brother who was a clumsy pyrotech.

They'd just reached Darling's office to make sure he'd eaten when they heard a loud crash inside. Rushing forward, Maris tried to open the door, but it refused to budge.

He pulled back with a curse. "The door's jammed."

Her heart pounded as she heard Darling on the other side, trying to get out, and she smelled smoke.

"Where's the release?" Zarya asked.

"Just tried it. It's jammed, too." Maris started coughing from the noxious smoke that filled the hallway, then his face went pale. "You smell that?"

Yes, she did.

Cursing, she looked around the hallway, trying to find something fast as she wrapped the scarf on her dress around her mouth and nose. They only had a few minutes before that poison killed Darling.

Her gaze went to the stairs.

That was it...

She ran to the huge table in the foyer where there was an

297

oversize lead vase of fresh cut flowers. Without breaking stride, she seized it, dumped the flowers and water out of it, then slammed the vase into the balustrade as hard as she could.

The iron spindle didn't budge. Shrieking in outrage, she summoned every ounce of strength she had and slammed the vase down again and again on the balustrade. *Break, damn you, break!*

Finally, the wood cracked. Yes! She dropped the vase and kicked one of the iron spindles out of the balustrade. Seizing the spindle, she ran back to the wall beside the door and used it to break open the plaster and expose the wiring beneath.

"Hold on, baby," she whispered, trying her best not to breathe the toxin in. Still it burned and hurt her throat. She could only imagine how much worse it must be on Darling who was trapped on the other side.

Maris helped her tear out the plaster. "We're not going to make it. He's probably already dead."

She refused to believe that.

They had to get to him. The alternative was unacceptable.

She jerked the wires out and started reworking them. "Don't you dare die on me, Darling Cruel!" she shouted at the top of her lungs. "I swear I'll follow you into hell to beat you if you do!"

It seemed like eternity had come and gone before the doors finally parted. Even so, they only opened an inch, then stopped. Working together, she and Maris continued to tug and push until they pulled them farther apart.

The smoke was so thick, it was hard to see. But as she started forward, her foot grazed something hard. Looking down, she saw Darling sprawled on the floor, just inside the doorway.

As she reached for him, Maris was there. He grabbed Darling by the arms and pulled him free of the room. Then he bent down and picked him up to carry him toward the reception hall.

Coughing, she ran behind them as the guards and firefighters finally came rushing toward them.

None stopped to check on their governor. Or asked about his condition.

Maris laid Darling down on one of the sofas, then pulled the mask off Darling's face. "Darling?"

His features pale, he didn't respond. Her heart stopped beating as terror filled her. *Please don't be dead. Please don't be dead…*

Maris placed his hand on Darling's carotid to feel for a pulse.

Zarya saw the agony in Maris's dark eyes as he looked up at her.

"We're too late."

Darling came awake to the bitterest taste imaginable in his mouth. It was so foul that before he could stop himself, his stomach heaved.

"Right here, sweetie."

Someone rolled him to his side and held a trash can for him while he purged his body of the toxin. It wasn't until he was finished that he realized it was Zarya who helped him.

"Leave him on his side for a minute."

Darling's vision swam to the point he couldn't see anything, but he recognized Syn's voice while someone, Zarya he hoped, stroked his hair with a gentle hand.

"It's all right, buddy," Syn said comfortingly from a short distance away. "We've got you."

Darling squeezed his eyes shut. "Where am I?"

"In your room. Can you see anything?" Syn asked.

He shook his head. "Eyes won't focus."

"That's probably not helping your nausea. Hang on."

Darling hissed as Syn gave him a shot in his hip. "Damn it, warn me before you hit the trigger!"

But at least it didn't take long for the drug to settle his stomach.

Syn gripped his shoulder. "All right, we're going to roll you back. Slowly."

As they turned him, the room spun so badly, Darling had to close his eyes to keep from being sick again. Once he was flat on his back, he let out a long breath as he tried to will his eyes to normal.

It was useless. They continued to violently shake and disorient him.

"What happened?" Darling asked.

Syn's voice was a fierce growl. "Some asshole launched a rocket full of Fledon into your office."

Darling slowly remembered the details of the attack as Zarya took his hand into hers. "I was locked in."

"Yeah," Hauk said irritably from Darling's blind side. "We know. You're lucky your girlfriend's trained. She saved your ass, boy. You owe her."

Darling tightened his hand around Zarya's. That was the one thing about her, in a fight, she was always levelheaded and resourceful. "Thank you."

She kissed him on the cheek. "Anytime, sweetie."

Darling opened his mouth to speak, then went into a horrible round of coughing.

Zarya let go of his hand as he struggled to expel all the poison out of his body. In between the coughs, he cursed at the pain it caused him. She hated seeing him like this. But she was so grateful she'd been able to resuscitate him that his coughing was music to her ears.

Syn put the oxygen mask back over his face. "Just breathe. Slow and easy."

Darling went completely limp.

As she panicked in concern for Darling, Syn held his hand up to her. "It's all right. I knocked him out again. He doesn't need to be coughing like that right now. He's likely to do more damage."

Hauk glared from his post on the opposite side of the room. "I want the balls of the cowardly bastard responsible for this."

"You?" Zarya asked, meeting his bloodlust head on. "I want them for earrings."

The Andarion smiled at her. "I really like you."

"Thanks." But her smile faded as she met Syn's grimace. "What's wrong?"

"I'm just wondering which of us is going to be the one to tell Darling that *you're* the reason he was attacked."

A pall covered Zarya all day as Syn and Hauk came and went from Darling's room while she and Maris watched over him. Syn's words hung heavy in her heart, and by the way Syn tended Darling, she could tell that Darling was in a lot worse shape than Syn was letting them know.

Please don't die. The one thing all of this had taught her was how much Darling meant to her. The thought of living without him...

How could she have forgotten how agonizing those weeks of not knowing where Kere was had been?

And now that she really knew him... his face, his past... it was so much worse. He was no longer her mythical, larger than life lover. Now he was human, and he'd carved an even deeper place into her heart.

What pained her most was the knowledge that this *was* all her fault. The Resistant members Darling had spared were trying to liberate her from his "custody." After his attack, they'd sent over a demand for her release.

I'm going to be the death of him. No matter how hard she tried to argue it, she kept coming back to that one basic fact. So long as she was with him, he was in danger.

But she couldn't stand the thought of leaving him. Especially not in the condition he was in.

Yet if she stayed, her allies—his enemies, would kill him.

"Maybe I should leave."

"Are you serious?"

Zarya hadn't realized she'd spoken out loud until Mari's question startled her. Swallowing the lump in her throat, she met his gaze on the other side of the bed. "How can I stay when I endanger him?"

Maris shot to his feet and closed the distance between them. "You can't go, Zarya. You can't. Do you not understand what it would do to him? He wasn't human until you came."

But she didn't believe that. "He was human."

Maris's face paled and when he spoke, it was in the sincerest tone she'd ever heard. "No, he wasn't. He was not the man you know." He pulled Darling's computer off the nightstand and turned it on.

After a few minutes, he handed it to her.

Scowling, she focused her attention on the video he'd pulled up. It took her a second to realize it was Darling she was looking at—something that filled her with dread. Whatever Maris intended to show her couldn't be good and she wasn't sure she wanted to see it.

Yet, she couldn't take her eyes off the screen.

Dressed in a long flowing cloak over a black battlesuit, Darling had the cowl pulled up over his head. His gold mask glowed in the dim exterior light as he headed across the back gardens, into the barracks where the royal guard took up quarters when they were on duty.

None of them bowed at his entrance. That, in and of itself, was an act of defiance and treason that was punishable by death, according to their laws. Each of those soldiers had sworn a blood oath to lay down their lives for their governor and his family.

But there was no loyalty on their faces that night. Several even spat at the ground near Darling's booted feet.

With a calmness she couldn't fathom, Darling swept his gaze around the room.

"What are you doing here?" their commander challenged Darling in a tone that would have had any aristo calling out for the pleb's arrest.

When Darling spoke, the most terrifying part was how calm and in control he appeared to be. "It's the Day of Reckoning. I'm here solely for those who have assaulted me. The rest of you can leave."

By the expression on the commander's face, it was obvious he was one of the culprits, and that he didn't see a threat in Darling's words. "We don't listen to you, *kieratun*."

Zarya sucked her breath in sharply at the insult that accused Darling of having slept with his father.

The commander lifted his chin arrogantly. "We stand together and intend to support whoever comes forward to dethrone *you*."

Darling slowly nodded his head. "Fine. Make sure you give Kere my best when you slide into hell." Faster than she could blink, Darling pulled out two League assassin short swords.

The commander drew his blaster and aimed it for Darling. Before the man could pull the trigger, Darling cut through him with an ease that was as swift as it was brutal.

Total chaos erupted as the guard corps finally realized that Darling was more than capable of delivering his justice by his own hands. And that that was what he fully intended to do.

They scrambled for weapons and the braver ones attacked him. With the same precise skillful moves she'd seen him use as Kere against the League, he tore his attackers to pieces. As they came for him, they learned what she'd known for years.

Nothing rattled Darling in battle. He *was* Kere—the god of death—and no one could stop him.

When it was finally over, Darling was wounded, but standing in the middle of several dozen bodies. With his head lowered like a feral predator, he scanned the area to make sure there were no more threats to him.

Once he assured he'd killed them all, he cleaned his swords off on his own sleeve and then returned them to the sheaths that were beneath his cloak. With the back of his hand, he wiped the blood from his exposed chin, and nonchalantly stepped over the bodies on his way out the door.

Darling didn't stop until he'd returned to the palace and met Maris in the back gallery hallway.

"You're hurt." There was no missing the concern in Maris's tone.

Darling didn't answer. Rather, he walked past Maris and entered the reception room so that he could open the bar and yank a bottle of Tondarion Fire off the shelf. He removed the top with his teeth, before he poured the searing alcohol over the wound on his arm. Then he took a deep draught of it.

Maris headed toward him. "Dar—"

Darling cut his words off with the point of a sword that he aimed at Maris's heart. He'd pulled it out so fast that her vision hadn't even registered his movements. It was almost as if Darling was a Trisani who'd manifested his weapon into his hand with his thoughts.

Maris froze while Darling drank half the bottle in a matter of seconds. "You can't keep this up, Darling. No one is going to let you live if you continue to slaughter everyone who's ever wronged you."

"Let them try and I'll burn it all to the ground and take as many of them with me as I can."

"This isn't a game."

Darling sneered. "It's never been a game, Maris. And I'm

through talking." He smiled then, but it was filled with bitterness and hatred. He said something to Maris that she couldn't understand before he lowered his sword and walked away.

Maris turned the video off and returned Darling's computer to the nightstand. "*That* was what we were dealing with before you came here."

"What did he say to you at the end?"

A tic started in Maris's jaw. " 'I won't forgive. I won't forget. Let hell open and rain my wrath down on them all. I will not be stopped and I have no mercy left inside me. I am death and I revel in the killing of my enemies. Bring me them all until I'm drunk on their blood.' "

Yeah, that was extreme, and that was the same man who'd overturned his desk in a fit of rage the night Maris had brought her here. "Weren't you afraid of him?"

"Honestly? I was at times. Afraid for me, but mostly for Darling." He glanced to where Darling slept on the bed. "If you leave, Zarya, he won't come back again. I know it. He'll be destroyed."

And if she stayed, her allies would do everything they could to kill him.

"Where is that rank little bastard!"

Her eyes widened at the sound of a shrieking female voice outside in the hallway. A second later, the doors to Darling's bedroom flew open to reveal a tall, auburn-haired goddess.

Zarya's jaw went slack at the sight. The pictures she'd seen didn't do Annalise justice. The woman was frighteningly beautiful.

And she was fiercely pissed.

Lise swept the room with an imperious glare before she stormed toward Darling with a furious snarl.

Zarya put herself between Darling and his sister. Not sure of Lise's plans or the source of her anger, she wasn't about to let the girl hurt him.

Just as Zarya thought she'd be attacked, Lise ran at Maris and punched him so hard in the jaw that his head snapped back.

"How could you? You sorry son of a bitch! I hate you! I hate you! I hate you!"

Completely dumbfounded, Zarya was frozen in total shock as the girl continued to assault Maris until he wrapped himself around her and held her tight against his body. Still, she fought, shrieking so loudly that it echoed through the room.

"Sh, Lise," Maris breathed soothingly in her ear. "It's okay."

Lise sobbed hysterically as she fought against Maris's hold.

Never had Zarya seen anything like this. Was there some kind of madness that infected Darling's entire family she needed to know about?

What had Maris done to Lise to cause this?

Syn came rushing in with an injector.

When he went to sedate her, Maris stopped him with a fierce shake of his head. "She'll be all right." He tightened his hold on Lise's body. "Breathe, little sister. Just breathe."

Tears flowed down her cheeks as her lips quivered. "I hate you!"

"I'm so sorry."

"No, you're not! You asshole!" She tried to hit him again, but he held her fast. Instead, she reared her head back, smashing it into Maris's face.

Somehow, he maintained his grip on her.

Lise shrieked again in frustration. "Do you know what it's like to hear that your brother's dead on a fucking news broadcast? Do you? Why didn't one of you call me, you sons of whores!"

Maris's patience with her never wavered. When he spoke, his tone was calm and soothing in spite of the bruises that were already forming on his face. "He's not dead, Lise. He's not. I swear it, sweetie."

Finally, Annalise started calming down. "W-what?"

As Hauk came into the room to check on the commotion, Maris dragged her toward the bed. "He's sleeping. See…" He led her hand to touch Darling's upper lip so that she could feel his breath against her skin.

Her tears fell even harder. The immense relief on her face once she realized her brother wasn't dead made Zarya's own eyes water.

Maris released her.

Lise turned on him and slapped him. "If you ever do that to me again, I swear I will gut you for it!"

Still, Maris didn't react to her blow. "I'm extremely sorry. It was a thoughtless thing to do, but I was more worried about Darling than calling you with the news, especially since he wasn't killed. I didn't think about the media reporting it, never mind them getting it wrong, and you finding out about the attack that way. It won't ever happen again. I promise."

Lise finally pulled Maris against her and held him close. She buried her face in his neck. "I'm so sorry, Mari. I didn't mean to hurt you. I was so scared. I thought he was gone and that I'd be left alone. He's all I have, you know?"

"Yes, I do, baby. He's all I have, too."

Sniffing, Lise squeezed him tight. "I love you. You still love me?"

"Not at the moment. I'm rather in pain. But after it fades, I'll probably be dumb enough to forgive you for it. Just don't do it again."

She kissed his cheek that was red from her punch. Laying her hand over it, she smiled at him. "What are you bitching about, anyway? You're from a warrior culture. Phrixians live to fight and clobber each other."

He arched a regal brow that said she was insane and wrong. "Hello? Gay man, here. I don't like the brutality, hence why I surrendered my commission." He turned her to face Hauk. "Next time, slap *him*. I think he actually gets off on it."

Hauk smirked. "Thanks, Mar. I will remember that."

"Am I wrong?" Maris challenged.

"No, but you don't have to tell everyone. You make me sound like I'm sick or something."

Smiling at their teasing, Lise wiped the tears from her face before she went to Hauk and gave him a hug, too. "How are you, D?"

"Better than you. You going to make it, little sis?"

"Maybe. I don't like being scared like this. You could have called, too, you know?"

"I'm pleading the Maris defense. I didn't even think about it. Sorry."

"You suck." Lise went to Syn next to hug him. "How's my precious baby boy and Shay doing?"

"They're great. Sorry we scared you."

"It's okay. *You*, I forgive since I'm sure you're the only reason I still have Darling right now."

"Actually, the credit goes there." Syn pointed at Zarya.

It was so strange to watch the play of emotions skim Lise's features in the same order they normally did on Darling's. The two of them had a lot more in common than just their hair color.

Finally, Lise settled on a confused countenance. "You saved him?"

Zarya wouldn't go that far. All she did was open a door. "We all saved him."

Syn shook his head. "Hauk and I weren't here when it happened."

"I couldn't get the door open," Maris confessed. "Zarya did. He'd have died had she not got in when she did."

"You're the one who dragged him to safety," Zarya reminded Maris.

"And you're the one who resuscitated him."

With a cry of joy, Lise threw herself into Zarya's arms and squeezed her so tightly, she was amazed she didn't break a rib.

"May the gods bless you for it. Thank you for saving my brother's life. You ever need anything, anything at all, call me. I won't ever forget what I owe you. I mean that."

Lise's zealous gratitude embarrassed her. Zarya wasn't used to people who showed so much emotion, especially so forcefully. "You're very welcome."

Lise gave her one more fierce squeeze. "I am so killing the beast when he wakes up." She flared from sorrow to gratitude to anger so fast that it was actually scary to watch. "He's determined that I'm never going to graduate. I swear. I was on my way to a chemistry test when I saw the news. Ugh!" She waved her hands around her face. "Whatever. I'll deal with it later."

Shaking her head, Lise fell right into the role of haughty princess, and yet there was something so adorable and at the same time vulnerable about her that Zarya couldn't help liking her. "I'm going to my room now to throw myself on the mercy of my instructors. Will someone please let me know the instant Darling wakes up?"

They all nodded.

Lise made a much more sedate exit.

"And people accuse *me* of melodrama," Maris mumbled as he rubbed his red cheek. "Sheez."

Nonplussed by what she'd witnessed, Zarya turned toward Maris. "Does she...um," she struggled to find words that wouldn't offend them or Lise, "Is she mentally stable?"

Syn laughed. "In theory, yes. But unfortunately, she inherited her uncle's explosive temper."

"Does everyone in Darling's family have it?" Zarya asked.

Maris snorted as he continued to rub his abused cheek and jaw. "Basically, yes. But Darling does a really good job riding herd on it most of the time. Though I've seen him go off and do some extreme things in the past."

Like kill his on duty guards...

Hauk laughed in agreement. "Yeah, he's normally really quiet and very slow to anger. To the point, I've had times I wanted to slip a mirror under his nose to make sure he's still breathing. But if you hit one of his trip wires, boom! He goes psycho on your ass. In fact, I once had to toss him over my shoulder to keep him from blowing up an entire bar."

That surprised Zarya. "Why?"

"They insulted Maris."

She scowled.

Maris patted her on the shoulder before he explained. "I was very rudely thrown out of the establishment, and I made the mistake of letting Darling know about it."

A bad feeling went through her. "What happened exactly?"

Syn answered in an angry tone. "They beat the absolute shit out of Maris, and gave him a concussion."

Maris looked sheepish now. "That's what I get for underestimating my opponents." He gestured toward Hauk. "And after Hauk stopped Darling from blowing up the bar, Darling stalked my attackers and returned the beating with good measure. He really doesn't cope well when his loved ones are hurt. Kind of loses all sense of reason and proportion."

"How so?" she asked.

Maris let out a gruff laugh. "Give me a bloody nose, Darling takes a limb."

Yeah, that was a bit extreme. Strangely though, it was one of the things she loved about him. "What will he do when he finds out his sister attacked you?"

"I don't intend to tell him that Lise bitch-slapped me. Even gay, I still don't want to admit a girl beat me up. Sheez!"

Hauk and Syn laughed.

But she didn't find it humorous. "It's not a fight if you don't strike back."

"True. Still, let's keep this unfortunate event between us," Maris whispered at her. "No need in upsetting Darling over it."

"Okay." Zarya didn't envy Darling having to deal with his volatile sister. But at least that emotional explosion had taught her one thing.

Lise loved her brother dearly. It was a shame that Darling didn't know how much.

The doors opened again to show Lise returning to the room. She pinned Zarya with a scowl. "You're Sorche's sister, aren't you?"

"I am."

Her frown deepened with confusion. "Why are you here?" Before anyone could answer, Lise threw her hands up and clenched her eyes and fists shut. "Never mind." She opened her eyes and dropped her hands. "I'm sure it's none of my business and Darling wouldn't answer me about it even if I asked. I just wanted to make sure I wasn't crazy... About you, anyway. The rest is still open for debate... Now I'm really gone." She made a very quick exit.

Hauk laughed deep in his throat before he spoke to Zarya. "Don't ask. We just go with her moods. Once you get used to her, she's actually very sweet."

"Not to mention, we're all responsible for ruining her. We have spoiled her rotten," Maris added. "Darling more so than the rest of us. But like Hauk said, she is a doll when she's not mad. And she has the kindest heart you'll ever meet."

That she definitely believed. No matter how odd this meeting had been, Zarya hadn't forgotten how giving and sweet Lise had been to her sister.

All of a sudden, the door opened slowly as if the person on the other side was hesitant about entering.

That definitely wasn't Lise.

Not sure who to expect this time, Zarya waited until it opened to show an extremely handsome man with red hair a shade darker than Darling's. Tall and well muscled, he was wearing Tavali battle gear. Something that was an impressive show of flagrant disregard for the law. The Tavali were essentially rogue pirates who preyed on the cargo of rich merchant fleets and League ships. They weren't an official group with any one leader, nor did they have allegiance to any planet or empire. Rather, they were a motley group who swore an oath to help and protect any of their brethren flying under their communal flag.

Because of the Tavali's less than legal activities, the League executed any and all they found in possession of their flag or gear. The same held true of most governments. So for him to come into a royal palace dressed like that said a lot about his courage.

And his stupidity.

Curious as to why one of their breed would be here, dressed for battle, she glanced around nervously at the others who didn't react to his presence at all.

He stopped next to Syn and purposefully kept his gaze away from the bed where Darling lay. "Is he alive or dead?"

"Alive."

He closed his eyes and let out an elongated breath—a sign that he welcomed the news. "What happened to him?"

"Assassination attempt."

Zarya frowned at Syn's stiff abruptness with the newcomer. He'd always been so open with everyone else that it was peculiar to see him so reserved around someone.

The Tavali cast a droll stare at Syn. "I knew that, asshole...Is he going to live?"

"He will."

The relief on the Tavali's handsome face was tangible. "Don't tell him I was here. I'm sure it'll only piss him off. Just please keep me updated on his condition. I'd really appreciate it."

Syn's features softened at those words. "You got it."

Inclining his head in gratitude to Syn, he turned to leave. After one step though, he stopped dead in his tracks. His gaze locked on the door as his expression turned dark.

Deadly.

Curious about his reaction, Zarya directed her attention to what had him captivated.

Ah...now she fully understood.

Drake stood in the open doorway, glaring at the Tavali as if he could go through him. And little brother was *not* what she'd expected from the stories she'd heard from Maris and Darling.

For one thing, he didn't appear to be a spoiled rich aristo. He held himself like a trained assassin who was aware of everything around him. Like a warrior ready for battle.

And Drake's unexpected presence slammed into her hard. Not just because he was probably four inches taller than Darling and muscular the way Darling had been before his torture, but because his features were identical to his older brother's.

Seriously identical.

Every arch of the brow, the long aquiline nose, the sharp cheekbones, and the intelligent blue eyes. They couldn't look more alike had Darling been cloned. But for their hair color and height difference, no one would be able to tell them apart.

It would have to pain Darling to see a face so flawlessly handsome, knowing that he'd look the same exact way if he hadn't been scarred. No wonder he didn't have any pictures of Drake past childhood.

Drake curled his lip at the Tavali. "Running out on us as usual, I see. Huh, Ryn?"

Ryn raked him with a sneer. "Don't start on me, *boy.*"

Drake went into the cocky role of a man who feared absolutely nothing and no one. One who knew he could stand his ground and give as good as he got. "Oh, I don't start shit, punk. I finish it. And there ain't no boy here. Just a man ready, willing, and able to kick your ass all the way back to the Garvon Sector."

Rolling his eyes, Maris let out an exasperated sigh. "Oh for goodness sake, would you two put it in your pants and stop measuring your overinflated members. Believe me, no one here doubts either of your manhoods." He moved to stand in between them. "Drake, apologize for being a twit, and Ryn, get your butt to your room, change clothes, and help your little brother out. Darling needs you."

They both looked at Maris as if he'd grown another head.

"Excuse me?" Ryn asked in a voice that said, "I know you did not just use *that* tone with me."

Drake was a little more verbose. "Are you high, Mari? I'm not apologizing for the truth."

Maris narrowed his gaze in anger. "Grow up, Drake. I have an Andarion here and I'm not afraid to use him. Trust me, he *will* kick your ass."

Zarya pretended to cough to cover her laughter. Hauk and Syn weren't so considerate. They laughed uproariously.

Drake glared at them.

But Maris gave him no reprieve. "You say you're a man? Prove it. Apologize like one."

"Why?" Drake gestured at Ryn. "He was the dick who—"

Exploding into action, Ryn stepped around Maris and grabbed his brother so fast that all Drake could do was gasp. He pinned Drake to the wall. "You better be glad Darling taught me not to strike out in anger. Otherwise, you'd be picking up teeth right now...*boy*."

His eyes sparking with fury, Ryn released Drake, then stepped back. "You're right, Mari. Darling doesn't have any other family he can depend on." He directed those words at Drake, then spoke over his shoulder to Maris. "I'll go deal with the media and gerents. Let me know if Darling needs anything." He rammed his shoulder into Drake's on his way out the door.

Fury bled from every pore of Drake's body. "I wish some tracer or assassin would put that bastard out of our misery."

Hauk hissed at him—something made even more ferocious by the flashing of his fangs. "That's your blood you're talking about, Drake."

"No blood of mine. He died to me the minute he walked out on us when we needed him. I'm not Darling." Drake said his name like it was an insult. "I don't forgive or forget a slight, especially not one done intentionally and with full selfish awareness."

But in spite of those words, Drake's anger melted into pain and grief as he looked to the bed where Darling lay. With a ragged breath, he crossed the room and knelt down so that he could place a hand on Darling's head. "Please tell me he's going to live, Syn."

"He will."

Tears swam in his eyes before he closed them and appeared to take a few minutes to whisper a silent prayer. When he finished, he opened them and glanced back at Hauk. "Where were his guards when he was attacked?"

"That's what we'd all like to know."

The unmitigated rage in his blue eyes scorched her, and it reminded her so much of Darling that it gave her a chill.

Drake laid his head down on the bed like a small child with a sleeping parent he didn't want to disturb. One he wanted to wake up and hold him, and make everything better.

Zarya felt her own tears gather at the way Drake stared at his brother. The love he had for Darling was so deep that it was almost tangible. This wasn't the image she'd had of Drake from what she'd been told about him. While there was no denying the fact that he was an adult, he held a deep vulnerability that made a mockery of his sister's.

Maris moved to put a comforting hand on Drake's shoulder. "He really will be fine. You don't have to worry about him. He's a fighter."

Drake nodded. "Believe me, I know."

"Did you bring your mother with you?" Syn asked.

Drake let out an aggravated sound deep in the back of his throat. "That's what took me so long to get here. I was trying to convince her to come with me. She adamantly refused. I know Darling's going to be pissed at me that I left her alone, but I don't care. After everything he's done for us, I couldn't stay there while he was hurt or dead...Damn the news. They had so many conflicting reports that I had to come and see for myself what had happened."

Then he did the most unexpected thing of all. He placed his head on Darling's shoulder and gave him what she could only describe as a little brother hug.

Her throat tightened at how sweet a gesture it was, especially coming from someone who was as fierce as Drake.

He stood and turned around, then realized there was a "stranger" in the room with them. A scowl creased his brow. "Who are you?"

"Zarya."

He went completely rigid. "Starska?"

She nodded.

Hatred flared in his eyes before he took an angry step toward her.

Hauk caught him with one arm and held him back. "Don't."

"She's the reason he was attacked!" Drake snarled. "What—"

"She's the reason he's alive." Hauk's tone was steady and calming. "But for *her*, you'd be picking out your brother's casket right now."

Maris nodded, then added, "Not to mention, Darling will paint your backside red if you harm one hair on his lady's head."

Drake turned his scowl to Maris. "What do you mean?"

"I spoke your language, little man. Quite plainly. What part of 'she's his lady' did you not comprehend?"

"All of it." Drake looked to the others before he spoke again. "I'm so confused," he breathed.

Hauk laughed. "Yeah, us, too. It's been a strange day all the way around."

Syn stepped forward. "Lise came in not long before you and Ryn. Why don't you go say hi to her?"

Drake put his hands on his hips. "Subtle like an exploding mine there, Syn. You might as well have said, 'Boy, get your ass out.'" He glanced back at Darling. "If anything changes, let me know."

Syn inclined his head to him.

No one spoke again until after Drake had left. Then Hauk looked at her and grinned. "They put the fun in 'dysfunctional,' eh?"

Zarya wasn't exactly amused by that. "I'm not passing judgment on them. It's not my place. But having met the three of them... it certainly does explain a lot about Darling."

Syn gave her a light hug. "I feel your pain. I married into an extremely screwed up family dynamic myself. But I have to say, Darling's family makes mine look normal in comparison—which scares the hell out of me most days."

Hauk let out an evil snicker. "Can't wait to tell Kasen that the next time I see her."

"You do and I'll make sure you have a nasty accident the next time you fly your ship."

Syn's threat didn't bother Hauk in the least. "That's all right, Rit. You'll just have to put me back together again. Be your punishment for it."

With a light "heh," Syn ran his hand through his long hair. "And on that note, I need to go update the rest of our screwed up family on how he's doing."

Hauk nodded. "I'll help."

After Hauk and Syn left, she turned toward Maris.

"What's that expression mean?" he asked. "And for the record, I didn't do it."

Laughing at his defensiveness, Zarya tried to reconcile the people she'd just met with the erroneous preconceived notions she'd had of them. "Just trying to take it all in. Darling has had a most complicated life."

"You've no idea, hon."

No, but she was beginning to, and like Syn with his in-laws, she was rather scared of Darling's. "I can't imagine dealing with the stress he's had. Having an uncle who treats you like you're mentally deficient and can't go to the bathroom alone, while the rest lean on you so hard that it's a wonder your back isn't bowed from it…"

How he had any sanity left was a miracle.

Maris gave a sympathetic nod. "True, but it was the lies he was forced to live with that cut him the deepest. Having to pretend to be gay and passive when it's not in his nature to be either…"

"I can't imagine."

"Oh I can, and it sucks to the extreme. The stress of it's unbearable…Only in my case, it was heterosexual and aggressive. I was truly a frightening warmonger in my earlier days."

His words caught her off guard as she tried to imagine someone as effeminate and gentle as Maris being tough and swaggering like the other warriors she knew.

Yeah…no. It just didn't work. He could *never* pull that off.

She wrinkled her nose teasingly at him. "You?" she asked with a laugh.

In that instant, his entire demeanor changed. His posture rigid and predacious, he moved to stand in front of her with an aura so powerful and lethal, she actually took a step back.

The scathing glare he raked over her body sent a chill down her spine. In that moment, she could easily see him killing someone.

When he spoke, his voice was an octave deeper and it rumbled from deep inside his chest. "You think I couldn't kick your ass, bitch? Never underestimate what I can do, and my willingness to do it." Now that was a warrior's growl that would rival any League assassin.

Then as quickly as he'd summoned it, he let it go and deflated back into the gentle man she'd grown to love.

"*That* was impressive," she admitted in an awed whisper.

Maris waved a dismissive hand. "Not really. I hated every minute of the years I was forced to live that way. I have eight brothers, a war-hero father, and assorted cousins and uncles who did nothing but throw women at me every hour of the day until I was ready to scream." He clutched his hands in his hair, then lowered them. "For that matter, I was even engaged once."

That caught her by surprise, too. "To a woman?"

He nodded. "Political alliance arranged by our fathers."

"What happened?"

Glancing toward the bed, he primly folded his hands in front of him. "On the day of the wedding, Darling and I were alone in the groom's chamber and I was so scared, I was shaking. My married future of lies stretched out in front of me, and it made me sick to my stomach."

Maris paused as he saw that moment again so clearly in his mind. Swathed all in black, Darling had been dressed more for a funeral than a wedding—something extremely apropos given Maris's feelings about the event.

Ever elegant and beautiful, Darling had stood there while Maris had paced back and forth with a lump in his throat so tight he'd felt like someone was strangling him.

As befitting his station, Maris had been in full dress battle gear, complete with the combat medals he'd earned. Back then, he'd been part of the Phrixian High Command as a fully commissioned officer—the very pride of his father.

Darling had watched him with a bemused expression. "Breathe easy, Mari. You look like you're about to pass out or puke."

"I'm trying." He'd locked gazes with Darling, seeking both forgiveness and strength for what he was about to do. "I can do this. It'll be easier, really. No one will expect me to whore around...as much, anyway. I can always say that I love my wife so I won't have to come up with excuses why I can't sleep with women anymore." If he made up one more STD to get out of bedding a woman, he was sure his father would have him permanently hooked to an antibiotic IV.

"True," Darling said.

Maris hesitated. "What's with that tone?"

"It's not my place to say. I'm your friend and I'm here to support you with whatever you do. You know that." Darling handed him a towel. "I think you're going to need another shower, though. At the rate you're sweating you're going to drown your bride at the altar."

"You're not funny."

"Really not trying to be."

Maris had wiped his hand across his forehead and grimaced as he realized Darling was right. He'd run marathons in the deepest heat of summer and sweated less. "How do I look?"

"Your pants are too tight, and you look like you're about to vomit."

That had panicked him even more. If he threw up like some green coward, his father would never forgive him. "What am I going to do, Dar? I'm about to be married...to a female person with female body parts. I'm going to have a wedding night and..." Unmitigated terror had filled him at the thought of sleeping with his wife for the rest of his existence. It was all he could do not to cringe. "Can you be me tonight? Please?"

"Pretty sure she'll notice."

Damn him for being right. But Maris wasn't quite ready to give up on that solution. "We could drug her and she'd never know the difference, that way we'd all be happy."

Darling gaped at his suggestion.

"Think about it," Maris said, really getting into the idea and all the possibilities that it would open. "We could. That way you'd have a woman and—"

"I'm not going to screw your wife for you, Mari. And I'm damn sure not going to drug her first."

"Fine, you moral asshole," he'd snapped in anger. Taking a deep breath, he braced himself for his duties. "I've had to sleep with women before. I can do this." But when he looked back at Darling, he'd seen the shadow in his friend's eyes of some unspoken emotion. "What?"

"I am not going to tell you how to live your life, Mari. The gods know I've fucked mine up so badly that I wake up every morning hoping it's all been one really long nightmare. But I keep seeing this as that one second when they handcuffed my mother to drag her away. That one instant where I screwed myself forever. If only I could take it all back or stop myself before I did it. And I keep hearing my dad's words in my head, *the worst decisions of your life will always be those that are made out of fear.*"

"What are you saying?"

Darling hesitated before he answered. "My moment of supreme

stupidity only impacted me. I was the one who was hurt by it, and I saved two people when I did it. But I'm the only one who's had to live with the lie and be bound by it. I just want you to think about the fact that when you walk down that aisle and tie your life to Tams, you will be forcing both of you to live with it. She wants a husband, Mari. One day, she'll want kids and they will be expecting a military father to train them. Are you ready to force your lie onto all of them *and* you, forever?"

Maris had growled angrily at him. "I really hate you."

Darling hadn't reacted to his hostility. "I love *you*, Mari. I always have and always will. And I'll be honest, I wouldn't wish my current existence on anyone, especially not you. You've seen what everyone has done to me and how they've all treated me because they think I'm gay. In your position, I'd marry her and deal with it as best I could. But at the same time, I know *exactly* how you feel right now, and how hard it is to walk a lie every single day of your life. This is *your* moment in the hallway, Mari. This one decision, either way, will viciously impact the rest of your life, and you will have to live with the consequences of it. Neither option will be pleasant for you. You are screwed both ways. But whatever you choose, I will be here for you. And I will protect you any way I can."

"But you won't sleep with my wife for me, you worthless beast."

"You know I can't."

Maris had sighed wearily as he debated what to do. "Would you sleep with me, then?"

"Maris..."

"I know, Dar. I know."

Even all these years later, Maris could still remember that nauseated feeling inside him as he'd walked down the aisle with Darling by his side.

Not to get married, but to tell everyone present why he couldn't. And *that* memory was one he never wanted to revisit.

Coming back to the present, he looked at Zarya. "To this day, I owe Darling everything. His support never wavered. I know he would have been there for me had I married her. Instead, he was there when I told my entire family and every dignitary present that I was gay. That was the worst moment of my life." He winced as he remembered their extremely unpleasant reactions. "My father even attacked him over it."

"Why?"

"Brace yourself," he said bitterly. "They thought it was all Darling's fault. That he'd converted me. To quote my father, I would never have been gay had that filth not infected me."

Zarya cringed as she saw the pain in Maris's dark eyes. She couldn't believe his family had thought such a thing.

"Would you believe my family even tried to sue him over it?"

She gaped. "What?"

He nodded grimly as he raised his right hand. "Swear to the gods." He lowered his hand and looked away from her. "You know that scar Darling has on his thigh? The one shaped like a star?"

How could she forget? It was the one that had allowed her to identify him when he'd been in their custody. "Yes."

"My eldest brother Kyr tried to castrate him on my wedding day. Luckily, Darling's a better fighter than Kyr is."

Her heart breaking for both of them, she pulled Maris into her arms and held him close. "I'm so sorry for what both of you went through."

Maris squeezed her lightly. "It's all right, though. Really. While the rest of my family refuses to speak my name, I have the best brother anyone could ever ask for. One who isn't afraid to let me be myself. One who wouldn't hesitate to die for me. In the end, I'm the luckiest bitch in the universe."

He stepped back to smile down at her. "Well, second luckiest. Personally, I think you have the number one slot. Want to trade?"

She laughed. "I love you, Mari. I really do. You're such a special gem."

Maris sighed wistfully. "If only you were a gorgeous man saying that to me, sweetie. Oh well...one day." He sobered. "I love you, too, Zarya. Thank you for saving him today."

"Team effort," she reminded him.

He shook his head at her. "You have a hard time accepting praise, don't you?"

"It makes me really uncomfortable."

"All right, then. You suck. Now, I'm going to check on Ryn to see if he needs anything while he deals with the firestorm over this."

Smiling, Zarya watched him leave. She really did love that man. But what she felt for him was nothing compared to what her heart held for Darling.

And she'd almost lost him today...

Worse, *she* was the biggest threat he had to his well-being and reign. Closing her eyes, she kept trying to blot out the image of the e-mail they'd received after his attack.

We are the Resistance and you are holding one of ours. There will be no peace and no quarter so long as you have her. Release Zarya Starska or we will burn the palace to the ground and destroy every aristo we find.

Protests had been breaking out steadily since the attack. Even now, there was a group of rabid protestors at the palace gates.

Because of her.

I have to leave him. In spite of what Maris said, and in spite of the pain it would cause her, she couldn't stay here.

For the sake of Darling's life, she would have to go. She knew it deep in her heart. But knowing what needed to be done and doing it when you didn't want to were two different things.

I don't want to go. She remembered how desolate she'd felt when Darling had gone missing. Remembered the nights of feeling lost and vacant. She didn't want to go through that again.

But if she didn't, he'd be dead, and then she would never be able to see him. Period.

I'll either have to live a life without him in it, knowing he's alive and well. Or live a life where he's dead.

Either way, she lost. There was no choice.

Somehow she was going to have to find the strength to break his heart.

And ruin the rest of her life.

14

"What the hell are you doing here? And dressed like *that*!"

Zarya jumped at the strident tone that startled her out of her thoughts. Not just because it was so angry, but because it came from the last person she expected to burst into her bedroom.

"Sorche? What are *you* doing here? Who let you in?" Unless Maris gave clearance, no one was supposed to be allowed into the governor's private wing without a full escort.

Her sister didn't answer. Instead, she rushed across the room to take her by the arm. Sorche pulled her toward the hallway door. "Look, there aren't any guards outside. I think we can make it out before anyone realizes you're gone."

Unsure if she should laugh or be insulted, Zarya gaped at her. "What are you talking about?"

Sorche lowered her voice to a tiny whisper. "I saw the news, okay? I know he's holding you against your will, and—"

Zarya refused to let her sister haul her across the room. She twisted her arm out of Sorche's grasp. "It's not against my will."

Sorche cocked her head. "The UCN said that he had mind control over you. Do you know who I am?"

Zarya gave her a droll stare. "My annoying little sister who has driven me insane since the moment she came into this world and threw up all over my favorite dress." She placed her hands on Sorche's shoulders and met her gaze levelly so that she could see Zarya was in full possession of her own mind. "I am here by choice, Sorche. That's why I don't have guards. I'm free to leave anytime I want to. I have the money and the means to leave."

"Then why are you here?" Fear sparked in her brown eyes. When she spoke again, her voice was barely audible. "You're going to kill the governor, aren't you?"

"No." Biting her lip, Zarya debated telling her sister the truth. While Sorche was extremely loyal, she could also be scattered, and extremely stupid at times. "I'm going to tell you something, but you have to swear on our mother's soul that you will never, ever breathe a syllable of it to another living being."

"Even Ture?"

"Even Ture."

Sorche considered it for a few heartbeats. "Then it has to be good. Spill it."

"Swear first."

Sorche nodded eagerly. "Okay, I swear it."

Now Zarya understood why Maris had hesitated with her. It was hard to let go of a confidence when you knew it would destroy the person you loved most if anyone else heard it. And while she trusted her sister, she was still afraid that by talking about this, she might do Darling harm.

But in the end, she knew she had to tell her sister the truth. Sorche wouldn't accept anything else. So taking a deep breath, she forced the words out. "Darling is Kere."

Sorche gaped at her disclosure. For several seconds, all she did was blink until she finally gasped, "*Your* fiancé Kere?"

"The one and the same."

"The Sentella Kere who is wanted dead by the League and—"

327

Zarya placed her hand over Sorche's mouth to keep her from carrying on. "You can't speak of this, Sorch. To anyone but me. Ever. Do you understand?" It would mean Darling's life if she did.

Sorche nodded, then pulled Zarya's hand from her lips. Her gaze danced around the room as she came to grips with the truth as to why Zarya was still here. "So where were you for the last year? Honestly?"

She didn't want to answer that, but she'd never liked lying to her sister either. "I was imprisoned." She didn't tell Sorche where because she didn't want her sister to hate Darling for it.

"I knew it!" Sorche grabbed her arm again. "I'm getting you out of here."

"Stop it!" Zarya snapped at her. "I can't leave him until I know he's going to live, okay?"

Sorche finally calmed down. "You really do love him, don't you?"

"More than my life."

Her sister rubbed Zarya's arm, offering her comfort. "All right, but I'm not going anywhere until I know *you're* okay. You hear me? While you might love him, I definitely love you."

She smiled at her sister's unnecessary concern. "All right. Now how did you get up here?"

"It wasn't easy at first. This obnoxious doorman was interrogating me. Thoroughly. Then this odd guy, dressed in an outlandish orange getup dismissed him and asked who I was and why I wanted to see you."

"Maris?"

"Yeah. He's . . . different, isn't he?"

Zarya laughed. "A little. So he showed you up?"

"Yeah." Sorche swept a curious gaze from the top of Zarya's head to her feet. "Now explain your clothes. I've *never* seen you in a dress before."

Zarya shook her head as she looked down at the filmy, light blue dress she wore. It flowed around her in a whisper of silk—to quote Maris. Sorche was right, it wasn't her usual style of a dark battlesuit. "It's called a day gown."

"Day gown?" Sorche pulled at the lightweight silk outer skirt. "I bet this thing cost more than a year's tuition."

Funny, Zarya had never put it in those terms before. Now she felt guilty for enjoying it. People were hungry and here she was, dressed up for no reason whatsoever.

Sorche sucked her breath in sharply. "I'm sorry, Zarya. I didn't mean to ruin it for you. Please smile again. You look beautiful in it. You do and it's about time you wore something really nice. I'm just not used to seeing you dressed like this. That's all."

She hugged her sister. "It's fine. Now let me find Gera and get you settled in one of the rooms."

Sorche hesitated. "You sure I can't kidnap you?"

She cringed at those words. But most of all, she cringed at the idea of leaving Darling. Ever.

You have to. No matter how much she loved him, she couldn't stay and endanger him. "Once I know he's going to live, I'll let you take me home."

Fearing he was blind—and would remain so—Darling opened his eyes slowly. As he blinked, the world came into focus. Not perfect, but it was back to what it'd been before his attack.

He breathed a sigh in relief.

Thank the gods...

Who knew you could be so grateful for a hazy view of the world? But he'd take fuzzy over nothing any day.

He lay on his back with a weight draped over his chest. Glancing down, he smiled as he saw Zarya sound asleep there with her arms wrapped around him in a tight hug. Now *that* had to be the most beautiful thing he'd ever seen. And it instantly set fire to his blood for many reasons.

Grateful to and for her, he brushed his fingers through her soft, mahogany hair.

She'd saved his life.

His head was still throbbing and much of what had happened was foggy, but one memory was crystal clear. The sound of her angry voice over the roar of the flames around him.

"Don't you dare die on me, Darling Cruel! I swear I'll follow you into hell to beat you if you do!"

He was a psycho bastard to have that mean so much to him. But it meant everything.

She really did love him.

And the truth was, he loved her, too. More than he could believe. More than he could stand at times.

For her, he would do anything.

So why did it have to hurt so much? Be so *damned* hard?

Because people let each other down. Always. No matter how much they love each other, someone always screws up.

And the more you love them, the deeper it stings...

It was a natural state of being. No one could ever live up to the expectations of someone else. Sooner or later, everyone failed and he was too tired of being disappointed to keep up the pretense that he wasn't.

She didn't disappoint you in this.

No, but it still didn't erase the past when she had, and in a much bigger way.

Why couldn't you have opened the door then, Z?

As bad as the fire had been, it was nothing compared to the months of hell her people had put him through.

Her actions today didn't ease that part of him. *You're not perfect yourself, you know?*

330

True. He'd done his own share of hurt where she was concerned. And she'd forgiven him for it, so why couldn't he do the same for her?

Because I'm a monster.

Physically and mentally.

But worse than that, he was an ass...

Zarya came awake to someone stroking her hair. Happiness shot through her as she realized what it meant. Lifting her head, she stared into those deep blue eyes that belonged to the most important person in her world. Never had she seen anything better. "How do you feel?"

"Did one of you drop me on my head?"

She laughed. "We only thought about it. Is your sight better?"

Nodding, he turned his head to look at the clock. "How long was I out?"

She cringed, not wanting to tell him. But he had a right to know and it wasn't like he wouldn't find out eventually. "Well...let me put it to you this way. You should be having surgery right now."

He handled the news better than she'd expected. It took a few seconds as he digested it, then he sighed. "Is it morning?"

"Yes."

Darling ran through his mind the fact that he'd been out for two days. While it didn't thrill him, there wasn't anything he could do about it...other than shoot Syn.

Maybe later.

Right now, he wanted to focus on the soft body pressed against his and on other matters he needed to attend to. "What have I missed?"

She wrinkled her nose and gave a playful cringe. "Mostly family tantrums."

His stomach tightened with dread. *Please tell me they're not here. Please...* "Pardon?"

As always, his luck fled out the door faster than a thief who'd just tripped an alarm.

"Your siblings are all here. Under one roof. Now I know why you chose not to have them around you while you healed. They can be…interesting, as I'm sure you know."

That he did. A multitude of adjectives went through his head for all three of them, and he was grateful she was being judicious and kind with her choice of words where they were concerned. Seldom was he so considerate. "I'm sorry you've had to deal with them."

"Don't be. Sorche's here, too. I'd much rather deal with your family drama than mine."

The catch in her voice concerned him. "Why is she here? Did something happen?"

Zarya shook her head. "She heard the same news report your sibs did and flipped out, thinking you were holding me here against my will. But I've got her calmed down and Gera gave her a room not far from Lise's. I hope you don't mind."

"Not at all. Your sister's always welcome here." Even though he'd never met Sorche, he felt like he knew her as much as he knew his own family. Most of all, since she was one of Zarya's favorite topics, he knew how much Sorche meant to her. For that reason alone, he'd be more than happy to set her up with a permanent residence here in the palace.

He rubbed his hand over his brow as he heard a dull roar through the walls. "What's that sound?" He would think it was his brothers and sister fighting, but there were too many voices for it to be the three of them.

And it wasn't loud enough to be Lise.

"What sound?"

He squinted as he listened again, trying to decipher it. "It sounds like people shouting."

"Oh." She bit her lip before she answered. "It is people shouting."

"And they're shouting... why?"

He saw the reluctance in her eyes. "You know the old adage, a single drop starts the deluge?"

"Yeah."

Zarya propped herself up on her elbow to look at him as she traced a small circle on his chest... one that was slowly making him crazy with lust as he wished she'd dip that hand lower and cup him. "Once word spread that you'd been attacked and were down, the people started rioting for every grievance they've ever had against you, your family, and their lives. Your gerents have no idea how to handle it, and Ryn is about ready to rally Tavali forces to put them down and shut them up—my paraphrasing, mind you. Ryn's language was much more... colorful and descriptive."

That sounded like his brother. When diplomacy failed, kill them all and let the gods sort it out. 'Course his wasn't much better. In fact, the only thing that really separated their philosophies was that Ryn wanted guns while Darling preferred high explosives. "Where's Ryn now?"

"Downstairs meeting with a group of social delegates."

Well, *that* iced his raging hormones. Damn...

Darling groaned out loud. "That's like asking a predator to guard prey." And he was the idiot who'd appointed Ryn to the position.

What was I thinking?

Basically that he had no one else he could trust.

Cursing himself for that particular piece of brilliance, he sat up and ignored the pain that burned through him.

Zarya scowled. "What are you doing?"

"Going to save my empire while I still have one."

She scooted off the bed to stop him. "You can't. Syn needs to—"

333

"Zarya," he said firmly, interrupting her. "Please. I can't fight everyone at once."

Growling her own frustration at him, she held her hands up in surrender. "Fine. What do you need me to do?"

"Help me dress."

Zarya paused at his suggestion. The last thing he needed to do was walk into a room full of people who wanted him dead. People who were itching for a chance to assault him, verbally and physically.

A wicked smile curled her lips as an idea struck her on how to keep him out of harm's way for a little longer.

She walked up to him and wrapped her arm around his neck, then pulled his head down so that she could nibble his lips while she gently scooted her right hand into his pants to fondle him. Her smile widened as she realized he was already hard and wet.

Pulling back, she whispered seductively, "Dress or *un*dress you, my lord?"

Darling's head swam as fire ran through his veins. Her fingers felt so good on him that it was hard to stay focused on duty. Especially when she dipped her hand down to cup and finger him.

Yeah, he'd much rather stay here with her.

Something that wasn't helped as she sank down to her knees in front of him and opened his pants.

You stop her now and I'll kill you.

But he had an empire to run. His id could wait.

No, I can't.

Yes, it could.

His legs went weak as she took him into her mouth and unmitigated pleasure tore through his entire being. For a full minute, he reeled from it.

The voices outside grew louder, reminding him of the job that awaited him.

Fuck the empire and everyone in it...

Yeah, that would be an intensely bad idea.

He really hated that stupid notion of the "empire comes first" his father had drilled into him as he forced himself to step back from her. The sight of her licking her lips in an open invitation was enough to kill him.

Stamping down the fire in his blood, he narrowed his eyes at her. "You *are* devious. Don't think I'm not on to you."

Any other time, it would work. But he couldn't allow her to distract him today or to know just how much power she ultimately had over him. He was completely weak and pliant when it came to her.

"Fine," she snapped irritably, rising to her feet. "Freshen up and I'll get your clothes ready."

Before he stepped away, he pulled her into his arms to give her the hottest kiss he could manage. One that had her wrapping her arms around him and clutching at his back. When he forced himself to pull away again, she was breathless.

Blinking, she stared at him with a hunger in her eyes that matched his.

He ran his hand along her jaw. "Don't you hate it when someone stirs a fire you can't quench?"

She narrowed those amber eyes at him. "You better be glad I'm still not over the close call you just had. Otherwise, I'd make you pay for that."

He grinned at her before he went to take a quick ice cold shower.

Darling hesitated before he opened the doors to the throne room. What if Zarya was right and his presence here worsened things? His people hated him. He knew that better than anyone. The plebs saw him as a selfish, entitled prick out to work them until they dropped while he became richer and richer off their backs. The aristos thought he was spineless and weak, and they laughed at him to his face. Thanks to Senator Nylan, Arturo, and his own desperate stupidity, none of them had even a modicum of respect for him.

Both groups viewed him with the utmost disdain.

Worse, his mask had been destroyed in the attack. If he walked in there, he would do it with *all* scars showing.

With Pip's name carved into my face.

Shame shredded his confidence while unwanted memories flogged him. Fingering his cheek, he stepped back and traced the raised scar. Even with his beard over it, it was plainly visible. Their contempt for him would only grow once they saw what had been done to him while he'd been powerless to stop it.

How helpless and pathetic he really was. If he couldn't protect himself, how could he protect his people? *That's exactly what they'll say.*

He winced as he remembered his guard corps spitting at his feet.

They all disdain me.

I can't do this. I can't be laughed at again.

In that one lonely heartbeat, every degradation and humiliation of his entire life slapped him hard in the face. He heard the laughter and ridicule that had been shoved down his throat since the day his father had died.

No one respected Darling Cruel.

I'm the punch line of all cocktail party jokes.

He closed his eyes in an attempt to blot it all out, and instead what he saw was his own brother's face as Drake sneered his contempt for him.

"I don't have to listen to you. You're not my father. You barely qualify as my brother. I swear, Lise has more testosterone than

you do. You're just a worthless piece of shit who cowers and grovels every time Arturo gets near you. I refuse to be like you, so pathetic, wasted, and scared that my own guards mock me for it. I will not give up or give in, and I damn sure won't belly crawl for someone else. So why don't you go find a cock to suck on, and get out of my face. Let me show you how a man handles things."

He flinched at Drake's angry words that'd been hurled at him when he'd tried one last time to stop Drake from confronting Arturo over embezzling part of their inheritance.

Only fifteen, Drake had thought himself man enough to fight.

And after Arturo had almost killed him for his adolescent stupidity and left the boy in intensive care, Darling had made the mistake of going to Ryn.

"You have to help us. Even though you're illegitimate, you're a direct blood descendant from the governor. The CDS can make a special accommodation for you to rule until I turn thirty."

Just like Drake, Ryn had sneered in his face. "Forget it. You're not dragging me back into that backbiting shithole. I've had enough of it. I don't want your throne or anything else to do with Caronese politics. For the first time in my life, I'm happy and I intend to stay that way." Ryn had tried to make him leave Ryn's apartment, but Darling had refused to go.

"He's going to kill them, Ryn. Don't you understand? They won't listen to me at all. Not my mother or Drake. No matter how much I beg or threaten them. Drake's only getting worse as he gets older. He thinks he can take Arturo head on. And I'm tired of running interference between them. Of deflecting Arturo's anger to me so he'll leave them alone. Please? I can't take it anymore. I can't. I'm through being their punching bag. I just want to go to sleep one night in my shitty life and feel safe. Is that really too much to ask?"

Darling had gestured to his arm that Arturo had shattered

when Darling had stupidly tried to kill him for what he'd done to Drake. "I'm still underage by our laws. And none of the other aristos will do anything to help us. Believe me, I've tried. The gerents are all too afraid of Arturo to back me without a stronger man to come in as my guardian. You told me that you'd be here if I needed you. I need you, big brother. We all do. Please, don't do this to me. I'm begging you for mercy."

Ryn shook his head in continual denial. "I love you, Darling. I do. But I'm not about to let you or anyone else drag me back to that hellhole. I'm not a politician and I don't want to be one. Just go home where you belong. They're your family, not mine. You deal with their psycho asses."

In that second of panicked desperation, Darling had looked down at the scars on his wrists from when he'd tried to kill himself and, like Drake, he'd let his fury get the better of his tongue. He didn't want to go back either. It wasn't fair that Ryn had his freedom while he'd have to wait more than another decade for his. He was tired and frustrated.

Most of all, he was through with being the sole defender while he had an older brother who should have been willing to help them.

Just as Drake had done to him, he'd verbally gone for Ryn's throat. "So that's it then? Captain Tavali. Lord Badass. At the end of the day, you're nothing but a selfish, scared asshole just like all the others in *your* family. I wonder what your friends would think if they knew what a spineless coward you really are?"

Darling had known exactly the buttons he was pushing and why they stung Ryn so badly. He shouldn't have done it.

But he'd wanted to hurt Ryn the way Ryn had hurt him by refusing to help. And it was too late to take those words back. Once they were out, they'd been a deadly challenge.

One Ryn had met with a furious snarl. He'd whirled on Darling then and grabbed him. They'd started fighting like two rabid animals. A fight that ended several minutes later when Ryn lifted Darling off his feet and threw him into the glass dining table. Because of his shattered arm that was in a sling and the other that was braced due to a sprain, Darling had been unable to catch himself. As a result, his face had taken the brunt of the fall.

In all the vicious beatings he'd had over the years, never had he seen so much blood. Felt more pain. The glass had torn through his body like a thousand razors. It'd taken the medics over half an hour to extract him from the broken pieces.

The whole time they worked to save him, Darling had prayed he'd finally bleed out and die.

But the gods had never been merciful to him.

Ryn had apologized repeatedly the entire time they pulled him from the glass and metal, but just like the angry words that had flown between all of them, it was too late to take it back. The damage had been done and it was permanent.

Their relationship had never recovered from that night. They were both ashamed of what they'd said and done.

Now those memories paralyzed Darling as he saw his reflection in the marble wall in front of him and he cringed inwardly.

His mother was right. He was hideous and disgusting.

Too ugly to look at.

Arturo's insults rang in his ears. They mingled with the hostile words and shouts he could hear coming from inside the throne room as his brother fought with the plebs.

But as his gaze went to the state portrait of his father that hung to his left, he remembered the brave little boy who'd stood at his father's tomb and had vowed that he would keep the things his father treasured most safe from harm.

The wife his father had loved above all things.

The children who'd been the pride of his heart.

And the empire that he'd worried and slaved over.

I won't let them suffer without you, Papa. I swear. I'll be the man you wanted me to be. No matter what, I will make you proud.

Darling had fought hard to protect his mother and siblings. Now it was time to keep the last part of that promise.

Taking a deep breath for courage, he lifted the cowl on his royal dark blue and gold robes so that it covered his head and shielded his face, then headed for the doors.

The moment they swung open, every eye in the room turned toward him. Wanting to run for shelter, Darling raised his chin and let the rank and mantle of noblesse oblige settle firmly on his shoulders.

This was what he'd been bred and trained for.

And as he stood there, he heard his father's voice in his head. *"The past is history written in stone that can't be altered. The future is transitory and never guaranteed. Today is the only thing you can alter for certain. Make the most of it."*

Ryn, who had changed out of his pirate gear in favor of imperial robes, rose from the throne where he'd been acting as pro tem. Maris, Drake, Syn, Hauk, and two other gerents stood to his left while a small group of plebs were on the right. His older brother bowed down before him. "Your Majesty."

The others followed suit.

Once they righted themselves, there was an absolute chill in the air as they faced him. Yeah, he was as welcome here as a fatal STD in a whorehouse.

But that didn't change the fact that he was their governor and this was *his* duty.

Darling focused his blurry gaze on the tall, skinny pleb standing closest to Ryn. He'd lay money that he was their leader. So he was the one Darling addressed first. "Care to enlighten me as to why you were shouting at my pro tem?"

The plebs paled. But the tall one didn't shirk in spite of his obvious fear. He took a step forward. "My name is Gerst. Svidan Gerst, Your Majesty. And we're from the workers' coalition." A bead of sweat rolled down the side of his face. "We are asking that our workday be shortened. Right now, we're working eighteen-hour days with no time off for illness or recuperation."

Ryn made a noise of frustration. "I was trying to explain to them that they need to take the matter to Lord Derkstig since he's the one who's in charge of setting labor standards."

Gerst grimaced at the mention of the gerent's name. "And we've taken it to him. His answer is to suck it up and be grateful we have jobs while others don't."

Just as Darling started to respond, the door to the main hall opened. Scowling, he watched as Zarya came in holding a little girl around the age of seven in her arms. Dressed in white, the little girl had curly brown hair that framed an angelic face.

He noted the panic on Gerst's features.

"See," Zarya said in a soothing, sweet tone to the child. "Your father's fine. Just like I said. No one's hurting him." She set the girl down so that she could run to Gerst.

Sobbing, the girl buried her face against her father's leg and held tight while the plebs rolled their eyes in obvious contempt.

Zarya curtsied to Darling. "Forgive our interruption, Your Majesty. There was a group of boys outside the gate who were tormenting her. They told her that her father was in here, being eaten by a monster. So she snuck into the palace, wanting to save her father from harm."

He would laugh if it wasn't so typical. "Maris?"

Maris came over immediately.

Zarya watched while Darling whispered something to Maris and Maris quickly left the room.

The girl's father peeled her off his leg and forced her to stand in front of him. "Drus, you have to leave now. I have important business to attend to."

The little girl sniffed and nodded. "I'm sorry, Daddy. I was just so scared you were hurt."

Zarya moved to take the girl's hand. "Come with me, sweetie." But before they left, she led Drus over to Darling.

With those voluminous, official robes that obscured his entire body, and the cowl covering his face and head, he did appear scary and fierce. Especially since no one could see or read his expressions.

However, Zarya knew the truth of him and he wasn't the minion of evil they feared him to be. "Drus, this is Governor Cruel. See what I told you, he's not a monster. He's just a man, like any other."

Darling knelt down on the floor and held his gloved hand out to her.

The girl stepped back to hide behind Zarya.

Kneeling down to her level, Zarya patted her on the back and turned her around to face Darling.

His damaged voice filled with patience, he tried again. "It's all right, Drus. I won't hurt you. I promise. You know, you remind me of my baby sister when she was a little girl."

Her eyes widened in awe. "*You* have a sister?"

"I do, indeed. Like you, she's very beautiful, and very dear to me." There was a smile in his tone as he spoke gently to her. "I also have a couple of very mean brothers, as well."

That made the corners of her mouth twitch as if she wanted to smile, too, but was still too afraid to try it. "Really?"

"Really. They're standing right there." He pointed toward them.

Drake and Ryn appeared less than amused by his description. But neither said anything to refute it.

The girl giggled.

Maris returned with a small box. He bowed formally as he presented it to Darling.

"Thank you, Lord Maris." Darling opened the box and pulled a small medal out that he held up for Drus to see. "Do you know what this is, Drus?"

She shook her head.

"It's called the Recognition of Honor and Courage. We give these to the soldiers who show exceptional bravery while under fire. Men and women who stand up for others even when it's really scary for them to do so." He tied a small knot in the ribbon to shorten its length. "I would like to present this to you."

Drus scowled at him. "Why?"

"Because you were terrified for your father. Even though you thought he was fighting a scary monster, you came inside to check on him, and I'm quite sure you thought you'd get into a lot of trouble for it."

She nodded vigorously. "Setchel said that I'd get fed to the monster, too."

"See," Darling continued, "that's extremely brave. Now if you'll kneel in front of me, I'd like to give you your award."

Zarya smiled as Drus knelt like an adult in front of her governor.

Darling held the medal up and performed the entire official ceremony. "It is with my greatest honor and gratitude that I, the 139th Governor of Caron Druxton Ambridate Darling Setonius Cruel, bestow this medal on you, Drus Gerst, for exceptional bravery while under the duress of fear and fire. May you live always to be a shining example to the people that when other lives mattered most, yours mattered least. It is for others that the brave will always gladly lay down their lives so that all our people can live without fear."

He placed the medal around her neck. "Now rise, Dame Drus. And let everyone know from this day forward that you are the bravest of the brave. You are the pride of the Caronese people and of her governor who thanks you for your courage and service."

Her beautiful features lit up as she cradled her medal in her small hands. Laughing, she launched herself at Darling. She hit him with such force that it knocked him back and caused his cowl to fall to his shoulders.

Drus's laughter turned to a terrified gasp as she looked up and saw his scarred face.

Zarya held her breath at the sudden tension in the room. The gerents and plebs glared with obvious disdain and aversion.

Eyes wide, Drus stared in dismay. "Did someone hurt you, Your Majesty?"

Agony and embarrassment burned bright in his blue eyes, but to his credit, Darling offered the girl a smile that was twisted slightly by the vicious scars across his lips. "They did."

"Then you can't be a monster."

Darling frowned. "How so?"

"Monsters can't be hurt by people, silly. My nan says so. You can only be hurt when you have a heart and monsters don't have hearts. That's why they steal them from others." Smiling at him once again, she leaned in to give him a quick kiss on his bearded cheek, then she patted it kindly. "I'm glad the beautiful lady was right. You are just a man and a very nice one, too."

Darling lowered his head and gave her a somber military salute. "Thank you, Dame Drus." He rose to his feet as Zarya came forward to reclaim Drus's hand.

She smiled down at the little girl. "Come on, sweetie. I'll take you to the reception room where we have cakes and cookies so that you can wait for your father."

Drus let out a squeal of excitement. "Cakes! Oooh, I can't wait. I love cakes."

Zarya paused at the door to watch Darling replace his cowl before he faced the men.

Her heart breaking for him and the pain she'd seen in his eyes, she led the girl outside.

As they were waiting, she allowed Drus to eat enough sweets that she was sure the girl's father would issue a death warrant for her. But it made Drus happy and kept the girl occupied while the men conducted their business. Over and over, Drus showed her the medal. She also showed it to any and every person who came anywhere near the room. Sometimes she even chased them down whenever they passed by outside in the hallway.

It seemed like an eternity had passed before the doors opened and the girl's father came to claim her. There was a happy light in his eyes as they took their leave.

The gerents, however, were another matter entirely. They appeared ready to slaughter someone.

Zarya went to the throne room to find Darling sitting on the throne while Ryn glared at him. Maris and Drake stood opposite of Ryn with Syn and Hauk beside him.

"The aristos are going to demand your head over this."

Darling shrugged at Ryn's dire prediction. "Then they should have taken care of the matter before it was brought to my attention."

"Let them have their strokes," Drake said drily. "I, for one, am proud of you, Darling."

Ryn passed a look of utter contempt to his youngest brother. "And you're a stupid little punk incapable of understanding the repercussions of one bad decision."

345

Drake moved to attack Ryn, but Darling sprang from the throne to catch him before he made contact. It was actually an impressive feat.

"Settle down," Darling said sternly as he forced his younger brother away from Ryn. "Now."

Hauk laughed unexpectedly. "You know, Ryn, I keep thinking back to what my father used to say to me. There are two kinds of people in this world. Those like my mother who can walk into the most backwater dive hole with the worst riffraff in the universe and in ten minutes, she'll have them baking cookies and singing love songs together. Then you have those like my father. The kind of man who could walk into an antiwar monastery and in ten minutes have the monks at each other's throats."

Ryn scowled at him. "What has that got to do with anything?"

Hauk jerked his chin at Darling. "Trust your brother. He's the best peacemaker among us. If anyone can settle them down, it's him."

Syn nodded in agreement. "Hauk's right. They were all about to set your clock until Darling came in." He met Zarya's gaze. "Great timing with the kid, by the way. You completely caught them off guard with that, and lowered their defenses."

"Not done intentionally," she confessed. "I wasn't sure what to do with the girl when I found her sneaking around the hallway, looking for her father. But I'm glad it helped."

Darling clapped Drake on his shoulder. "You need to get back to your mother."

Zarya didn't miss the way Darling referred to his mother or the fact that Drake didn't think it was unusual.

"Not while I'm needed here."

"You aren't needed," Darling said, not with malice, but patience.

Drake clenched his teeth. "You know, I may be emotionally stunted, but there's nothing wrong with my mental capacity."

Darling smirked. "Obviously there is, or you wouldn't be arguing with me."

Still, Drake stood his ground. "I'm not leaving. Not this time. I'm not a child anymore, Darling. It's time you stopped treating me like one."

Darling silently cursed at his brother's obstinacy. Even though he wanted to choke him for it, the kid was right. Still, it was so hard to see Drake as a man when he was used to protecting him. "Fine. Stay if you must."

Drake inclined his head to him with a respect he'd never shown Darling before.

"So what's the next step?" Ryn asked. "You pleased a handful of plebs today, but the gerents will all have seizures when they hear that you sidestepped Derkstig, and sided with the workers over them."

Ryn was right. They would have a tantrum to make any infant proud.

"I didn't side with the plebs. I only did what was right and decent where they're concerned."

Ryn snorted. "They're not going to see it that way."

Again, he was right.

Darling considered his options for a few seconds. It was the last thing he wanted to do, but it was something he should have done weeks ago. If he wanted to move forward as governor he couldn't postpone it any longer. "I need to call a meeting with the CDS."

Ryn's eyes widened in alarm. "You sure about that?"

No... The last thing he wanted to do was voluntarily walk into a room where he would be considered a laughingstock by everyone in it. It was why he'd been postponing it.

But he had no real choice. He'd have to meet with them and let them know that they still had their places with the new regime. That he was willing to let bygones be bygones, and to move forward without going after them for the past.

He nodded, then looked past Ryn. "Syn, how fast can you repair my face using Prillion?"

Ryn was aghast at his question. "Are you out of your mind? You do know that shit's illegal, right?"

Darling shrugged nonchalantly. "I'm sure the Tavali"—he cast a meaningful look at Ryn—"can lay hands on it. And it's not illegal in *my* empire."

The look on Syn's face called him all kinds of stupid, but he thought it over before he answered. "I could have the bandages off in about seventy-two hours, but there's no guarantee that one surgery will make that much of a difference. Might not make any improvement at all. That being said, there is a new procedure with skin nanos that might accelerate it and do better than standard reconstruction. It's still experimental though, and I've not used it. I'd have to call in a few favors to get someone to the table who might be willing to try it. But again, I can't guarantee anything. And I don't know how your body will cope with *any* of it. We won't have a clue until you're under and you know how risky that is."

Yes, he did.

But at this point, he'd rather be dead than continue living with his current disfigured face. He saw the panic in Zarya's eyes that told him she didn't want him to risk it at all. Gods, how he wished the rest of the world held her heart. That everyone could see past the ugliness and judge him for something less petty.

It was why he loved her.

Unfortunately, others weren't like that and he knew it better than most.

"Not like you can make it any worse," he said under his breath. He spoke louder to Syn. "Do what you can, as fast as you can. I'll call the meeting for the end of next week." He turned back to Ryn. "Can you run things while I'm down?"

He didn't miss the reluctance in Ryn's eyes, but for once his brother agreed to help him. "I'm willing to try. You going to kick my ass if I screw something up?"

"Probably."

"Oh well then," Ryn said with exaggerated enthusiasm, "by all means, let me get started right away."

Zarya suppressed a smile at Ryn's sarcasm.

Darling ignored it entirely as he walked over to Syn. "How long do you need to prep?"

"I can have you in surgery in about four hours from now. Or we can wait until tomorrow morning."

Darling's gaze locked with hers. She wished she could read his mood, but he gave nothing away. "I want it over with. Please, get started on the prep."

"You sure?" Syn asked.

He nodded.

"All right. Hauk and I will jump on it. See you in four hours at HQ." They headed for the door.

Darling glanced to Drake. "I really wish you'd go home."

"I am home."

A fierce tic started in Darling's jaw. But he didn't say anything more about Drake's refusal. "Can you and Zarya give me a few minutes alone with Ryn and Maris?"

Drake inclined his head to him before he offered his arm to Zarya.

Surprised by the unexpected chivalry, she tucked her hand into the crook of Drake's elbow.

As they started for the door, Darling stopped them. He cupped her cheek in the palm of his hand. "You understand why I'm doing this, right?"

"I do, but I don't agree with it, and I really wish you'd at least wait until tomorrow. You've barely had time to heal from the attack."

His gaze softened before he leaned down to kiss her.

Zarya held him to her when he started to pull away. "Don't you dare die on me."

He nuzzled her cheek. "I know. You'll follow me into hell and beat me if I do," he whispered in her ear.

"You know as stubborn as I am that I will, too."

He kissed her cheek. "I'll be up in a few."

She nodded before Drake led her from the room.

Drake didn't speak until they were alone in the back hallway. Then his entire demeanor turned stiff and icy as he pulled her to a stop. "Why are you here?"

His accusatory tone brought up all of her defenses. "Excuse me?"

He raked her with a suspicious glare. "I'm trying to understand what I saw just now. I've heard every rumor from you're Darling's kitchen slave, his military prisoner, his political hostage, to the most ludicrous of all that says you're his mistress. What exactly are you to my brother?"

That was a difficult question to answer. While she had no doubt that Darling loved her, she wasn't sure what that meant exactly.

Yes, he'd proposed to her, but since they'd gotten back together, he hadn't breathed a single word about marrying her again. Nor had he asked her about her missing engagement ring that the slaver had taken from her. There was no talk about having a future together—not the way they used to talk about it for hours on end.

When they were alone now, all she could focus on was the shadow of mistrust that would darken his eyes. That unguarded look of painful torment.

But most of all, Darling's words haunted her.

"When it's just the two of us and we're alone, I can forget what happened, and I'm better. Then just as I think I'm all right, it all comes barreling back and kicks me in the crotch. I can still hear

you laughing out in the hallway when I needed you most. And honestly, it hurts all over again. I feel betrayed. I know you didn't do it on purpose, but my feelings don't have ears and they don't listen to my head."

Which meant she had no idea where she currently stood with Darling. Honestly, she was too scared to ask lest she find out just how little he trusted her.

So she settled on the simplest truth. "I'm the woman who loves him."

Drake's expression said she was completely insane. "You know he's gay, right?"

"He's not gay."

He laughed until he realized she was deadly serious. "Since when?"

"Always."

Drake scoffed. "You don't know my brother very well, then."

She had to bite back her own laughter. "Trust me. I know him better than most, and I definitely know him better than you do. Darling only claimed to be gay to save your mother's life."

"Bull. Shit."

"No. Truth," she said, duplicating his sharp staccato. "You can ask Maris if you don't believe me. He's the one who helped Darling pull the ruse off all these years."

For a moment, she thought Drake might vomit as he finally accepted the truth. He looked positively green with sickness as he stepped away.

"Are you okay?"

He shook his head before he pinned her with a brutally cold stare. "Are you sure? Positive?"

"Absolutely. No doubt in my mind. He and I have been sleeping together for over three years now."

Once again, he shook his head as if he couldn't grasp the

possibility that Darling had lied to him. Rage blazed deep in his blue eyes. Never had he looked more like Darling than he did right now. "I should go in there, and beat the utter shit out of him."

She scoffed at his bravado. "I think you'd find that extremely hard to do. I've seen him fight. If there's anyone better, I haven't come across them."

Drake held his hand up and laughed. "Are you sure we're talking about the same person? Darling never fights. He hates it."

"And again, I'm telling you that I have seen him in battle. Many times. Bloody and fierce. He never hesitates. Your brother is a major badass with a capital 'B.' He's a fully trained assassin with all the skills *that* entails. How do you think he took your uncle out so easily and held the guards at bay?"

Drake still looked like someone had sucker punched him. "I'm such a stupid bastard," he breathed. "How could I have missed seeing it?" He winced as if some bad memory had slapped him. "Damn, the shit I've said to him over the years for..."

Whatever it was, he didn't finish naming it.

She rubbed his arm comfortingly. "Don't beat yourself up, Drake. Siblings fight. It's what we do."

"No," he breathed. "Not like I did. Until I was fifteen, I was a total asshole to him, in ways you can't begin to imagine. I honestly don't know why he even speaks to me, never mind tolerates my presence, now. You know how he got that long scar on his face, don't you?"

"He fought with Ryn."

"Yeah. Because of *me*." The pain that one word betrayed was so deep that it put an instant lump in her throat for him. The self-loathing in his eyes was hard to look at. "That fight would *never* have happened had I not been a first-rank bastard."

"I don't understand."

Drake ground his teeth so viciously that his jaw muscles protruded. "I was only eight when my father died, and honestly, I barely remember the man. Still, I didn't want to go back to school after the funeral. I wasn't ready. I needed my family around me, especially my mother, but Darling made me leave. He literally picked me up and carried me out of my room and forced me onto the shuttle without any explanation other than I was better off at school."

She felt terrible for Drake. It had to be awful to be so young and alone after something so tragic. She knew how lost she'd been when her parents had died. The only thing that had kept her going after her father's death had been Sorche.

"He was trying to protect you."

Drake pierced her with a cold glare. "That's *not* what he said to me. Ever. All I heard from him was that I needed to keep my grades up and stay at school. Every time I turned around, he stopped me from coming home on holidays and at breaks. He'd arrange for me to stay in the campus dorms or with people I barely knew, and I hated him for it. I kept trying to call my mother, but she wouldn't talk to me either. In one heartbeat, I was an orphan no one wanted, and I had no idea why my entire family had abandoned me and left me to the care of strangers."

That would have been hard on anyone. The anguish in his eyes reminded her so much of Darling that it was all she could do not to pull him into her arms and hold him. "I'm sorry, Drake."

He didn't comment on her sympathy. Instead, he continued. "Then, on the very night when I was *finally* allowed back here during one of my semester breaks, my mother was arrested in front of me. Next thing I know, my brother confessed to the world that he was gay."

"How old were you then?"

"Ten. I didn't even know what gay meant. But I was quickly educated." His gaze burned into hers and the agony there rivaled every bit of the pain that Darling carried. "You have no idea how bad it was. Arturo was so angry over it, that both Lise and I were rounded up and sent back to school that very night, still in our pajamas. Once people found out, which was pretty much immediately, the kids at school were merciless to me over it. All I heard from everyone was that it ran in the family, and that I would be or was already gay, too. From that day on, it was a constant fight against everyone I knew as I tried to prove to them that I wasn't anything like Darling."

Anger whipped through her. "Darling—"

He held his hand up to silence her defense of his brother. "Don't go there. Again, you weren't here in those days. You have no idea what I went through and you didn't see or hear the things I did. And if all that wasn't degrading enough, when I was thirteen, I was going to be honored at school for good merit and for maintaining the highest student body GPA for that year. Something I'd worked my ass off for. Night and day. Then what happens? The day before the ceremony, Darling gets caught screwing Senator Nylan, and that shit went instantly viral."

Now it was her turn to feel sucker punched. "Excuse me?"

He nodded bitterly. "Oh yeah. There were pictures and videos of the two of them circulating everywhere. You couldn't get away from it or miss it. Everyone knew about it. Because of Darling's scandal and the fact my school didn't want to even admit they had a Cruel on their roster, *my* award that I'd worked so hard for was yanked. I lost my position on the school team and in our student government. They put *me* on probation, and I was pulled from the regular residence hall and put in with the social rejects and delinquents. Meanwhile, Darling ended up in a mental institution over it."

That was *not* the story Maris had told her. Did Maris not know or had he outright lied to her?

Drake continued with his angry tirade. "For years, Darling was in and out of them. Whenever I talked to my mother about it—which was only twice a year if I was lucky—all she'd say was that Darling had a lot of problems, and that Arturo was trying to help him with them. And I believed her. I had no reason not to. The only member of my family who called every week to check on me *was* Arturo, who told me that I was always welcome to come home anytime I wanted. He said that Darling had snapped after my father's death and gone crazy. That he was addicted to drugs and alcohol, and that I shouldn't waste my time worrying about him. I almost never heard from Darling and when I did, he was either drunk or high—I couldn't tell which. But his words were always slurred, if not completely incoherent. All I could ever make out for sure was his insistence that I stay as far away from here as I could."

Zarya rolled her eyes at his assumption. Most likely those conversations came while Darling was on pain medication for the beatings Arturo routinely gave him.

Or the meds they pumped into him whenever he was in an institution.

Drake laughed bitterly. "By the time I hit fifteen, I was basically psychotic from everything I'd been through. I couldn't stand any of them. Not my mother, my sister, and definitely not my brother, whose every scandal rained down on *my* ass like a firestorm. I didn't want to be in school anymore and deal with that shit, and I hated Darling in a way you can't imagine. The handful of times I'd seen him over the years, he was either so effeminate or so terrified of his own shadow that he repulsed me. Every time I turned around, Lise would call saying Darling had tried to kill himself again. I prayed every night that his next attempt would not only be successful, but come sooner rather than later..."

Wanting to slap him for that last comment, Zarya gaped at

another tidbit no one had mentioned. What else didn't she know about Darling's past?

Drake drew a ragged breath. "I never saw Darling that he didn't have his head down and his arms wrapped around his body as if he was trying to become invisible. He'd cower and cringe if anyone came near him. He wouldn't look anyone in the eye. Not even me. I thought he was a worthless coward, and I have called him every insult you can imagine."

Tears welled in her eyes as she realized that what Drake had seen was the aftermath of Darling's rapes and abuse. The times in his life when he'd needed his family most of all.

The times when they'd all let him down and left him to face it.

Alone.

She tried to tell herself that Drake, who was three and a half years younger than Darling, had been far too young to realize what was going on, but still she was mad at him for being so selfish and stupid.

"The summer I turned fifteen," Drake continued, "if all of that wasn't bad enough, I found out that Arturo was syphoning off our inheritance. When I asked Darling if he knew, he sounded wasted as usual. He told me to let it go and not worry about it—that it was no big deal. Furious over his cavalier attitude, I signed myself out of school and came home. I'd intended to stay here and be taught by a tutor like he was so that I could keep an eye on our money before Arturo stole it all. Darling met me at the front door on my arrival and told me I needed to leave immediately and go back to school. He had bruises all over his face and a busted lip. I asked him what had happened, but he wouldn't answer. He wouldn't even look at me. You know what I said to him then?"

"No." She wasn't sure if she wanted to know.

He curled his lip in self-disgust. "Next time you give head, you should wear protective gear."

Fury tore through her. "Why would you say that to him?"

His eyes blazed with hatred, but she wasn't sure if it was for him, Darling, or for both of them. "Because at least once a day, *every* single day for years, someone e-mailed me photos of a naked Darling being groped by a man old enough to be our grandfather, with some kind of insult for both of us tagged to it. They didn't stop until Darling and Syn became tight, and Syn hacked in and deleted every online copy. You have no idea how humiliating it is to be laughed at for something your brother did that you had no control over. How many times other men propositioned *me* because of it. I was sick of hearing and seeing it."

Zarya couldn't make any sense of that. Maris had told her that Darling had never experimented. Had those pictures been forgeries?

Or was there something about Darling that Maris didn't know?

"Anyway," Drake continued, "I pushed past him and went to my room. He dogged me every step of the way there, telling me that I had to leave before Arturo found out I was in the palace. He said that Arturo would kill me if I mentioned the missing money to him. That Arturo would be furious at me for coming home without permission. I didn't know the man Darling described. Arturo had never been violent toward me in any way. Never raised his voice. So I stayed. And that night...I found out fast why Darling's face looked the way it did and why Darling was so skittish of Arturo. Even with my fight training, Arturo beat me unconscious, and just like Darling had warned, he damn near killed me. I didn't even get a chance to accuse him of his theft before he had me on the floor."

"What did Darling do?"

Drake clenched his eyes closed as if he were reliving that night. But he didn't answer her question. At least not right away. "When I finally came to after the beating, I lay in the hospital, feeling sorry for myself, thinking that I had no family who gave a shit about me. No one came to check on me or call. Not until two days later. I was still in ICU on a ventilator, unable to speak. Darling came in, looking even worse than he had the night he'd warned me how stupid I was. His eyes were so swollen and bruised, he could barely open them. He had one arm in a sling, and the other one in a brace from a third-degree sprain. He was just a krikken kid, too. You know? I still don't understand how he could hold himself up in that condition, never mind move. Yet with all that pain, he'd come to see me even though he should have still been in bed himself.

"I found out later from Maris that once Darling had called the medics for me, he'd gone after Arturo with everything he had and that Arturo, after beating the shit out of him, had thrown him down the main palace stairs. As soon as Darling had been able to get out of bed, he'd come straight to the hospital to sit with me, so that I wouldn't be alone there. And do you know what Darling's first words to me were?"

She shook her head.

"I'm so sorry I couldn't protect you better. I promise I won't let him get a hold of you again." Tears swam in Drake's eyes. "After all the mean, awful shit I'd said to him over the years. After being a complete and utter dick whenever I was around him, he apologized to me. *Apologized.* Like it was somehow his fault I was an idiot who wouldn't listen. And it was then that I found out why his speech was always slurred when he called me at school."

"Because of his pain meds..."

He swallowed hard. "No, it was from the way he had to hold his mouth to speak around a busted jaw and loose teeth. You talk about feeling like a worthless piece of shit...It killed me that I wasn't able to tell him how sorry I was for *everything.* That I couldn't tell him how grateful I was he'd saved my life. That I didn't care what anyone else said or thought about him. I was finally proud to call him my brother. Most of all, I wanted to tell him that I loved him, too."

Drake drew a ragged breath. "Three days later when they finally took me off the ventilator and moved me to a regular room, he went to beg Ryn to help us. Something he'd never done before. But Darling was so afraid I'd go after Arturo again, that he was willing to sacrifice his dignity to keep me safe. So the fight they got into that scarred him so badly was over *my* dumb, stupid, igno-rant ass."

His gaze haunted, he cleared his throat. "That beating I took opened my eyes to a lot of things. I realized then that Darling had kept us at school so that we wouldn't be in the line of Arturo's fury, while Darling was forced to live here and bear the brunt of it. Day in and day out. And instead of saying thank you for it, all I'd ever done was insult him because I was too busy listening to lies about him rather than bothering to discover the truth for myself. To this day, I don't understand how he stood living here, or toler-ated us. He has every right to begrudge us every breath we take, and yet he doesn't. And now you're telling me that all this time he wasn't even gay..." He cursed under his breath. "If that's true, then explain to me where those photos came from."

"I don't know. I have no idea. But I know, beyond a shadow of a doubt, that Darling wasn't a willing participant."

Glancing down the hallway, Drake focused his gaze past her. He went ramrod stiff.

She turned to see Darling approaching them.

Darling hesitated as he saw them together in the hallway, not far from his room. "Is something wrong?" he asked her.

She smiled to allay his fears. "Not at all. We were just talking."

Suspicion hung heavy in Darling's gaze. "About?"

"The fact that you're not gay, you asshole," Drake snarled at him. "Why didn't you ever tell me?"

Darling shrugged with a nonchalance she was pretty sure he didn't feel. "You enjoyed insulting me over it too much. I didn't want to take away your only creative outlet."

"You are such a bastard. I'm serious, Dar. Why didn't you say something?"

Darling sobered. "I know your temper, Drake. I couldn't risk you popping off at the mouth about it to someone who might tell Arturo."

Arms akimbo, Drake glared at him. "Thanks for the vote of confidence. Appreciate it."

"What are big brothers for?"

"Apparently not much," Drake breathed. "I'm going to tell Lise to get ready to leave for your surgery. I'll see you two later."

After Drake left them alone, she wrapped her arm around Darling's as they continued on to his room. "Drake really loves you."

"I know he does. Most of the time, I love him, too." He opened the door to his bedroom and allowed her to enter first. "And I can tell by the look in your eyes that something's bothering you. What's wrong?"

She hesitated inside the room. "I probably shouldn't say anything."

"Never stopped you before."

"True." But this was extremely personal and she wasn't sure how he'd react to her asking about the photographs. Fact or fiction, it had to be something that had caused him a great deal of pain over the years. As bad as Drake thought his agony was, she was certain it couldn't compare to Darling's.

Part of her didn't want to dredge it up, but the other part of her wanted to know the truth.

Darling scowled at her. "You know you can talk to me about anything."

Yeah, but she didn't want to hurt him. He'd been kicked enough.

Taking a deep breath for courage, she forced herself to broach a topic she was sure was brutal. "Drake mentioned something about photos of you and—"

He cursed so foully it broke her words off. By his furious expression, she knew she didn't have to finish her sentence.

Darling knew exactly what she was talking about.

"Why the hell would he mention *that* to you?"

"Because it was why he felt justified in insulting you when he was younger."

"Of course it was," Darling sneered. " 'Cause everything's always about Drake."

She didn't comment on his hostile words. "So what happened?"

Darling flinched as his memories went to a place and time he never wanted to think about again. Something he did his damnedest to never, ever remember. In a life filled with degradation and pain, that entire ordeal reigned supreme in total humiliation.

Why can't I live that one afternoon down?

Every time he thought it was buried, it came back like a vicious curse.

Now Zarya knew about it, too.

He winced. "I was stupid."

"How so?"

He wanted to curse her for her insistence. But then, that was Zarya. Whenever she wanted something, she wouldn't give up until she got it. "I'm going to kill that little bastard for telling you. Please, don't make me relive it, okay?" Darling wasn't sure if he could survive it again.

It hurt *that* much. Even all these years later.

Why the hell wouldn't it die?

Nodding, Zarya caught him against her and held him close. "I'm sorry I asked. You don't have to tell me. It's fine. You're allowed to have your secrets."

In the moment, he'd never loved her more, and as he'd done hundreds of times in the past, he found himself telling her something he'd never told anyone else.

Even though it shredded him to do so.

"By Caronese law, once I turned sixteen, I was old enough to choose another guardian to be the Grand Counsel instead of Arturo. For several months, I debated on whether or not to leave everything alone or replace him. Finally, I decided it was time to do it."

"Why did you wait so long?"

"By that time, Arturo had tightened the noose around me to the point I couldn't breathe. I was seldom allowed contact with anyone from the ruling class. Not my mother, my siblings, or even Maris. And you have to have a guardian who is a natural-born Caronese aristo with the right bloodline. More than that, I needed one willing to stand up to Arturo. Most weren't, and I knew it. He kept everyone around him so intimidated that they didn't dare."

Zarya listened as he stepped away and paced a small area in front of her. "So what happened with Senator Nylan?"

Darling flinched as if the name itself struck him like a blow. "He was a distant cousin on my father's side, and I knew from past encounters with him that he thought I was...pretty." He spat the word out. "He'd made several lewd remarks and offers to me over the years after my father's death."

Her heart broke at those words.

He glanced at her and she saw the torment that scarred his soul worse than her men had scarred his body. "I just wanted the pain to stop, Zarya. Just for one minute of my life. I was so tired of being beat on, locked up, and drugged. I thought it would be easier to be some man's kept whore than another one's punching bag. And by then, I'd learned that Arturo wasn't just beating on me. He was raping my mother—something he'd been doing since the night he killed my father. He used me against her, the same way he used my family against me. It's why she hates me so much. Why she hasn't been able to look at me since I was twelve years old. Every time she hears my name, she flinches because of what he did to her. I figured that since everyone already thought I was gay, what would it matter? Anything had to be better than the hell we were in."

She pulled him into her arms so that she could comfort him. "What happened?"

He actually trembled from the pain of his memories as he laid his head on her shoulder and held her close. "I told Nylan I was willing to be...mentored by him any way he wanted if he would assume my guardianship. He said that he didn't buy things sight unseen. So he made me take all my clothes off in front of him."

"Oh baby..."

"Yeah..." Darling's voice was barely more than a whisper. "He walked around me, looking me up and down, like a piece of meat in the market. I wasn't allowed to cover myself while he inspected me from head to toe. I felt so humiliated that I thought I was going to vomit right there. He moved to stand behind me so that he could fondle me, and he told me to moan out loud like a whore for him. To tell him how much I craved him and to beg him to touch me even though all I wanted to do was run."

She tightened her arms around Darling's waist, wishing she could burn that memory out of him forever. No wonder he seldom made a single sound whenever they had sex. It probably reminded him of that day. "You don't have to say anything else, baby."

He nuzzled his cheek against hers. "There's not much more to tell. I had no idea the sick bastard was recording the whole thing.

When I failed to get hard for him, he told me that he'd have to think it over and get back to me. He watched me dress and I left. By the time I got home—after I'd thrown up a couple of times— he'd sent pictures of us to Arturo, telling him I was the best and tightest piece of ass he'd ever had. And that while it was tempting to assume my guardianship, I needed someone with a firmer hand to control me."

She could only imagine how that went over. "Why would he do such a thing?"

"To get back at me for all the times I'd turned him down over the years. He wanted me humiliated . . . and he succeeded."

Never in her life had she wanted to kill anyone more than she did Nylan. Damn him for his cruelty.

Darling winced. "Arturo met me at the door, and then put me through it. Hoping he'd finally kill me, I spat the blood out of my mouth and laughed at him. I told him he hit like a girl. And that I'd whore myself to any man who'd get him out of my life. As bad as I'd been beaten before then, it was nothing like that night. I didn't think he'd ever stop. At some point, I passed out. When I came to, I was in a mental institution."

"Maris said it was done to cure your homosexuality."

He laughed bitterly. "That's what my file says, and it's what I let other people think. But it was done to teach me a lesson about trying to find another guardian. Not that I needed it. Believe me. After what Nylan did to me, I wasn't about to try again. Besides, I knew no one would ever help me. No one cared. I'd been stupid for even trying. I was just so desperate that I was willing to do any- thing. And those pictures were posted *everywhere*, by both Arturo and Nylan. They haunted me for years. Every time I thought I could put it behind me, someone would slap me in the face with them. Every member of the Caronese aristocracy has seen them and they've all had something horrendous to say to me over it."

She couldn't imagine anything worse. It'd been bad enough to experience it, but to have other people dredge it up constantly and throw it in your face...

Glancing down, she saw the scars on Darling's wrists from his suicide attempts that Drake had told her about. Her hands trembling, she lifted his so that she could kiss them. "How many times did you—"

"Three. It was part of the reason everything was taken out of my room and I was strip-searched every night. Why my guards would randomly come in at all hours to wake me. The gods forbid, I should die and escape my hell."

She laid her hand against his cheek. "I'm glad you're still here."

Darling's stomach tightened at the love he saw in her eyes. But it wasn't enough to take away the misery of those memories. Nothing could.

Yet she helped him in ways he'd have never thought possible. Like Maris, she didn't judge him by his mistakes. Nor did she hold them against him. Or use them to hurt him. They didn't make him less in her eyes.

For that alone, he was eternally grateful.

She kissed his lips. "I'm so sorry for what they did to you, and I swear I will never, ever speak of it again or mention that bastard's name. May he rot in hell for eternity."

He tightened his arms around her. "I've never told anyone what really happened, Z. Not even Maris. I'm sure he's seen the photos, too, but he's been decent enough to keep silent about them. Too bad Drake couldn't."

While he loved his brother, there were times he couldn't stand him. Why would Drake have told her about the most horrific event of his entire life?

Why couldn't Drake leave things alone?

"Hey," Zarya breathed, stepping back and forcing him to look at her. "I love you, Darling. I really do. It's that capacity you have to care about others more than you care about yourself that has always drawn me to you. You've been my hero from that first moment when you risked your life to climb out onto my roof to get my cat for me, to the moment when I first saw Kere carrying Timmon to safety. The rest of us ran for cover during that ambush, but you ran into it, knowing we had soldiers pinned down. I've never known anyone braver than you."

"I don't feel brave." Most days, he just felt like complete and utter hell.

Zarya kissed him lightly on the lips. "And that's what makes you so wonderful. You don't see the beauty that is you. I hate that you focus on your handful of flaws."

Why shouldn't he? "Everyone else does."

"Screw them if they do," she said as her anger blazed in those beautiful amber eyes. "Do you really care what they think? Are any of them that important to you?"

"No. But it doesn't stop it from hurting."

Zarya blinked away the tears in her eyes. "You're right. But my father used to have a saying. 'Don't let them steal your day.' *Never* give them that kind of power over you. They're not worth it."

Darling let those words soothe him, along with her fingers that toyed with his hair against his collar. In his mind, he saw an image of her as a little girl on that day when they'd first met, crying and begging for her big brother to save her cat. Wanting to play ball outside, Gerrit had callously brushed her aside and ignored her pleas.

But those tears and her concern for her pet had touched him even as a boy. Unable to walk away from her misery, Darling had gladly braved the high-pitched roof of her father's mansion to make her smile.

It was the first time in his life that he'd felt heroic. She'd been so grateful. So thrilled. She'd even hugged him for it, then given him the cookie she'd been saving for herself.

His siblings had always taken his help for granted. He could give them the entire universe and they'd think nothing of it. As for his parents, they expected it of him, and were extremely disappointed whenever he failed to help someone.

But not Zarya. She had never failed to make him feel so incredibly special and courageous. It was why he'd always begged his father to take him along whenever his father visited Lord Starska. As soon as Zarya saw them coming into the palace, her entire face would light up and she'd run as fast as she could to say hi to him.

In all the years they'd been apart, he'd never forgotten the way she made him feel.

Welcomed. Appreciated. Noble.

Loved.

It had been the same when he, as Kere, had been working with the Sentella on a rescue mission to save the Caronese Resistance members who'd been pinned down on a remote outpost. Since he hadn't heard a single word about any of the Starskas in years, he'd assumed Zarya was long dead, or that she was so deep in hiding that he'd never see her again.

He and Hauk had volunteered to get as many of the Resistance soldiers out as they could. Smoke and enemy fire had been thick all around them.

While Hauk secured the rear, Darling had gone on ahead. He grabbed the first soldier on the ground that he'd come to and pulled him back to where the bulk of the Resistance's troops had been pinned down for hours.

There in the midst of utter chaos, with hell itself raining down on them, Darling had stared into that pair of amber eyes that had haunted him as a boy.

Zarya had smiled up at him with that same, exact look she'd

SHERRILYN KENYON

worn when he saved her cat—the look that made some unknown part of him soar.

"Thank you!" she'd breathed with such sincerity that he'd glanced behind him to see if she was talking to someone else.

Momentarily stunned by the way she smiled at him, he'd taken a shot to his shoulder that had sent him into the wall next to her. Cursing, she'd sprung to her feet and opened cover fire to protect him from the Caronese guard corps.

He'd been in love with her ever since.

But never in all the talks about childhood they'd had since their first meeting as adults had she ever mentioned those long ago afternoons he'd spent with her as a boy. He'd assumed that they had meant nothing to her. That her hatred for his family had destroyed all remnants of what, to him, had been some of the happiest moments of his life.

He cupped her cheek in his hand. "You remember us as children?"

Her smile widened. "I remember *you*."

"Why did you never mention it?"

She grimaced. "Like yours, my childhood memories are too painful to visit, so I try to never go there. Not because they were awful, but because we were so happy before your father died, that it hurt too much to remember them. Until I met you as an adult, I never thought I'd ever be happy like that again."

Darling inhaled her scent as he savored the sensation of her arms around him.

Right now, his entire world was in chaos. His people were revolting...in more ways than one. Life was changing faster than he could handle.

The only constant he had was Zarya.

Nothing good ever lasts. If he'd learned nothing else in his life, it was that one fact. Every time he'd found solace or comfort of any kind, it had been ripped from him. It was why he should have never proposed to her. Had he refrained, he could have saved them both a year of utter hell.

Yet he wanted this relationship to be real. Most of all, he needed it to last.

But in his heart, he knew the truth. This was temporary and soon the gods would divide them again as they always did.

He wasn't meant to have Zarya. He wasn't meant to be happy. Whenever he tried to make his life better, the gods made it worse.

Just don't let her die. He could handle anything except that.

Closing his eyes, he held her tight against him, knowing that all too soon he'd have to let her go for good.

Senna listened as the remnants of the Resistance met in a dive hole not far from where the Workers Coalition had been rallying. No more than a few moments ago, Gerst had returned from the palace and disbanded them.

She narrowed her eyes at Hector. "I told you Cruel has mind control. Now you have proof of it."

Hector nodded angrily. "He is far more cunning and dangerous than his uncle ever was." He slid his drive toward her. "Those are his medical records from when he was committed. He's extremely unstable. Anything can set him off and as far as I can find out, he still has bombs planted all over the city that could explode at any moment."

"Then how do we bring him down?"

Hector shook his head. "He should never have survived our attack. We have to get him out of the way so that our ally can seize the throne."

She couldn't agree more. "What about Starska?"

"We need to accept the fact that she might be lost to us. There's no telling what he's done to her by now. How much damage she's taken."

"We can't leave her with him."

"What do you suggest?" Hector asked.

Senna fished her own small drive out of her pocket and slid it toward him. "I have a way to bring him down once and for all, and to get our leader back. Cruel won't even know what hit him. I promise you, next time, he will die."

15

Zarya had known that Darling, as Kere, had an extended family where the Sentella was concerned. But honestly, she'd had no idea exactly how massive it was. Not until they walked into the Sentella's central headquarters and literally everyone they came into contact with took a minute to speak with him and wish him well.

And she meant *everyone*. From the cleaning staff to the soldiers to the engineers. Everyone they saw seemed to know him, and most shocking of all, he knew them. Darling asked about them, their families and friends, and mentioned details that showed he not only remembered who they were, but that he cared about their lives, too. That all of them meant something to him.

If she'd ever had any doubts about what a great governor he'd be, this alone would have allayed all fears. Standing back to watch him interact with his people, she was stunned by just how generous and kind Darling really was.

In some ways it was hard to rectify the fierce warrior she knew him to be with the man who was able to soothe a little girl's fears and to greet every worker with a smile and a handshake.

He absolutely amazed her.

"They like him best," Hauk whispered in her ear as they were

371

stopped yet again so that Darling could talk to one of the engineers. "Notice how they all ignore me like I'm not even here."

Maris snorted. "It's because you always threaten to eat them."

"Well there is that," Hauk said with a fang-enhanced smile.

She had no idea why, but she really liked the acerbic Andarion.

He leaned over to whisper to her, "Still...Darling's their favorite."

Zarya laughed at Hauk's feigned pout.

In fact, it took them so long to get down the hallway, that Syn ended up bringing a stretcher for Darling.

His tone dry, Syn pulled Darling's shoulder and urged him toward it. "Get on here. Lie down. And don't say anything."

Darling rolled his eyes before he obeyed.

Winking at her, Syn covered him with a sheet. "I don't know what we're going to do with Lord Social here."

"I vote we shoot him," Hauk said with an evil smirk.

"You know, there's nothing wrong with my hearing. Right, Hauk?"

Hauk grinned at Darling's comment. "Yeah. Like I care."

"You will when I send you a special gift that's wrapped with wiring."

"Children..." Syn had the voice of a stressed parent. "Let's not fight."

"Yes, Dad," they said in unison.

She glanced over her shoulder at Maris who was following them. Drake and Lise were behind him.

"They're always like this," Maris mouthed to her.

Shaking her head, she wasn't quite sure what to make of this more playful side of Darling. As Kere, he'd been reserved and formal whenever he interacted with her soldiers. Ruthless and lethal with his enemies. As governor, he'd been stern and fierce. Guarded. With Maris, like her and his younger siblings, he was protective and strong. Ever watchful and ready to attack anyone who hurt them.

In private, she'd seen glimpses of this playful side of his personality, but he'd never been quite this open and at ease, even with her. It was like a part of him had waited for her to betray or hurt him. Like he feared that she'd reject him if he acted goofy around her.

Yet here in the heart of the Sentella, while on his way to a risky surgery, he was completely at ease and relaxed. Even with people as deadly as Syn and Hauk. His behavior reminded him more of how his brother and sister acted around him.

But then, Darling knew they would kill or die for him just as he would for them. He trusted Hauk and Syn, she realized. Fully.

More than he's ever trusted me. And that stung on a level so deep, she had to force herself not to flinch from it. They owned a part of Darling that she could never reach.

"Are you okay?" Maris asked her.

She nodded in spite of the fact it was a lie. She wanted Darling to give her this side of himself, too. To be so comfortable with her that he could be silly and childlike without reservation.

As they entered the waiting room, Zarya slowed. Trepidation filled her at the sight of all the unfamiliar people gathered there to see Darling.

Nykyrian Quiakides she knew immediately by sight, but only because his face had once adorned more wanted lists than hers and Darling's combined. Given his extreme height and long white-blond hair that was braided down his back, he was a hard man to miss. And while he was no longer a League assassin, he still wore the dark sunglasses that kept anyone from seeing what he was looking at or who he was targeting.

Next to him was an extremely pregnant redhead. She put her hand on Darling's arm to stop Syn from taking him straight into the operating room.

Pulling the sheet back, she tsked at him. "Don't tell me they couldn't get you here any other way."

Darling laughed. "Ah, you know. It happens."

The woman took his hand into hers, sending a little wave of jealousy through Zarya. "I know Syn will take care of you, but… I love you, sweetie. God speed and keep you." She placed a kiss on Darling's forehead, then stepped back.

"Don't worry," Maris whispered in Zarya's ear. "Kiara's an old friend of Darling's and she's married to the tall blond killer dwarfing her."

In spite of Maris's kindness, Zarya was beginning to feel like an outsider. Even as long as she and Darling had been together, there was still a lot about Darling she didn't know. And the people here brought that home with a vengeance. Not only did she not know who they were, she wasn't sure what they meant to him.

The next to stop Darling was a rather large group.

She could identify the tallest of the men, but again only by reputation. Dressed more like a Tavali pirate than royalty—right down to the blaster strapped to his lean hips—Caillen de Orczy was the Exeterian prince and heir to his father's empire. He'd been hunted a couple of years back when the League had erroneously accused him of assassinating his father and the Qillaq queen. For weeks, no one had been able to go near any news broadcast without seeing his face.

Tall, dark, and exceptionally gorgeous, Caillen had his arm around a brunette woman who was holding a little girl. Asleep on the woman's shoulder, the girl looked so much like her that it had to be her daughter.

And if Zarya didn't miss her guess, the red-haired woman beside Caillen was Shahara Dagan—one of the most lethal tracers in the business. Her name was synonymous with death, and anyone who carried a bounty on their life knew exactly who *she* was.

You'd be a fool not to. No one wanted to tangle with Shahara. Most of all, they didn't want to be pursued by her.

Shahara held a toddler boy in her arms. He blew Darling a precious kiss before laughing and bouncing in his mother's arms. Then he practically jumped from Shahara to Syn who caught him and held him tight against his chest before he kissed the boy's cheek.

Zarya's jaw went slack as she realized the boy looked just like Syn.

"Syn has a son?" she asked Maris.

"Two, actually. The other was with his first wife."

She arched a brow at that disclosure.

"It's a really long story," Maris added.

The boy launched himself from Syn to Darling who sat up to catch him. Squealing, the boy wrapped his little arms tight around Darling's neck and hugged him close like he was another father.

"Hey, little guy," Darling said with a laugh. "Look how big you've grown."

The boy laughed and bounced in Darling's arms.

Her heart melted at the sight. Especially when Darling tickled him, then kissed his cheek. In that one moment, she could see Darling as a father...

"Dang, Shay," Darling said to Syn's wife. "What have you been feeding my boy? He weighs a ton."

"He does not," she said defensively. "He's perfect for his age. Absolutely perfect."

Darling made a face. "He's also smelly."

Shahara narrowed her eyes at Darling and then Syn in turn. "If you two weren't heading into surgery, I'd make one of you change him." She clapped her hands at the boy. "Come to Mama, Devy-baby."

The boy arched his back and fell into her arms.

"I'll change him for you," the man with her group said. He looked at the shorter of the two women with Shahara. "I need to practice. I'm sure Tess is going to make me change more than my fair share."

The woman who must be Tess grinned. "Oh baby, you know it. But look on the bright side, Thad. You still have a few more months of freedom before Devyn has a cousin."

Groaning, Thad carried a laughing Devyn out of the room.

Tess and the taller woman with brown hair came forward to wish Darling well and give him a quick kiss on the cheek.

The last group that stood in front of the operating room doors was all male and all feral testosterone.

Among them was Ryn who had returned to wearing his black Tavali gear. In fact, all four of them belonged to that renegade pirate group. An Andarion who reminded her of Hauk, a blond human male, and another man with dark hair whose features were similar to the woman with Prince Caillen.

All four of them touched Darling on the shoulder or bumped knuckles with him, but none of them spoke. It was as if their bond to him was such that no words were needed.

As Syn started to take him through the doors, Darling made him stop. Still sitting on the stretcher, he crooked his finger at her.

Heat exploded over her face as everyone turned to stare at her with great curiosity. Trying not to notice, she went to Darling.

He took her hand into his and offered her a grim smile. "Here's to hoping, right?"

Her stomach tightened as a wave of fear for him consumed her. "I still wish you wouldn't do this."

Cupping his hands around the one he held, he led it to his lips so that he could kiss her fingers. He nipped one, sending a chill along her spine that made her wish they were alone. She leaned down to kiss his lips.

When she pulled back, he winked at her. "I'll be fine," he promised. "After all, someone besides Sorche has to harass you." He held on to her hand until the hospital staff stopped her from entering the operating area. Even then, he gave one last squeeze before he reluctantly released her hand.

Tears swam in her eyes as he vanished from her sight and the doors closed, separating them. *Please don't die on me...*

The mere thought made her light-headed and ill. She couldn't bury another person she loved. She couldn't.

Maris wrapped his arms around her shoulders and held her tightly. "Have faith. He'll be fine, Z."

Leaning back against his chest, she brushed her hand over his arms. "He better be, Mari. I'd hate to have to kill Syn."

In the next instant, she was surrounded by people who were hammering her with questions so fast that she couldn't distinguish any one of them. She was so grateful that Maris held her, otherwise she'd be terrified.

A loud whistle split the air.

They all turned to look at Nykyrian. "Yes, everyone. Darling has a *girl*—as in fully female—friend. Her name is Zarya. Try not to run her off. Darling will be most unhappy with you if you do."

The muscular brunette who was holding the little girl elbowed Caillen in his stomach. "I told you Darling wasn't gay. Next time, you'll listen to me, won't you?" Smiling sweetly, she stepped forward to offer Zarya her hand. "I'm Desideria Denarii de Orczy."

Zarya tried not to gape at the impressive pedigree displayed by that single name. "The Qillaq princess?"

"Was. Now happily Exeterian." She rubbed Caillen's stomach where she'd elbowed him. "And this is my most wonderful husband Caillen and our daughter Lillya who will wake up eventually and say hi."

Before Zarya could absorb that, Thad returned to hand Devyn back to his mother.

Taking her son, she stepped forward to introduce herself. "I'm Shahara, Syn's wife and Caillen's oldest sister. And I hate to mention this on our first meeting and all, but if you try to kill Syn, I'll really hurt you."

Zarya wasn't sure what to make of that, but one thing was certain. Shahara meant it.

Maris was right, there had to be one heck of a story as to how Syn had ended up married to one of the most lethal tracers in the Nine Systems. And how that tracer was related to an Exeterian prince...

It was enough to boggle the mind.

Shahara tickled the chin of her son, making him laugh out loud. "And this exceptionally handsome boy genius is our baby Devyn—the most spoiled child in the entire universe."

He squealed happily at Zarya as if he agreed completely with his mother's description for him.

Shahara held her hand up to the women who were with her. "These are my sisters Kasen and Tess. And Tess's husband, Thad."

Zarya did her best to commit all of them to memory. "Nice meeting you."

The other red-haired woman stepped forward with a regal grace that was impressive. "I'm Kiara Quiakides and the fiercely stern blond on my right is my husband Nykyrian. And we have other kids, but this," she rubbed her hand over her distended belly, "is the only one with us right now. The others are at home, hopefully not making their nannies too crazy."

Nykyrian let out an intimidating grunt. "If Adron sets fire to his room one more time, I vote we make him live outside in a tent."

Everyone laughed. Except Kiara who appeared to actually consider it.

Ryn led the group of men over. "These are..." He hesitated as if he couldn't think of how to introduce them to her. "Hell, I don't know what to call them that's fit for mixed company. They're family, too." He indicated the dark-haired man next to him. "Chayden Aniwaya is Desideria's older brother."

Chayden flashed a wicked grin at his sister. "I would stand near *her*, but she not only elbows, she kicks."

Desideria made a sound of extreme annoyance, then smiled. "Oh it's true. I do."

Zarya laughed at them, wondering how a prince could also be a Tavali pirate...

The insanely handsome blond with them stepped forward without an introduction and offered her his hand. "I'm Nero Scalera."

A strange rush went up her arm as she made contact with him. It was as if he had some kind of aura so powerful, it sizzled in the air around them.

"Hi," she said, hoping she didn't betray her unease. There was something about Nero that was truly frightening. Even more so than Nykyrian, and that was saying something.

Hauk draped his arm over the other Andarion. "This is my socially inept, evil older brother Fain."

"Who is destined to become an only child in the near future." There was a wicked glint in his eerie eyes as he narrowed his gaze at his younger brother.

Hauk took his threat in stride. "Nah, you love me and you know it."

"You go on and believe those lies if you want. I know the truth and it doesn't scare me."

"All right." Chayden broke them apart. "Hauks behave. I don't want to have to wash blood out of my clothes again today. I'm out of fresh shirts."

"Don't worry," Desideria said to Zarya in a loud whisper.

"You'll eventually learn all of our names and quirks. It took me awhile to keep them straight myself."

As Zarya glanced around them, trying to remember who everyone was, she noticed one person was missing from the group.

Jayne. That wretched bitch who'd sold her...

Thank the gods for small favors. She was one person Zarya didn't want to ever see again.

But that good grace didn't last more than about an hour.

Sitting between Sorche and Lise, who were studying while they waited for Syn to update them, Zarya had just started to relax when the door opened.

Jayne came in with a smile on her face.

A smile that died the instant she met Zarya's gaze. Growling something that had to be a curse in whatever Jayne's native tongue was, she rushed toward Zarya.

Zarya shot to her feet, ready to battle the woman until one of them was dead.

But before Jayne could reach her, Nykyrian caught Jayne by the waist and tossed her over his shoulder with so little effort that it was truly frightening.

And impressive since Jayne was not only tall, but well muscled.

"Damn you, Andarion!" Jayne said between gritted teeth. "Put me down!"

Nykyrian tightened his grip on her as she tried to kick him. "Not until you get a hold of yourself."

Jayne made a sound of supreme agitation before she settled down. Somewhat. "What's *she* doing here?"

Drake answered. "Apparently seeing my brother..." He slid an insidious glance toward Zarya. "Among other things from what I've heard."

Zarya's face flamed.

Jayne froze as she looked around the gathered men for confirmation. "What?"

"Yeah." Drake grinned up at Jayne since Nykyrian had yet to put her down. "And if you harm her, Darling will probably hurt you over it."

Scowling, Jayne looked to Maris. "Mari? Is Drake lying to me?"

"Not a bit. About *any* of it. Darling will have your rump for a chew toy if you harm one hair on her head."

Jayne grumbled in that unknown language, but she was much calmer now.

Nykyrian finally set her back on her feet, then put his hands on her shoulders to steady her. "You okay?"

She nodded. "You know, boss, I really hate it when you do things like that to me."

"I know. But I didn't want our youngest brother-in-arms to send you a special package wrapped in wire."

"Fine." Jayne moved to stand in front of Zarya while all the men watched on nervously, ready to grab her again if they needed to. "I'm completely baffled by your presence here, and why Darling isn't gay anymore, but for his sake and the fact that I love him like a brother, shall we put the past behind us and try to be friendly enemies?"

What Zarya would rather do is bury the hatchet between Jayne's eyes. Yet the woman was right. For Darling's sake, they needed to be at least cordial to one another.

"I'm good with that." Zarya shook Jayne's proffered hand.

Jayne leaned in to speak to her in a low tone. "If you hurt Darling at all, I will slice open your throat and bathe in your blood."

Zarya gave her a taunting smile. "Good luck with that. It didn't go so well for the last person who tried it."

There was a grudging light of respect in Jayne's gaze. With an assassin's salute, Jayne stepped back, then moved to stand with Fain and Nero.

Lise came to stand behind Zarya and patted her hand affectionately. "If it makes you feel any better, Jayne doesn't like me either."

How could anyone not like Lise?

Well, her tantrum with Maris notwithstanding, Lise was usually an angel. "Why?"

"I threw up on her when I was a kid and she never got over it. That woman can hold a grudge like no one I've ever seen."

Great. Just what she needed. One more person wanting her dead.

Not wanting to think about that, Zarya laughed at why Jayne would hate Lise.

Lise resumed her seat next to Sorche who returned her e-ledger so that she could resume her studies.

With the drama over and nothing else to do, Zarya sat down and tried to rest as best she could. At least here in Sentella headquarters, which was guarded better than any palace she'd ever heard of, there was no threat of harm to any of them. Not to mention, she was surrounded by some of the best fighters ever born.

Hours ticked by slowly as everyone waited for any word on Darling.

Once the babies became bored and fussy, their mothers took them home and left the rest of them to pace, sit, play games on their mobiles, and crack a few random jokes.

Lise sat quietly, studying while Sorche ended up leaning against Zarya's shoulder so that she could nap on her.

Every so often, Lise would have to get up and move around to alleviate the back pain left over from her attack. An attack Zarya tried not to think about. Especially as she watched the young woman suffering so miserably from it. Worse, was the knowledge that Lise would have to cope with it for the rest of her life. But to her credit, she didn't complain at all. She'd walk a bit, stretch and then discreetly take medicine when it must have become truly unbearable for her.

Maris had left a few minutes ago to get more drinks for Zarya and Lise.

Zarya wished she could make time go faster. She couldn't stand not knowing what was happening to Darling on the other side of those doors.

Kiara sucked her breath in sharply, then put her hand over her stomach.

Nykyrian, who'd been standing with the men, shot over to her with a most inhuman speed. Something made twice as impressive given the fact that his back had been to his wife. That man had some scary observation abilities. "Are you all right?"

Kiara grimaced. "Technically yes. But..." She glanced to Lise and blushed. "These seats are making my back hurt and the baby's doing somersaults."

Nykyrian held her hand in his. "You want me to take you home?"

Kiara bit her lip as she scanned the room. "Let me walk around a little while. I think that would help."

"Okay." He helped her up, then the two of them left.

Lise sighed as she watched them go. "Do you ever think about having children?" she asked Zarya.

"Sometimes. What about you?"

"I really hope I'm sterile."

The sincerity and alacrity of Lise's tone shocked her. "Why?"

Lise gave her an arch stare. "You've met my family. Why would I want to pass on our damaged chromosomes to some poor innocent child? That desire alone would mark me as a bad mother."

Feeling terrible for the girl, she squeezed Lise's hand. "Sweetie, there's nothing wrong with any of you. It's amazing how well adjusted the three of you are given everything you've gone through."

"Still, I don't think I'd ever want that kind of responsibility. No one can control when they die, and the last thing I want is to leave an unprotected child to someone who might hurt it. Most of all, I live in fear of looking at my child one day and hating its guts."

Zarya was astonished by Lise's words. "You would never do that, honey. Parents love their children."

Lise scoffed at her. "You haven't met my mother. She hates us—Drake and Darling more than me, but still...In her mind, we trapped her and she resents it. Had she not had us, she'd have been allowed to return home to her people after my father died and remarry. Instead, she was stuck in perpetual mourning until Darling took over and pardoned her from her vows."

Only the reigning governor could allow the former governor's consort the privilege of leaving mourning behind and having a normal life, free of her royal obligations to her dead spouse. Even then, he couldn't do it until the second anniversary of the former governor's passing.

In the past, the governors had always pardoned their mothers as soon as they could. Only Arturo had been cruel enough to make sure that Natale was tied to them without hope of a pardon.

Lise took a deep breath. "Darling keeps telling me that before our father's death, Momair was extremely loving and kind. But I have no memory of her being anything other than a bitter, resentful bitch."

Frowning, Lise glanced toward the operating room doors. "Sometimes I think it's harder on Darling since he has memories of having a real mother, than for me and Drake. We don't remember her being nice or giving. But when Darling talks about the past...you can see in his eyes how much he misses the parents he had. Sometimes it makes me wish that I remembered them, too. Instead, all I know about my father is what my brothers, mostly Darling, tell me. And I have no concept of being mothered by anyone except Darling and Maris."

Zarya had to smile at that. "They are good at that, aren't they?"

Lise nodded. "The saddest truth? I wouldn't know anything about makeup or clothes at all, but for Maris. He was even the one who went with me to buy my first bra."

Zarya laughed. "Seriously?"

"Oh, yeah. I'd asked Darling to go with me, but he'd been so offended that Maris had volunteered. At the time, I thought it was solely because he didn't want me growing up. Now…"

"It would have been extremely awkward for him," Zarya finished, trying to imagine Darling in a women's lingerie boutique. Although, he did have a deep appreciation for it…

Teasingly, she rubbed her arm against Lise's. "If it makes you feel any better, Maris is the one who taught me, too."

Lise laughed. "If you ever get a chance, you really should go shopping with him. I've never seen anyone get so excited about shoes." The humor faded as she turned serious again. "I know Sorche doesn't remember her mother, but do you?"

"I do."

Lise considered that for a moment. "What was it like?"

Zarya wasn't sure what she meant. "What was what like?"

"Having a mother. Was she kind?"

Zarya couldn't speak for several seconds around the lump in her throat that those words caused. It'd always saddened her that Sorche couldn't remember their mother. But Lise's was alive…

I will never understand Natale. How could she neglect her children so?

"She was wonderful. I'm sure we fought, but I don't remember it at all. I only remember her laughing and hugging us."

"I'm so sorry, Z."

Her apology startled her. "For what?"

"Everything my uncle did to you." Lise glanced over to Sorche who was snoring ever so softly. "I know how much Patrice and Rachelle meant to Sorche. She said that you and Rachelle were very close."

Zarya clenched her teeth against the wave of pain that crashed through her at the mention of her sisters. She even missed her brother's meanness. "We were."

"Sorche talks about them all the time, but she said that you don't."

Tears welled up in Zarya's eyes, blinding her for a moment. "I can't," she said with a short sob. It was why she'd blocked out those memories of Darling's visits when they'd been children. She missed her family so much that when she looked back, it felt like something gutted her. She still couldn't believe they were gone.

That she'd never see them again...

Lise wrapped her arm around Zarya's shoulders and hugged her. "I get it now."

Zarya cleared her throat. "Get what?"

"You and Darling. You've both had the weight of the universe on you for a long time. From the cradle, my father filled Darling with responsibility. And my mother shoved so much on him that I'm surprised it didn't break his back to carry it all. Meanwhile, your father made you responsible for the entire Resistance, as well as Sorche and Rachelle."

Strange, she'd never thought of it that way. She'd never considered her sisters a burden. But Lise was right. She and Darling did have that in common.

"Darling was the only parent I've ever known and Sorche said that you've been her only mother."

Zarya glanced down at her little sister. "Yeah, but I never minded."

Lise fell quiet for a few seconds. "I wonder if Darling ever did."

"Did what?"

"Minded us." Lise flinched.

"Is your back all right?" she asked, worried about the pain she saw on Lise's face.

Lise nodded. "It's not the back. I flashed on Darling and all the times Arturo would start toward me or his daughters, and Darling would put himself between us, giving us time to escape while he drew Arturo's attention and fire to him. It had to bother him, didn't it? But he never said anything about it. Not once."

Zarya took her hand and held it gently. "He loves you, Lise. Dearly. So no, I don't think he minded at all."

"I really need to be nicer to him."

Smiling, Zarya started to respond, but the operating room door finally opened.

Her throat went dry as Syn came out, looking pale and shaky. Exhausted. Without a word, he went over to Nero and pulled the flask off his belt. Tipping his head back, he took a deep swallow.

Nykyrian and Kiara returned a second before Maris joined their group.

Terrified of Syn's behavior, Zarya gently pushed her sister off her shoulder, got up and went over to him. "Is Darling all right?"

Syn returned the flask to Nero, then nodded. "I've got him stabilized. For now."

Hauk scowled. "What happened?"

Syn ground his teeth. "We lost him three times on the table and had to resuscitate him." He glared at Nykyrian as if it was somehow his fault. "Damn you half-blooded mongrels. You make it hard as hell on us to treat you. None of you react to anything like you're supposed to."

Half-blooded? Those words echoed in her head. She frowned at Syn. "Darling's human, isn't he?"

Syn didn't answer her question as he continued his report. "Because it's Darling, we're not sure how well the new procedure will take. But I did a little more work on his internals while I had him under. The additional stress shocked his system, which was *really* stupid on my part. However, I knew the chances of getting him back on the table would be slim, so I wanted to get as much done on him as I could." He pulled the surgical cap off. "I seriously hope I haven't made a mistake."

Nykyrian placed a comforting hand on his shoulder. "You're the best there is, Syn. He'll be fine."

Syn's gaze doubted that confidence.

"Can I see him?" Nero asked.

"He won't be awake for a while."

Nero refused to be daunted. "But can I see him?"

"Sure."

When Syn went to show him the way, Nero stopped him. "I got it. You stay here with the others."

Syn frowned, but didn't argue as Nero left them in the waiting room and vanished through the doors. "Damn. I should have grabbed his flask again."

Fain handed him his. "My shit's better, anyway. Nero's a cheap bastard who has no taste buds."

Syn saluted him with the flask.

Caillen tsked as Syn took a deep drink. "You wouldn't be doing that if Shahara was here."

"Damn straight. She'd kick my ass sideways and you better not tell her I did this. *I* will kick yours if you do."

"Don't make it a habit and I won't."

Zarya glanced at Maris who'd been eerily quiet through everything. "How long before Darling wakes up?" she asked Syn.

He shrugged. "There's no telling. His metabolism is faster than most so he burns through medication like nothing I've ever seen. It's why it's so hard to put him out medically and why you never want to try and drink him under the table...After we rescued him from the Resistance, I went through most of the pharmacy in one week alone just to keep him in a coma so he could heal."

His gaze touched on everyone who stood around him. "There's no need for you guys to hang. I've got him under tight observation and he's not going to want to talk to anyone when he wakes." He jerked his head toward the hallway. "In fact I'm going to crash in my office for a while."

Lise walked over to Fain. "Are you staying, or heading home?"

"Why?"

"If you're staying, I'd like to sleep and shower on your ship."

"Sure."

Drake cleared his throat. "You're not going there alone, little girl. Not with Fain's reputation where women are concerned."

She rolled her eyes at her brother, then looked at Zarya. "I'll pay you money to kill him."

Chayden laughed. "Well, if you want your brother killed, you're in the right place, but asking the wrong person. I think everyone here, but Zarya, is a trained assassin."

"Drake's not trained," Lise said flippantly.

Zarya saw a nervous light flash in Drake's eyes before he caught himself.

Frowning, she wondered what he was hiding from the rest of his family. Obviously, he'd been trained by someone. But the three of them were gone before she could ask about it.

The others followed suit.

Syn yawned before he looked at her and Maris. "I'm going to bet that you two aren't leaving."

"No," they said in unison.

He scratched at the back of his neck. "C'mon. I'll have a cot brought into Darling's room for you to sleep on," he said to her. "And I'll send your sister down to the empty office next to mine that has a couch she can crash on."

"Thank you."

He inclined his head to her as he led her toward the doors. "Should I have one brought for you, too, Mari?"

"No, thanks. But I will go back for the drinks I left when I saw you come in." Maris touched her elbow. "I won't be long." He squeezed her lightly before he took his leave.

Once they were alone, she pulled Syn to a stop. "What aren't you saying about Darling?"

"Really nothing. I'm just worried."

Which worried her. "About his dying?"

"Partly, but that's not my biggest fear." There was a haunted, chilling light in his black eyes. "You weren't here when I took the bandages off his face and he saw the scars your people gave him. He didn't cope well, Zarya. Not at all."

That she could believe. Who would have? "He's still not coping well."

Syn snorted. "Do you blame him?"

"No." Her throat tightened as she thought about the constant pain Darling lived in, and all the damage that had been done by his own allies. "I'm not sure I would cope as well as he has, all things considered."

"Yeah," Syn breathed. "So I'm nervous as hell about what we might find this time and how he's going to react if there's little, or gods forbid, *no* change."

Honestly, so was she. But she refused to consider that. If it happened, they'd deal with it. "I don't care what he looks like."

"Yeah, but *he* does." Syn sighed in disgust. "You know why he grew his hair over the scar?"

"He hated the sight of it."

Syn laughed bitterly. "Yeah…That's the simple answer. The truth? We were in a restaurant when Darling was twenty-one, maybe twenty-two, having dinner and celebrating the fact that we'd been able to repair all the damage on his face except for that one scar…which given the severity of what we started with was damn incredible. I know Ryn didn't do it on purpose, but damn… Darling's face was awful before the surgeries…Anyway, Darling was finally so happy that he looked human again. It was the first time he'd been out in public since he was scarred by his fight. While he was in the middle of thanking me for repairing him, the manager came over and asked if we'd mind moving to a corner table so that Darling could face the wall."

She scowled in confusion. "Why?"

The rage in that black gaze scorched her. "Some of the diners had complained. They'd told him that seeing Darling's face was making them lose their appetites. If I live to be a thousand, I'll never forget the way Darling took *that* news. He looked like someone had kicked his teeth in. So he covered the scar with his hand and literally wilted in front of me. I punched the son of a bitch for it, but the damage was done. Darling was so embarrassed that he left immediately."

Her own fury ignited. "People can be so mean."

"Don't even go there with me," Syn said between clenched teeth. "I've seen a side of people you better pray God you never do. Anyway, after that Darling wouldn't go into public without a crash helmet covering his entire face. Not until his hair grew long enough to hide the scar. Even then, it was years before he stopped holding his hair in place with one hand to make sure nothing exposed it."

"I understand. Believe me, I know exactly how self-conscious he is of it."

Nodding glumly, he led her down the hallway. "I really hope, for his sake, this surgery works."

So did she. With every part of her.

They slowed as they reached a room that had a strange orangish-red glow coming out from the bottom of the door.

What in the Nine Systems?

They exchanged a questioning scowl before Syn opened it. The glow vanished the instant he touched the handle.

Zarya followed him into the room to find Nero standing on the other side of Darling's bed.

But that wasn't what held her attention. Her stomach shrank into a tight knot as her gaze went straight to Darling. There were numerous monitors hooked to him. But it was the bandage covering his entire face that scared her. She couldn't make out any part of his features.

"Did something happen?" Syn asked Nero.

"No. Why?"

Syn looked like he started to say something, then he reconsidered. "Never mind."

Zarya paused as she noted the way Nero stood, and the expression on his face. It was so similar to one of Darling's that it startled her. They had the same eyes. Not the color, but the shape of them. While Darling's were blue, Nero's were gray. Their noses were also very similar.

If she didn't know better...

Nero arched a brow at her. "You okay?"

She mentally shook herself and wondered if she was imagining it. "I am."

"Uh...yeah. I should probably warn you that you can't lie to me." His tone was level, but there was a peculiar note in it. "You're stressed and you're scared. You really should relax and calm down."

Her suspicion ran rampant at his words. "What do you know that I don't?"

He glanced to Syn. "I have an answer about one of your concerns for Darling."

Syn quirked a curious expression at Nero. "Which one?"

"Darling *can* father children."

Those most unexpected words left her completely breathless. Was he implying...

She closed her gaping jaw. "Excuse me?"

Nero gave her a lopsided grin. "For the baby's sake, you need to rest, and yes, I'm exactly what you're thinking I am."

Trisani. A chill went down her spine. She'd never met one before. Few people had since they'd been hunted to the brink of extinction. But everyone knew about their legendary psychic abilities. Abilities that were so great, most of them were killed in their youth before they could develop them. Others were kept as drugged slaves and ruthlessly used. An even larger number of them had been experimented on to the point they willed themselves dead.

Now they were an endangered species.

Nero turned toward Syn. "Can you give us a few?"

"Sure. I need to see about a bed for her anyway." Syn left them alone.

Nero folded his arms over his chest. "And to answer your earlier question from the waiting room, Darling's my cousin. But only Syn knows that, and only because of Darling's surgeries. We had to tell him since he needed to know exactly what he was dealing with whenever he operated on Darling. Due to the hostility toward our people, it's not something we *ever* talk about."

"Then Darling knows he's partially Trisani?"

He nodded. "Don't fret, though. Darling's a good eighty to ninety percent human, genetically. He has just enough of our DNA to screw with his metabolism and genetics. But that's a good thing. It's the only reason he wasn't hurt worse by what the Resistance did to him. Had he been fully human, he wouldn't have survived it."

While she was grateful Darling was still alive, those words hit her hard. Had he been completely human, he would never have been forced to endure so much. "Can you tell me what's going to—"

"No," Nero said, cutting her off. "My powers don't work that way. The future is in constant flux and I don't have the ability to pinpoint the decisions you'll make that impact it. I can see several outcomes, but I won't know which one is correct until it comes into being."

That made sense, but she hated that he couldn't tell her what would happen. "Which is why you're telling me to rest."

"Exactly. And I can tell you what is fact. Such as, Darling loves you more than anything. I know you love him the same."

Those words should make her happy and yet... "Why do I have a bad feeling there's a *but* in your tone?"

"You know the but." His voice was eerily calm and distant. "It haunts every second you breathe." Nero looked down at Darling. "He has the ability to be the greatest governor in Caronese history. But he will step down to keep you with him. Drake's not old enough to lead yet, and Ryn can't lead because of his mother's bloodline."

"Could you?"

Nero shook his head. "I'm related to him on his mother's side."

Which meant no. Inheritance was only traced through the males.

Zarya's heart sank as she considered what Nero was really saying. "So you're telling me that I need to leave him."

"I'm not telling you anything." He stressed the last word. "It's not my life to live. Any more than it's my decision to make. If you stay with him, his enemies will come at him with everything they have, and it will be fierce. If you leave, he will follow you. Especially since you carry his child. His throne means nothing to him compared to you. It never will."

Honestly, she didn't like the sound of those options. No matter what, Darling lost.

Nero approached her slowly. "I didn't mean to add to your stress, Zarya. But I thought you should know. It's not going to be easy."

Nothing ever was.

She swallowed against the pain inside her. "Have you ever been in love?"

"I've made a lot of mistakes in my life."

Zarya didn't miss the fact that he avoided answering her question.

Or was he saying that love was a mistake?

"But you know," he continued, "in all the regrets I have, the one thing that never bothered me were the decisions I made with my heart. The rational ones, the ones I made while I was scared or desperate, those hammer at me constantly."

She didn't know why, but she had a bad suspicion that someone had hurt him in the past. Terribly. A betrayal so foul that he couldn't even speak of it.

She glanced to Darling, and tried to decide what to do. "I don't know if I can leave him."

"Then you shouldn't."

Yes, but how could she stay if it caused him to be attacked?

She placed her hand over her stomach and considered the baby that was there. But for Nero, she'd have no idea at all that she carried a part of Darling with her. "How far along am I?"

"A little over a week."

Oh yeah... he had to be messing with her. There was no way he could know that. "And you can tell?" she asked suspiciously.

He winked at her. "I'm much more reliable than any pregnancy test."

Still, she wasn't ready to believe him. "Have you ever been wrong?"

"Nope. You can bet on me any day."

Then I'm pregnant. The reality sank in slowly. A part of her was so happy, she could fly. But the rest of her was terrified and stunned.

Although, she shouldn't be *that* surprised. It wasn't like she hadn't known it would be a possibility given what they'd been doing, and the fact that they hadn't been using protection... Something they'd always used when he was Kere.

Funny how she hadn't even thought about her pregnancy shots having run out before Maris bought her. She'd always been so conscientious about it. But since their reunion, she'd been focused on so many other things that the possibility hadn't even occurred to her.

I'm going to be a mom for real.

Her thoughts drifted for several minutes as she fully accepted the weight of that reality and responsibility. There was a piece of Darling inside her. Right now. A part that would grow into a baby she hoped looked just like him...

What are we going to name you, little one?

Yeah, that, too, was scary. What if she screwed it up? All of the Caronese aristos had unreasonably long names like Darling's. Her full name was Escadara Marahn Zarya Clotile Starska.

What if her child hated the name she gave it as much as Darling hated his?

And with that fearful thought, she remembered what Darling had told her about Nero. "Are you really the one who named him Darling?"

He gave her a sheepish grin. "His mother technically, but I was the one who suggested it."

"Why?"

"In Trisani, Darling's the name of our north star. It's what we use to guide us home and to find our way through the dark. When I suggested it, I wasn't thinking about the Universal definition. As I said, I've made a lot of mistakes in my life. But I don't count that as one of them. Darling, however, does."

Yes, he did.

Still, Darling didn't have to go by it. "Out of all the names they gave him, why did his parents choose that one to call him by?"

"When he was a child, everyone used it as an endearment for him to the point that we thought nothing about it. It wasn't until he was a teen that it became a source of ridicule. *That* is what I feel guilty about. I never intended him to be mocked for it. But it, like the rest of his past, is what has made him the empathetic ruler Caron needs."

Darling certainly was that, but it made her wonder… "You said you can see multiple outcomes for people?"

He nodded.

She hesitated before she asked a question she probably shouldn't. But it was one she had to know. "What would have happened to Darling had his father lived?"

Nero stared into space with a glassy look in his eyes before he answered. "He would never have been scarred. He'd have grown up very spoiled and happy."

"Selfish?"

"No," he said empathically. "That was never in him. But to address what you truly want to know, he wouldn't have the bitterness that he has now, and while he would have been sympathetic to his people, he wouldn't have the degree of understanding that he has."

His next words stung her. "He would have married young, in his late teens, and been very happy."

But Darling wouldn't have married *her*. A part of her wanted to know who his bride would have been. The other part didn't want her name for fear she'd hunt her down and punch her over something that hadn't happened in this lifetime.

Either way, there was one truth she couldn't deny. "He would have been much better off."

Nero screwed his face up. "Maybe...In some ways."

"In others?"

Nero released an elongated breath. "We're all victims of someone else's hatred, Zarya. And survivors of our own bad decisions. Had Darling not gone through what he has, he would never have been able to love you to the depth that he does. Plain and simple."

"But he no longer trusts me."

Nero laid a gentle hand on her shoulder. "For better or worse, our pasts and experiences are what define us. But they don't have to rule us. In time, all hurts can be forgiven. It's only when you add to them that they can't."

She paused at his unexpected wisdom. At first glance, Nero looked like any other live-by-the-crotch-of-his-pants Tavali rogue. And yet...

"There's a lot more to you than you show most people, isn't there?"

He shrugged nonchalantly. "That's true for most," he said with a wicked gleam in his eyes. "But I'm a lot older than I look. I've lived through things far worse than Darling has. You'd be amazed at how much forgiveness the heart is capable of."

"Love isn't what scares me," she admitted. "It's hatred I fear." She jerked her chin toward Darling. "And I've seen what it's capable of more times than I've seen people forgive. It's that cold viciousness that drives out all humanity that terrifies me. I don't want him to ever feel that for me again."

"Have faith in yourself, Zarya. And have faith in Darling."

Before she could comment, the door opened to admit Syn and Maris.

Zarya fell silent. While she didn't mind Maris knowing her fears, she wasn't as sure about Syn. Darling trusted him implicitly. But she didn't have his allegiance and she barely knew him.

Nero inclined his head to them. "I'm going to rest for a while. I'll be nearby if anything changes."

"Later." Syn moved to check Darling's readouts while Maris handed her a bottle of water.

"How are you holding up?" he asked her.

"I'll be better once he's awake."

Maris squeezed her hand before he went to stand in the far corner.

"So how did you meet Nero?" she asked Syn. "Through Darling?"

"Through prison," he said in a matter-of-fact tone like someone who was answering with, "at the market" or "at a friend's house..."

She froze at *that* unexpected answer. Was he serious?

"He's not joking," Maris said as if he, too, were Trisani.

Still, she was aghast that both of them were felons. "Do I want to know what you two were in for?"

Syn's eyes flashed with anger. "Being born. Both of us. You'd be amazed at how many people the League locks up for no reason whatsoever."

"Actually, I wouldn't. I've heard the stories."

"Yeah, well, I lived them. Believe me, it's much better having them told to you." Syn made a few adjustments, before he turned toward them. "I'm going to rest, too. I've got the alarms set. They should have a bed in here for you soon. If you need anything, buzz me."

Maris inclined his head to him. "Thanks, Syn."

After thanking him, too, Zarya went to the bed while Syn left them.

Once they were alone, Maris returned to stand beside her. "It's hard to see him like this, isn't it?"

She nodded. "How many times have you been with him in a hospital?"

"More than I care to remember. But the worst had to be when he was seventeen."

"Was that when he was knocked through the table?"

"No. Before. It was a while after his first confinement in a mental institution."

She scowled. "What happened to put him in a hospital?"

His expression grim, Maris took a sip of water before he answered. "His first attempt to kill himself. Like Lise, I found out about it from a news report right after I'd come in from a training exercise. It's why I wasn't upset at her for overreacting. I know how bad it is to hear something like that from a stranger who's reporting it with a sickening gleam in her eye."

Sighing, he capped his bottle. "By the time I got to the hospital, I was so mad at him for not calling me first, I could have killed him myself. What I didn't know then was that Arturo had taken his link from him. Darling had been prohibited from talking to anyone, for any reason, including his mother and especially his family. Between that, having been raped, and his nightly strip searches that were every bit as humiliating and invasive as his rapes, Darling had been unable to cope with it all. The thought of enduring another thirteen years of hell like that had been more than he could stomach, so he broke the mirror in his bedroom and used the fragments to slash his wrists."

Tears welled in his eyes. "I'd never seen Darling like that before. When we were in school together, he'd always been so strong and happy. Nothing got to him. Ever. Whatever came at him, he stood ferocious before it and dared it to try and knock him down. That was the Darling I was expecting to beat to a pulp for being stupid. And then I opened the door."

Clearing his throat, he wiped at the tear that had fallen down his cheek. "His face battered, Darling had looked so pale and defeated. So broken…"

He bit back a sob. "Since the doctor was afraid Darling would try to kill himself again, he'd ordered Darling strapped to the bed like some kind of animal or criminal. They'd braced his arms so that it wouldn't touch the bandages over his cuts. Darling was so ashamed of it all that he wouldn't even look at me. He kept staring out the window with these dazed, glassy eyes that said he didn't want to be here anymore. And he was there all alone. No family. No friends."

"I'm so sorry, Maris."

He shook his head. "My pain is slight compared to his. But that had to be the hardest year of his life. I can't imagine everything he went through in just a handful of months. I still don't know how he survived it all."

"That was the same year that…" She hesitated. Maybe she shouldn't bring it up. The last thing she wanted to do was hurt Darling any worse.

"That what?" Maris prompted

There's no way Maris doesn't know about it. He knew everything when it came to Darling and Drake had told her that the photographs and videos of Darling had circulated far and wide. So she forced herself to say the name that burned in her throat. "Nylan."

Maris's nostrils flared in anger. "How do you know about that? I know Darling didn't breathe a word of it."

Just as she thought—Maris knew him better than anyone. "Drake told me."

"I swear that I, who profane violence, am going to cut that boy's tongue out one day," he said under his breath. "Why would he tell you about that?"

"He was explaining why he'd hated Darling when he was younger. Why he refused to believe me when I told him Darling was straight. He said that he'd seen proof otherwise, and he used that as his example."

Maris mumbled under his breath in Phrixian—a habit he always had whenever he was really mad about something. "Just please tell me that you didn't ask Darling about it."

She cringed. "I did."

More Phrixian.

Trying to soothe him, she touched his arm. "If it makes you feel better, Darling is grateful to you that you've never mentioned it to him."

"It doesn't and why should I?" He prissed daintily. "Drake is an idiot. I now have irrefutable proof of his supreme fatuousness. It was obvious to anyone with a brain what had happened." He hissed like a cat. "Which explains why Drake didn't get it...From the moment I heard about the scandal, I knew Darling would have to be beyond desperate to go to that pervert."

He set the water bottle down on the tray next to Darling's bed. "You can't imagine the disdain and ridicule Darling's been subjected to because of it. There were so many jokes that went around—jokes that were sickening. I was in militia training the first time that video was shoved in my face. I was so angry, I clocked the moron who was laughing when he showed it to me."

It had to be bad to motivate Maris to such an act. "People can be extremely vicious."

"Believe me, Zarya, I know. I am a gay man, remember? They've let me have it plenty."

He jerked his chin toward Darling. "Some of the old jokes are still floating around and are retold anytime he makes an official appearance."

"Such as?"

He turned a pale shade of green and made sure that Darling wasn't awake before he whispered to her. "I'm only telling these to you because you *will* hear them, and I want you prepared for the sheer, brutal nastiness of it…" He lowered his voice even more. "What's the difference between Darling Cruel, the wind, and a vacuum?"

She drew her breath in sharply, dreading the answer.

Maris held the same look of disgust that she felt. "A vacuum only sucks. The wind only blows. But Darling sucks, blows, and swallows."

She screwed her face up at the sheer cruelty. No wonder Maris had punched someone. Something like that would motivate her to even worse actions.

Sighing, he told her another one. "What's the difference between a toilet and Darling? The toilet doesn't follow you around after you use it. Then there's my personal fave. What's the difference between Darling and an oven? An oven doesn't moan out loud when you stick a piece of meat in it."

Her stomach shrank in horror. "Oh my God, that's disgusting."

"Trust me, there are a lot more than those three and I've thankfully forgotten most of the worst ones. But I'm sure Darling hasn't. There's nothing people love more than to laugh at someone else's misery, and they belly-rolled over his. They didn't care that Darling was in pain and that they were making it worse."

Licking his lips, he glanced away from her. "What kills me

most, though, is that it was obvious in the video that Darling was crying, scared, and humiliated the entire time. But to them it was just *hilarious*. Bastards!"

In that moment, she honestly hated people for their cruelty.

Before she could comment, the alarm to one of Darling's monitors sounded.

Maris rushed to it and blocked her ability to read why it was going off.

"What is it?" she asked.

"Darling's heart just stopped."

16

Darling came to slowly. Exhausted and in pain, he tried to open his eyes, but the bandages left him in complete darkness.

"Is he awake?" That was Hauk's familiar growl.

"Darling? Can you hear me?"

Zarya. How could anyone mistake that precious, angelic voice? He heard the monitor for his heart speeding up. It quickened even more when he felt her soft hand clutching his.

Voices exploded so that he couldn't quite make them all out.

"Hey! Give us the room," Syn demanded over the sudden pandemonium.

The voices grew louder an instant before they stopped entirely.

When Zarya started to let go of him, he tightened his grip on her hand to keep her with him.

"Syn?" she said gently.

"Yeah, okay, you can stay. The rest of you need to leave for a few minutes."

Zarya kissed Darling's fingers. "I'm right here, baby," she whispered in his ear. "I'm not going anywhere."

Another hand slid under his free one. By the large, rough feel of it, he knew it was Syn's and not Zarya's tiny, delicate hand. "Hey, bud. Tap once if you're alert enough to understand me."

Darling did.

"Good. You scared the shit out of us again. Thanks so much. It's really an honor to be your doctor." Syn's sarcasm was so thick, it could double as insulation for a bomb shelter. "But we're glad to have you back. Are you in pain at all? Once for yes. Two for no."

Darling tapped once.

"Okay. Once if it's severe. Two if you can live with it."

It was severe, but Darling didn't want to be incoherent so he tapped twice.

Syn scoffed at him. "Yeah, your blood pressure's calling you a liar. That being said, I'm assuming you want to stay awake for a bit. So I'm not going to give you anything unless your blood pressure worsens." Syn removed his hand. "Since you're awake, I want to remove your breathing tube so that you can talk. I'm going to send Zarya out while I do it. Is that all right?"

Darling used League sign language to agree.

She sandwiched his hand between hers before she released it. "I won't be gone long."

As soon as she cleared the room, Syn numbed Darling's throat so that he could slide the tube out. Darling tried not to gag, but it was hard.

And it was a fight he ultimately lost.

"Here." Syn turned him to his side fast and held him there until his stomach settled down. "It's all right. Don't worry about the mess. Just breathe easy, little brother."

Darling laid his head down, grateful he couldn't see. "I don't know how you do what you do. How many years did you go to med school to learn how to clean out bedpans, anyway?"

"Ha, ha. Instead of being a smart-ass, you should be kissing mine. Anyone else would have left you to code."

"No offense, Syn, but right now, I'm wishing you had." Darling rolled over slowly until he was on his back again. "How bad was it this time?"

"You don't really want to know. Suffice it to say, if this doesn't take, there won't be another attempt. I'm not ever putting you under again. You can find yourself a new doctor who doesn't care if you live or die."

That news kicked him hard. He could tell by the brutal pain in his chest that felt like someone had stomped the crap out of him that he'd died on the table.

More than once.

"Seriously. How many times did you resuscitate me?"

"Enough that I'm glad I don't pay the power bill here."

Darling rubbed at the area over his heart that hurt the most. "Remind me to sign a DNR next time."

"Like I'd pay attention to that? Yeah. You go right on and waste your time." Syn ran his hands over Darling's body, examining his abdomen.

A new feeling of dread consumed him. "What did you do there?"

"I attempted to repair some of your internals so that you might be able to go to the bathroom without trauma."

That would be better than fixing his face.

Almost.

"Did it work?" Darling asked.

"We'll know when we get some solid food back in you."

"Oh goody. Can't wait for that."

Syn snorted. "You better be glad you're already busted up. Otherwise I'd make you pay for all this sarcasm you're spewing."

Yeah, right. Syn was a top graduate from the School of Sarcasm himself. Not to mention the small fact that he knew his friend would sooner cut his own throat than hurt him.

Darling groaned out loud as Syn touched a tender spot. "That's attached, you know?"

Syn didn't say anything as he kept going with his examination.

While he worked, Darling's thoughts went to what concerned him most. "When will the bandages come off?"

"I'd like to leave them on until the morning. Since I used a Prillion and Prinum combination, you should be as good as you're going to get by then."

Darling's stomach clenched hard at the thought of what they might find once he was unwrapped. *Please let this work.*

He couldn't stand the thought of going through the rest of his life with Pip's name carved into his face. *I just want a chance to be normal.*

Just once.

Between the fight with Ryn and his torture, he couldn't remember a time when he hadn't flinched at his own reflection. A time when people hadn't stared at him in distaste.

Don't think about it.

The surgery was done. Either he was better or he wasn't. There was nothing any of them could do about it now. It was what it was. All too soon, he'd have the answer…

"How long was I out of it?" he asked Syn.

"Not quite seventy hours."

Damn. He was getting tired of being unconscious. "How much of that was spent in surgery?"

"Let's just say if I'm ever on that table that long, I hope I have a few tag team doctors for it. You're lucky I'm used to not sleeping."

That was an understatement. Syn and Nykyrian were the only ones he knew who could stay awake longer and more alert than he could. Truly impressive. "Remind me, I need to send Shahara flowers for letting me keep you away from her for so long."

Syn placed a comforting hand on his shoulder. "You owe her

more than that. She and Kiara have been taking shifts keeping your woman and sister from climbing the walls. But at least Lise took a nap. Zarya hasn't slept since you've been here. She's refused to close her eyes for anything more than a blink. Maris either, for that matter. They're both about to collapse."

Darling wasn't sure if he should be angry, flattered, or disturbed by that news. While he never wanted them to deprive themselves for anything, even him, a part of him was thrilled that they cared that much. It was selfish—probably wrong—but his heart swelled with the love he had for the two of them. They were his life.

He felt Syn move away from the bed. "Do you want me to let everyone in or keep them out?"

"Can you send in Ryn, Zarya, and Maris first?" He needed to speak with them away from the rest of the group.

"Sure." Syn's steps drifted away.

"Hey, Syn?" Darling called, hoping he caught him before he left the room.

"Yeah?"

Darling hesitated. He owed the Ritadarion a debt that couldn't be repaid. Over the years, Syn had patched him up and pieced him back together more times than he could count. And while Syn never said the words, he knew that Syn couldn't stand to see someone he cared about suffer. It was a "weakness" Syn's father had ruthlessly used against him when he'd been a kid. It was why Syn had become a doctor. Having seen his own sister die, he'd wanted to have the ability to heal anyone he loved.

To keep them safe.

And Darling knew what it did to Syn every time he died on the table and Syn had to go through the fear of his not waking up. The fact that Syn would continue to put himself through that so that Darling could keep his genetics a secret...

That was true friendship.

409

"Thank you. For everything."

Syn snorted at him. "You might want to save that gratitude until we see how much it helped."

"Even if I'm still a freak, I appreciate it. Most of all, thank you for being my friend."

Syn let out a low whistle. "Damn, I better double check the meds I have you on."

Darling laughed, then grimaced as pain lanced through him again. Closing his eyes, he tried not to think about his face remaining the same as before.

I won't be able to take it.

But the saddest part was that he knew he would. Somehow he'd find the strength to endure it, even if it killed him. After all, it wouldn't be nearly as hard as having to face the other aristos after Nylan and Arturo went viral with his video.

Anything was easier than that.

Besides, he should look on the bright side. *At least no one wants to screw me when I'm scarred.*

No one except Zarya.

Her name had barely flashed through his mind before he smelled the sweet warmth of her perfume. She took his hand again.

"Syn said you could speak?"

He cleared his throat, which was still incredibly sore. "Are Maris and Ryn with you?"

"We're here." They were on the other side of his bed.

Darling rubbed her hand, and braced himself for her reaction. "Ryn? Would you mind taking both of them home for me?"

"No!" Zarya snapped.

Maris's tone was even sharper. "We're not leaving."

He ignored their protests. "If they won't go on their own, have Nyk stun them."

Maris cursed him in Phrixian while Zarya sputtered in indignation.

Darling held his hand up to silence them.

Zarya made a sound that he'd only heard her make toward her sister whenever Sorche really angered her. "Oh don't even think that imperial gesture works on me, boy."

He smiled at Zarya's rage. "I'm too weak to argue with the two of you. Z, please. Have mercy on me and go rest. In case this doesn't work, I want to have time to come to terms with it on my own before you see me, okay? I just…I want to face it without an audience. And Mari, you're the only one I trust to keep her safe for me. Please. I'm begging you both to go home and get some sleep. For me."

Zarya wanted to argue, but the pain in his voice kept her from it. Darling was being honest with them and while she was worried sick about him, the last thing she wanted was to add to his stress. Not to mention, she had a baby to think about now.

Torn between caring for their baby and staying with Darling, she met Maris's gaze.

He hesitated before he nodded.

"All right," she relented. "We'll go. But you better not get worse after we leave. I meant it. I will skin you alive if anything happens to you."

"And I will hand her the knife to do it," Maris added.

Ryn crossed his arms over his chest. "I'll hold him down for you both."

"Thanks for the support," Darling said drily. "Your warm, loving words mean so much to me."

Ryn laughed. "Anytime, little brother. My pleasure."

Darling frowned at the term Ryn hadn't used for him since before the fight that had left him scarred. It was weird to hear Ryn call him that after all this time.

411

But even more unexpected was his next words. "Mari? Zarya, would you mind letting me have a word with Darling alone?"

"Sure." Zarya kissed the palm of his hand before she left.

Maris touched his shoulder, then followed after her.

As soon as they were gone, Ryn moved to stand beside his bed. Though he didn't touch him, Darling could feel his body heat.

Darling braced himself for whatever bad news Ryn was about to dump on him. "Is something wrong with the empire?"

"Other than the fact that the gerents and Resistance are trying to remove you from power?"

Darling let out a short, bitter laugh. "I'd only be surprised if they weren't. Arturo made sure long ago that they'd never respect me as their governor." The bastard had gone out of his way to guarantee that should, by some miracle, Darling reign, it would be as hard on him as possible. But that wasn't what concerned him. "How are you coping with it all? I can have Nyk step in if you're tired of the crap."

"He's not Caronese."

"Neither are you. At least that's what you've always told me."

Ryn shifted his weight to his other leg as his throat drew tight over those words and the regret they gave him. There was no anger in Darling's voice. Only a calm acceptance that cut him all the way to his blackened soul. He'd much rather deal with Darling's anger that set fire to his own and made him feel vindicated.

This...

It ignited his guilt and that hurt most of all. Of all the people in his world, Darling was one of the last he'd ever intentionally hurt. There was a time when Darling had looked up at him and respected him.

A time when Ryn had respected himself.

But that was a long time ago and the one thing his harsh life had taught him was when it was too late to try. All he had now was a desire to be the brother Darling once thought he was.

He stared at the bandages that kept him from reading Darling's features. That, too, reminded him of the worst night of his life.

If I could have only one thing…

It would be to have his little brother whole again.

Licking his suddenly dry lips, Ryn spoke from the deepest part of the heart he never gave to anyone. Ever. "You have no idea how many times in my life I've wished that I'd been the brother to you that you've always been to Lise and Drake. I know sorry doesn't even begin to cover it. But I am so sorry for what I said and did."

"You've nothing to apologize for." The sincerity in Darling's voice didn't help his guilt at all. "I went for your throat and you went for mine. I started it and you finished it. That's what we were taught to do."

"Not against family. Dad taught us to protect each other. I should have never lost sight of that. Not even in my anger."

"My mother was merciless to you, Ryn. Arturo even more so. I don't blame you for not wanting to step back into that shit after you'd gotten away from it. For years, I hated you for abandoning us, but I get it now. You were just a kid, too. I was wrong to even ask you to take on Arturo. He'd have crushed you."

Yeah, right. That bastard wouldn't have stood a chance against him. And that wasn't the reason why he'd declined.

That was something he'd never share with anyone. Not even his brother.

"I doubt that, Dar. But since I didn't try, we'll never know. I was selfish to deny you, and it was wrong. Like the rest of the family, I abandoned you when you needed me most." He stepped closer to the bed. "But I swear to you that I won't *ever* do it again."

"Ryn—"

"Darling, it's okay," he said, interrupting him. "And before you say anything more out of guilt or remorse or whatever else you might feel...I...I apologize with full knowledge that you're the one who turned me in to the League."

Darling froze for several seconds as those words echoed in his ears. All these years, he'd felt so bad about having done that to Ryn. It'd been so wrong. So cold.

He'd always hated himself for it, and that one act had taught him well about striking out in anger. Especially against those he loved. Ryn had lost three years of his life for that.

What he'd done to Ryn had been every bit as bad, if not worse, than what Ryn had done to him.

"When did you find out?" he asked.

"While I was in prison. It's why I didn't speak to you for a couple of years after my release. I was afraid I'd kill you if I did. But like you said, I started it. You finished it. In time, I forgave you for it."

How? Darling wasn't sure he'd ever be able to forgive Ryn had Ryn sent him to jail. "What I did to you was far worse than what you did to me."

"No, it wasn't, little brother. I was a trained assassin in a League prison. While it definitely wasn't fun and I've no wish to repeat the experience, I wasn't defenseless. Besides, I respect the venom. It was a brilliant payback, and I'd much rather you had done that than sicced Nykyrian on me. While I survived prison, I wouldn't have survived his blade."

"Still—"

"No, Darling. You spent a lot longer in your prison than I did in mine, and you had no way to fight back. While I had a fairly happy childhood, yours was cut in half and made absolutely miserable. I abandoned you to a hell no one should have endured. You have more than earned your place as governor, and I wanted you to know that I intend to do everything I can to back you. You need soldiers, assassins, whatever, I will bust hell's gates wide open to get them for you. On my life, I mean it. I won't let you down this time." Ryn cleared his throat before he spoke again. "Is there anything you need me to do right now?"

Darling swallowed as emotions surged through him. He'd missed those days when he'd been a kid and had looked up at Ryn like Ryn had all the answers to the universe. Like his big brother was some mythic hero, capable of any feat. While he'd never feel that way again, this, in some ways, was better. For the first time since their fight, he felt like he had a brother he could depend on. "Please get them home, and don't kill Drake."

"I can't promise the latter, but I will make sure both Maris and Zarya get some rest."

"Thanks, shilo."

Ryn squeezed him on the arm. "Get better fast. I won't keep your empire straight for Drake."

Darling had no doubt about that. The two of them had never gotten along. They were way too much alike. And he'd spent his entire life attempting to make peace between them.

Closing his eyes, he savored the silence even though he missed Zarya in a way that was inhuman. She was his breath.

His heart.

His…

He opened his eyes, but it was too late. The Trisani in him that was so unpredictable had already seen a glimpse of the future. A future that terrified him.

It wasn't his death he'd seen.

It was Zarya's. And unlike Nero, he didn't see multiple outcomes.

He only saw the one and that meant it would happen without fail…

17

Alone in Zarya's dark room, Darling frowned at her empty bed. As soon as Syn had given him medical clearance to leave the hospital and he'd finally come to terms with the surgery's results and accepted them as best he could, he'd headed straight home to find her.

But she wasn't here.

Sad disappointment overwhelmed him. Her room looked as if no one had been in it at all. And that left him feeling as empty as her bed. Absolutely desolate. It was like a part of him was gone, too. And the hole it left inside him ran all the way to his soul.

Where is she?

Sadness turned to panic as he realized that there was no sign of her clothes or anything else to suggest that she'd returned home after she left him in the hospital. A bad feeling rushed through him as he remembered his premonition of Zarya being killed.

Could they have been attacked?

Was Maris missing, too?

Visions of Annalise's brutal assault went through his mind. Only the image of his sister lying on the ground, soaked in her own blood, turned to one of Maris and Zarya. He struggled to breathe through the pain of it.

Why hadn't he thought to check on them?

You stupid, self-absorbed bastard… He should never have allowed them to leave without him. He should have kept them by his side so that he would know they were safe.

Damn you, Ryn. If he'd allowed them to get hurt…

I'll kill you this time. I swear it!

Calm down, Dar. Don't jump to conclusions.

After all, it was the middle of the night here. Yes, her room was empty, but maybe it was nothing bad.

Maybe, she was…

His searching gaze went to the door that connected their rooms. Could she be in his bed, instead? It seemed like a long shot, and yet…

His heart hammering, he crossed the room and pushed the door open. Gripping the knob for support, he stood absolutely still as a slow smile curled his lips. Relief hit him so hard that he thought for a minute his knees might give out.

Lying curled in the center of his giant bed, Zarya looked tiny in comparison. Her long dark hair fanned out across his pillows while her faint snore warmed him.

See, dumbass. She's fine.

Best of all, she was still here.

He glanced around his room, taking in all of the extremely feminine personal items she'd invaded his masculine domain with over the last few weeks. It'd started out small…a pink hairbrush on his dresser and flowered toothbrush in his bathroom, followed by a few elastic headbands she used at night to pull her hair back whenever she washed her face or read to him. Then the small collection of flavored glitter lip balms that lay on a tray beside his bed. Her scented lotions and his favorite perfume that she wore for no other reason than to make him crazy with lust. Even some of her shoes were strewn near his bed.

And she'd draped one of her sheer nightgowns and a frilly pink robe over his navy settee. An image of her wearing the gown electrified every hormone in his body.

That thought pushed his relief away as desire burned through him. He closed the door and slowly crossed the room to his bed, undressing himself as he walked.

Zarya sighed contentedly at the sensation of a warm, naked male body pressing up against hers. Mmm, she'd always loved the way Darling felt whenever he snuggled behind her at night.

Until she remembered the fact that Darling wasn't home. He was still at the hospital.

Who was in her bed?

Her eyes flew open as fear and anger mixed inside her. With a warning hiss, she started to turn over only to have that lean, ripped body tighten around hers, pinning her to the mattress.

"Sh, *misa*, it's me," Darling breathed in her ear, using the Caronese word that meant "my most precious one." Her throat tightened. The surgeries had done nothing to change his damaged throat at all. In a way, she missed the refined, melodic cadence of the voice she'd fallen in love with. But she was getting used to his gruffer tone. The only drawback was that it often caused him to sound angry even when he wasn't.

She covered his hand with hers. "I'm going to beat you if you don't stop sneaking in on me like that." His warm, masculine scent should have told her instantly who it was, but still...

"I'm sorry." He nuzzled his face against her hair. "I didn't want to wake you at all." She might believe him if he wasn't teasing her nipple with his thumb through the black shirt she wore, and if a certain extremely hard part of his body wasn't resting against her hip.

She reached for the lamp, but he stopped her.

"I want to hold you like I used to. Before there was any kind of hurt between us. When it was just you and me in the dark. No past. No pain. Just two people who were madly in love with each other."

"I'm still madly in love with you."

He didn't respond to her words. Instead, he nibbled her earlobe while he unbuttoned her shirt and spread it open so that he could cup her breast in his warm palm. "So why are you sleeping in my bed and not yours?"

Closing her eyes, she savored the way he felt holding her. "The same reason I'm wearing your shirt. I missed you too much to sleep in my room. In here, I can feel your presence and pretend that you're with me and not far away." She buried her face against his pillows. "I can smell you, too."

And she'd wrapped herself up in his shirt to feel as close to him as she could without his being home. While it wasn't the same as being held by him, it'd been a close substitution, and one that had allowed her to finally go to sleep. Honestly, it scared her just how much he meant to her. How much it hurt when he wasn't here.

For hours after her return, she'd wandered around the palace like a grieving spirit. Aching. Lonely. Terrified of what would happen to her if he didn't return. She couldn't imagine a life without him in it. She couldn't. The mere thought of losing him was enough to make her hysterical.

How could any man wreak such havoc with her sanity?

He trailed his hand over her hip and stomach until he found the most private part of her body. Zarya sucked her breath in sharply while his fingers delved deep inside her. He nuzzled his face against her shoulder, scraping her skin with his whiskers as he removed his shirt from her body. She'd grown so used to his beard that it was strange to feel his skin on hers again.

"Can I see you?"

"Not yet," he said gruffly. "I'm not ready. I'd rather make love to you like we used to."

In the dark where she couldn't see him at all.

Her heart sank. Poor Darling. The surgery must not have worked. Tears gathered in her eyes as she ached for him. "I don't care what you look like."

"I know." He rolled her over onto her back, then he took her breast into his mouth. Her stomach fluttered with every stroke of his tongue. Gods, how did he manage to do that? She reached to cup his face, but he caught her hands in his, then lifted them over her head so that she couldn't touch him.

"What are you doing?" she asked.

His lips tickled her as he smiled against her skin. "I know what you're up to. You were trying to feel my features."

Heat scalded her cheeks at having been caught. He was right. "So I'm not to touch you?"

"Not yet." He continued to trail his lips over her flesh, blazing a hot trail everywhere he went.

Her body on fire, Zarya moaned out loud at how good he felt as he moved lower, down her belly and to her thigh. He nudged her legs apart. She bent her knees and opened herself up for him.

He nipped her thigh before he took her into his mouth. Her senses reeled as he licked and teased until she could barely stand it. Arching her back, she reached over her head to grip his headboard. Still, he tortured her with absolute pleasure.

A few seconds later, she cried out as her release came so fast and powerful that it made her shake all over.

Darling laughed as he continued to wring every last spasm out of her.

She expected him to enter her then, but he didn't. Instead, he took his time teasing and licking every inch of her flesh. It was as if he was starving and she was the only thing that could satiate his hunger.

Her heart thundering, she reached to cup him. This time, he didn't stop her.

He sucked his breath in sharply against her ear while she explored every inch of his hard cock with her fingers. For a full minute, he rocked himself against her hand. Then, he pulled away and rolled her over, onto her stomach. He pulled the largest pillow under her hips, lifting her up.

"Now what are you doing?"

His answer came as he gently spread her legs and returned to teasing her with his mouth and fingers. She shuddered with every lick and stroke. She wanted to touch him so badly, but in this position, she couldn't reach his body at all.

She cried out loud as he made her entire body hot and alive. He felt so incredibly good. His tongue flicked around and into her over and over until she couldn't stand it anymore. She came again, even more fiercely than she had the first time.

Still, he continued until she was weak with ecstasy. She started to move to touch him, but he stopped her. "I need you inside me, baby. Please."

Darling savored the sound of those words on her lips. No one had ever made him feel the way she did.

Like he mattered. Like she missed him whenever he wasn't around. It was stupid, he knew. But so few people had ever loved him at all.

The fact that she'd wrapped herself up in his shirt and bed...

He wanted to give her everything. To make her so happy that she never regretted being his. For the whole of his life, he'd been resented and begrudged by those around him. No matter what he'd done or sacrificed for others, it'd never been enough to make his family happy. Most of the time, they'd used his actions as a reason to hate or curse him.

But not Zarya.

She saw not only the real him, but what he wasn't, and she loved him for it. It made no sense whatsoever. She baffled him at every turn. Sometimes she even infuriated him. And right now, he wanted to wrap himself up in her arms and never leave them.

He nipped her buttocks before he laid himself over her and entered her from behind. She cried out as he went deep inside her warmth.

Darling sucked his breath in sharply at how good she felt under him. He didn't know what it was about her, but she made him feel so possessive and protective. She was his and he never wanted to share even a nanosecond of her with anyone else. He buried his face against her neck, inhaling the sweet scent of her skin and hair.

She ground herself against his groin, meeting him stroke for stroke with a heated demand that matched his own. And that, too, made him smile.

"I love you, Darling," she breathed.

Those words ripped him apart. They gave him a strength he'd never known before. Most of all, they weakened him. She owned him, body and soul.

For her, he would kill.

For her, alone, he would die.

And when he came a second later, he cried out from the sheer force of it and the intense emotions she made him feel against his will.

Damn her for it!

Zarya smiled at the fierce sound of his release as he shuddered against her. He'd never done that before. Never. Not once in the entire history of their relationship.

And now she knew exactly why he'd never made a sound before.

Nylan, and others, had humiliated him over it. Made him beg to be touched when all he wanted to do was run away.

Could it possibly be that she'd helped him heal that part of his past?

I hope so. She would give anything if she could erase those horrible memories...

His breathing ragged, he collapsed against her, pinning her to the bed. He let out a contented sigh, then went completely limp against her.

She reveled in having his weight press her into the mattress. "Did you fall asleep on me?"

"No," he said quietly. "I just want to be inside you for a few minutes longer."

"Feel free to stay there as long as you want."

He smiled against her shoulder as he brushed a callused hand over her skin. "We're going to look really strange trying to walk around like this."

"That we would."

Darling kissed her on the cheek before he pulled away.

Still, he wouldn't let her turn on the lights. Instead, he took her hand into his, and there in the dark, he slid something cold onto her finger.

Zarya froze as she mentally flashed back to the last time they'd been together before his torture. Back to the night he'd proposed to her. "What is—"

He silenced her with a kiss. "I want to try again with you, Zarya. Will you marry me?"

Tears stung her eyes as her love for him overwhelmed her. But it was the uncertainty in his voice that really made her ache. How could he doubt her feelings for him after all they'd been through? "You know the answer to that. Of course I will."

"Then you can turn on the light and see what you're going to be tied to. If you change your mind, I won't hold it against you. I'll definitely understand."

She blinked back her tears. "I don't need the light to see you, Darling. Your heart shines brighter than any sun ever could." She reached for his face.

He dodged her hands, then flipped the lamp on.

Since he had his back to her all she could see were the scars marring his skin. The assassin skull and snake tattoo on his shoulder... She ran her fingernails up his spine until she buried her hand in his soft red hair.

He kept his head bent so that his hair fell over his face. His entire body was tense as if he dreaded her reaction. How could he fear her being so petty?

A part of her wanted to tell him she was pregnant, but she hesitated. Assuming Nero was right, she wasn't even far enough along for it to show up on a pregnancy test.

Not to mention, Darling had enough to cope with right now. She didn't want to burden him with anything more.

Bracing herself for the worst, she brushed the hair back from his right cheek, then froze at what she found there.

He swallowed hard before he glanced up sheepishly.

For a full minute she couldn't speak as she stared into his all but perfect features. It was incredible. There was only a faint telltale scar over the left side of his face from where he'd fought with Ryn. Barely noticeable now.

She cupped his face in her hands as she studied him. It was like meeting a stranger.

He had another faint scar at the top of the right arch of his lips where one of the worst injuries had been caused by the muzzle they'd forced on him. And a hairline scar just over his left brow.

But there was no trace of Pip's name or any of the other scars that had been so deep and painful.

Swallowing hard, he licked his lips. "Are you okay with me?"

Was she okay? Was he serious?

Syn had done the most amazing job ever. In her wildest dreams, she'd never imagined how good-looking Darling really was. While he did share features with Drake, his were definitely more refined and masculine.

"You're beautiful."

He pulled his long hair down over the left side of his face. "It's better, but—"

"Darling...you can't see the scars."

"Yes, you can." He brushed his hand over his right cheek where Pip had carved his name. "It's better though. But they're all still there."

Her heart broke for him and the fact that they were so branded in his mind that even with them gone, he still saw them clearly. "No, baby, they're not."

"I'm not *that* blind, Z. I know they're still there." Suddenly, his eyes started jerking back and forth—something they did whenever he was really stressed. He pulled away from her so that he could lie down and close them. He pressed his thumb and forefinger against his eyelids as if that would somehow magically make them stop.

Tears choked her. "Darling, you really can't see them. I swear it."

Darling wanted to believe her. He did, but he wasn't stupid. He knew how people treated those who were disfigured. Those who were broken.

They were cruel and mean.

Most of all, they were unforgiving.

And soon he'd have to face the gerents and hear all their bullshit... *I should have killed more of them.*

On second thought, he should have killed them all.

A knock intruded on his thoughts.

"You rest." Zarya reached over him to get her robe and wrap it around her...

Covering himself with a blanket, he tried to read the clock, but his eyes wouldn't stop jumping long enough for him to focus.

"Did I hear Darling come in?" Ryn asked from the doorway.

"He's resting."

"I know it's late, but it's really important. Otherwise, I wouldn't be here."

"Let him in, Z." Darling kept his eyes closed, but he could sense Ryn moving into the room until he was next to his bed.

"Wow," Ryn said in an awed tone. "Syn did a great job. They're completely gone. How do you feel?"

He was still a little sore—like he'd worked out too hard, but the medicine had done a remarkable job of healing him. "I've felt worse. So what's got you stirred up in the middle of the night?"

Ryn made a sound of irritation. "Fain just shot over an e-mail that's been circulating through everyone's in-box. I thought you needed to know about it."

Darling's gut clenched. *Please don't let it be that fucking video again.* While it'd been years since a copy had shown up—thanks to Syn's tech skills—Darling had always lived with the fear that someone would rerelease it. "What's it about?"

Ryn handed him his mobile.

"I can't read it right now. I've got a bad headache." He should probably tell his brother the truth about his eyesight, but the fewer people who knew about a weakness that could kill him, the better.

Ryn took it back. "Fine, I'll read it..." He cleared his throat. "'The governor is the most sadistic bastard to ever breathe our beloved Caronese air. Every second he lives is an affront to any decent being in this universe. As all of you know, the League will not help us. Not while he and the rest of the noxious aristos pay them to turn a blind eye to their murderous crimes. The governor is so sadistic and cruel that his own guards refuse to do their due diligence and protect him. His gerents live in fear of his wrath and insanity. Reliable sources have told me how they cower at the mere mention of his name. And well they should. I have witnessed both firsthand, and I bear the bruises and wounds to prove it. Every night I bleed anew from his incessant beatings and every morning, his staff is forced to clean my blood from the walls and floors while I am kept as his own personal pet to be tortured at his leisure. I beg you, my brothers and sisters, to rally as much fire as you can to help me forever end the reign of Cruel. Ever your leader…" Ryn paused for effect, "Zarya Starska."

She gasped as Ryn finished.

Bitterly amused, Darling opened his eyes to stare at her as best he could. "Something you need to tell me, sweetie?"

Zarya was aghast at his nonchalant tone and his question. Horror filled her. "I didn't write that. I swear!"

Ryn handed his mobile to her. "It's a scan of someone's handwriting. You recognize it?"

Her jaw went slack as she read the words that she'd never even considered writing. "It looks like mine, but it's not. I haven't touched a computer except to read it or hand it to Darling." Terrified of what he must think, she met Darling's unstable gaze. "Darling, I promise you that—"

"Relax, Z. I'm not stupid." He closed his eyes and covered them with his arm. "If you wanted me dead, you've had more than enough chances to kill me. Instead, you saved my life, and I'm pretty sure the shower incident was an accident."

Relieved at his sanity, she sat down on the bed, then returned the mobile to Ryn. "Thank the gods you're reasonable."

Ryn scoffed at her. "Yeah well, that doesn't change the damage this thing is doing to his tarnished reputation. It's gone viral as hell. The civs and the Resistance believe it's real, especially since someone posted photos of your bathroom with broken glass and blood everywhere—including one of your nightgowns that was soaked in blood. And I have to admit, it's gruesome. In response to those photos, the Resistance is sending out e-mails, saying that if you're not released into their custody within a week, they're going to bomb the palace, drag Darling out and set fire to him on the steps of the CDS building. Meanwhile, everyone—and I mean *everyone*—is panicking with fears of how many of them are going to die in the cross fire."

Of course they were. Darling couldn't blame them. He'd be worried, too, if he didn't know the truth. "Do we know anything about this Hector who's leading the Resistance?" he asked Zarya.

"We didn't have a Hector."

Ryn sighed in disgust. "You do now."

Zarya sputtered. "Where did he come from?"

"I have Syn working on that." Unfortunately, Darling had had to pull Syn off that research to repair his face.

Could the timing for all this suck more?

Probably.

But honestly, all he wanted to do was spend one sedate night with Zarya and forget about politics. Instead, he was forced to deal with unnecessary drama. And for what?

One man's grab for power? Or some misguided humanitarian who believed the idiocy he spewed?

At the end of the day, the answer didn't matter. He had to squelch this before it got any bigger. As Nyk would say, *Coura dona eck nonyun.* "A headless snake doesn't strike."

Darling let out a tired breath. "I'll move the meeting to tonight and try to nip this shit before it worsens. If I take Zarya with me, they can all see for themselves that she's unharmed and not being held against her will."

"All right, but I'm calling in some backup. Just in case."

Zarya appreciated Ryn's offer, but... "You know, the Tavali are going to stand out a bit at the CDS."

"Not Tavali." Ryn tucked his mobile in his pocket. "Sentella. No one will question if Nyk and Caillen are there."

She liked that thought, and he was right. While they weren't Caronese, they *were* aristos. It wasn't unusual for foreign dignitaries to attend such meetings.

And there was another one who'd be even better than having them there. One who would know immediately if an attack on Darling was imminent. "What about Nero?"

A panicked look flashed across Ryn's face before he caught himself. "You know about Nero?"

Afraid she might have given away Nero's secret, she backpedaled. "Do *you*?"

Darling let out a short, bitter laugh. "If you're asking about the family connection, Z, we know. It's also why he can't go near any aristo. If anyone recognizes him and who he really is, he's screwed."

"No," Ryn corrected, "we're talking beyond screwed to the infinite level. He'll be hunted even worse than he already is."

Zarya was trying to follow their conversation, but she was missing something. "Okay, now I think I'm lost. He's your cousin. I don't see why that would endanger him." It seemed to her that being related to a family as powerful as the Cruels would be a major asset to anyone who wasn't a Resistance member.

Ryn gave her a droll stare. "It's not being our cousin that endangers him. He's the last surviving member of the Trisani ruling family. Sole heir. In theory, he could petition the League to have his family lands and money returned to him from the humans—and I use that term loosely—who stole it from them after they enslaved everyone he was related to, and locked him in prison."

"Why doesn't he?"

Darling answered before Ryn had a chance. "Even with his powers, he wouldn't live long enough to enjoy it. He's much better off keeping a low profile."

"But doesn't that threaten your mother, too?"

Darling yawned before he answered. "It would if anyone knew she was related to the Scaleras. But once it became open season on the Trisani, her family did a hell of a job erasing their ties to them. The only reason we know about it is because of the genetic deformities I have."

She frowned. "Is that why you avoid medics?"

"No. I avoid them because they have a long history of assassinating my family."

"It's true," Ryn concurred. "Our grandfather was poisoned and murdered when a med tech came here to give him a routine vaccine."

She winced at that fact.

Ryn indicated where she was sitting on the mattress. "He died right there."

She shot off the bed. "Ew!" Glaring at Darling, she had an awful case of the sudden creeps. "Couldn't you have told me that?"

Darling laughed. "Sweetie, there's barely a corner in this palace where someone hasn't died or wasn't murdered."

He had a point. Still...

Ew!

Ryn pulled his mobile out of his pocket and checked it for a message. He looked back to Darling. "I would suggest beefing up your security, but they're not real fond of you. At this point, I wouldn't be surprised if one of your own guard didn't try to assassinate you."

Anger whipped through her at his reminder. "I don't under-stand that. They protected Arturo." Who had to be the nastiest piece of work to ever breathe. How could they have served him and not Darling? Were they that stupid? "What do they have against Darling, anyway?"

"You mean aside from the fact that he killed a third of them when he took the throne?"

While she'd seen him go after the guard courtesy of Maris, that number stunned her. "Is that true?"

"No... It was more like half of them."

Ryn let out an evil laugh. "I'm speaking from experience. *Never* get on Darling's bad side."

"Payback's a bitch." He dropped his hand to pin her with a cold stare. "I owed them for sixteen years of abuse and fourteen years of rude, invasive, and sadistic body cavity searches. Let's just say, I'm not a forgiving man. The old excuse of 'I was ordered to do it' didn't sit well with me. I expect more out of my guard than someone who ruthlessly violates a defenseless kid under orders and then laughs about it and throws it in his face every time they see him." His eyes still jerking, he glanced toward Ryn. "Because of that, I wouldn't trust them anyway. They've never thought much of me... other than as a punch line to a tasteless joke."

Ryn held his hands up in surrender. "Hey, I commend you for weeding out the gene pool, even though I have to say that I enjoy polluting it myself. It doesn't say much for their substandard intel-ligence that none of them thought ahead to what would become of them once you were governor."

"They were counting on my being shoved aside in favor of Drake inheriting. No doubt, they still are."

Ryn snorted. "Well to that, all I have to say is... surprise."

"And they were. Though in retrospect, killing so many of them probably wasn't the wisest move I've made. Oops."

Oh, his humor was bad. But then, he'd always had a dark side. Another knock sounded on the door.

"What the hell?" Darling growled. "Did I miss a memo? Who opened my bedroom for public access?"

Laughing, Zarya went to the door to find Hauk there, along with two extremely tall men flanking him. "What are you doing here?"

Hauk flashed a wicked, fanged grin at her. "So good to see you again, too, lovely. Thanks for the warm welcome. 'Preciate it."

Her face flamed at her unintended rudeness. "I'm sorry, Hauk. It's just late and most people are in bed."

He leaned down as if to impart a secret to her. "In case you missed it, I'm not people." Looking past her to the bed, he jerked his chin toward Darling. "And I've come to protect Lord Hard Head."

"Pardon?"

"Is Darling still awake?"

She stepped back so that he could see Ryn. "He is."

Hauk headed for the bed. "Fain sent me a note about what's going on with the locals. I'm here with backup."

Darling growled. "Not helpless, people."

"Not people, human," Hauk said in an exasperated tone.

Darling made an obscene gesture at him. "I thought I got rid of you when I left the hospital."

Hauk clutched his chest as if those words wounded him. "Aww now, Dar, you're going to hurt my feelings."

"You don't have feelings."

"True. Just think of me like a bad STD. I always show up at the worst time." He glanced back at Zarya. "So much for your hot date, huh?"

Darling groaned. "You are ever a pain in my ass, Hauk. Should I reset the timers on my explosives in the city? Might give the

Resistance pause if they think I'm going to take them or their families with me."

Ryn shook his head, but didn't comment on Darling's threat. "I'm sure you need to rest. Get some sleep and we'll take care of everything else."

Hauk moved to sit in the chair near Darling's closet.

Arching his brow, Darling scowled. "What are you doing?"

"Taking my post."

"Yeah...no. Get your hairy ass out."

Hauk scoffed at Darling's protest. "Let me be honest with you. Nyk scares me. You don't. Not even a little. Besides, you'll sleep better with a bodyguard."

Zarya stepped forward. "He has a bodyguard."

Hauk raked her with a less than complimentary grimace. "You'd be dead before you could scream."

"Try me."

When he stood up to confront her, Darling laughed. "I wouldn't do that if I were you."

"You're not me." Hauk moved to pin her.

Zarya dodged, and twirled out of his reach. She grabbed the blaster off his belt and angled it at his head. "Like I said, he has a guard."

A light of respect darkened those eerie Andarion eyes. "All right then. It's settled. Zarya will watch you and I'll be outside should either of you need anything."

She held his blaster out to him.

"Keep it."

"Thanks." Zarya set the blaster down on the nightstand as the men finally left her alone with Darling again.

Darling rubbed his hand over his forehead. "This wasn't how I wanted to come home to you."

Zarya quickly exchanged her robe for the shirt she'd been

sleeping in. "I don't mind...so long as you come home." She'd take him any way she could get him, scary friends and all.

She slid into bed and leaned back against the padded head-board before she parted her legs for him.

Darling moved to rest his head on her thigh. He lay on his back, looking up at her as she brushed her hand lightly through his long, tangled hair.

The beauty of his repaired face still stunned her. He was exquisite. "I'm going to have to get used to you all over again."

A stricken look furrowed his brow. "What do you mean?"

She smoothed his features with her fingertips. "It's nothing bad, sweetie. I was just repeating the fact that Syn did a remarkable job."

Darling fell silent as he surrendered himself to her soothing touch and tried not to think about the fact that she deserved a man who was whole. Not a scarred piece of shit like him. He took her hand in his and held it against his cheek. The scent of her skin was enough to make him light-headed. He'd spent his entire life aching for someone to hold him when he was hurt.

As a teen and young man, he'd only trusted Maris with his weaknesses. While he knew his friends wouldn't hurt him, Syn, Nyk, Hauk, Caillen, and Jayne weren't the most sympathetic of beings. They had their own damaged pasts to deal with, just like him. Because of that, he'd tried to keep his bitching to a minimum.

Then there had been the perpetual fear that if he told them exactly what was going on at home, one of them would kill Arturo for hurting him and he'd lose his family over it. A fear that seemed stupid now given the fact he'd finally found a way to murder his uncle and bypass the law Arturo had put into place.

Why hadn't he acted sooner? If he'd only come up with the bomb idea when he was a kid, he could have saved himself years of abuse...

But then even if he had murdered Arturo, there was still the matter of his being virtually enslaved to whomever replaced his uncle's guardianship.

His luck, it would have been someone even worse.

Someone like Nylan.

He flinched at the thought while Zarya traced the line of his brow with her fingernail. She sank her hand into his hair. He turned his head so that he could breathe her scent in and let it drive the past away.

Everything was so different now. He stood on new ground with a CDS who hated his guts even more than Arturo had.

And tonight he'd have to face all the Caronese gerents...

Pain racked him as he remembered the last time he'd been forced to attend a Caronese symposium. It'd been unbearable.

Granted even a regular gathering of multinational nobles wasn't the joy of his life. But at least when other empires were present, the mocking was kept to a minimum. The Caronese didn't believe in airing their private ridicule to strangers.

Yet when it was just them...

He didn't want to think about what was to come.

Why couldn't Nylan do him the favor of dying already?

But the gods had never been friends of his. Rather, they intended to keep the bastard alive for no other purpose than to serve as an eternal reminder that Darling was nothing more than a stupid piece of shit.

The memory of their laughter at the last gathering still rang in his ears... *"What's the difference between Darling Cruel and a rooster? In the morning, a rooster says, 'cock-a-doodle-doo' while at night Darling says, 'any-cock'll-do.'"*

"Are you okay?" Zarya's voice cut through his misery to bring him back to the warmth of her touch.

"Just thinking about the meeting tonight." He looked up at her.

"Maybe you shouldn't go to it." The last thing he wanted was for her to overhear one of those stupid, juvenile jokes.

Anger flashed in her eyes. "I do know etiquette, Darling. I'm not going to embarrass you."

His heart sank at her mistaken assumption. "It's not that," he quickly assured her. "I don't know how *they'll* react to *my* presence. The last thing I want is for them to insult you because of me."

She leaned down and kissed his lips. "I don't care what they think of me. None of them are worth a minute of my time, and I will not waste one thought on worrying about them when I'd rather spend it thinking about you."

Darling wished he could banish them so easily. Instead, they kept rushing his mental blocks and slamming them to the ground. "I'll have Maris there to get you out if it gets bad."

"Who'll protect you?"

"They won't physically attack me, Zarya."

"Yes, but physical blows heal a lot faster than psychological ones."

Darling didn't respond this time.

Worried about him, Zarya glanced down to see that he'd fallen asleep in her lap. Smiling, she brushed the hair back from the left half of his face so that she could study the surgery without Darling watching her. She couldn't believe the difference it'd made. Syn was a certified genius when it came to medicine.

Darling was absolutely devastating. Those very faint scars actually enhanced his beauty. Without them, he'd lean more toward pretty than ruggedly handsome.

No one would ever mock his looks now.

But that wasn't what concerned her most. If Darling didn't make peace with the gerents tonight, he wouldn't be governor long.

One of them would have him killed.

18

Unmitigated panic ripped through every part of Zarya as she stared at herself in the mirror. She didn't know the woman there. It was a complete stranger gazing through her amber eyes.

One who absolutely terrified her. Even though she had a royal and noble bloodline and had been taught the ways of the aristocracy, Zarya Starska wasn't an aristo. She could only vaguely recall those days.

No, she was a soldier. A Resistance fighter. One who was more at home on a battlefield than walking through the land mines of social barbs and verbal slaps. While she technically knew how to behave at a royal function, she hadn't been drilled on those behaviors since her mother's death. All she knew intimately now was raw survival.

A survival instinct that told her to run.

I don't know if I can do this.

She blinked her eyelids that were heavy from the makeup Gera had applied. Her maroon dress was so tight, she could barely breathe. Strapless, it was trimmed in gold and dark blue—the royal Caronese colors.

According to Gera, Darling would be dressed in dark blue, and this dress had been made to complement his official state formal attire.

I'd run for the door, but in these shoes, I might break my leg.

For that matter, she wasn't really sure if the delicate lace high heels that had been dyed to match her dress really qualified as shoes. But, she knew for a fact that her sister would kill to own a pair of them.

Her door opened. She expected it to be Darling or Maris.

Instead, it was Gera. She had a strange expression on her face. One that never boded well for Zarya's sanity or sense of norm.

"Did we forget something?"

Gera smiled. "No, Mistress. You look like an absolute vision. Any man would be honored to escort you." She brought whatever she'd been hiding behind her back around so that Zarya could see a burgundy leather box.

Zarya cocked a curious eyebrow as a wave of nervous trepidation went through her. "What's that?"

"His lordship gave it to me for you to wear tonight." Gera presented it to her much the way Darling had given his medal to Drus.

Zarya stared down at her new engagement ring. The center stone was dark blue with the side stones a deep, blood maroon that matched her dress. She'd only ever owned three pieces of jewelry in her entire life. Her mother's ring that she'd given to Darling, and the two engagement rings Darling had given her.

And since two of them had been violently stolen...

"I don't really wear jewelry."

Gera refused to be daunted. "You'll want *this*. Trust me."

When she didn't move to take the box, Gera opened the lid to show her the most magnificent necklace she'd ever seen in her life. It looked as if it'd been made to match her ring. Red and blue stones were laced together with tiny gold gems to form a collar that held one obscenely large, perfect red teardrop.

Gera handed her the matching earrings, then took the necklace out of its box. She moved behind Zarya so that she could fasten it around Zarya's neck.

All Zarya could do was gape at something that probably cost more than a small planet. Why had Darling sent it to her?

She covered the stone with her hand—it was so large, she couldn't even close her fist around it—while Gera worked with the catch. "Is this his mother's?"

"No, Mistress. Lady Natale has all of her jewelry with her at the Summer Palace. His lordship went down into the vault to select these for you."

Vault?

Zarya frowned. "I don't understand."

"These are part of what his lordship inherited when his father died," Gera explained. "Every lady of the empire is given her own jewels by her husband. When she passes, she may will them to someone or return them to the vault so that they remain the governor's property and go to her child who inherits. This set belonged to his lordship's great-grandmother. They were given to her when she birthed his grandfather. The center teardrop is the largest blodesteen ever cut."

Those were the rarest of all the precious stones in existence.

Zarya picked it up to stare in awe of the priceless gem that was worth even more than she'd originally thought.

"Her ladyship always wore this set for all state functions, and at all celebrations. She claimed the blue stones were to calm her nerves and the red to inspire her husband to become even greater than he already was. If you've been down the north hallway, you've no doubt seen her wearing them in her state portrait. They were her most prized possession."

Gera moved to put the earrings on.

Zarya kindly stopped her. "I can do it. Thank you, Gera."

Inclining her head, Gera took her leave.

Zarya fastened the earrings, then went straight to Darling's door. Knocking, she didn't wait for him to respond before she pushed it open.

She froze instantly.

Holy mother of all shoes...

Darling was absolutely startling in his regal beauty. The navy uniform, trimmed in gold and maroon, made his eyes an even darker shade of blue. His valet had cut his hair so that it no longer fell over the left half of his face. Rather, the much shorter style curled around his collar and formed a perfect frame for his chiseled features. A style that left both of his eyes visible.

And braided into his hair so that it fell from behind his right ear was his harone—the three graduating strands of jewels that designated his status as a royal governor. The longest strand was made of red stone beads with every sixth bead being yellow. At the end hung a larger briolette cut of navy blue. The next strand up was dark blue with every fourth bead being yellow. The briolette on it was maroon. The shortest strand was red beads with every fifth bead blue. Its briolette was yellow.

An aura of lethal, regal authority bled from every part of him. Unlike her, he was completely at ease with his nobility, and he looked every bit the powerful ruler that he was. She'd never found an aristo sexy, but Darling wore that title well. There was no arrogance to him, only a deep self-assurance that was as erotic as the hot look in his eyes as he stared at her.

"You are stunning, my lady." He all but growled those words.

"And you are exceptional."

His valet cleared his throat to get Darling's attention. "Majesty? Is there anything else you require?"

Darling glanced to his left where his valet waited. "You're dismissed."

After a slight bow, the man quickly took his leave.

As soon as he was gone, Darling wasted no time closing the distance between them so that he could kiss her.

Zarya breathed him in, wanting to feel him naked against her skin. But she knew better. They couldn't afford to be late to this meeting.

Reluctantly, she pulled back. "If you mess up Gera's hard work, she might poison us both."

One corner of his mouth twitched. "If not for the gerents, I'd be willing to risk her wrath." He picked her hand up and placed a sexy kiss to her fingers. "Did you need something? You looked kind of pissed when you came in."

His syntax was the only part of him that betrayed his Sentella training. The rest of him was all arrogant emperor. In the past, men like him had repulsed her. But now that she knew him so well and had walked on the inside of his privileged world, she understood that it was a shield he wore just like the body armor they chose whenever they went into battle. And in a way, that was exactly what he was about to do.

Only his weapons wouldn't be knives or blasters or bombs or gases. He would be fighting with his words and wit. With his ability to effectively argue his side, and to show the fallacies in his opponent's logic. A different battlefield, but the outcome was the same.

The winner dictated the future of the people she'd spent her life fighting for.

That detached arrogance he cloaked himself with was a vital shell that, just like the red tinged black battlesuits the Sentella wore, kept his opponent's from knowing when they'd wounded him, and how deeply their blows had struck.

Funny how she'd never known that until lately.

Now she fully understood. And she knew from her own

experience that words always cut deeper than any weapon forged by man.

The only thing that was sharper and that scarred more was the selfish actions of those you loved when they made it crystal clear that they cared more for themselves than they did for you. Especially when it was someone you trusted to always put you first.

And that pain was what she felt right now. "I'm not pissed," she said slowly, answering his question. "More curious." She ran her hand over the exquisite necklace. "Why did you loan this to me?"

He frowned. "Didn't you read the note I sent with it?"

"It didn't come with a note."

His eyes flashed with anger, then settled into a look of disappointment. "It's not that important, I guess. But they're not a loan, Zarya. They're a gift."

Go on, keep talking, buddy. Dig yourself in deeper.

"Why?" she asked, hoping she was wrong.

That turned him defensive, which made her suspicions grow. "Do I have to have a reason to give you a present?"

"If you're giving it to me because you don't want me to embarrass you, then yes."

Darling choked at her unexpected, and highly erroneous assumption. Indignant, he glared at her. "How could I *ever* be embarrassed by you?"

"I know I'm technically no longer an aristo, but—"

"Zarya..." He placed his hands on her arms and stared into her amber eyes, hoping she could see how sincere he was. "You *are* an aristo. Your father may have been stripped of his titles and money, but your blood is as noble as anyone's in the CDS, and it's as royal as mine. I picked that set for you because I thought they'd be beautiful on you and I was right. Most of all, when my valet brought in my harone, it dawned on me that you didn't have any jewelry of your own. I wanted to give you some because I thought it would make you happy. That was the only thing that motivated me. I swear."

Zarya wanted to weep as she heard those words. And here she'd tainted his beautiful gift. Suddenly, she felt stupid for doubting him when he had never given her a reason to.

Rather, she'd attacked him out of her own insecurity and for the views that had been held by her last boyfriend.

"Damn, Zarya. Can't you at least try to look like a woman when we go out? The last thing I want is for someone to think I'm dating a man or a hobo."

It wasn't fair to Darling when he had never once said anything negative about how she dressed or looked. "I'm sorry, Darling. I didn't mean to be so shrewish."

He kissed her lightly on the cheek. "It's all right. My nerves are shot, too. I hate doing shit like this just as much as you do."

Clenching his teeth, he went over to his dresser and picked up a pair of darkly tinted glasses. Not quite as dark as sunglasses, they shielded her ability to see his eyes.

She scowled in confusion. "I thought you didn't want anyone to know your vision was impaired."

"I don't. But in the event I have to read something, I can't afford to let them know that I have a problem. Plus, if my eyes start jerking, I definitely don't want them to see it...I'm hoping these will help me keep both secrets."

That made sense.

"They look great on you, by the way."

Darling appreciated her compliment. But even so, he had a terrible feeling about the meeting tonight—it was the same uneasy feeling he'd had the night before Clarion's attack. Every instinct he possessed told him something bad was going to happen.

443

I won't let it.

And yet even as that thought finished, an inner part of himself laughed at his arrogance.

Fate is a bitch, but she always has a wicked sense of humor.

Please, don't let me be her punch line tonight.

19

Darling paused outside the Grand Assembly room of the main CDS building. He could hear the roar of the gerents and their spouses through the strains of the orchestra music. There were four Sentella soldiers dressed as Caronese guards in front of him, waiting for his signal to open the door for his admittance.

C'mon, Dar. You've done this a thousand times in the past. So what if they mock and laugh? You're now their governor.

He had the power of life and death over all of them...

Zarya released his arm and moved to stand at his back, next to Maris. Since she wasn't Darling's wife yet, protocol demanded that she and Maris trail him. Anything else would be seen as a slap to the aristos.

He glanced over his shoulder to offer her a smile he didn't feel.

But the sight of her cheered him exponentially. Dressed in the royal Caronese colors, she was breathtaking. Her strapless gown trailed behind her on the floor, giving her a regal look as she tucked her gloved hand into the crook of Maris's elbow. The royal jewels sparkled around her neck, but they were no match for her warm amber eyes.

Against his will, his body hardened. *Great, just what I need. Walk in there to face those bastards with a hard-on.*

"You two ready?" he asked them.

Maris covered her hand with his. "Lead on, my lord. We will follow you anywhere."

"Hell it is, then," Darling mumbled under his breath.

With a deep breath to brace himself for the coming slaughter, Darling signaled the guards to open the doors. Without a word, they obeyed.

Hating this with every fiber of his being, Darling forced himself to step forward.

The moment they entered the hall, all sound immediately ceased and every eye in the room focused on him as he made his first public appearance.

Zarya feared she might pass out as she saw the number of aristos in attendance who stared at them with contempt and disdain. Somewhere in the crowd, Drake and Ryn were here, but she couldn't see them anywhere.

"Breathe easy," Maris whispered to her. "Remember, they're not looking at us. They're picking apart Darling."

Trying her best to suppress her laughter at that, she wrinkled her nose at him. "You're so evil."

"Yes, but it's true. We'd have to light ourselves on fire to catch their notice right now. Even then, I'm not sure if it'd work."

Laughing as they followed Darling through the crowd, she saw heads leaning together as people began to gossip.

Darling paused next to the majordomo and spoke in a tone so low, they couldn't hear him.

The majordomo cleared his throat before he announced them. "All hail his exalted and esteemed lordship, High Governor Cruel."

The room bowed to him.

Looking every bit the part, Darling followed his guards to the elegant throne that was centered against the left wall on a small dais.

Once he was seated and everyone had regained their feet, the majordomo spoke again. "The Andarion ambassador, his most honorable High Lord Maris Sulle and the most venerated Grand Marleena of Starrin, High Lady Zarya Starska."

Shocked to the core of her being, she'd have fallen had she not been holding on to Maris. The last time she'd heard someone referred to as the Grand Marleena of Starrin, it'd been her mother. Her father had been the Grand Marle.

Had Darling reinstated her title?

He must have, otherwise it would have been illegal for her to use it. But why not tell her?

It didn't make sense.

Maris tightened his hand on hers as he led her to stand before Darling's throne. He bowed low while she curtsied in front of their governor.

Darling inclined his head to them.

After rising, she and Maris moved to stand to the right of the dais as all the gerents and their spouses came forward to follow suit and pay respect to their governor.

"Don't you look smashingly gorgeous!"

Zarya turned to see a tiny brunette. She threw her arms around Maris's neck and hugged him close.

Smiling at her, he kissed the woman's cheek, then smoothed one of her curls that had fallen out of place. That action was so intimate, that it momentarily shocked Zarya.

"I pale in comparison to you, my dearest love," Maris said, his grin widening. "But then you were always exquisite."

The woman tsked at him. "You better be careful, Mari, lies like that will get you into trouble."

"As long as it's the right kind, I don't mind at all." He gave a nod to Zarya. "Have you met the Grand Marleena?"

"No, I have not." The woman spoke breathlessly in a tone that said she thought meeting Zarya would be scandalous.

Maris kissed the woman's hand before presenting her. "Zarya, this absolutely ravishing beauty is Tamara. Tamara, Zarya."

Zarya smiled at the petite woman. Maris was right, she was so gorgeous that it left Zarya feeling without. But she wouldn't hold that against her, not when she seemed to be so much fun. "It's a pleasure to meet you, Tamara."

"Call me Tams, hon, everyone does." She frowned as she looked past Zarya's shoulder. "Ugh, I'm being summoned." Irritated, she glanced to Maris. "We need to have a girl gab session and catch up, Mari. I'll find out where our placards are and switch them so that we can sit together during dinner. Later, my precious." She kissed him on the lips before making her way through the crowd.

Flabbergasted by the entire encounter, Zarya arched a curious brow at Maris. "Who is she exactly?"

More to the point, *what* was she to Maris? Because their entire interaction had been very strange.

Maris gracefully pulled two glasses of wine from a passing server's tray. He handed one to her before he answered. "Tams was the woman I left standing at the altar."

Zarya choked on her wine as those unexpected words rang in her ears. *That* had been Maris's former fiancée?

She couldn't believe that Tams would be so nice and pleasant after such a humiliating ordeal—it was the kind of experience most women dreaded...And all the women Zarya had known would have still wanted to claw out Maris's eyes.

"Pardon?"

He saluted her with his glass. "It's true. And that was how I knew for a fact that I was gay. No question about it. If ever a woman would have attracted me and compelled me to be a breeder, it was she."

His gaze went to Tamara as she and her husband were introduced to Darling. "She is truly beautiful, inside and out, in a way that very few people are. Besides Darling, she's one of my best friends and has always been such. May the gods bless her. Rather than being scandalized and bitter, she actually thanked me in the chapel for being honest and not trapping her into a celibate marriage of convenience."

If nothing else about Tams was gracious, *that* alone would have made Zarya love the woman. "I'm so glad she was decent about it."

"No kidding. Aside from Darling, she was the only one who was. The rest of her family wanted my testicles on a platter."

Giggling at his vivid imagery, Zarya daintily picked up a small hors d'oeuvre from the tray a waiter presented to her. She'd just bitten into it when another aristo approached them. At least, she *thought* he was an aristo. While he was in uniform, he had the bearing and presence of one.

Not to mention, he was amazingly handsome. Dressed in a formal black League uniform, he wore a pair of opaque sunglasses covering his eyes. His long black hair was braided down his back—the mark of a high-ranking assassin. He appeared ready to kill, but his features softened as he inclined his head to Maris.

Was he one of Maris's former boyfriends? Darling had told her that Maris went through men faster than most people changed their socks.

"You look so happy, Maris. I hope it's not a façade."

Maris's features were unreadable, but his body was rigid and cold. "I am happy, thank you." His gaze dropped to the sleeves of the man's uniform. A slow smile curved his lips. "I see you made assassin's rank like you always wanted. Are you enjoying it?"

True to his training, the assassin didn't betray a single emotion. "It's not exactly what I thought it would be. But I can't complain. And you..." He broke his stern countenance to laugh. "Darling made quite an impression with the High Command when he nailed every assassin Kyr sent in to kill him. It was highly impressive. Are you the one who taught him how to fight?"

"Not I. Nykyrian Quiakides."

"Ahhhh." The assassin returned to his cold demeanor. "That explains a lot, actually."

Maris indicated Zarya with his glass. "Zarya, allow me to introduce you to Deputy Agent Safir Jari."

The assassin stiffened. "*Chief* agent, actually."

"Oh Saf, I'm so sorry." Maris finally relaxed into the man she knew and loved. "I so did not do that as an intentional slap to you." He gestured to the embroidery on Safir's sleeve. "I never could keep the League ranks straight."

Safir smiled. "I know, Mari. Dad used to get so mad at you whenever you'd screw them up."

Zarya had to catch herself to keep from gaping at the unexpected disclosure. This was one of Maris's many brothers?

Really? Other than the black hair, they didn't really favor. Except they were both exceedingly handsome.

Maris swallowed as a dark shadow clouded his gaze. "I take it he still won't speak my name."

Safir's face mirrored Maris's pain. "Mom, either."

Maris glanced around the room uneasily. "You should go before someone photographs you speaking to me and sends it to them. I don't want you to have to deal with that."

Safir bowed respectfully to him. "Before I go, I should warn you that Kyr will be here tonight."

A tic started in Maris's jaw. "Why?"

"League High Command wants to hear what Darling has to say. It's why I'm here, too."

"Are they going to make an attempt on his life?" That would be the natural assumption.

Safir made a subtle gesture she assumed was a Phrixian sign of trust. "I wasn't given those orders, and to my knowledge no one else was either. We're simply here to observe. Nothing more." He paused next to Maris and placed his hand on Maris's shoulder before he leaned in to whisper something in his ear.

Zarya frowned as Maris responded in an equally low tone.

Stepping back, Safir offered her a stiff, formal bow. "It was an honor meeting you, my lady."

"You as well." She curtsied to him.

Once he was gone, she lifted a brow at Maris. "One of your many brothers, I presume."

Maris nodded. "My youngest. He's also the only one of them who will still talk to me…when he can."

It saddened her to hear that, especially since it was obvious that Safir loved his older brother. How tragic for their parents' prejudice to divide them so. But it wasn't her place to judge. She refused to be like others and hate someone when she didn't know what demons drove them to their beliefs.

She watched as Safir was hailed over to a group of gerents who greeted him warmly.

While she watched them, she reviewed their conversation. "When he said 'Kyr,' did he mean Kyr Zemen, the prime commander of the League?"

Maris drained his glass in a way that was more akin to his military training than to the fastidious man she knew him to be. "One and the same. Unfortunately. Bloody damn wanker bastard."

The venom behind those words had to spring from a personal

grudge between them. She'd never seen so much hatred from Maris before toward anyone.

Not even her.

"How do you know him?" she asked.

"He's my oldest brother."

That news floored her. Completely. "Are you . . . what? No. Not possible. Well, I guess it's possible, but . . . why do all of you have different surnames?"

He plucked another glass from a passing tray. "Unlike other cultures, Phrixians aren't born with their surnames. We earn them. Zemen means 'strength through adversity.' Jari is 'honor in battle.'"

Ah . . . She hadn't caught the different nomenclature earlier because she hadn't realized when they were introduced that Safir was Maris's brother. "And Sulle?"

He gave her a twisted grin. "'Invincible.'"

Her eyes widened at that.

"I really was a soldier, Zarya," he said simply. Then he held his hands wide to show her his body. "Underneath all this fashionable, sexy attire is a bitch who knows how to kick ass and smack people around with the best of them."

She still had a hard time reconciling Maris's playful personality with that hard military persona. Even though he'd shown it to her, he hadn't held it for very long. She just couldn't imagine him as a warrior.

He reached for another hors d'oeuvre.

A tall brunette woman stepped out of a passing group to pause by Maris's side. She swept him with an amused, but cold smile. "So, Mari, I have to know something."

"Yes, Cretia?"

She pinned Zarya with a glacial stare. "What does she do for you and Darling? Is she around to coach you on how to be a woman, or are you two instructing her on how to give blow jobs?"

Zarya saw red. Before she even realized what she was doing, she lunged at the woman.

Maris caught her with one arm and pushed her back.

"Oh," Cretia said, raking her with a smug sneer. "She's your bodyguard. I get it now. Makes sense, since she has more testosterone than both of you combined." She drifted off.

Zarya glared at him as he finally released her. "You should have let me rip her hair out by the dyed roots."

Maris tsked at her. "Oh please. The last thing you want to do is get her acidic blood on your beautiful dress. Think of the poor designer who'd curse you for the affront to his hard work."

"Yes, but the dry cleaner would thank me." She made an obscene noise at the direction the woman had vanished in. "I can't believe how rude she was."

"That was exceedingly mild, thanks to her infantile intelligence. And look at it this way, they're all going insane with curiosity. Not to mention, jealousy. None of them can figure out why we *both* walked in as his royal escorts, wearing official Caronese court garb."

He had a point. It was actually illegal for anyone other than a member of the governor's immediate family to wear the royal colors together unless it was a national holiday or they had a special dispensation from the governor.

By having them in his colors and entering with them, Darling had made a very public statement about his feelings where she and Maris were concerned.

Maris jerked his chin toward the dance floor. "Let's really get under their skin and rub their noses in it, shall we?"

Laughing, she set her glass down, then took his proffered arm and allowed him to lead her toward the other dancers.

Once they reached the floor, he swept her into his arms and masterfully guided her through the elaborate steps.

*   *   *

Bored beyond human endurance, Darling glanced away as he tried not to roll his eyes at the ancient gerent in front of him who was droning on and on about the good old days under the reign of Darling's grandfather.

As he glanced around the room, his gaze was drawn to a bright flash of maroon—a color only one woman had permission to wear tonight.

The moment he focused on Maris and Zarya as they danced together and laughed, his blood began racing. If anyone other than Maris dared to hold her like that and make her appear so deliriously happy, they'd be searching the dance floor for their body parts.

As it was, Darling was captivated by her beauty and vitality as they swirled together. Strange how, in all these years, he'd never known that she could dance. Never mind, do it so well.

He went instantly hard.

Desperate to be the one who added the color to her cheeks and make her laugh like that, he excused himself, then headed to the dance floor. In the back of his mind, he was well aware of the gossipmongers who watched and ruthlessly shredded his every movement. As governor, he wasn't supposed to dance at all. It was considered beneath his position.

However, he was a different breed than his predecessors. Tradition had a place in the world.

But it wasn't here tonight.

Maris pulled her to a stop as he saw Darling's approach. With an extremely formal bow, he surrendered her to Darling's custody.

Her face lighting with a smile that set fire to every part of him, Zarya took his hand and allowed him to pick up where Maris had stopped. "I didn't think you were allowed to do this."

"Fuck them," Darling said nonchalantly. "What good is being governor if I can't dance with the most beautiful woman here?"

Zarya's blood raced as he dipped her low. The strength of his arm supporting her made her think of other times when he'd held her in private. Something that made her even more breathless than the quick dance.

His lips were so close to hers that it was all she could do not to kiss them. He straightened her, then twirled her around, and brought her back against the front of his hard body. Her head reeled from the sensation of all that power surrounding her as they moved in perfect synchronicity. With each step, she could feel how much he desired her as her hip brushed against his groin. It left her even more breathless and weak.

She turned to face him. "You keep doing that, my lord, and we're going to really scandalize them."

The grin on his face made her heart soar. "I'm game if you are."

The music quickened.

Darling spun her around again, faster and faster. Never had she danced like this. She could feel the muscles in his arms bulging as he gracefully guided her around the room. The wonderful scent of him made her senses reel.

Everything and everyone faded except him. It was as if only the two of them existed. She was completely captivated by the heated look on his handsome face, and the warmth of his touch.

When the music finally stopped, he supported her entire weight with only one arm. His hair disheveled, he had beads of sweat falling from his temples. Bent in an arc, she stared up at him as he cupped her face with his left hand. His breathing was as ragged as hers. In that moment, she was desperate to taste him. This time, she couldn't resist those lips that held the tiniest hint of a smile.

Sinking her hand into his soft, red hair, she pulled his mouth to hers so that she could kiss him.

Darling's head spun as Zarya explored his mouth with a hunger that left him even harder than their dancing had. Oh yeah, this was what he needed...

It wasn't until he heard an off-key note that he remembered they weren't alone.

In fact, they were the center of everyone's attention. He gave her one last second before he pulled back and regretfully returned her weight to her feet.

Zarya went completely still as she straightened and became aware of all the mocking gazes fixed on them. Heat scorched her cheeks.

I look like the biggest slut of all time...

In public.

Why didn't the universe provide rotating black holes on planets that could swallow people whole when they needed them to?

"Don't let their bitter viciousness steal your happiness," Darling whispered in her ear before he placed a tender kiss on her cheek. Tucking her hand into the crook of his arm, he led her toward his throne.

Arms akimbo, Maris gave them both an angry, condemning stare while he tapped his foot against the stone floor. "You *never* danced with me like that."

Zarya scowled as she tried to understand why Maris was so upset at her. "We only had the one dance."

"He's not talking to you, love," Darling said in her ear.

Oh...

She laughed at Maris's exasperation.

"Governor?"

Darling turned toward the gerent leader who was trying to keep the venom out of his sneer and failing miserably. Honestly, someone should have told him that it was never a good idea to provoke a man who possessed the skills to gut you.

He answered the leader with only a brow raised in warning to let the man know he needed to pick another tone.

The gerent leader paled a degree before he spoke. "It's time to start our meeting."

There now... much better attitude.

Until the leader's gaze slid to Zarya in a way that said he thought she was on the level of something that needed to be flushed out an airlock. And that set fire to Darling's temper.

Don't punch him... It took everything Darling had not to. But it wouldn't go well for him to show off his temper right now. It would be the biggest mistake he could make.

You say one word to her and I swear, politics or not, you're on the floor, asshole.

The leader must have sensed that he was dancing with the devil. He cleared his throat and changed to a more respectful demeanor. "That is if you don't mind, Majesty."

Taking a deep breath, Darling gave him a curt nod. "Gather them, then. I'll be there shortly."

As soon as the gerent was gone, Maris wagged his eyebrows at Darling. "Train them right from the start."

"Working on it." Darling turned to face Zarya. Even though she appeared every bit the lady, there was a light in her eyes that showed him just how vulnerable and uncomfortable she was here. He hated leaving her, but he had no choice. "I'll be back as soon as I can, I promise. Caillen, Nyk, Kiara, and Desideria should be here any minute to help keep you two entertained and out of trouble."

As if on cue, and dressed in Caronese guard uniforms, Hauk, Chayden, and Fain walked through the doors and headed straight to Darling. Something that caused the delegates and their escorts to start gossiping all over again since it was obvious the two hulking mountains weren't human and therefore definitely *not* Caronese soldiers.

Thank the gods they'd finally arrived, now he wouldn't be so worried about Zarya and Maris and could focus on his task of dealing with pompous assholes who hated him.

As soon as the entire group reached them, Hauk gave Darling an arch stare. "Damn boy, there's nothing to be *that* nervous over."

Darling was completely baffled by his comment. "Excuse me?"

"You're sweating like you ran a marathon."

Amused by that, Darling shrugged. "I'm sure Zarya will fill you in. Right now I have to meet—"

"You're not going in without us," Hauk insisted.

Darling opened his mouth to argue, then caught himself.

While Hauk busted on him as if he were Darling's older brother, he, like the rest of the Sentella High Command, was extremely protective of him. There was no way the Andarion would allow Darling into an arena with that many enemies and not be there to pull him out if things went bad.

No amount of argument would sway the Andarion. Hauk was even more stubborn than Drake and Zarya combined.

Then, Ryn gave him that big-brother-knows-best stare that didn't help his temperament in the least. "Chay is coming to the meeting, too, as the Qillaq ambassador. And we're"—he indicated Drake and himself—"going in with you. Let the bastards know up front that for the first time in decades the Cruels are united. They're not going to be able to use one of us against the other. Ever."

Those words meant a lot to Darling, especially since his brothers were dressed in royal colors. And he knew exactly how much Ryn hated being in the middle of politics.

Not to mention, Ryn had a most valid point. If the gerents saw their solidarity, it would help squelch the idea that they might be able to use Drake to overthrow Darling.

"Okay. Let's do it." Darling paused long enough to kiss Zarya's hand. "I'll return as soon as I can."

"Good luck."

He inclined his head to her before he performed a military turn and went to the conference room with his brothers and friends two steps behind him.

Zarya didn't know why, but it hurt to be left behind. She wanted desperately to follow and make sure that Darling was all right.

A stupid thought really, given who he was and the soldiers with him. They could definitely handle anything thrown at them.

Still...

A small furor erupted at the doors.

Afraid of what that might signify, she stood on her tiptoes to see over everyone's heads. Something she didn't have to do long. Two seconds later, literally, Nykyrian and Kiara entered with Caillen, Desideria, and Syn right behind them.

The gathered nobility exploded into a chatter of excited whispers.

"What's the Andarion heir doing here?"

"Isn't that the Exeterian prince?"

"That's Desideria Denarii, the Qill princess."

"Oh my God! That's Kiara Biardi, the dancer!"

"Yeah, and she's here with her father, the Gouran president. I saw him a few minutes ago in the washroom!"

Dozens of such comments circled around her. Comments that came to an abrupt halt when all the people they were talking about joined her and Maris.

Kiara grabbed her into a tight hug. "Sorry we're late." Stepping back, she patted her stomach. "For the record, when you get pregnant, you don't just get morning sickness in the morning, and it doesn't always stop after the first trimester... Oh the lies they tell us."

Zarya smiled at her, grateful for her warm friendliness. "Well, for someone who's been sick, you look stunningly gorgeous."

Kiara returned her smile. "Thank you."

"Where's Darling?" Nykyrian asked, scanning the crowd around them.

Maris sighed. "The meeting started right before you got here."

"Oh goody," Caillen said in a tone that dripped sarcasm. "We arrived just in time for the boredom. So glad we rushed to get here. Yeah, us!"

Desideria glared up at her husband. "Caillen, cut the sarcasm."

"Can't help it. It's the primary service I offer to everyone not wearing my wedding ring." He flashed a wicked grin at his wife who rolled her eyes in response.

Syn sniffed like he was crying. "Awww, Kip," he said to Nykyrian with an exaggerated pout, "our little baby's all grown up and being political... We did such a good job with him. I'm so proud."

Nykyrian scowled at him. "What the hell's wrong with you?"

Sobering, Syn held his mobile up for Nykyrian. "I hacked their security feed. Wanna spy on Darling with me?"

"I definitely do." Zarya stepped closer to Syn so that she could watch Darling in action.

Syn adjusted the volume until it was loud enough for them to hear, but not be overheard by the rest of the room.

Looking so powerful and sexy that she wanted to take a bite out of him, Darling sat stoically on his throne in the council room while the gerents ranted about their mistreatment at his hands.

"You do not make those kinds of decisions without us," one of the older gerents railed at him. "*We* control the workers. We're the ones who set their hours and their pay, not you."

Darling betrayed no expression whatsoever. He waited calmly for the senator to finish before he posed a question of his own.

"And when the workers refuse to heed your orders and enter their plants to do their jobs, who would you call to negotiate?"

Ryn stroked his jaw with his thumb. "That would be *you*, Majesty," he said to Darling just in case the others weren't bright enough to know the answer.

Another senator rose to his feet with a smug expression. "We didn't need you. We'd have handled it ourselves. The protestors would have been fired and replaced."

Darling nodded thoughtfully. "On average, how long does it take to train a new worker on equipment and company procedure?"

"Not long," the first gerent answered. "A few hours. Tops."

Darling's face was a mask of bitter amusement. "Obviously, you've never had to work a job or run unfamiliar equipment. It takes a few *weeks* to become comfortable and *basically* competent. It's months, if not years before they're as productive as the current staff, who have been working those jobs, ironically enough, for years. And then there's the problem of who would train those new workers if all the old workers were fired?"

The gerents didn't like having logic thrown at them.

Darling glanced around the crowd as they sputtered indignantly. When he spoke again, his voice was calm and level. "By negotiating what, to anyone with a conscience, is a humane work environment and schedule, I saved all of you millions of credits in the long run, and I kept the factories opened without drama. Even if you have to hire a few thousand more employees due to the shortened workday, you're still better off than you would have been had you fired the existing staffs. Those who are proficient in their jobs will happily train the noobs, and there's no loss in productivity. I can send you all the statistical charts on the projected savings."

"You had no right to do this!"

A tic started in Darling's jaw, but there was no other physical evidence to betray his irritation. "I have no right to protect my people? Is that not, by the very definition, what a governor is supposed to do?"

"You've overreached your position!"

Darling frowned. "So none of you are truly angry that I negotiated with the workers? You're upset because I didn't drag you out of bed in the middle of the night to have you agree with what I did... Very well. In the future, I'll make sure to call all of you in and disrupt your days and nights with bullshit. Works for me... Ryn, make a note."

"Stupid cock-sucking faggot." It was impossible to tell where that angry voice came from.

Darling didn't react to the insult in any way. Instead, he smiled coldly. "My father always said that you know the absolute second you've won a fight. It's when your opposition has run out of logic with which to battle, and the name-calling commences. But really, how unimaginative of you. There are thousands of other insults that are so much more creative and demeaning. And I would actually respect you if you had the nerve to stand by your convictions and face me when you insult me." He scanned the crowd with a sneer of contempt. "Homosexual or not, no one can ever accuse *me* of cowardice. If I'm going to insult someone, I at least have the balls to do it to their face."

The gerents began shouting in outrage.

Zarya's eyes widened as fear for Darling tore through her. "They're going to eat him alive."

Syn shook his head. "Oh no... Wait for it."

She was aghast at his nonchalance. "For what? The bloodshed?"

True to Syn's words, Darling allowed them to scream for several more minutes.

Finally, he rose to his feet. They quieted instantly, with the majority of them scanning the room to see where Darling had positioned his guards. Which made sense since anyone else would have called for their arrest.

Instead, Darling took a deep breath. "I seriously hope that all of you have gotten that out of your systems. We can sit here and you can insult me, my parentage, my lifestyle, hell, let's even throw in the color of my shoes for good measure, or we can do what we're supposed to do. Take care of our people."

With a fierce set to his jaw, he swept the delegates with a condemning countenance. "I know under Arturo's reign that many of you took liberties you shouldn't have. I know he arrested or exiled anyone who didn't agree with him, and confiscated their lands and titles. Those who supported him were given the luxury of his turning a blind eye to all their activities, no matter how illegal or immoral. So long as you paid his fees, he left you alone."

Darling paused to let that seep into their collective minds before he spoke in a cold tone. "I am not my uncle. I am not my father, but I do subscribe to the twenty rules he taught me from the cradle. One, if you're afraid to fight, then you'll never win. Two, in times of tragedy and turmoil, you'll learn who your true friends are. Treasure them because they are few and far between. Three, know your enemies, and never become your own worst one. Four, be grateful for those enemies. They will keep you honest and ever striving to better yourself. Five, listen to all good advice, but never substitute someone else's judgment for your own. Six, all men and women lie. But never lie to yourself. Seven, many will flatter you. Befriend the ones who don't, for they will remind you that you're human and not infallible. Eight, never fear the truth. It's the lies that will destroy you. Nine, your worst decisions will always be those that are made out of fear. Think all matters through with a clear head. Ten, your mistakes won't define you, but your memories, good and bad, will. Eleven, be grateful for your mistakes as they will tell you who and what you're not. Twelve, don't be afraid to examine the past, it's how you learn what you don't want to do again. Thirteen, there's a lot to be said for not knowing better. Fourteen, all men die. Not everyone lives. Fifteen, on your deathbed, your greatest regrets will be what you didn't do. Sixteen, don't be afraid to love. Yes, it's a weakness that can be used against you. But it's also a source of the greatest strength you will ever know. Seventeen, the past is history written in stone that can't be altered. The future is transitory and never guaranteed. Today is the only thing you can change for certain. Have the courage to do so and make the most of it because it could be all you'll ever have. Eighteen, you can be in a crowd, surrounded by people, and still be lonely. Nineteen, love all, regardless of what they do. Trust only those you have to. Harm none until they harm you. And twenty... Never be afraid to kill or destroy your enemies. They won't hesitate to kill or destroy you."

The gerents glanced about nervously.

Darling met Drake's gaze and his brother gave him a nod of proud approval. "Number twenty is the only thing I share with my uncle. But unlike Arturo, I don't believe in torture. I don't believe in imprisonment. I trade in execution. You come at me, expect to die."

"Are you threatening us?"

"No," Darling said simply. "I'm stating my policy for all of you to hear and to know. You're well aware of how I came to power. That I cut Arturo's throat and dared his guards to arrest me. You've seen my punishment for those who were foolish enough to underestimate me, and those who harmed my family. So long as I breathe, that won't change."

One of the older gerents stood to address him. "And what of the Resistance leader? You say you don't believe in imprisonment and yet you hold her prisoner."

Zarya bit her lip in trepidation of Darling's answer.

He didn't hesitate with it. "The Grand Marleena is free to do whatever it is she desires. She's been granted a full pardon. Her family lands and all their titles have been reinstated to her and her sister."

That news floored her. Why hadn't he told *her* that?

The gerent screwed his face up into a mask of disbelief. "Then why is she still with you?"

Darling smiled. "Hell if I know. But she has agreed to do me the honor of becoming my consort and wife."

That news caused another violent wave of protests.

"She's a criminal!"

"Her father was a traitor!"

"Death to the Resistance, and all its members!"

"How could you even think about marrying an outlaw?"

"You insult us with that choice!"

"Have you not seen what the Resistance has done to this empire?"

"No wonder you were confined to a mental ward. You're insane!"

Variations on all the above rang out in a harsh cacophony.

Until Kyr Zemen stepped forward. Dressed in full League battle gear, he only broke from one League tradition. He didn't have on a pair of sunglasses. Most likely due to the eye patch he wore over his right eye. Though to be honest, he didn't need the sunglasses to be sinister. He pulled it off with an aura of I'll-kick-your-ass-so-hard-your-ancestors-will-feel-it. In fact, he hemorrhaged stone-cold cruelty from every pore of his body.

Now that she knew he was related to Maris, she saw the similarities in their features. Aside from their shared height, Kyr also had that indefinable intensity of personality. But where Maris had black hair, Kyr's was a deep chestnut brown that gleamed with reddish highlights.

And the sneer on his face questioned Darling's mental capacity. "You did *not* get League sanction to pardon her."

Darling shrugged nonchalantly. Something that was either extremely brave...

Or incredibly stupid.

"Since she's only wanted by my government, I didn't have to seek your approval."

Kyr tsked at him. "You should have consulted us anyway."

The smile on Darling's face was absolutely frigid. "Last time I read the laws, the Caronese governor wasn't a pawn of the League's. Rather we're a sovereign empire."

Kyr gave him a hostile glare that was tinged with something that appeared to be hope. "Are you declaring war on us?"

Darling deftly sidestepped that loaded land mine. "By stating Universal law? I don't see how. Are you declaring war on the Caronese?"

He narrowed his eye on Darling. "I detect a note of rebellion in your tone."

But Darling refused to be cowed. "And I detect a note of contempt in yours."

Maris sucked his breath in sharply. "Darling...don't goad the devil. He won't take it well."

Zarya didn't comment on Maris's warning as she continued to watch and listen to the meeting.

A slow, sadistic smile curled Kyr's lips. "Perhaps you see your own sins in the actions of others. I believe *your* psychologists and therapists"—that was a low blow to bring up Darling's past in front of the others—"would call that projection."

Darling didn't rise to the bait. He stayed eerily calm under fire. "Again, I say to you that I am not my uncle. If I was to declare war, or should I ever rebel, there won't be any guessing. It will be clearly stated and unmistakable."

The heat in Kyr's eye said that he was begging for Darling to take a single wrong step. "I only have one other question for you, Governor." Could he have put any more contempt into that title?

"And that is?"

"What does your *boyfriend* have to say about your upcoming marriage to a woman?"

The room erupted with laughter and mockery.

A taunting grin curled Kyr's lips. "It must be so confusing for you at night when you have to figure out which part of her anatomy to tap."

The rage in Darling's gaze was unmistakable, but to his credit, he kept it in check. Something that amazed and mystified her.

"What was it you accused me of a moment ago?" Darling asked Kyr. "Oh yes...projection. I do believe, dear Commander, that your sins are now aired before all."

Everyone in the room sucked their breath in, waiting for Kyr to attack.

Instead, he took a single step forward. "You're playing a dangerous game with a most lethal opponent."

Darling's expression dared him to make a move. "You're talking to someone who experiments with explosives in order to wind down at night. Believe me, I learned a long time ago exactly how much pressure to apply in order to achieve the desired result." He stared at Kyr's eye patch. "Not to mention Nykyrian Quiakides taught me well."

Syn snickered at Darling's comeback. He jerked his chin to Nykyrian, then explained to her the significance of Darling's comment. "Just so you know, Zarya, Kip's the one who injured Kyr's eye."

She let out a low whistle at Darling's nerve in bringing that up.

Kyr stepped back. "I bid you well, Governor. And I leave you to the care of your empire." He swept his gaze around the gerents, then finally pinned it to Ryn. "May you follow in your father's footsteps."

Darling took that veiled threat in stride. "Thank you, Commander. And may you reap all the fruits of your diligent work."

Zarya held her breath as Kyr glared at Darling, then turned and stormed from the room. The rest of the League soldiers fell in behind him.

Syn shook his head. "Our boy is something else."

She couldn't agree more, but his fearlessness terrified her. "Remind me not to ever try to verbally outmaneuver Darling. He's good."

Maris winked at her. "You have no idea. He's like lightning in everything he does." He paused and gave her a quick once-over. "Well, not *everything*. But it's good that he takes his time with *that*."

Heat stung her cheeks. Unwilling to comment, she returned her attention to Syn's mobile.

There was so much tension and animosity in that room that she felt terrible for Darling. She couldn't imagine having to stay so controlled while facing so many people who loathed her.

The gerent leader stepped forward. "You still haven't told us what you intend to do with the Resistance...my lord governor."

Wow, it was impressive how he made that title sound like an insult.

"I will deal with them."

Laughter rang out again from the group.

"As you dealt with them before?" His features smug, the leader swept his gaze around the room. "I wonder whose name they'll carve into your face this time."

Rage darkened her sight at that verbal blow. She started for the counsel room, but Maris stopped her.

"You can't go in there," he warned.

"So I'm supposed to stand here, listening to them attack him and do nothing? You're asking too much of me, Mari." She gestured to Syn's mobile. "That was *so* wrong."

Worse, it was unbelievably cruel.

Sadness darkened Maris's eyes. "But it's not the worst he's had to suffer. Believe me."

She winced at a truth that made her want to kill someone. It was one thing to be told about the horrors Darling had suffered. It was another to watch it happen.

Syn turned his device off. "That's enough of that." He glanced to Nykyrian. "You know, I can find that man's address. Accidents happen all the time."

"They do, indeed," Nykyrian said with a sigh, "but unfortunately, Darling would explode if we interfered with his governorship."

Syn growled deep in his throat. "Damn shame that."

"Yes, it is." Zarya was far from satisfied. "Can I at least kick the gerent some place that counts?" She glanced to Syn. "I can always say that, too, was an accident."

Syn laughed. "You're such a perfect addition to our crew."

Maybe, but she couldn't get past one truth that kept slapping her in the face. "I'm a detriment to Darling, aren't I?"

"No," Maris said firmly. "If not for you, we wouldn't have him at all. You weren't here, Zarya. You didn't see him when he was first released from the hospital."

"He's right about that." Caillen jerked his chin toward the mobile. "That is not the same man who was walking around wired in explosives, daring people to attack him. He's sane again. And I have to be honest, I didn't really think anyone could reach him and bring him back to us."

Indignant, Maris stiffened. "Is that why you told me to do it?"

Caillen grinned impishly at him. "I figured you were the least likely to be gutted if you failed."

"Oh thank you, Cai. You're so considerate."

Zarya started to speak, then paused as she caught sight of Kyr in the doorway. He was staring a hole through Nykyrian.

Syn nudged Nykyrian slightly to get his attention. "Look, Kip. Your friend wants to say hi."

Nykyrian scoffed. "Damn, you're slow, Syn. He's been eyeballing me for about five minutes now."

Syn snorted. "*Eye*balling. Ar, ar. I get it."

Unamused, Nykyrian released an elongated breath, but Zarya thought it was funny.

Sick, true. Still...

She sobered as Kyr and his four League escorts came over to them. Given the way he'd been staring, she expected him to approach Nykyrian.

Instead, he stopped in front of her and raked her with a sneer. "What are *you* doing here?"

She gifted him with her best eat-crap-and-choke smile. "I was personally invited by the governor. You?"

Caillen started laughing, then had to quickly pretend to cough as Kyr glared at him. And she couldn't help noticing the amused quirk to the corners of Safir's mouth. A quirk he quickly hid before the others saw it.

Returning his attention to Zarya, Kyr curled his lip. "No wonder the air in here is stale."

Nykyrian scoffed. "Little boy, don't. Darling already cleaned your clock. I think you've had enough humiliation for one night. But if not... I am willing to hand you your other eye."

Yeah, that comment didn't go over particularly well. Part of her expected Kyr to go for Nykyrian's throat. But apparently his common sense held sway over his suicidal tendencies.

"One day, Quiakides, we're going to tangle again."

Nykyrian quirked a humorless smile at him. "Oh you better hope not. Next time, I won't be merciful."

"Neither will I." Kyr's attention went past Nykyrian's shoulder to where Maris stood. "Gods, you get more disgusting every time I see you. Have you had surgery yet to become a woman? Not that anyone could ever tell the difference."

Maris tsked at him. "Oh, my brother...you always under-estimated me. That's all right, though. I have the satisfaction of knowing that I'm the only creature alive who has ever knocked Nykyrian unconscious. Instead of insulting me, you should have teamed up with me. Then you could have killed him and com-pleted your assignment, and not have that ugly blemish on your record. That must really suck for you. But I wouldn't know. My military record is flawlessly perfect."

This time, Safir was the one possessed of a coughing fit.

Infuriated, Kyr responded to Maris in Phrixian.

Maris made an air kiss at him.

If looks could kill, Maris would be a stain on the wall. Kyr swept her entire group with a withering grimace. "I shall see all of you later."

"We're so looking forward to it," Caillen called after him. "Fuck you very much, Commander. Have a good day."

As soon as Kyr and crew were gone, Maris let out a low whis-tle. "Poor Saf. He's going to get the dog end of every assignment for the next year or more."

Zarya hated that for him. Unlike Kyr, Saf had seemed like a decent enough...assassin.

Pushing that thought out of her mind, she turned toward Nykyrian. "What exactly did you do to him?"

"I gouged out his eye."

She'd known that, but... "Why?"

Kiara answered. "Nykyrian doesn't like to be grabbed from behind. Luckily, I'm much shorter than what his muscle memory accounts for, and as a former dancer, I have exceptional reflexes." She looked down at her stomach. "Well, not so much right now. But..."

Nykyrian gave his wife a droll stare. "I've never once harmed her. Kyr, on the other hand, came at me and made the mistake of being alone when he did it. Don't come barking at my door unless you have a fierce bite."

Before anyone could respond, one of the ladies came over and cleared her throat. "Now that the meeting is wrapping up, we'll be sitting down for dinner in a few minutes." She bowed to Caillen and Nykyrian. "We have prepared places for both of your highnesses and your wives."

"Thank you," they said in unison.

The hostess curtsied again, then left.

"Who was that?" Zarya asked Maris since he seemed to know everyone. And most importantly, he knew their secrets.

"That would be Lady Nylan."

Zarya's jaw dropped. "As in..."

Maris inclined his head. "Since the senator's one of the oldest members of the CDS, she's the delegate wife who's been hosting the social part of all their meetings for decades."

Meanwhile her husband...

Zarya didn't want to think about that. She was too afraid of what she might do to the man. How could anyone be married to someone like that? *I will never understand people.*

Most of all, she'd never understand their cruelty.

Everyone began adjourning for the dining room.

Nykyrian, Kiara, Caillen, Desideria, and Kiara's father went in first since they were considered guest dignitaries. Something that confused her.

"Why aren't you considered a foreign dignitary?" she asked Maris.

"They don't like me."

She popped him playfully on the arm. "I'm serious."

"So am I."

She didn't believe that until they started to enter the dining room. Lady Nylan met them at the door and pulled them aside.

Her gaze cold, Lady Nylan put on a false smile. "Because of the unexpected guests, we ran out of place settings. As a result, we've set a small table for the two of you, outside of the dining room. That is, if you don't mind."

Zarya loved when people said that, knowing they weren't about to take a negative response. She felt like protesting just to rub the woman the wrong way, but the last thing she wanted to do was cause a scene and embarrass Darling any more than what had already been done to him.

"Of course, my lady," Zarya said, proud of herself that she kept her disdain from showing.

"Please, follow me." Funny how her tone completely disagreed with that formal civility.

Maris rolled his eyes behind the hostess's back. "We don't want to sit with those apes anyway," he whispered to her.

Agreeing completely, Zayra came to an abrupt halt as she saw the small side table that had been pulled out for them. "Small" being the operative word. It must have been an end table in the conference room. The chairs were tiny foldaways with stained gray cushions. And while the linens were clean, they, too, were stained in places.

It was the ultimate slap in the face. But for Darling, she'd be throwing a tantrum over it.

Instead, she smiled at the woman and graciously sat down while Maris followed suit. *Never let them know how much they've hurt you. Don't give them the satisfaction.* Her father had raised her on those principals and she held them tight. Starskas didn't flinch or bitch.

They got even.

Lady Nylan left them.

Zarya picked up her napkin and placed it primly in her lap. "They don't think much of us, do they?"

Maris shrugged. "Fine with me. I don't think much of them either." He pulled one of the two hard breadsticks out of the water glass someone had put it in, and held it out to her. "You better eat up, sweetie. I'm pretty sure they won't have extra food for us either."

"You okay?"

Darling nodded at Drake as they walked down the quiet hallway with Ryn, Chayden, Hauk, and Fain. "I'm glad to be done with it."

For the first time in Darling's memory, Drake looked at him with respect. "They weren't as bad as I thought they'd be. And you...you were incredible. I can't believe how well you handled them."

"Yeah well, when you spend your entire lifetime being a verbal punching bag, you learn how to effectively strike back when you need to."

Ryn rubbed at his temples. "I don't know about you guys, but I swear I have a migraine. I wish I could blow off dinner."

"You know we can't." Darling allowed Drake and Chayden to lead them into the dining room.

Like Ryn, he had a vicious migraine of titanic proportions. But at least Nylan hadn't said a word during the session. He'd been waiting for the bastard to speak up and firebomb him in public.

Miracles do happen.

Instead, Nylan had simpered and smirked the entire time. Which was fine by him. Smirking he could handle. One word from the bastard and he might have snapped.

May the gods help them then.

As they entered the dining room, he scanned the crowd for Zarya or Maris.

Neither was present.

A bad feeling went through him. Hoping he was wrong, he went straight to Kiara and Nykyrian who stood off to the side with Caillen, Syn, and Desideria.

"Where are Maris and Zarya?" he asked as soon as he reached them.

Fury burned in Kiara's eyes. "They were seated in the hallway near the kitchen."

Darling scowled at the news. "What?"

"Yeah," Syn said bitterly. "Nylan's wife said that the additional guests"—he indicated their small group—"caused them to run out of seats at the main table. So the two of them were given seats outside."

Forget what he'd just gone through. This...*this* angered him more than anything else ever could. "Bullshit. They could have added an extra leaf while we were in session."

Caillen held his hands up in surrender. "He's just repeating what they were told."

"Fuck this shit." Darling stormed past them, ready to go to war. Before all was said and done, someone was going to lose their head over this.

Literally.

20

Laughing at Maris's joke, Zarya felt a chill go down her spine. She sobered as the skin on the back of her neck crawled like a living creature.

When she turned her head to see Darling's furious glower while he stalked toward them, she understood the uneasy knot in her stomach. This wasn't the levelheaded politician who'd met with the gerents.

This was the feral soldier, Kere. And he was out for blood.

Maris rose at Darling's approach. "What's going on?"

Darling broke out into a furious rant in Phrixian...one day, she was going to have to learn that language. It was aggravating to have no clue what they were saying around her.

Maris attempted to calm him, but Darling was having none of it.

Ignoring Maris, he turned toward her. "Come, Z. We're leaving."

She hesitated before she stood up. "Aren't you supposed to be with the gerents?"

"Yes," Maris hissed, "he is. If he fails to attend dinner, it'll be viewed as an affront to them."

"And what is this," Darling gestured angrily toward them and their table, "if not an affront to *me*?"

Maris scoffed. "It has nothing to do with you. This is a slap at me and you know it."

"I totally disagree. But let's say you're right. It's still a slap at both of us, and I won't tolerate them treating the two of you like this. I won't."

Maris folded his arms over his chest. "Baby, you're overreacting."

Darling started to protest, but Zarya cupped his face in her hand and stood up on her tiptoes to nibble his jaw. Yeah, that made his thoughts scatter to the point he could barely remember his own name. His knees went weak and he lost all resistance to her.

Then she whispered in his ear. "You were magnificent tonight. Don't ruin what you've achieved with something that's as trivial as their pettiness. Besides, I like it here with Mari. He's highly entertaining."

At the moment, the only thing he wanted was to find a bed.

Or a closet.

But she wasn't some crass prostitute selling her body for drugs. She was a high-born lady who was going to be his consort. He wouldn't treat her that way. And by the gods, he wouldn't let anyone else either. "They've insulted two of the people I value and love most in this universe. Would you really have me forgive that?"

"Yes, I would." She gently pushed him back a step. "Go on in there and don't worry about us."

He debated what course of action he should take. On the one hand, he wanted to break someone's ass. On the other, he knew Zarya and Maris were right. No one would remember why he left the meeting tonight. They'd only remember that he'd turned his back on his gerents and insulted them.

"We're really fine," Maris said, reiterating her stance. "They did us a favor with this. We're having a great time out here."

Darling ground his teeth as another wave of fury ripped through him. "I'm still pissed."

Zarya winked at him. "Trust me. I know the feeling."

"Yes, she does," Maris concurred. "We all had to stop her from storming the session earlier."

Darling's frown deepened. "What do you mean?"

Zarya gave him a mischievous nose crinkle. "Syn hacked the security feed so that we could check up on you. I don't know how you stayed so calm. I commend you for it. It was extremely impressive."

Not really. It amazed him that they were all so stunned by his behavior. It wasn't like he was Hauk, and prone to ripping people's arms off whenever they upset him.

His ascension to power notwithstanding, he'd always been level-headed and calm.

"Yeah, well, when you spend your entire life being insulted, you get desensitized to it. I don't think Arturo ever used my real name. After a while, it gets boring and you learn not to pay attention to it. As for the gerents, I'd have to care about their opinions where I'm concerned in order for them to hurt me. Since I couldn't care less... Let them make themselves giddy with their own stupidity. I've got better things to worry about."

"I was still impressed by your demeanor and composure." She gave him a very light push. "Now go, before you cause another scandal."

He dipped his gaze down the cleft of her breasts that swelled over the top of her dress. Yeah, he'd much rather be naked with her in his bed than deal with a bunch of egotistical assholes.

"I wouldn't mind causing one with you," he whispered in her ear.

She kissed his cheek again. "Go on. Get out of here."

He gave her a courtly bow before he took his leave.

Still seething, Darling went back into the main dining room.

Glancing at Caillen, Drake, and Nykyrian, an idea hit him. He approached the three of them with a wry twist to his lips. "Ready to start some shit?"

"Depends on the shit," Drake said.

Caillen grinned evilly. "Point me to the toilet, and let me in."

Nykyrian ignored that comment since it was vintage Caillen, who loved nothing more than messing with the heads of the aristocracy, and irritating everyone around him. "What's the plan?"

Darling took a step back. "Follow me. I know a way to rectify the slap I've just been given, and deliver one right back." He motioned one of the passing servants over.

"Yes, Your Majesty," she said respectfully, bowing before him.

He put on his kindest, most regal tone. "It has come to my attention that we're two places short at the table tonight. Princes Nykyrian and Caillen have graciously offered to make room by having their seats moved closer to their wives. Likewise, I am more than content to share my space with both the Grand Marleena and Lord Maris. I would deeply appreciate it, and would consider it a personal favor, if you would accommodate us."

The woman beamed in joy at being able to help the governor. "Absolutely, Your Majesty. It would be my deepest honor." She rushed to it.

Nykyrian gave a low laugh. "You are evil. I love it."

Desideria and Kiara approached them with reservation.

Kiara scowled at her husband. "It positively scares me whenever you laugh in public. What did we miss and what has all of you huddled here?"

Nykyrian indicated Darling with a tilt of his head. "Our boy there just firebombed our hostess."

Her eyes gleamed with satisfaction as she faced Darling. "Good. I hope you let her have it with all barrels."

The moment the servant returned with two others to start moving seats and adding place settings, Nylan's wife came running out to challenge them.

The lead servant pointed to Darling.

Fury flashed in her eyes at being thwarted, but Lady Nylan checked it before she walked over to them. "Your Majesty, I beg your indulgence and tolerance in this matter. But given Princess Kiara's delicate condition, I don't think it's wise to—"

"I'm pregnant, my lady, not infectious," Kiara said, interrupting her. "Since I count Lady Starska and Lord Maris among my closest friends, I don't mind sharing my space with them."

"I couldn't agree more," Desideria chimed in. "Zarya is a true gem. But if it causes you distress, we would be most happy to join them in the hallway."

Nykyrian nodded. "Feel free to move all of our settings there."

The countess inclined her head respectfully. "That won't be necessary, Your Highnesses. I'm sure we'll be able to find them a suitable spot."

Darling cleared his throat to get her attention. "One on either side of me."

She stiffened in anger. "Excuse me?"

Darling made sure to keep his tone flat and even. "You heard me, my lady. I expect my senior adviser and fiancée to be seated with me."

She went pale with the news. "Fiancée?"

"Yes. Lady Starska and I are to be married. And I am sure she will be moved by your graciousness toward her."

Darling wouldn't have thought it possible, but her face turned even whiter.

Lady Nylan grabbed a waiter. "I need the man and woman in the hallway moved in here immediately. Do not drag your feet."

Kiara winked at Darling. "You are so incredibly sneaky. I love it."

He glanced over to Nykyrian. "I learned from the best."

In under three minutes, Maris and Zarya returned to the dining room.

Zarya gave him a suspicious stare as she neared them. "What did you do?"

Darling blinked innocently. "What makes you think *I* did anything?"

Maris snorted. "The way the waiter behaved—like he was afraid for his life."

Darling shrugged. "No idea why. I merely made a request."

"Sure, you did," Maris said with a short laugh. "I've heard your requests. They're positively wrong."

Zarya wasn't sure what to think as she was shown to a seat next to the head of the table. Maris was seated across from her. *Please tell me that seat belongs to Darling.* Or at least one of his friends. The last thing she wanted was to be beside one of the nasty gerents who glared at them.

"My lady?"

She looked up as an older gentleman stopped beside her. His face was so wrinkled that he reminded her of a suit someone had dug out of the back of their closet. His gray eyes were cold and he smelled like rotten camphor balls. "Yes, my lord?"

"I just had to meet the woman who could turn a gay man straight. I didn't think it was possible, especially someone as licentious and effeminate as our governor. Believe me, I know how much he loves a good hard cock in his ass. Congratulations."

His rudeness stunned her silent. She sat there, slack jawed, trying to think of an appropriate response that wasn't crude or profane.

For once, nothing, absolutely nothing came to mind. She simply reeled from it.

"Hey, Nylan? We need you over here for a second."

He left her side.

So that was...

Gaping like a fish, she looked at Maris for corroboration on the man's identity.

"Yeah," Maris said with a snarl, "he's *that* bastard."

Darling returned to her side immediately. "Are you all right?"

She started to tell him what had happened, but she didn't want to upset him. Given the past, she wasn't sure Darling wouldn't kill him for saying that to her.

Forcing a smile to her lips, she nodded. "Where are you sitting?"

He indicated the chair between her and Maris. *Thank the gods for that favor.* She wanted out of here so badly that she could taste it. But what bothered her most was the knowledge that this would have been her life all along had her father's titles not been stripped.

She would have been just like the other women who passed judging sneers at her and Maris. Those who wouldn't even speak to them. Frigid. Callous.

Mean.

That thought made her blood run cold. For the first time in her life, she was grateful that she'd been raised outside this realm. She'd much rather have eaten bread sandwiches with her father for weeks on end than have been fed like this every day if putting up with them was the price for it.

It just wasn't worth it.

Once Darling was seated and dinner began, it did get better. At least as long as she ignored the stares—most of which were hostile—that the gerents and their spouses directed at them.

And as she ate, she became acutely aware of how Darling and Maris interacted with each other. For some reason, she'd never noticed it before.

But tonight...

She saw them through the eyes of a stranger. While she had no doubt they'd never slept together and that Darling was completely straight, she finally understood why others didn't believe it.

He and Maris were completely relaxed with each other, even in the midst of all the animosity around them. In fact, with his hand on Darling's shoulder, Maris was leaning in to whisper intimately into Darling's ear while Darling laughed at whatever it was Maris said to him. They were practically cheek to cheek. And the smile on Darling's face whenever he looked at his best friend was tender and warm. Some might even say it was adoring.

And there was no mistaking the love in Maris's gaze every time he looked at Darling, which was often. He hung on everything Darling said.

Likewise, Darling doted on Maris almost to the extent he did her. And while she knew it was because they were family, it would be easy to misconstrue their affection for each other if you didn't know the truth of their relationship.

"Are you jealous?"

Zarya blinked as she realized the gerent beside her was talking to her. "Excuse me?"

He indicated Maris and Darling with his knife. "Are you getting jealous of them?"

She screwed her face up at him. "Not even a little."

"Hmm...I commend you, then. I don't think I could share my wife with another woman without it making me completely crazy." He took a sip of his wine. "So I take it your upcoming marriage to the governor is politically motivated. Makes sense. You help him quell the Resistance, he reinstates your title and wealth. You both win."

She was livid at his audacity. "That's not why we're getting married. I didn't even know he was Darling Cruel when we were first engaged."

Yeah, okay, that sounded extremely farcical and unlikely when said out loud. But it was the truth.

He laughed at her. "Are you terminally stupid? Or do you think I am? How could the leader of the Resistance not know the face of your enemy?"

Heat scalded her cheeks, and it seriously angered her that she couldn't set the man straight.

"Z?"

She turned to see Darling watching her closely.

He slid his gaze to the gerent. "Is everything all right?"

Forcing herself to smile past the knot in her stomach, she nodded. "Fine, sweetie."

Darling took her hand into his. "If you're not feeling well, we can leave at any time. Just say the word." He lifted her hand and pressed her palm to his lips. The fire in his gaze was unmistakable as he inhaled her scent and held her hand like a sacred object.

She savored the warmth of his lips on her skin, and it made her ache to take him home and pick up where they'd left off before coming here. And by the way Darling stroked her palm, she knew he felt the same way.

No, she had no doubt whatsoever about his sexual orientation or his devotion to her. "It's all good."

For the rest of the meal, Darling kept his hand on hers and made sure that the gerent didn't speak to her again.

As soon as the meal was over, he rose and, breeching royal protocol, held her chair for her.

"Wow," someone said near them. "You'd almost think he *was* straight given the way he treats her."

"It's all a show for us. Don't be fooled. Nylan has always said that he gives the best head of anyone he's ever slept with."

"Yeah, I heard he moans like a bitch in heat whenever you screw him, and that he prefers to be the sub who takes it up his ass."

She felt Darling tensing at their whispered insults. So much for his telling her that those comments didn't bother him.

She started for the gossipers, but he tightened his hand on hers. "Let it go."

"But—"

"It's fine, Z. Really."

She ground her teeth as anger burned deep inside. "It's not to me."

"You know the difference between the governor and the Aris, don't you?" This time, she suspected the gerent talking wanted her to overhear him. Yet his question made no sense. The Aris was a League station that had malfunctioned and crashed into a base on Nera V when she and Darling were children. It'd been one of the worst tragedies in League history.

"What?" another gerent asked.

"The Aris went down on only two thousand men."

She headed for Hauk.

He arched a brow at her approach.

"Give me your weapon. Now." She held her hand out for it.

He laughed. "I would love to, but Darling would kick my ass if I did."

"I'm going to kick it if you don't."

Darling pulled her back against him. "It's okay, Z. They always do this. I really am used to it."

"You're their governor. They should respect you."

He gave her a teasing grin. "This from the leader of the Resistance?"

Guilt over that gnawed at her. How could she have ever sanctioned anyone to fight against him? She wanted to beat her own butt for that.

Meanwhile the jokes echoed around them until she wanted to scream.

"C'mon," Darling said quietly. "Let's go. We're done here."

Still, it infuriated her.

But in the end, she knew he was right. Attacking them over those insults would be a bad mistake. If Darling went crazy on them, they could petition the League to have him removed from power. Even jailed.

Or institutionalized.

Most likely, that was why they were doing it. They wanted to goad him into attacking.

Unwilling to give them any kind of satisfaction, she followed Darling and tried to ignore them, too.

With his friends and family in tow, he led her down the hallway to where they'd checked her wrap on her arrival.

Darling had just put it on her when another gerent laughed at them.

"Yes, but you have to envy him *that* ass. You know, she'd have to be one hell of a lay to get him hard for her. I bet that whore can suck the glaze off porcelain."

Even though Darling wore those dark glasses, she saw the flash of unmitigated fury in his eyes. Now, she finally understood where his strength came from. She could take insults against her. They didn't matter. It was only the ones against him that made her livid.

Zarya cupped his face with her hands and forced him to look at her and not the man who'd insulted her. "Let it go, Darling. He's not worth it."

Darling forced himself to listen to her and to calm down. She was right. He needed to walk away. He couldn't afford to attack them.

That was his thought until the gerent spoke up again. "Make sure to give her your number, then. A cheap skank ass bitch like that would hike her skirt and open her legs for anyone."

With a snarl of rage, Kere slammed down on him. One second, Zarya held him.

In the next...

21

Darling went for the gerent's throat so fast that no one could stop him. By the time they realized he'd made it past Zarya, he had the man on the ground, repeatedly pounding his head against the floor with a fury so strong, it crackled in the air around them.

Zarya was amazed the man's head didn't split open given the force Darling used. While she had seen Darling fight as Kere many times, she'd honestly forgotten just how ferocious he could be. This was a side of him that she never saw in private.

And he was about to kill the man on the ground.

Moving with an incredible speed, Nykyrian pulled Darling off the gerent and hauled him back. But that didn't last long.

Using a move and strength no one expected, Darling flipped Nykyrian off him with an ease that was nothing shy of a miracle, especially given how much larger Nykyrian was. The throw caused Darling's dark glasses to fly off his face and shatter on the floor.

Stunned by the unexpected counterattack, Nykyrian landed against the far wall in an unceremonious lump. When Hauk went in for a try, Darling caught him by one arm and slung the Andarion in the opposite direction. He cut through two of the gerent's bodyguards before he returned to ruthlessly beat the man who'd insulted her.

"He's going to kill Giran," Maris breathed by her side.

By Darling's lethal expression, she believed it. But what could they do? She glanced over to Nykyrian who was back on his feet and trying to assure his wife that he wasn't hurt.

Three gerents moved in to stop Darling. Bad mistake on their part. It was only then that she realized he'd been holding back when he fought the gerents' guards and Nykyrian and Hauk.

There was no such mercy for the nobles. Obviously, he'd been wanting a piece of them for a long time.

Darling caught the first one with a punch so hard, it made a resounding thud against the man's chest and sent him straight to the floor. The second one took a hit to the nose that shattered it. The gerent staggered back, screaming like a girl on a playground as he cupped his face with both hands. The third lost his knee to one swift quick.

And as Darling cut through them with an ease that was scary, the nobility around them panicked more.

"He is insane!"

"You see! He has no right to rule."

"Where did he learn to fight like that?"

"Did you see him throw the assassin and his own guard?"

"May the gods help us with him in power."

"We're doomed!"

"No wonder Arturo kept him in institutions. He must have been terrified of him since he was a kid."

As their comments and anger against Darling built, she knew she had to do something.

Fast. But what?

Suddenly, a stupid idea came to her.

Before she could think better of it, she grabbed Darling's arm as he went for Giran again.

He turned around, his hand raised to strike her, too. Just as she thought he'd put her through the wall behind her, he caught himself. His breathing ragged, he stared at her and lowered his hand. The agony on his beautiful face hit her like a blow. He cupped her head in the palm of his hand, then gently pulled her into his arms.

She hugged him close as his heart pounded fiercely against her breasts. He continued to cradle her head and hold on to her like she was his lifeline.

Maris approached them slowly. "Are you better?" he whispered to Darling.

His eyes started jerking. "No. I didn't get a chance to kill the bastard." He turned in Giran's direction. "No one insults my lady. No one."

Nykyrian wiped the blood from his lips as he neared Darling with a look that said he craved retaliation. Luckily, he didn't give in to his anger. "We need to get you both out of here. And whatever you do," he said to Darling, "say nothing else." That last sentence came out as a fierce growl.

Darling inclined his head to him.

As they started walking, the gerents noticed Darling's eyes.

"He's blind?"

"No wonder he had on sunglasses."

"How can a blind, insane man lead an empire as powerful as ours?"

"I wouldn't trust him to lead a herd of dogs to water. Never mind lead us."

His jaw locked to keep from responding to their erroneous speculations, Darling allowed his friends to escort them from the room. He kept his arm around her waist as if he was afraid of letting her go.

Once they were clear of the building, Caillen released a low whistle. "That was a strategic blunder the kind of which *I* normally make. You know, Dar...the ones *you* usually crawl my ass over when I do them?"

"Yeah," Ryn agreed. "That little explosion of temper just cost us every nano-inch of ground we'd taken."

Darling glared at Ryn. "I don't care."

Ryn scoffed. "Hope you feel that way in the morning."

"I will. Trust me."

Hauk tested his teeth with his thumb. "I forgot how hard you punch, you little bastard. If I lose a tooth, I'm taking it out of your hide."

Kiara cast Darling an evil grimace. "Better be glad I'm pregnant. I'm not exactly fond of seeing my husband thrown into walls, especially since we were only trying to help *you*."

Drake sighed. "I understand why you did it, Dar. But damn... this is one ugly mess."

Darling glanced at her. "You want to pile on here with your opinion against me, too?"

Zarya shook her head. "Not at all. I totally get why you did it. I just wish I'd punched a couple of them for what they said about you. It seriously pains me that I didn't. Can I please go back and break on them?" She started back for the building.

Smiling, Darling caught her against him and turned her around to keep her moving forward.

Damn him. It wasn't fair that he got to pound on them when she was the one who really wanted a piece of their hides.

"We all get why he did it," Syn said. "There's not a one of us who wouldn't have done it had it been our better half they insulted. Honestly, I'm only surprised you kept him from killing them."

Nykyrian put his arm around Kiara. "Me, too."

"But," Ryn inserted, "it doesn't change the fact that it was a political blunder on an epically stupid scale."

And by the time they made it back to the palace, the extent of that blunder was making itself known. The gerents had called a press conference the moment they'd left the CDS, and were using videoed outtakes of the fight to show Darling attacking Giran for what appeared to be no reason whatsoever.

Darling cringed every time Zarya pulled up a feed to view it. *If I'm not deposed over this, I'm banning all mobiles from the meetings from here on out.*

The commentator smirked at the camera. "As everyone can clearly see, the new governor is out of control. We have reports that he drove the League High Command out of the meeting and threatened to go to war with them, as well as his own gerents. Senator Giran has been released from the hospital. According to witnesses, he was blindsided by the governor for making a passing comment to a friend that had nothing to do with politics. The governor and his staff have refused to take any of our calls or to comment on the matter in any way..."

Zarya shut the newsfeed off. She couldn't take any more of their one-sided slant. Dear gods, the journalists didn't care at all about the truth. They only cared about persecuting an innocent man.

Darling lay on his bed with the heel of his hand pressed against his jerking eyes. Wearing only a pair of pajama bottoms, he held a bloodied cloth in his other hand from the nosebleed that had finally slowed down.

She crossed the room to sit beside him on the bed. "I'm so sorry, Darling."

He removed his hand from his head to pin her with a grimace. "Sorry for what?"

"Causing this awful mess. I should have stayed here and let you go alone."

Darling hesitated at the catch in her voice. The last thing he wanted was for her to think that any part of this was her fault when it wasn't.

Or worse, for her to think that he blamed her for it when he was more than aware of who the moron was.

Pulling his palm away from his eyes, Darling laid his hand against her cheek. "Baby, you didn't do anything wrong. I was the dumbass who let his temper get the better of him when I knew better. The only thing I regret was that you had to hear them insult you."

And he hated the fact that she'd heard the ugliness about his past. Why couldn't people just let it go? Why did they have to use a past mistake as a weapon against him to...

Is that not what you've done to Zarya?

He froze as that realization slapped him hard across the face. Zarya had made one mistake in their relationship—granted it was a doozy, but...he was still judging her for it and occasionally, holding it against her.

For the first time, he saw things through her eyes. What would he have done had *he* been their leader, and she the one who was missing-in-action while he had no idea where to search for her? Right now, his soldiers could be torturing someone and he'd have no knowledge of it whatsoever.

My office isn't across the room from them.

Still...

Even if it was, he wouldn't know. He got that now. Fully.

I'm such a krikken idiot...

"Z?" He pulled the cloth away from his nose to make sure it wasn't bleeding anymore.

Zarya sat next to him with his computer on her lap. "What, baby?"

"Can I ask you something?"

Zarya looked up immediately at his change of tone. There was a note of such seriousness, that it made her heart pound. Had she done something to hurt or offend him? "Sure," she said while every part of her dreaded whatever was on his mind.

"Why didn't you ever check on me while your men held me?"

Not that again...Her anger snapped to the forefront that he wouldn't let this go, but she forced it down. He wasn't accusing her this time. In fact, there had been a note of pain in his voice and it was the first time he'd asked this question.

Biting her lip, she searched for the best words possible. *Please, God, help me find a way to make him understand that I hadn't meant to hurt him. Ever.*

She knew he couldn't see her or her reaction, not while his eyes were jerking. So she set the computer aside and took the cloth from his hand so that she could clean the remnants of blood from his face.

As she did so, her gaze dropped down to his chest where the scars from his torture screamed their own form of accusation at her. The worst ones were the burn scars on his nipples and groin. It was inhuman what they'd done to him. Who could blame him for holding it against her?

Tears blurred her vision."Honestly Darling, I was so consumed with looking for Kere, that you as the prince never entered my mind. Not even as a passing thought. Every day I didn't hear from Kere, I panicked more because it wasn't like you to not have any contact with me for days on end. All my attention was spent trying to get the Sentella to tell me something about Kere's whereabouts. I left hundreds of voicemails on your mobile and with the Sentella. Did you never get them?"

"No. Syn cleared them while I was in the hospital." Darling fell silent as he tried to reconcile what she said with his memories of being in Resistance custody. "You never sounded like you were looking for me." She'd sounded happy every day. Like she didn't have a single care in the world.

"That's because you heard the voice of the Resistance leader— the soldier who couldn't afford to let anyone know her weaknesses. No matter how I felt, I couldn't let them see it. But I swear to you, Darling, I was screaming and crying inside for fear of your death—you can ask my sister, if you doubt me. Or Ture. They'll tell you that I wasn't human. My mental state was so bad that they came over every weekend to stay with me so that I wouldn't hurt myself."

She traced the scar on his chest where Timmon had branded him with a hot chain. "And I know I shouldn't have left you there without checking on you. I hate myself every time I think about you in that room, starving and suffering at the hands of the people I entrusted you to. I know it's not the same as your having gone through it, but I promise you, you're not alone in that hell. A part of me dies every time I see a scar on you that I could have... that I *should* have stopped." Her voice cracked. "You are the most important person in my life. The only one I can depend on and when you needed me most, I wasn't there for you. I—" Her words broke off into deep, heart-wrenching sobs. "Why didn't I just open that damn door? Why?"

Darling pulled her against him and held her tight. "It's all right."

"No. No, it's not." She was crying so hard now, that her entire body was shaking. "I let them hurt you. I did. And now—"

"Shh baby," he said, hating himself for upsetting her like this. "I swear I will never, ever bring it up again."

Zarya believed him, but it didn't change the fact that when he slept, *if* he slept, he still had horrifying nightmares over it.

I failed him in the worst way imaginable.

"I'm so sorry, Darling."

Tightening his arms around her, he kissed her cheek. "You want to know the truth?"

No. Not if it was worse.

But before she could speak, he continued. "I would gladly suffer all of that and more if at the end of it, I knew you'd be waiting for me."

She cried even harder. How could he feel like that? How? They'd torn him up so badly that Syn had barely been able to piece him back together.

"I was trying to cheer you, Z. Not upset you more."

"I know." She hiccupped. "I just...how did you survive it?"

Leaning back, he pulled her into his lap and held her with her head tucked beneath his chin. The warmth of his body soothed her more than anything. "At first, I thought you'd recognize me. After all the times that damned scar showed through my hair when I didn't want it to, the one time it could have served me, it didn't show at all. You got to love irony, huh? Anyway, once they chained me, I kept thinking you'd come in, see the scar and know me."

"And when I didn't come?"

"In the beginning, I clung to my anger—the same way I survived the mental institutions. I told myself that I was going to get out and then I'd have the throat of everyone who'd hurt me. But the bad thing about anger is that it's not sustainable. Eventually it burns out and the pain swallows it until there's nothing left but a hollow shell. All you want is to die and when you know you can't, you find this fucked-up place inside you where all you do is survive. Minute by minute. Second by second. You try not to think about anything or feel anything. You just get through it one heartbeat at a time, as numb as possible."

"You so didn't deserve it."

"No one does, Zarya. But sooner or later, no matter who you are, life uses everyone as its whipping boy. You didn't deserve to lose your family or be given to a slaver. You damn sure didn't deserve to have your brother die in your arms."

No, but it wasn't the same. While Gerrit still haunted her, none of those had been the unrelenting hell of excruciating pain he'd lived through. He'd had no let up at all. And that was what amazed her about his strength.

"I love you, Darling."

He nuzzled her hair with his cheek. "I love you, too."

Zarya savored the feeling of his fingers brushing through her hair as his heart thumped slow and steady beneath her cheek. And as she inhaled the warm scent of his skin, she understood what he'd meant. She, too, would walk through hell itself so long as she knew he was on the other side.

She never wanted to hurt him again. But as her gaze went to the computer that had begun to play another news segment, she cringed. While they weren't physically flogging him, this was every bit as unrelenting.

And it, too, was because of her. *Why do I have to cause him so much pain? Shouldn't love be easy?*

Suddenly a whiny voice filled the room. It was a tech worker being interviewed by a reporter. "I think the governor is insane and shouldn't be in power. While I was never fond of the Grand Counsel, he didn't scare me. This new governor terrifies the daylights out of me. What with all that happened tonight, I'm afraid to let my family out of my house. We can't go to war with everyone. Someone ought to tell the governor that. We need a leader who isn't crazy."

Darling groaned out loud before he reached to close the computer. "I'm thinking I should blow up the CDS building to give them something else to focus on."

She snorted. "Call me whacky, but I don't thinking killing more people is going to allay their insanity fears where you're concerned."

"I can wait until the building's unoccupied...or better yet, call in Giran and Nylan, then set it off."

She laughed in spite of her tears. With his warm hand, he wiped them from her cheeks.

"Don't worry about this, Z," Darling said, grateful that her tears had finally stopped and that she was calm again. "If I've learned nothing else in my life, it's that we will get through it." Eventually.

And compared to the whole Nylan scandal and some of his other traumas, this was mild. At least the gerents were afraid of him now. They were no longer laughing in his face.

They were still trying to depose him, but they weren't laughing while they did it. That made all the difference...

Yeah, right.

"How do we fix this?" she asked.

"Hell if I know. At this point, I think the best thing for me to do is to keep my head down. At least then I can't screw up anything else."

"You're not funny."

"Really not trying to be." He sighed. "I knew, given what Arturo had done to me and my reputation, that this would never be an easy transition. I always expected the gerents to protest my governorship and to mudsling to the point I contemplated murder."

But what he'd never considered was coming to power after he executed his uncle...with his bare hands. And what that would do psychologically to the people who hated his uncle as much as he did, and with a lot less reason to do so.

He'd hoped to have at least *some* of the gerents back him, and he'd relied on the mistaken belief that the people would welcome him in after living under Arturo's greedy fist.

However, after tonight, that wasn't going to happen. *So much for allaying the gerents' fears.*

Now, everything was so much more complicated than he'd ever anticipated. While he'd known Caronese people didn't like him, their unreasoning animosity was slowly shredding what little confidence he had.

And that could ultimately tear the empire apart.

One match, and the gerents would now ignite the fires of rebellion against him.

I swear, Dad, I will protect the things you love most...That naïve promise haunted him.

"Maybe I should abdicate and let Drake take over." Everyone loved his brother...

She pushed herself up to give him a scowl that resonated, 'are you stupid?' "You can't. Drake's not old enough to rule, and Ryn won't take on guardianship for him. The rest of the gerents... they're selfish bastards out for themselves. They don't care how their decisions affect other people. You're what this empire needs. Not them."

Her loyalty touched him deeply, especially since he knew what she truly thought of the Cruel family and their elongated reign. Over the years, she'd ranted against all of them repeatedly. *"The best thing that could happen for this empire would be a gas leak in the palace that took all of them out at once."*

Yeah, those words had been hard to swallow. But he'd more than understood her malice, and he'd never held it against her.

Still unsure of what would be best, he turned on the wall monitor. Immediately, it showed Giran being interviewed. Through his shifting vision, he saw that Giran's eyes were blackened and his nose taped. There was a white bandage wrapped around his entire head. He looked awful.

I should have hit him harder...

Giran licked his bruised lips. "We have to remember that Governor Cruel comes from a long line of unstable genes. Why do you think all of them have been assassinated? Our latest leader is the worst of them. I've released his medical file for public review. Right here"—he held up the mobile reader in his hand—"the psychologist says that Governor Cruel had to be restrained due to his violent outbursts, and this while he was sedated..."

He glanced down at his mobile so that he could read the report verbatim. " 'Patient Cruel is showing no improvement or remorse for his past behavior, whatsoever. He continues to be belligerent, lunging out against the staff and cursing all of us. He's resistant to our best efforts to rehabilitate him. Yesterday, he broke the arms of two guards. When asked how he felt about putting them in the hospital, he responded that he not only enjoyed it, but that he'd gladly do it again. And that if he was able to, he'd harm me as well.' "

Zarya gaped at Darling.

His features darkened as he clutched the remote in his hand. Vicious memories of that event rushed through him and he wanted blood for it. He returned her shocked expression with a fierce growl. "They were violating me with a pole and the doctor stood there watching, telling them to be more sadistic with it. When they hit me in the arm with the pole, it knocked loose one of my restraints. As soon as I had my arm free, I beat the shit out of them. And yes, I enjoyed it. Every second of it, and every scream they let out while I did it. My only regret was that they sedated me before I could kill them."

Zarya felt sick at what he described, and at the shame that tinged the anger in his jerking eyes. Damn that bastard for dredging up something so foul.

Still, when one didn't know Darling's side of the event...

"I understand, but it sounds so bad from the doctor's point of view."

"Of course it does. You don't really think he'd put in a report that his treatment was to sanction the brutal rape of a patient, do you?" He cursed under his breath as the reporter continued to question Giran about his mental capacity and inability to lead them.

Zarya cringed with every word. The saddest part of it all was that Darling would never set the record straight. His shame and horror over it ran too deep.

And she couldn't blame him for it. In his place, she wouldn't breathe a word of it either.

He gestured toward the monitor with the remote. "They're taking everything out of context and spinning it to annihilate me. It's..." His voice trailed off as his eyes widened and his face went stark white.

Zarya turned to see a naked teenaged Darling with Nylan. Maris was right. Darling was crying and it was painfully obvious that he wanted no part of Nylan's groping. Her stomach tightened to the point she thought she'd be sick as she grabbed the remote from his hand and turned it off.

Horrified agony was etched deep into his features.

She felt as if *she'd* been hit with a blow. "Darling?"

He didn't move. His gaze on the floor, he sat there as if he were comatose.

"Sweetie?"

Still, he didn't respond in any way. It was as if the pain was so great that all he could do to survive it was to withdraw from everything. Even her.

Wanting to soothe him, she reached to brush her hand through his hair.

He jerked away. "Don't touch me!" Those snarled words brought tears to her eyes. Pain bled from every pore of his body. He was aching on a level she couldn't imagine. No one should ever be so hurt.

Darling couldn't think as memories surged and brought him to his knees.

But the worst was having Zarya see it...

Why would the gods do this to him? Why did they make her see his shame?

Needing to withdraw from her and the pain of his past, he slid off the bed and headed for the bathroom. He only took three steps before his jerking vision unbalanced him and sent him to the floor.

He ground his teeth as his fury mounted. *I can't even walk myself to the fucking toilet...*

Arturo had been right after all. He was a useless piece of shit, unfit to breathe, never mind run an empire.

Suddenly, Zarya was there, helping him to his feet.

With no choice, he allowed her to put him back in bed. Something that didn't help his ego at all. *I'm so worthless...*

She brushed the hair back from his face. "Bad things happen to decent people, Darling. It's so wrong, but—"

"Don't you dare patronize me!" he snarled.

"I'm not. Believe me, I'm not." She gestured toward the bedroom door that led to the hall. "My mother and sister were killed in this palace. Brutally. Why? Because they dared to ask an old friend for mercy. A *friend*. Someone my mother had known most of her life. A man we'd all sat down to dinner with. She didn't deserve that any more than you deserve what was done to you."

"I know that, Zarya. I do. Just as I know the horror and shame of that video won't kill me—even though I've wished a million times that it would. I've been forced to live with it being thrown in my face for years. I...I just need a minute to catch my breath and cope, okay?"

Zarya hesitated. Did he really need to be left alone? She wasn't sure. But then he'd never asked that of her before. Surely he wouldn't send her away if he needed her.

Deciding to give him some time to himself, she relented. "All right, sweetie. I'll go see Maris. Call me if you need anything."

He responded with a single nod.

Her heart breaking for him, she left his room. Fain and Hauk looked up from where the two of then were sitting on the floor, against the opposite wall.

In spite of Darling's wishes and protests, the men had stayed to guard him should any of the gerents or people try to harm him after tonight's events.

She paused beside Hauk as she studied the three strange pyramids in his hand. "What are you doing?"

"Playing Squerin."

He said it like she should know exactly what it was. "I've never heard of it."

Fain laughed. "It's an old Andarion game. From the way Dancer plays, I don't think he's ever heard of it either."

"Stop calling me that," Hauk growled at his brother.

Fain scoffed at his anger. "I'm not about to call you Hauk. Sorry. My name, too, and it gets confusing as hell whenever I'm around you. Every time someone yells out for you, I think they're calling me. So your parents named you something stupid. Take a stone from Darling, and deal with it."

"I'll take a testicle, all right, but it won't be from Darling." He glared meaningfully at his brother.

Zarya wrinkled her nose at their sudden hostility. "I feel so bad. You two were playing nicely until I bothered you. I didn't mean to cause a fight."

Fain reached for the pyramids. "Don't take it personally. We're Andarion. Which means we're perpetually pissed off."

"Yeah," Hauk agreed. "We're always fighting about something, even if it means making up a fight over nothing."

She laughed. "All right, then. I'll leave you to it."

Before she could move, Hauk jerked his head toward the bedroom door. "Is he okay?"

Zarya wasn't sure how to answer that. Like them, she was worried about Darling and how he was coping with this unending barrage of insults and public ridicule. "Depends on the definition. I don't think I'd use the word 'fine' per se. But he's coping better than I would."

"Then why are you leaving?" Fain asked.

"He wanted a few minutes alone. So I thought I'd go see what Maris was getting into."

Hauk rolled the pyramids onto the floor. "Ah...take your time. Don't worry about Darling, we'll keep our ears open."

Coming from Andarions, who had incredible auditory abilities, that made her feel better. Until another thought occurred to her... She outwardly cringed as she realized that they'd probably heard *everything* that had happened between her and Darling.

Fain looked up and froze. "I can tell by your expression what you're thinking and no, we weren't eavesdropping while you were in the room with him. We think more of the two of you than to do that, and we figured if you needed us, you'd holler."

That made her feel a lot better. "Thank you." She blew him a kiss before she continued on her way.

When she started down the ornate wing where Maris lived, it suddenly struck her that this was now her home, too. If she married Darling, this was where she'd live out her life, birth her children, and most likely die...

In a palace.

The mere thought froze her in place.

And it wasn't just any palace. It was the palace of an enemy she'd spent her entire adulthood trying to ruin and overthrow.

A foreign sensation washed over her at that realization. *What am I doing?*

For a moment, she couldn't breathe as it all slammed into her with a clarity she'd lacked before.

She really was engaged to the Caronese governor...

To the most powerful person in their empire. One of the most powerful people in the entire universe. Darling ruled the second largest empire in history.

And *she* would be his crowned consort.

Now there was something you didn't get to do every day.

Her heart pounded as she looked around at all the gilding on the crown molding over her head. At the portraits of Darling's ancestors and their cold gazes that seemed to judge her as insufficient.

If she married him, her picture would hang here as well. Forever. Generations of Cruels, staff, and visitors would look up at her, just as she'd done at all of them.

Her stomach hit the floor as cold panic bit her viciously.

You don't have to stay here, you know. You can always go home. Return to her old life.

Granted, she'd have to find a new cause to fight for since she was probably the only Caronese alive who didn't want to overthrow the new governor. But she didn't have to stay here.

Darling had kept her apartment for her. He'd given her the keys, money...

I want you with me because you want to be here. You're free to leave at any time. I won't stop you. Those words still choked her whenever she thought about them. She'd asked him why he'd kept her place after he'd been freed, but he'd refused to answer. Deep inside, she suspected it was more a matter that he had a hard time letting go of the things he loved. And while he'd been furious at her, that apartment had been a place where they'd been happy together.

That was where she'd assumed she would live with Kere once they married.

Zarya looked down at the huge ring on her finger. While similar, it was very different from the first one he'd given her. The one that had been stolen by the slaver...Darling had never once asked her about the first ring.

She tried her best not to think about the fact that while he'd lost his finger trying to keep her ring with him, she hadn't fought the slaver to keep Darling's ring at all.

*Please tell me that ring wasn't sentimental to him...*That fear and guilt were what kept her from asking him about it.

"Mistress?"

She jumped at the deep voice behind her.

Jerking around, she saw the new captain of Darling's guards there—Darling had killed the former one. "Yes?"

He bowed respectfully to her. "Forgive me, Mistress, if I scared you. I saw you standing here and just wanted to make sure you were all right."

Smiling, she nodded. "I was just thinking about some things. Sorry. Apparently, I got so lost in thought that I stopped walking."

He started away, then hesitated. After a few heartbeats, he turned back to face her. "Do you mind if I ask you something?"

His question piqued her curiosity. "Not at all."

"I, um, I don't know if you remember me or not, but I was the guard who carried you up to the mistress's room when you hurt your ankle."

Her face heated up at the reminder. How could she *ever* forget something like that? "I remember."

Regret and shame filled his eyes. "Given what's being said about everything the governor's done to you in the news, I wanted to apologize if I've hurt you or caused you to be hurt in any way. If there's ever anything I can do to help you, please let me know."

Her smile melted into a scowl. "I don't understand."

He stepped closer so that he could whisper to her in a low tone. "If you need help escaping, Mistress, I—"

"Oh good grief, not you, too."

Now it was his turn to frown. "How do you mean?"

She would laugh if it wasn't so ridiculous. "Captain, I'm not a prisoner or a slave or anything else that's bad." She held her hands up to show him her skin. "Do you see any bruises on me?"

"No, ma'am."

"Do I look abused in any way?"

"No, but—"

"There are no buts." She patted him lightly on his arm, grateful and offended by his concern. "How long have you been a guard for the governor?"

"About four years."

"Four years," she repeated, thinking about how many things had changed in her life in such a short period of time. In some ways it seemed like an eternity and in others, like a blink.

"Do you know, Captain, that I've known the current governor far longer than that? In fact, he was a member of the Resistance before he took the throne."

His jaw went slack. "What?"

"It's true. I swear it."

"I don't understand. If he was one of the Resistance, then why did they take him prisoner?"

Her stomach knotted at that question. "They didn't realize who he was. And neither did I. Not until it was too late. Because he was the prince, whenever he fought with us he didn't dare show his face. Yet he was there by our sides. Battle after battle. He fought for all of us against his uncle. Many times. Both here in the palace and out on the streets. I can't tell you how much money and blood he's spent and shed in defense of his people."

He shook his head in denial. "I don't believe it. When he came to power, he slaughtered so many who were innocent."

"Innocent?" she asked in disbelief. "You said you'd been here

506

for four years. Were you not aware of what was done to him under his uncle's reign?"

He looked away, but not before she saw the horror in his dark eyes. "I heard some stories from others. But I never saw anything myself."

"Stories or bragging?" she asked him.

His face turned bright red. "Bragging mostly."

She didn't even want to contemplate what they'd said. It wasn't often someone was given a free reign to brutalize a member of the aristocracy with impunity. "I promise you the stories you heard didn't do the reality justice. When he came to power, Darling only attacked the ones who'd hurt him. It's why you're still a captain and why he never went after you. I'm going to wager that you never once did him harm."

His gaze told her that she'd guessed correctly. "What about the gerents, then? Why are they rebelling against him?"

"They're angry that Darling changed the amount of time they can work their employees into the ground. All of this was caused by that one, simple thing." She gestured down the hall that led to where she'd left Hauk and Fain. "You've seen the men and women who've come in here to protect and watch over Governor Cruel. Do you know who and what they are?"

"I'm not sure. But I think I heard a couple of them say Sentella and Tavali."

"Exactly. Do you truly think they'd protect a monster?"

"Yeah, I wondered about that."

"You shouldn't," she assured him. "I promise you, they would be the first to kill Darling if he was the animal the media said he was. For that matter…" She lifted the hem of her dress to show him the small blaster she had sheathed in an ankle holster. "I've been armed since His Majesty was attacked in his office. I stay awake while he sleeps. If he were hurting me in any way or posing a threat to our people, I promise you, I would have killed him myself."

"The news says that he's brainwashed you."

She scoffed. "Do you really think that?"

"But I've heard you scream while you've been here. A lot."

Heat stung her cheeks again. "It wasn't from pain. I assure you."

"What about all the blood in your room and his that the house-keepers clean up on a daily basis?"

"It's not mine, and it never has been mine. It's from the governor when we change his bandages or he gets nosebleeds...which he gets a lot." She left off a couple of other causes since she doubted Darling would want a stranger to know his business. "Not one drop of the blood has ever belonged to me. A simple DNA test will show that."

There was still doubt in his eyes.

She opened her mouth to further allay his fears, but before she could speak, something shattered loudly. At first she couldn't tell where it came from.

Not until Fain and Hauk jumped to their feet, then kicked in Darling's door.

In that instant, she knew.

Darling was under attack.

22

By the time Zarya and the guard made it to Darling's room, the fight was over.

Darling stood over the bodies of two assassins while Hauk cursed in his effort to get Darling to show him the wound on his side.

Holding a wadded up shirt against the injury, Darling smacked at Hauk's hand. "I'm trying to stop the bleeding, asshole."

Unperturbed, Hauk acted more like a patient mother than a bodyguard. "I want to see how bad it is."

"It's fine, Hauk. Believe me, I've had a lot worse. It glanced off the rib and didn't go deep." Darling's nonchalance left her speechless. But then, she'd seen him as Kere handle some rather nasty wounds without reacting to them either.

Fain shook his head at Darling and Hauk as they continued to argue over the shirt. "Just call for a medic, Dancer, damn. Leave the boy alone."

"No," Darling snapped. "No medics. I don't trust them. I'm not about to let one of them treat me, especially given all the shit going on right now."

Fain made an obscene gesture at him. "Not one of yours,

dumbass. I wouldn't trust them, either. Call the Sentella. Didn't I see a medic come in with them?"

Hauk shook his head. "I don't think so."

Darling nodded at Fain. "Kerste came in about four hours ago."

"Isn't he a gunner?" Hauk asked.

Darling rolled his eyes, which had thankfully stopped jerking— she didn't want to think about what would have happened had they been doing that while he fought his attackers. "No. He's medical. Don't you remember? He's the one who stitched your leg that time when you went after those bounty hunters who'd been preying on kids."

"Oh yeah." Hauk's scowl deepened. "Then why did he come here?"

Darling gestured sarcastically to the shirt that was now saturated with blood. "Syn wanted someone close to me in case something misfired after the surgery."

"Ah." While Hauk pulled out his link to call Kerste, Darling gave her a small smile to let her know he really was all right.

Then he looked past her to his guard. "Captain Harren? Would you please contact the sentries and make sure that none of them were attacked by the assassins? I don't want one of them lying under a bush, bleeding out because they haven't been missed yet."

Zarya wasn't sure why it surprised her that he knew the guard's name. But the expression on Harren's face was comical. It was a mixture of disbelief, shock, and a big dollop of fear and trepidation.

"How do you know my name, Majesty?"

"I know everyone's name," Darling said matter-of-factly. "Especially the ones like you, who are decent and who take pride in doing their job well." He glanced to Zarya, before he returned his attention to Harren. "I also know you have a thing for my sister. And if you want to talk to her or ask her out, you need to.

Otherwise she's going to think you're a depraved stalker the way you watch her every time she comes home."

Harren's face turned bright red. "You wouldn't be offended if I asked her out?"

"Hardly, and neither would she. Her last boyfriend was a mechanic in the Sentella." He jerked his chin toward the open window, then returned to their original topic. "The assassins came in through the north side. Preskitt and Xheris have that patrol. Since they're not due to check in for another twenty minutes, you might want to start with them and make sure they're okay."

By his expression, she could tell that stunned Harren even more.

Before Harren could move to obey, Darling turned to get away from Hauk. The moment he did, the assassin tattoo on his back was plainly visible. Harren gasped audibly.

Darling faced him. "Is something wrong, Captain?"

He gestured toward Darling's back. "You have a soldier's mark, Majesty?"

Hauk gave him an arrogant smirk. "Sentella, actually. It's a trained assassin mark."

"You're a member of the Sentella?" Harren asked Darling.

It was Hauk who answered. "He's been with us since almost the beginning."

Harren gaped in her direction before he met Darling's gaze. "I'll have all of the patrols check in immediately, Majesty."

"Thank you."

Harren bowed respectfully. "You're welcome, my lord. And I'll personally see to it that there are more patrols added to secure your chambers."

"I appreciate your diligence, Captain." Darling gestured at the bodies on the floor. "But as you can see, I can take care of myself."

Harren appeared to want to argue, but as the Sentella medic

brushed past him, he gave Darling a formal military salute. "Call for me if you need anything at all, my lord."

Zarya had a sudden childish urge to say "I told you so" to Harren, but somehow she managed to keep it inside.

After he left, Fain let out a low whistle. "Either you're winning them over, Dar, or he hit his head. Hard."

"I vote for head injury." Darling dropped his shirt to the floor so that the Sentella medic could tend him. "Hi, Kerste. How's your daughter doing in her new school?"

Kerste smiled. "She's adjusting well. Thanks for asking." He pinned each of them with a pointed stare. "Now, if we could have the room, it would be a lot easier to seal this."

Fain inclined his head to the larger of the two bodies lying on the floor. "I'll take fat ass," he said to Hauk, "if you can grab the other."

"Uh-huh, give me the bloody one while you get the broken neck. Thanks, big brother." Groaning in protest, Hauk took his by the legs so that he could drag him toward the hallway while Fain threw the other body over his shoulder.

Zarya started to ask them about waiting for investigators to inspect the bodies, but then reconsidered. It wasn't like they didn't know what had happened.

While Kerste tended Darling, she followed the Andarions outside. As soon as they had the door closed, the brothers started searching the assassins for credentials and information.

Hauk took the hand of the one he'd carried and put the dead man's index finger against his mobile. After a few seconds, he cursed. "Not a pro team. This one is...or rather, was a mechanic." He reached for the other man's hand and scanned it. "This was an out-of-work programmer." He glanced at her over his shoulder. "I think they belong to you, Princess."

"How so?"

He handed her his mobile.

Zarya scanned the man's file, then winced. They were both Resistance fighters. Newly recruited. She tried to use Hauk's device to access Resistance files so that she could find out more about them and their mission, but someone had blocked her access.

So she went to the bounty sheets. Since those were public, she had no problem finding the contract out on Darling's life. It made the one for Kere look like a joke.

"This is ridiculous." She handed the mobile back. "Who is this Hector?" And how dare he lead her men.

Hauk slid his mobile back into his pocket. "No one can find out anything about him. And I do mean no one. We figure it's an alias. But we can't link it to anyone."

Yeah and neither could she. Yet there was something about it that was niggling in the back of her mind. Something familiar.

What was it?

Before she could think of an answer, blaster fire sounded from outside, in the yard below.

Deafening alarms rang out everywhere.

I've got to do something to stop this. It didn't matter who Hector was. *She* was still technically the Resistance leader. And this Hector knew it as well as she did. Why else continue to use her name to call their people to action?

Her mind whirled with possibilities and courses she could take. But no matter what, she kept coming back to one simple fact. If she could get the Resistance to fight *with* Darling against the gerents as they should, then the gerents would have no choice except to accept him as their governor.

Easier said than done. Neither side trusted Darling. Nor were they trusting her at the moment either.

But if she were to show up without Darling...

Maybe she could talk some sense into them.

She left Hauk and Fain to their cleanup while she went to her room. As she paced the floor, planning, she could hear the news from Darling's room.

"Since the governor was pulled out by his security during the meeting"—*Could they get anything right?*—"the Resistance forces have been setting fires and vandalizing corporate buildings. Entire staffs are staying inside their offices like prisoners since they're too scared to even attempt to leave while under this latest round of protests. As a result, the gerents are begging for League intervention to quell the rebel protestors and bring Governor Cruel into line. Maybe even dethrone or assassinate him."

Her heart pounding, she tried not to hear any more. This was such a disaster.

Unfortunately, there was nothing she could do about it tonight. Darling would never agree to let her go to the Resistance alone and if she took one of his people with her, or worse, him, they would never believe she wasn't under his influence.

No, this was going to take careful planning and execution if it was to work.

And time was running out...

"While the League refuses to comment on whether or not they'll intervene, we did hear from a source who doesn't want to be identified that the League is rallying their soldiers and assassins for an attempt on the palace."

She could hear the seconds ticking away. If she didn't persuade her people to see the truth, Darling was going to be fed to the wolves.

God help him.

To save his life and his throne, she was about to throw herself straight into the heart of his enemies.

She placed her hand on her stomach as she considered the baby Nero had told her about. She still didn't have any symptoms at all.

Darling will kill me when he finds out.

If anything happened to the baby, she would never forgive herself.

But what choice did she have? There was no way she could stand by while he was attacked repeatedly because of her.

They'd been lucky this time. His eyesight had been normal when the assassins struck. But what if she'd been with Maris and they'd attacked an hour ago?

Darling would be dead.

His nosebleeds disoriented him. His eyesight crippled him. The two combined...

He couldn't make it to the bathroom alone. Never mind fight off a trained assassin. If those two had been League assassins and not Resistance fighters, tonight's attack might have had a different ending, too.

There was no way she could stand by and do nothing while he was under attack. It just wasn't in her.

The door that connected their rooms opened. Darling paused in the doorway, staring at her with an adoring gaze that set fire to every part of her. Shadows played across his beautiful features as he watched her watching him. As always, he held so much intensity and command of everything around him that it sent a chill over her.

He was every bit the fierce soldier and regal politician.

Most of all, he was the one person she couldn't live without. If his capture had taught her anything, it was that her life was empty and miserable without him in it.

And as she stared at him, she remembered how good his lips tasted. How much she loved being in his arms.

How much she loved *him*.

This was the father of her child...

The only man alive she would kill or die to protect.

"Are you all right?" He approached her slowly, almost bash-fully. Something so out of character for him that it instantly charmed her.

It also struck her as odd that he'd ask after her well-being when he was the one who'd been stabbed. Her gaze dropped to the bandage on his side that was already marked with his blood. "Worried about you," she admitted.

"Don't be. I have no intention of leaving you anytime soon."

But she was going to leave him. She had to. If she was lucky, and the Resistance cooperated, she'd be able to return to his side.

If she wasn't...

She would never see him again.

23

Two days later, Zarya paused as she navigated her way through the charred remains of a burned-down building. Historical and regal, it had always been one of her favorites. When she'd been a little girl, her father had brought her here for cherished birthday meals.

Oh how she'd loved the cake they'd serve her with sprinkles and carved chocolate bunnies...

She touched her stomach, wondering what joyful memories like that she'd give to her child. *Please, let every one of them be good.*

Most of all, she hoped that everything went as planned so that she could get back home before Darling realized she was gone.

Over the last few years, she and Sorche had begun meeting here as well. Since it was close to Resistance headquarters and to the engineering firm where Sorche worked, it'd been a logical place to get together.

Now it, like most of the people she loved, was gone. Nothing more than a faint memory...

Her heart ached as she stood at the remains of her favorite table where she could keep her back to the wall and watch the door.

She'd been sitting right here, in her usual chair when she'd told Sorche about her engagement to Kere.

Laughing and crying, Sorche had oohed and ahhed over her ring while taking her to task. *"Only you would obligate yourself to a man and not know who he really is or what he looks like. Really, Zarya...Someone must have dropped you on your head as an infant. And by that I mean more than once."*

She smiled at the memory.

Until her gaze went to the burned remains of a painting that had hung near the register. It was of the owner's daughter.

Please tell me everyone got out of here alive.

Saddened by the waste around her, she swept her gaze to the horizon where even more fires blazed from dozens of buildings and homes. Thanks to the Resistance and the gerents, Taranyse— the outpost where the Resistance was headquartered—was being systematically torn apart in a show of power between the two factions.

For that matter, the Resistance seemed determined to tear down anything in their path. People. Buildings. Furniture. Rodents...It didn't matter what. If it got in their way, they set fire to it. It was like they were drunk on destruction.

But she knew there was more to it than sheer havoc. Rather than protect the people as they'd sworn to do, the Resistance was hoping to either draw Darling out so they could assassinate him, or cause so much furor that it forced the gerents or League to kill him.

Meanwhile, since the gerents couldn't use the professional Caronese guard without Darling's approval and sanction, they'd activated the Citizen Army to fight against the Resistance. Something that had resulted in a bloodbath on both sides as the Resistance and CA clashed all over the empire.

And though Darling condemned their actions, he wasn't officially in control of the CA. Only the CDS was. He could ask his citizens to lay down their arms and return home, but at the end of the day, the only way to force them to stop was to call out his guard and arrest every member of the Citizen Army. Something he wasn't ready to do...yet.

And if that wasn't bad enough, the CDS kept begging the League to step in and quell the rebels. To throw Darling off the throne and replace him with one of his distant cousins. Nylan, Giran, and crew had promised Kyr that if the League declared martial law here, they would take power and make the CDS fall in line with all League laws and objectives.

May the gods help them all if the League came in.

Poor Darling had tried to placate both groups without the League's interference, but neither the gerents nor the Resistance would cooperate. The only allies he had currently were the workers who were unable to convince the other two groups that Darling was a leader worth following.

At this point, it was only a matter of time before the League came in and enslaved them all. But Darling would be the one most hurt. Once they slaughtered all the Resistance, the League's next course of action would be to imprison Darling for the rest of his life.

Or execute him.

I'm the only shot he has.

"Z?"

She jumped at the sound of a familiar voice cutting through her thoughts. Ready to fight, she turned to find Ture there. "Oh thank the gods. You scared me to death."

He checked the time. "Isn't this when you told me to meet you?"

Trying to calm her racing heart, she placed her hand over her chest. "It is. I was just lost in thought for a minute."

So glad to see him again, she walked into his arms and gave

him a tight hug. "It's so good to see you, Ture. I've missed you so much! Thank you for coming. I owe you one giant whopping favor for this."

He squeezed her back. "You know I'd do anything in the world for you, doll."

She kissed his cheek, then stepped back to make sure he was wearing the uniform correctly. May the gods love him, a cook by trade, he wasn't up on military protocol or dress.

A little over six feet in height, Ture had short brown hair that he'd put reddish highlights in. His vivid gray eyes were a stark contrast to his deeply tanned skin. But as always, he was breathtakingly gorgeous.

Today however, he wasn't impeccably dressed. Standing up the collar of his battlesuit and then rearranging the order of his "rank," she tsked at him. "You look so uncomfortable right now."

He patted at the collar she'd fussed at. "Well, this would be like you in a sequined pageant dress and five-inch heels." He stepped back, showing off his battlesuit with a macho swagger. "But I do look smashing in it, don't I?"

She grinned at his play. "Yes, you do, honey."

He plucked at his front breast pocket. "I have to say though that I've only dreamed about getting men out of one of these. Never once did I consider how to put one on." He made a face at her. "However, I now totally understand that warrior gait they all have."

"How so?"

He reached around and tugged at his pant leg. "This stiff fabric crawls into dark places it shouldn't...if you know what I mean, and after our thong conversation a few weeks ago, I know that you do. Dreadful really. I don't comprehend how they stand it and fight. Then again, it's probably what incites them. Nothing about this drab uniform is comfortable. I would fight, too, if forced to wear it. If for no other reason than to get my butt out of it." He gestured to the blaster at his side. "And this thing only shoots light beams. I was afraid to even attempt to grab a real one. My luck, I'd blow off my leg. Or at least a toe. Probably the one I need for balance. Or worse yet, another part of my anatomy that I'd miss even more."

She laughed again at his dissertation. He carried on in a way that strangely reminded her of Annalise. But in his borrowed uniform, no one would ever guess that he was gay. Not that many people ever did. It was actually quite comical to watch women come on to him in his restaurant.

"Just look like your normal self and you'll be fine...but don't reach for the toy."

Ture put the safety strap over the toy blaster. "I will do my best for you. Now, what exactly are we doing?"

"The impossible."

"Good." He wrinkled his nose. "I haven't done that in a while. I can definitely use an exercise in futility. How considerate of you to think of me."

She let out an amused "heh" at him. "By the way, if we live through this, there's someone I *have* to introduce you to."

Ture cocked one haughty eyebrow. "If he's your delicious, but highly insane lover, I think I'll pass. I so don't want to deal with that kind of drama. Thank you very much."

"Not Darling. You would like him though, I promise."

He made a noise of profound disagreement.

Biting her lip, she debated the sanity of doing this...again. The last few days had been agonizing as she went back and forth on whether or not she should even think about attempting to contact her soldiers who seemed hell-bent on ending their world.

Talk about insanity...Whoever their new leader was, he wasn't thinking clearly. And he definitely hadn't considered the repercussions for his actions.

You can't run now, Z. You're doing this for Darling.

She couldn't let herself forget that.

Please, let this work. She didn't know of another way out.

With a breath for courage, she led Ture away from the restaurant's ruins and down three blocks until she reached the "secret" entrance for the Resistance offices. To an outside observer, it appeared to be a law office. And there were actually lawyers who subleased offices from them. But if you went to the back lifts from the street level, and punched in the right code, it would take you deep into the basement where they worked.

As they entered the building, she had no idea how far they'd get before Resistance security stopped them. But she was going to try.

For once though, there was no security on the door. How weird…

She didn't stop until she reached the lifts. Then, to her complete shock, the control panel accepted her old access code and handprint.

This can't be good…

Why wouldn't they have changed it?

Nervous, she reached down to touch the new tricom Darling had given her to keep her safe while all hell broke loose around them.

His ultimate sign of trust, and one that had let her know he'd meant what he said about not holding the past against her anymore.

Ture leaned forward to whisper in her ear. "Should you be able to get in?"

"No," she whispered back, trying not to be too rude. It was sad when a civ knew more about military protocol than the current Resistance leader. "Whoever Hector is, he's an idiot."

For one thing, especially if they really thought she was being held against her will and tortured, their offices should have been moved. That would have been her first action after they were attacked by the Sentella. Then *all* of her codes should have been blocked, not just her online access.

Who would have ever thought she'd be grateful for stupid?

The doors opened to a hallway that was even more familiar to her than the one in her apartment flat.

A weird feeling tickled her stomach as she stepped out and glanced around. This building...this light gray hall had once been her home. In fact, she'd spent most of the last eight years right here. Night and day. *This* had been her life.

She'd never thought to leave it.

And as she stood there, ghosts from her past haunted her. She heard the voices of her dead friends. Saw images of Darling dressed in the full black battle gear of Kere, walking by her side as they discussed how best to irritate his uncle.

It was just down the hall from here that he'd first made love to her...

Gods, how she missed him.

But the one memory that burned brightest and hardest was the one of Darling being dragged away from the hangar...

In that moment, she felt like a stranger here. Like she didn't belong anymore.

She was no longer the woman who'd been so determined to bring down the Cruel family. Yes, she still wanted to save and protect her people. She still wanted them to be free of those who would exploit or harm them.

But now she knew that the best way to achieve that would be with Darling as their governor.

Ture placed his hand on her shoulder. "Are you all right?"

Not really. But she didn't want him to know that. "Yeah. I'm just a little concerned that we've made it this far and no one's greeted us. We should have been swarmed the moment we came in."

No sooner had the words left her lips than a shout rang out, followed by a red-tinged blast that narrowly missed her face.

"Stop!"

She froze instantly and held her hands out so that the man could see she wasn't a threat. Ture followed suit.

"Put your weapons down!"

Zarya smiled as she finally recognized the angry voice snarling orders at her. "Ferin? Is that you?"

He hesitated before he answered. "Zarya?"

"Yeah. It's me."

Still he didn't come out from his cover. "What are you doing here? And who is that with you?"

"It's Ture. A friend of mine. And I thought you guys wanted me back. Was I wrong?"

"You can't trust her. She's been brainwashed by our enemies."

She didn't recognize the second man's voice. It was a deep, guttural tone—the accent native to the western part of the empire. Was he the mysterious Hector?

"No one's brainwashed me." She took a step forward.

Another blast came within inches of her face.

She stopped moving instantly, but what her attacker didn't know was that his shots weren't scaring her. They were pissing her off.

"You shoot to kill. Not to warn." Her father's voice was loud and clear in her head. But today, she couldn't listen to him. Instead, she had a psycho to disarm.

"Are you Hector?"

"I'm the Resistance leader now," he said without answering her question directly. "*You* abandoned us." The venom in that tone had to come from personal betrayal. Nothing else made sense. A stranger shouldn't be so hostile toward her.

And yet, she still couldn't place his voice.

"Who are you?" she tried again, holding her arms up over her head to let them know that she posed them no threat.

At first she didn't think she'd get an answer.

Then, out of the darkness emerged the last person she'd ever expected to see again.

Pip.

For a full minute, her emotions paralyzed her. Shock. Anger. And a hatred so bitter, she could taste it. She wanted to claw his eyes out over what he'd put Darling through.

But all that being said, he looked like someone had already tried to kill him.

No. Rather he looked like they'd succeeded.

A vicious scar ran over his left cheekbone and the jagged, horrific one across his throat must be why his voice sounded the way it did. It appeared Darling had stabbed him right below the Adam's apple, then ripped the knife across his entire neck. How Pip had survived such a savage attack, she couldn't imagine.

Had she not seen what he'd done to Darling, she'd feel sorry for him. But there was nothing inside her except contempt. "Why are you calling yourself Hector?"

He narrowed his eyes on her. "It's my real name. But you never bothered to learn that, did you? No. I was too far beneath you for you to notice me."

Now that really made her mad. While she lacked Darling's impressive recall with people's names and background, it didn't mean she didn't care. "That's not true. I never treated you that way. Ever."

"Didn't you? Clarion told me how you reamed him for taking the royal prick prisoner. You were siding with them from the very beginning. First chance you had, you went running right back to your inheritance, didn't you, Princess? Once an aristo, always an aristo. None of you care about anyone but yourselves." He gestured at his face. "Look what the bastard did to me!"

Zarya had to struggle to keep herself calm, but it wasn't easy. Not when she really wanted to gut him where he stood. Lowering her hands very slowly, she took a second to turn on the tricom... just in case Pip was as insane as she thought him to be. "What happened to you is awful. I admit that. But what was done to Darling—"

"Look at the way you use his name," he sneered at the others who were still hidden by their cover. "You sicken me, you sorry fag whore!"

Oh that was it! How dare an animal like him judge *her*. "Then we're even, Pip. The sight of you makes my skin crawl and it has nothing to do with your scars or your classification. You make a mockery of the uniform you wear. You're the one who doesn't believe in our cause. Instead, you use our colors so that you can practice your depravity under the guise of being normal when you're not. No human being could do to another what you did to Darling."

With a cry of outrage, he leveled his blaster at her. "That's it, bitch. You're dead." He pulled the trigger.

The blast headed straight for her. Out of reflex, she jerked her hands up and cringed in expectation of being blasted. But just as it would have struck her, it hit the tricom's force field. The shot broke apart and rebounded through the hallway, seeking out all the men in hiding.

It caught Pip straight in the chest and sent him flying into the wall behind him.

Whoa...

No wonder Darling had been so pissed off about his attack. It looked extremely painful to be hit by whatever it was the tricom generated.

Yet none of her soldiers moved or cried out. They were absolutely frozen.

"What did you do to them?" Ture asked in an awed tone.

"I didn't. It's a device that was made for me." How fitting that it would be used against the ones who'd trapped Darling with it.

Ture let out a low whistle. "Well color me impressed, and please, don't *ever* use that device against me. I'll be a good boy, I promise."

Not even Ture's attempt at humor could quell her anger. Rather it mounted with every step she took closer to Pip and the others. They lay on the ground, eyes open. The only clue she had that they were still alive was the faint rise and fall of their chests as they breathed.

That made her think of Darling lying like that on the ground and what Pip and the others had done to him while he'd been helpless against them...

Wanting blood, she went to stand over Pip. "Now, if I were you standing over Darling after I'd paralyzed him, I'd be calling *your* beloved little sister a bitch, and I'd start bragging about how I shot that same defenseless young woman in the back and killed her while she was running away from me...'cause shooting a fleeing woman in the back is such a manly thing to do. Then, I'd strip you naked so that I could steal from you."

She ground her teeth to staunch the bitter pain those words welled in her throat. With every syllable, she wanted vengeance for Lise and the agony that poor girl would have to cope with for the rest of her life because of Pip.

But most of all, it was Darling's misery that drove her on. "And while you lay there helpless, staring at your sister, I'd cut your finger off and make you eat it. Then I'd put a torture device in your mouth and carve my name into your cheek." She sneered at him. "You talk to me about *your* hatred. You don't even know the meaning of that word. But I do. And I will not apologize for being on the right side of this fight. And to clarify that for you, the right side is *not* yours, Pip. At no time has the Resistance *ever* been about cruelty."

She glanced around at the others on the ground. "This organization was founded to stop a tyrant from abusing his power. Now let me reiterate that last bit slowly so that *you* can understand it. The Resistance was founded to stop a tyrant from abusing his power. We weren't founded to become the tyrant who abuses others. How dare you do such a thing in my name. You have dishonored my father, and you have awakened the ugly side of *me*. Do not mistake my kindness for weakness. I assure you, I don't have a weakness."

More soldiers came running, arms at ready.

As they neared her, they slowed, then stopped. The sight of their comrades on the ground while she and Ture stood over them, unarmed, confused them.

"Zarya?" Someone shouted her name in relief while others questioned her identity.

She focused her attention on the one who knew her... Titon. He'd been one of her younger members, and because of that, she'd doted on him.

"It's me, sweetie," she said with a calmness she didn't feel. "I'm here to stop this madness before it's too late."

His face ashen, Titon shook his head. "It's already too late."

"What do you mean?"

Before anyone could answer, an explosion knocked all of them off their feet.

Sighing in irritation, Darling held another cloth to his nose while he listened to reports of Resistance rebellion as they set fire to more businesses. He'd been trying to negotiate with their current leadership, but none of them would talk to him.

This has to stop.

Maris had already warned him that the League was moving in at the request of the CDS. *Stupid bastards...* Once the League declared martial law, the Caronese were screwed. He didn't even want to contemplate what it would take to get their empire back from Kyr.

How stupid could the gerents be?

Oh wait, he'd known many of them most of his life. That single question in and of itself was moronic.

See what happens when you hang out with them? They suck out your IQ and leave you stupid, too. Yeah, Giran alone could reduce his intelligence by thirty points in under two minutes.

"My lord?"

Lowering the cloth to hide how saturated it was in blood, Darling glanced over to the door of his office where Gera stood, fretting in the doorway.

He forced the irritation out of his voice and smiled at her. "Yes, Dame. What can I do for you?"

She hesitated before she entered the room. "I'm not sure if I should be mentioning this, but do you know where her ladyship is?"

Gods, what had the bitch done now? Did he even want to know? "My mother's at—"

"Not the dowager, my lord," Gera said, cutting him off. "Lady Starska."

It took Darling a second to realize who Gera was talking about. How could he have forgotten Zarya's title?

Because he didn't think of her that way. She was much more intimate to him than her title made it sound. But then Gera was nothing if not formal.

Darling wiped at his nose to make sure it wasn't bleeding anymore. "She said she wasn't feeling well, and went to her room."

Gera swallowed audibly. "She told me the same, but when I went to her room to check on her, she wasn't there."

That wasn't unusual. Zarya didn't like being alone. He suspected it was from the same kind of ghosts that haunted him—old memories that refused to let him rest. "She's probably with Lord Maris."

"I already asked him, Majesty, and he hasn't seen her either."

Okay, *that* concerned him. Zarya very seldom ventured away from *both* of them. "Did you check with her sister?"

"Yes, Majesty. Lady Sorche said that the last time she spoke to her was at dinner last night."

His throat went dry as he noticed Gera nervously clutching something in her left palm. "What's in your hand?"

Biting her lip, she approached him slowly. "I went to her room to see if maybe she was in her bathing chambers. While there, I started picking up a few things she had scattered about and..."

She placed her hand on his desk. "I found this in a drawer."

Don't panic.

It was hard not to. And when Gera pulled her hand back and he saw Zarya's engagement ring, he felt like someone had kicked his stones straight into his throat.

Don't jump to any conclusions.

"She must have forgotten to put it back on after her bath this morning."

Yeah, that must be it. Zarya didn't forget her ring often. Just every now and again. It did happen. It wasn't necessarily a bad thing.

Just a forgetful one.

"Perhaps...but still I'm worried about her, Majesty. Given all the madness that's going on...you don't think someone's kidnapped her, do you?"

Okay, the panic beast was no longer stalking. It now had him on the ground and was stabbing him hard. Where was she? "Let me check with my sister. Maybe Lise—"

"I already called her, my lord. She said that she hadn't talked to Lady Starska since day before yesterday. The same was said by both Lord Drake and your friends Hauk and Fain."

And he hadn't seen her since early that morning...

His heart racing, Darling rose to check it out himself, but before he could take a single step, his office door flew open.

It was Giran.

Nothing could have shocked or appalled him more than to see that noxious bastard in his home. "What?" Darling asked drily as he tried to keep the contempt he felt from showing on his face. "Did hell freeze over?"

It must have for the gerent to be here alone.

Now armed with a guard to attack and dethrone him—*that* would have made sense. But for the gerent to be here as he was...

Yeah, this could not be good.

Giran grimaced as he stepped into the room and ignored Gera completely. "This isn't funny," he said to Darling with a note of hysteria in his voice. "We have a bad situation here."

No, shit. Most of it caused by *him*.

What? Did the genius just wake up and realize that calling in the League was a blunder of epic proportions? It ranked up there with inviting a pack of mountain lions in to kill the mouse in your basement.

Not that it mattered to him right now. Giran was the last person Darling wanted to deal with. The bastard was lucky he was still upright and not gutted.

Disgusted by the gerent, Darling started past him. "I'm a little busy with something else."

Giran stopped him. "Your Majesty, please..."

Those words and the sincere pleading beneath them stunned him into complete shock.

Hell really had frozen over.

"What's happened?" Darling asked, dreading the answer. It had to be extremely bad for Giran to address him with respect.

Giran's eyes teared up. "The League...they've declared martial law on us. As a result, they've moved a large number of their troops into Taranyse."

Great. He needed that like another body part that spasmed out of his control. He ground his teeth. "Are you happy now?"

An actual tear fell down the man's face. "Majesty...the League overran Resistance headquarters and then went for the council building where they've set up their own people to rule us."

No surprise there since that was League SOP. Darling had tried to warn them that this would happen.

Their response? They'd laughed in his face and publicly insulted him through the media. With this particular asshole being their ringleader.

He'd started to remind Giran of that, when Giran spoke again. "Every gerent who was inside the CDS building on Taranyse was arrested and taken into custody..." His voice cracked from emotion. He locked gazes with Darling. "They have my son, my lord. And my younger brother."

Even though Giran's brother had been one of Darling's worst critics, he winced at what was most likely being done to both of them while Giran was here. A Caronese noble in League custody ranked right up there with Darling Cruel being held by the Resistance.

"Did you contact the League?" he asked Giran.

"I tried. But the agent I spoke to said that they were all considered radicals who are being held to secure the peace, and that so long as the League was here, they would remain in custody. She also intimated that if I persisted or protested, I'd be viewed as such and seized, too."

Darling gave him a droll stare. "Did you not know this?"

Giran sniffed back his tears as he ignored Darling's question. "My son was only there so that he could go home with my brother after the meeting and visit with his cousins. He's barely fifteen, my lord. Just a baby."

Darling ground his teeth. A kid that age wouldn't do well in a League prison. Especially not with an uncle who most likely had never been in so much as a fistfight to protect himself...

Gods have mercy on that kid.

"I don't understand why they did this. The League was supposed to help us."

Darling wanted to ask him what form of hallucinogen he'd consumed. *Please tell me you're on something.* The thought that he'd be sober and do this...

Honestly, it had to hurt to be *that* stupid.

Giran cleared his throat. "Did you know that when the League is invited in by the ruling body of a planet or empire, they are allowed to take over all facets of the government, and place all of the reigning aristocracy, not just the ruler, in League prisons?"

Again, no shit...

"Yes, I did. What? Did you sleep through your government classes?"

Giran raked his hand through his hair. "There were so many laws to read and remember. And they were ever changing. I never could keep half of them straight. And honestly, they were so boring that I usually cheated to pass the classes."

Darling let out a short, bitter laugh. "Yes, they were extremely dry and boring, and in between my sucking off thousands of men, stealing the money from our treasury and embezzling funds from the pleb schools, getting shanked and filmed every afternoon by Nylan, all my stints in and out of mental wards where I, as a boy your son's age, beat the staff to the point they were all terrified of me, and raping and brainwashing the Resistance leader I'm only marrying for political reasons, I committed every single one of those laws, our laws and my father's code, to memory. And in between my numerous extracurricular activities, superhuman that I am, I've kept up with every change to every law that has been made in my lifetime."

Shame filled Giran's eyes over Darling's sarcastic reminder of what he and his brother had been publicly alleging every time a news camera came near them. "I'm so sorry I said those things about you, Majesty. It...*I* was wrong to do so, and I apologize deeply."

Pride must have choked him hard to admit that. And the fact that he did, that he was here begging for Darling's help after attacking him so viciously, also let him know just how desperate Giran was. Not that he blamed him. If someone had *his* son, he'd bust Kere's domain wide open to get him back.

Gods help whomever was dumb enough to touch someone *he* loved.

Still, Darling wasn't as forgiving as his father would have been. Not after everything they'd been doing to not just him, but those he loved.

Giran's words and actions, in particular, resonated loudly in his memory.

"You publicly and cruelly insulted my fiancée, and then aired the most humiliating moment of my entire life to everyone who might have missed it, all the while insulting my integrity, intelligence, and sanity with lies you knew to be untrue. Why should I *ever* help you?"

Giran averted his gaze, but not before Darling saw the agony and shame he was trying hard to hide. "You're right. I shouldn't have come here for a favor. I have no right to ask you for anything. What I did to you was beyond cruel and it was wrong. And I'm ashamed of the fact that I took pleasure in hurting you."

Yeah, right. The only thing Giran was ashamed of was that after having held Darling's head down and rubbing his nose in the past, he now had to belly crawl to him to get his son released.

Tears fell down Giran's cheeks. "I only pray that whoever has possession of my son is showing him the compassion I *should* have shown you."

There, Giran had finally stumbled onto the magic phrase. Darling wanted the bastard to admit to not only him, but to himself, what he'd done and how wrong it'd been. And why it was wrong. It was the only way to make sure Giran didn't do it to someone else.

"Scars are there to remind us of the price we pay when we learn a vital lesson. Never hide them, Darling. Revel in the fact that you've grown as a person. Embrace the newfound knowledge you learned about yourself."

His father's words rang in his ears. No matter the situation, his father always knew what to say or do to make it better. How he wished he had one tenth of what his father had possessed.

Instead, he stumbled through his life blindly, hoping he was doing the right things.

Giran started for the door.

"I didn't say I wouldn't help you," Darling said coldly. "I only wanted you to understand that I'm under no obligation to do so, and that I have every reason to turn my back on you as you did me when I went to you and the CDS in good faith, expecting you to help me do the right thing for our people."

"I understand," Giran breathed. "Honestly, I'm not sure if I'd help me if I were you, given what all we've done." He met Darling's gaze with a burning sincerity in his eyes. "And this is a favor I won't forget, Majesty."

Darling inclined his head to him. "Good, because if I succeed in getting them back, you are to set the record straight with the media about my past. I want you to recant every lie you've spewed.

535

More than that, I expect you to support and back my governorship before the rest of the gerents and CDS."

Giran's lips quivered. "If you save my son, Your Majesty, I will spend the rest of my life making sure no one ever questions your decency, mercy, or reign. I will give my life for you."

"Good. 'Cause I need you to rally the CDS to an emergency session as soon as possible. The steps I'm going to have to take are severe and extreme. It's a move I don't want to do without the full support and knowledge of the CDS."

He bowed low. "I will see it done, my lord. You are truly an asset to the people. May the gods bless you for your benevolent mercy, and give you the longest and happiest life imaginable."

Darling scoffed at his obsequious fawning. The only reason Giran was here was for his son. If anything went wrong or Darling failed in his mission, he'd be the first to lunge at Darling's back. "Don't flatter me, Giran. I know what you really think about me when you're not worried about your kid. Everyone in the universe knows since you've been extremely verbose about it. And I would rather have your sincere hatred than unctuous friendship any day."

Giran straightened and let his aristocratic mask slip so that Darling could see his real emotions. This wasn't an aristo in front of him. It was a father who was terrified of losing his son because of his own stupidity. "Sincerely, Darling, thank you for at least trying to help me. I do mean that."

"Let's hope the gods listen to your prayers." Because they had very seldom listened to his. "Now, go. Every second wasted is one more your son lives in danger."

Giran left immediately.

Darling turned to Gera who was still waiting for orders about Zarya. That was the only thing that...

His gaze went past Gera to the monitors he'd had on for the last few days so that he could watch the news and stay abreast of the Resistance attacks, and the gerents' confederacy of dunces.

All four of the wall mounts showed clips of a League raid on his territory. It was one thing for Giran to tell him. Another to see it in full color. The League soldiers were shooting indiscriminately into crowds of innocent people, and shoving bystanders around. Men, women, and children.

How dare they! Those were his people.

He'd tear them apart for this.

But that anger fled as he saw the one thing that sucker punched him. It was a video of Zarya in cuffs, being led out of the Resistance HQ and placed into a transport by League soldiers.

His stomach lurched.

Grabbing the control off his desk, he turned the sound up.

"…League command is refusing to comment or speculate. But again, they have routed the Resistance and taken all of its leaders into custody."

They flashed to one of the League high commanders. "We were invited here by the members of the CDS, and we have now taken control of the cesspit of the Caronese Empire. The CDS is no longer the ruling body here and they will be required to submit to our rule until such a time as we deem they are safe."

"And what of Governor Cruel?" the reporter asked.

"Since we have been provided with proof of his diminished capacity and known ties to the Resistance, we are relieving him of his duties. If he refuses to surrender himself to our custody, we will be forced to issue a bounty on him and arrest him."

That actually made Darling laugh. "Bring it, punk. But you better stock up on body bags." He wouldn't go down without a fight.

He locked gazes with Gera.

"How did they capture her?" Gera asked.

"I don't know. But don't worry. I *will* get her back."

She gave him a kind smile. "I have faith in you, my lord."

He wished he shared that faith with her. Because once he set his arrogance aside, he knew the truth. Going up against the League was suicide. It was one thing to defend himself against random assassins sent in to kill him.

It was another to take an army up against them.

Darling clutched at the remote. To get Zarya back now would require the kind of bombastic lunacy people wrote warning fables about.

Great. Arturo was right. My only purpose in life is to serve as a warning to others...

His gaze went to another monitor that showed Zarya from a different angle. There was no fear showing on her face at all. She walked with the grace and dignity of a queen.

But he knew her well enough to recognize her fear. Underneath her icy façade, she was terrified and she had every right to be. Much like with Giran's son, a woman in League custody never fared well.

Touch her and so help me, I will kill every one of you...

"Hold on, baby," he whispered. "I'm coming for you." Even if it meant his life.

The saddest part? He'd be damned lucky if that was all they took.

24

"We're so dead."

Running her fingers over the restraints on her wrists, Zarya took a deep breath as she tried to stay strong for the men and women around her. Even though Pip had been the Resistance leader for almost two years, she'd worn that responsibility a lot longer.

And not to be arrogant, but a lot better. If she could get the Resistance members to trust her again, she might be able to get all of them out of this alive.

As for the aristos in the prison shuttle with her . . . they were terrified, too. Someone needed to give them hope.

"We're not dead yet," she said with a conviction she didn't feel. "Stay strong. Don't let them defeat us."

"We're League prisoners," one of her men sneered. "Do you not know what's going to happen to us when we land? What they're going to do to us?"

Hopefully, they'd be a little more merciful than Pip and crew had been to Darling.

Not wanting to think about that, Zarya patted the man on his shoulder, trying to calm him. Darling would remember his name. But while she recognized his face from missions they'd done together in the past, she couldn't recall his name or position no matter how hard she tried. "I do. And I'm one of the primary ones they'll focus their attention on...But I also know people who've survived their custody, and they were a lot younger and more inexperienced than we are. Plus, I know for a fact that Governor Cruel won't allow them to keep us."

Pip sneered at her. "You're about to learn a harsh lesson, little girl. You're nothing to him. Just another replaceable whore." He raked a harsh glare over her body. "Probably not even that. I've heard his tastes run more along the line of pretty young boys."

She met his glare with one of her own. "You know *nothing* about him. And if you refer to him again with anything other than the utmost respect in your tone, you won't have to worry about prison or the League. I'll fucking kill you with my own bare hands."

Those words had the effect she wanted them to. Everyone sucked their breath in and held it. No one had ever heard her use such language before. It wasn't in her nature.

But she was through watching others insult Darling when all he'd ever done was try to help them.

Her conviction fortified by that rage, she scanned the soldiers and aristocrats around her. "We are not pawns. We are not victims. We are Caronese—one of the greatest races in the United Systems. And we're warriors for a cause. *All* of us. I've bled with most of you and mourned injustice with you all. Yes, the League has us for the moment, but the fight doesn't end here and neither do we. Others have defied them and lived."

"Who?" one of the aristocratic women challenged her. "Name me one they haven't killed."

"Nykyrian Quiakides."

Furstan, who'd been one of her more trusted commanders, scoffed. "We're not trained assassins. He survived only because he was one of them."

"True. But I've met the man many times and while he is a great fighter, I saw our governor toss him flat on his butt in a fight."

Half the Resistance laughed in mockery, but she could see the doubt in their eyes.

"I saw him do it," one of the aristos said. "I was there and she's right. The governor got past him like he was a civ."

"I saw it, too."

That quieted the dissenters.

She nodded at them. "That's right. Darling was trained to fight by Nykyrian himself. He is a soldier well—"

One of the men snorted derisively, interrupting her. "He's a stupid faggot. He can't protect himself. How—" Before he could finish those words, Ture got up and punched him so hard, the man went sprawling to the deck.

His nostrils flared, Ture stood over the man with his fists clenched. Never in her life had she seen him like this. For that matter, she'd never known Ture to lose his temper before. Not over anything. He was normally the most laid back person imaginable.

"I have news for you, breeder," he growled. "Just because we're homosexual doesn't mean we lack the physical strength of men. We can still fight. Most of us better than you, because we've had to defend ourselves our whole lives from jerks who think it's funny to attack us. There's a big difference between not wanting to or liking to fight, and not knowing how."

Zarya pulled Ture back and separated them. She patted him on the shoulder in sympathy and passed him a silent look that said she not only approved, but was proud of him.

However, they couldn't afford to fight among themselves. They had the League for that, and she was sure they'd be more than willing to lend a hand in the beatings.

Right now, they needed to stand together or else they'd die alone.

As Ture resumed his seat, she returned to the subject. "I know the governor better than anyone. He will not tolerate the League coming into his territory and taking his people prisoner. Not for *any* reason. He *will* come for us."

The woman to her right shook her head. "No offense, but he has to find us first. Have you any idea how many prisons the League runs? Over a thousand on hundreds of planets and outposts. No matter how angry or determined Governor Cruel is, it could take him years to locate us."

Yeah, okay in her exuberance, she'd overlooked a few small details. That was definitely one of them, and with the League, those prisons were impregnable.

And with that, came a whole new fear.

Instinctively, Zarya placed her hand on her stomach. It was also League policy that any child born to a female prisoner would to be taken away for assassin training. If it had any kind of abnormality, it was killed immediately after birth.

More than that, her child would have Trisani in its DNA. Would the League view that as a defect? Or worse, would they sell her baby into slavery or experiment on it?

And once they tested the child and found it was part Trisani, they'd test her. And when they found no trace in her genetics, they'd know that Darling and his family were partially Trisani...

Panic seized her. It would mean the death of them all.

They can never know I'm pregnant.

But that wouldn't last. As of today, she'd officially missed her period. By now, she'd be far enough along that they'd be able to detect the pregnancy with either a scanner or blood test.

Panic rose inside her so strong that for a moment, it took her breath.

She refused to give in to it. *Darling will find me. He will.* As unlikely as it seemed, she had to hold on to that belief. He wouldn't let her down...

The way she'd failed him.

Tears filled her eyes as she finally understood the true horror of his confinement at their hands. The one person who should have been hunting for him, who should have saved him from his torture, had walked by a thousand times outside the very room where he was imprisoned. And he'd heard her there over and over again.

Oh gods...

How would it feel to hear him on the other side of that locked door while she languished in here with no prospect of escaping?

It was one thing to be told something horrific.

It was another to experience it.

How could he ever really forgive me?

The fact that he'd spoken to her at all after his release was a miracle. How he could still love her was beyond her comprehension.

I'm so sorry, Darling. Her only hope was that she lived long enough to really make it up to him.

"What do you mean, you can't find her?" Darling glared at Syn. "Her location has to be in their system. They make a record of every fart one of them takes."

Screwing his face up at Darling's crudity, Syn gestured toward his laptop. "I'm looking, but I'm telling you, it's not there. For some reason, probably intelligence, they didn't file a log on her. There is nothing in their system to let me, or anyone else, know where they've taken her. They've all but deleted any evidence of her ever having lived."

And they all knew what that meant.

The League intended to execute her and since they had no real evidence to convict her on, they wanted no trace of it. If they didn't find her soon, it would be too late.

Frustrated and terrified, Darling looked over to Nykyrian who was pacing in front of Darling's desk. "Where do they normally take political prisoners?"

Nykyrian shrugged. "There are over two hundred and fifty prisons for political inmates. But the problem is, she might not be in one of those. While she is an aristo, she's also a criminal in their eyes. With or without evidence."

Which brought them back to square one. She could be in any prison on any planet.

Damn them!

It'd already been over two weeks that they'd been searching for her. Two. Full. Weeks.

Darling had paid out more than six million creds in bribes to any- and everyone who might have even a kernel of information about her or her location.

Nothing.

When Nero had heard about it just hours after she'd been captured, he'd tried to find her with his powers and had almost burned up his brain in the process. But for Syn, he'd have died. Poor bastard had gone into a coma while attempting it and had developed a vicious migraine that no amount of medication could cure. Fifteen days later, he was still unable to open his eyes in any kind of light.

At least he tried. For that, Darling owed him and he wouldn't forget it.

Syn slapped at his keyboard. "They're determined that no one is going to find any Caronese prisoner. It looks like they've scrubbed that word from their vocabulary. I've never seen any-thing like this."

And Syn had been professionally hacking files since he was a small child. If Syn couldn't find an e-trace, no one could.

What are they doing to her? That thought was never far from his mind. If he hadn't been insane before all of this, fear for her life was quickly stealing what little sanity he had left.

"She's on Brinear."

He started at Maris's deep voice as his old friend stepped through the door of his office. "What?"

Maris hesitated before he spoke again. "My source came through. It took him a few thousand creds, but he finally got the information, and he verified it. She's definitely there, under extremely heavy security."

Gods bless Safir. If anyone ever learned that he'd helped them, he would be torn into pieces. "I'll make sure he's reimbursed."

"He doesn't want the money. He only wants to do the right thing."

"Then he needs to surrender his commission," Nykyrian said bitterly. "Trust me. It's a dangerous game he's playing. The bad thing about the League, every assassin is out for themselves and they're real quick to throw you to the wolves if they think it'll advance their rank even a single decimal of a point."

Maris nodded. "I know. I was raised with the head asshole himself."

Nykyrian clapped him on the back. "And for that I'm infinitely sorry."

"Yeah, most days, me, too."

Syn closed his laptop. "All right, then, folks. We have a location for attack. Give me an hour and I'll have the facility mapped, then we can plan our next move."

Darling nodded. "I'll try to rally my troops."

"And I'll get the Sentella scrambling," Nykyrian said.

Ryn finally stirred from the sofa he'd been lying on for so long that Darling had assumed he'd gone to sleep. "I'll go motivate the Tavali."

Grateful for that offer, Darling knew it took a little more than just the promise of a good deed to motivate the pirate brigade. "Tell them any who fly with us will get a full pardon from the Caronese Empire for any past crime, except murder, pedophilia, or rape. And I'll give them a free pass to fly through our territories for the rest of their lives, so long as they don't prey on our people or ships."

Ryn gave him a cocky grin. "You are by far the better politician. That'll motivate their sorry asses in a way I could only dream. Even without the Sentella and Caronese Armada, you're about to have one hell of an army, ready to lay down their lives for you."

"Let's hope they don't have to." Darling gave them a short nod before he made a sharp military about-face and headed for the door.

Maris fell in beside him. "She's going to be fine, Darling."

He wished he had Maris's faith. But that had been kicked out of him when he'd told himself every day that his friends would find him and release him from hell. Meanwhile weeks had gone by while he'd hung in his cell in utter agony.

Now...

Darling didn't believe in much of anything, except the universe's willingness to screw him over.

Please let her be all right. Thoughts of her being brutalized tortured him even worse than his own memories. Every hour they didn't rescue her had him living in fear that she was being raped and beaten while calling out for him to help her.

Just like Lise when she'd been shot...

His panic rose so high that for a moment, he couldn't breathe. *Please don't let my eyes start jerking.* Though there was no real rhyme or reason to when they'd start, they seemed more inclined to do it whenever he was stressed.

He glanced askance at Maris. "Did Safir give you any information about her condition?"

"No. He tried his best to find out for you, but he couldn't access that. He did say that he'd cautioned Kyr against raping her when they'd taken her into custody."

Darling clung to the thread like a lifeline. "Do you think Kyr listened?"

"Honestly? I don't know. I hope and pray for her sake and yours that he did."

Darling's throat tightened. "Did he know if she's one of the ones being tortured?" The League had bragged to the media every night since they'd raided the Resistance's HQ that they were "interrogating" the Resistance leaders in an effort to find the rest of their members.

"He couldn't answer that either. Sorry."

Darling ground his teeth as pain shredded his gut. "As bad as Kyr hates me . . . I hope he's not taking that out on her."

"You know, he's not so—"

"Don't lie to me, Mari," he said, cutting him off, "and tell me he's above that. We both know better. I have the scar to prove just how bad his temper is. He didn't get to the top of the League high command by showing mercy to those he perceived as enemies. He got there by carving his way through a mountain of bodies."

Maris winced at the truth. "He wasn't always like that, you know. He was a kid once, too."

"I know." Like Maris, he remembered when Kyr had been in possession of the soul he'd sold to the League for vanity and glory. Granted Kyr had never had much of a sense of humor, but he'd been fair.

Decent.

Until something had happened shortly after Kyr turned seventeen.

In one summer, he'd turned from being an insecure, average teenager into a cold-blooded soldier.

I guess my father's old adage was right. "*Whenever you take the shot, Darling, two men die. The man you targeted and the man you used to be. Once you draw first blood, you can never go back to the way you were. It will always change you, and never for the better.*"

After that summer, Kyr had locked up emotionally, and had never been the same. For the longest time Darling had felt sorry for him.

Until that one moment that was forever etched into his memory.

Even now, he could see Maris walking barely a step in front of him, toward the altar where Tamara was waiting for the ceremony to begin.

But the moment her gaze had met Maris's, fear had etched itself onto her face.

The old priest had breathed an audible sigh of relief. "Ah, there you are, Maris. We'd begun to—"

"Forgive me, Holiness. But there's something I need to say." Stopping just in front of the priest, Maris had looked to Darling for support.

Dressed in his Phrixian uniform, Maris had been the epitome of a fierce regal war hero. Except for the perspiration on his brow and upper lip—perspiration that worsened as he turned toward Tams. She'd been exquisite in her blue and gold gown that flowed around her lush and abundant curves. Darling could tell by her expression that she knew what was coming.

And why.

She'd reached out to touch Maris's arm, and offered him a kind smile. "It's okay, sweetie." Biting her lip, she'd glanced to Darling, then back at Maris before she'd whispered to them. "I've had a feeling for quite some time that you two were more than friends."

Maris had taken her hand into his and kissed it. "I do love you, Tams. I'm just not *in* love with you. I'm so sorry."

Her eyes had glowed with her love and respect for him. "Don't apologize, Maris. Not for this. And not for being you. I'm only grateful you're doing this now instead of later when it would have been too late to undo it." She swept her gaze to her parents who were scowling a hole through all three of them. "My father might kill you over it, but I for one can't thank you enough for not tying me into a marriage where I could never have the one thing I want most."

Children.

Unlike him and Maris, she wanted a house full of them.

When they had turned around toward the crowd, Maris's father had shot to his feet. "What's going on here?" he growled. "Why aren't you facing the priest? Maris, explain this!"

"We're not getting married, Father. Sorry."

That hadn't gone over well with his father. "What do you mean, you're not getting married? You've made a commitment. Now be a man and honor it."

A tic had started in Mari's jaw. "I *am* honoring my word, Father. I promised Tamara a long time ago that I would never do anything to bring hurt to her heart. It's why I can't marry her."

Her parents had started shouting then that there was nothing wrong with their daughter, and the crowd had gone crazy with accusations against both bride and groom, as well as their families.

His father's face had turned bright red from rage. "Boy, you better turn around right now and—"

"I'm gay, Father. And I can't enter into marriage with Tams when I know I can never be the husband she wants or deserves." The moment those words had left his lips, silence ripped through the entire building.

For a full minute no one spoke or moved. Hell, Darling didn't think anyone even breathed.

Then the cacophony returned at twice the volume and violence it'd been before. Out of nowhere, Kyr had lunged at Maris. Acting on pure instinct, Darling had grabbed Maris and pulled him out of his brother's reach.

Kyr had whirled on him then, and they'd fought for a few minutes, until Kyr had stabbed at Darling's groin, narrowly missing it. The knife had gone straight into his thigh. But instead of pulling it out and trying again, Kyr had twisted the blade, then plunged it into his thigh again and again…three times, causing a star-shaped scar.

Darling couldn't remember the insults Kyr had growled out at him as he'd stabbed him. But he'd never forgotten the momentary fear of thinking Kyr had sliced through his femoral artery, and that he'd be dead within seconds.

Since that day, they'd been bitter enemies.

Yet none of that changed the fact that Kyr was Maris's older brother. A brother Maris had once worshiped and looked up to.

Now as they walked down the hallway to set up a fight to the death against Kyr, Darling draped his arm around Maris's shoulders. "I know you still love your brother, Mari."

He would never begrudge his friend those feelings.

Maris took the hand Darling had on his shoulder and held it tight. "Family is so complicated."

Darling laughed bitterly. "Tell me about it."

Maris pulled him to a stop, then turned Darling to face him. "But *you*…you've never once disappointed me. You've always been a much better friend to me than I have ever been to you."

Darling scoffed. "Completely not true. I wouldn't be here if not for you. I'd have died a long time ago and you know it." He fell silent for a moment as he remembered all the times in his life Maris had been there for him…Like supporting his weight after they'd freed him from the Resistance. Visiting him in the hospital after his suicide attempts and his uncle's violence. Of Maris sitting with him for hours after Darling had buried his father...

Most of all, he remembered Maris braving his fury to return Zarya to his life.

For that alone, he owed Mari more than he could ever repay.

"At the absolute worst moments of my life, Mari, you've always come through for me. Always." Just like now. His entire world was falling apart and spiraling out of control.

And instead of running from the suicide mission they were about to embark on, Maris was standing by his side. Ready for battle.

While life had done its best to drive him to his knees and break every part of him, Maris had been his sole support who never faltered or hesitated.

Maris pulled him into a tight hug. "We're going to get our lady and bring her home, Darling. I promise you."

Darling clung to Maris as all of his fears and emotions shredded him. It was a weakness he'd never allow anyone else to see. Tears swam in his eyes. "I can't live without her, Mari," he whispered. "I can't. She has to be all right. The thought of anything else..."

Maris tightened his arms around him.

"I am so incredibly confused."

Blinking away his tears, Darling burst out laughing at Drake's befuddled exclamation from the opposite hallway. With a shake of his head to clear his vision, he leaned against Maris and met his brother's fierce scowl. "Yes, little brother, I'm *that* confidently heterosexual that I can hug my best friend in public and not feel awkward while doing it."

"Yeah, I can hug a guy, too. Just not nipple to nipple." Drake shivered in revulsion. "That's just a little too much bromancy for me, thank you very much."

Laughing, Maris held his hand out to Drake who took it

without hesitation. He pulled Drake toward him, then hugged him with one arm while keeping their crossed hands trapped between their bodies so that their chests didn't touch. "Don't worry, Drake. Even nipple to nipple, you wouldn't turn me on."

His expression offended, Drake stepped back. "I don't believe you for even a second, Mari. I ooze sexy animal magnetism."

Darling rolled his eyes at Drake's arrogance. "Excuse me, little brother? Not to tear down your epic ego or anything, but...Mari and I have gotten more women as gay men than you have ever gotten with all that oozing sexy animal whatever."

Maris concurred, then stepped forward to whisper loudly. "And if it is oozing, sweetie, you really should see a doctor about it. I'm told they have medication for things like that nowadays."

"Oh dear gods, what did I just walk in on?" Annalise pressed her hands to her ears and started singing out loud as she continued on her way down the hall, past them.

Maris gave Darling a lopsided grin. "I think we may have scarred her for life."

Darling shrugged. "I wouldn't worry about it. I'm pretty sure I ruined her years ago." Grateful for the temporary break in the melancholia that had been his life since Zarya had been taken, he met Drake's gaze. "Did you need something?"

"Yeah. I was coming to let you know that Giran has finally assembled the CDS in the south council hall. They're waiting for you."

Maris sighed. "Do you know what you're going to say to them?" he asked Darling.

If he'd been his father, Darling would have had a prepared speech ready. Something profound, that would unify the people and build their confidence.

Unfortunately, *he* flew by the seat of his pants, and would rather speak from his heart.

"Not a clue."

"Oh good." Maris elbowed Drake. "You get the drinks and I'll bring the snacks. This is going to be a great show."

Darling wasn't amused. He felt more like he was heading toward an execution.

Might as well get it over with. Besides, whatever he said wouldn't matter to more than half of them. They were going to hate him regardless. There was nothing he could do or say to sway them to his cause. With a deep breath, Darling changed course for the south hallway. Instead of going to his guard to rally them, he was now going to try and...

Not get politically assassinated in the media again.

It didn't take him long to reach the south hall where everyone waited. Maris and Drake stayed at his back while his real royal guards opened the doors for his admittance. He was still getting used to them doing that, and treating him with respect and deference—something Harren had somehow miraculously induced. But it was hard to undo a lifetime of ridicule in just a few weeks. A part of him kept waiting for their contempt to kick in.

Just as he waited to hear it from the assembled gerents as he entered the chamber hall.

They remained quiet with only a few of them throwing belligerent glares toward him. Ignoring them, he descended the row of stairs to take his throne at the front of their seats. Maris moved to stand to his right while Drake stood on his left.

The gerents sat down after he did.

And still not a single sound could be heard. Not even the rustle of fabric.

Giran came down the main row that divided the room. He bowed low before Darling, then moved off to the side so as not to give Darling his back—an act of supreme reverence and respect.

Clearing his throat, he went to the podium to address the others. "I want to thank all of you for coming out so quickly."

Darling would dispute two weeks as being quick, but he held his tongue. No need in being the first one to start the name-calling. *See what happens when they don't fear you'll blow them up? They take their sweet time with assembly.* Unlike the first time when he'd been able to get them together in only a few hours...

"As all of you know," Giran continued, "we are being occupied by foreign soldiers, and many of us have family who are now in League custody as political hostages to guarantee our cooperation. Governor Cruel—"

"He's the problem!"

"They wouldn't be here if not for him!"

"I say we give him over to the League, then they'll release our people."

Giran held his hands up to silence the angry barrage. "*We* are the reason the League is here!" He shouted over them until they settled down. "The governor had nothing to do with this. He knew what would happen if we asked for their intervention, and he tried to stop us. *We* are the ones who invited them in without his consent or knowledge."

He swept the crowd with a fierce scowl. "And I know no one in this room is stupid enough to really believe that all the League wants is Governor Cruel. In fact, it is my concrete conclusion that he is *the* only hope we have of getting our families back, ever— something he has graciously offered to do. For. Us. And I think we should listen to what it is he now proposes."

A few people let out noises of disapproval, but those stopped as soon as the doors opened to admit what appeared to be the entire Caronese royal guard.

For a moment, Darling expected them to attack or arrest him. He'd never seen that many guards at once, except at state functions or during arms' displays. And anytime more than two approached him, he'd been seized and thrown to the ground, then hauled to wherever his uncle was waiting for him.

But they didn't attack.

Instead, they came forward to sink to one knee before his throne, and respectfully bow their heads. Darling had an urge to turn around to see if Nykyrian or someone else was standing behind him. But his throne was pushed against the wall. There was no one there.

They really are kneeling to me.

What a mind freak that was...

High Commander Brenton rose to his feet and snapped to a military formal stance. "We are here, Your Majesty, to support whatever military action you wish to take." He swept his arm out to indicate the men and women with him. "All of us have taken a new blood oath to lay down our lives in service for you. Long reign Emperor Darling Cruel!"

The soldiers with him let out a cry of support.

Yeah, the god Kere was definitely wearing snow gear today.

For them to call him emperor was the ultimate show of respect and support. It was a title reserved for only a small percentage of his family. And no Cruel in the last thousand years had been deemed worthy of it. Unlike governor which was an inherited title, emperor could only be conferred by a unanimous vote between the guard and the five leaders of the CDS.

Stunned to the core of his being, Darling looked over to Captain Harren. He was sure the captain was behind this. He had to be.

Ever since the captain, under Darling's orders, had found that both Preskitt and Xheris had been viciously wounded by the assassins who'd attacked Darling, his attitude had changed. But for his following Darling's orders, both men would have died. And since Xheris was his younger brother...

Harren had become a major advocate for Darling.

After the soldiers stood and took up positions inside the hall in support of him, Darling rose to his feet. It wasn't until that moment that he realized he wasn't in the robes of a governor. He was actually wearing his red-tinged black Sentella battlesuit. And he'd forgotten to put his tinted glasses on. If his eyes started jerking, they'd all know.

This wasn't the smartest thing he'd ever done.

Saddest part? It wasn't the dumbest thing he'd ever done either...

He could only imagine what he must look like dressed to kick the League's ass with his governor's harone still in his hair. His ancestors had to be rolling in their graves.

Oh well...

This was his reign... short though it might prove to be.

Clearing his throat, he braced himself for what he was sure would be a less than stellar reception.

Don't get used to the title of emperor, boy. After this speech, they just might unanimously decide to yank it.

Even so, Darling stood strong before them. "Just a few minutes ago, we learned the location of where our people are being held. It's taken longer than we'd hoped to find them, but nevertheless, we can now move forward with our plans."

They started chattering around him. Some in support. Some...

Not so much.

Darling held his hand up to silence them. "I know most of you in this room truly believe I'm insane. The good new is, I am. But not for the reasons you think. A sane man would gladly sacrifice his people to the League and bargain with them so that he could stay in power no matter what. A sane man wouldn't even begin to contemplate what I'm about to undertake."

"What are you going to do?" someone shouted.

Darling glanced in the direction of that unknown voice. "Bring our people home."

They laughed.

He ignored their ridicule. He was used to it, after all.

Once again, he silenced their protests. "I'm not asking any of you to risk anything." He turned his attention to the royal guard. With Ryn and the Tavali backing the Sentella, he no longer needed them. "And that includes my soldiers. They're free to stay home and protect our citizens from the invaders."

To his shock, the majority of his guard protested the idea.

"Our job is to defend you, Emperor!"

"The emperor is the heart and soul of the Caronese people! He's not a martyr to be sacrificed!"

Warmed by those shocking statements, Darling continued. "In the event I fail, I have a video that will be given to the League, telling them that I acted without knowledge or approval of the CDS. It renounces my titles, and names my brother Drake as my successor, with Ryn continuing on as Grand Counsel until Drake's majority. I wanted all of you here so that I could personally assure you that the well-being of this empire is my greatest concern, and I would never do anything to jeopardize my people. The Caronese are my life. And by the gods, I will not tolerate anyone coming into my territory and kidnapping my people out of our government buildings for any reason, and then to hold them hostage..."

He would mention the Resistance, too, but he knew no one in this room cared that they'd been taken. Most were probably happy about it. And mentioning their capture might even alienate some of the CDS.

Darling saw the pain in Giran's eyes as the gerent watched him. He was terrified for his son and well he should be. "The League has issued a command that I surrender governorship to them. If I do so, they will step in and replace me."

A cheer of approval went up.

Yeah, now that was what he'd expected when he walked in...

Darling wanted to laugh at the morons. *I should step down.* That would teach them an invaluable lesson.

But unfortunately, he couldn't do that to them.

Giran scowled at his "friends" and their mockery as they called for the guard to arrest Darling and hand him over to the League.

"Gerents?" he shouted. "Do you not understand what that would mean for us?"

Utter silence filled the hall.

"We wouldn't have a faggot for a leader!"

"Enough!" Giran roared. "I will not stand by and see our emperor insulted!" He pinned several of them with a brutal glare. "If the League steps in, *all* of us are replaced. Do you understand me? The CDS will be disbanded. Immediately. Our titles will be confiscated and those of us here in this room will join those already imprisoned."

That finally got their attention. Yeah, the bastards didn't like that thought at all.

A deafening roar broke out until Giran let loose a fierce whistle. "Let's hear from the emperor what he intends to do for us."

He and the rest of the room looked to Darling.

Darling clasped his hands behind his back and eyed them coldly. "My plan is simple. I intend to walk right into the heart of League territory and ram their dictate for our surrender down their throats."

The royal guard cheered. But the gerents weren't quite so enthusiastic.

"They're not going to let you walk in and take our people out," a woman sneered. "They'll come for us."

Darling shrugged with a nonchalance he didn't feel. "They might. But it's not likely. As far as the League will know, the attack won't be sanctioned by the Caronese," he reiterated. "The Sentella will be leading it."

"Why would the Sentella put their lives on the line for us?"

Because I'm one of its founding members, imbecile...

But he could never say that out loud. "It's what they do. Everything is already in place. Nemesis and Kere are standing by to start the assault as soon as I give them the clear. Something I didn't want to do without consulting all of you first."

Giran gave him a fierce military salute. "I am with you, my lord. May the gods speed and keep you. Most of all, may they give you the strength to save our people and bring them home."

The royal guard let out a resounding sound of approval.

But the gerents...

They remained quiet for so long that Darling began to wonder if he hadn't bored them to sleep.

Finally, Lady Tehrshin rose to her feet to address him. "I remember my father telling me when I was a girl that the League would never act against any nation. That all they wanted was to keep us in peace and health. But over the years, I've watched as they lost sight of their mission. Now I am one of those who is directly affected by their actions. They hold my only son for no reason whatsoever. Today I am the one who suffers. But tomorrow, it could be anyone in this room. They need no reason these days to kill or suppress. I support you, Your Majesty, and I commend your courage. Would that all men possessed it. May the gods bless you always, Emperor."

"Here, here," Lord Sirisk said as he, too, came to his feet. "Long reign and health to Emperor Cruel."

Suddenly, one by one, the gerents stood up and gave a formal nod of approval.

Astonished by their unexpected reversal, Darling stood before them, trying to absorb the fact that for the first time in his life, they were with him.

Not against him.

Releasing his pent-up breath, he returned their salute with one of his own. "Thank you for your support in this. Now I'm off to finish preparations."

With those words spoken, he quit the room.

Drake and Maris ran to catch up to him in the hallway.

"Wow," Maris breathed in awe. "That was something I never thought I'd live to see."

Drake nodded in agreement. "It was incredible. *Emperor* Darling. I can't believe they're with us."

Darling wasn't so sure about that. At any moment, he expected one of the gerents to betray him. *Dear gods, I've become as jaded as Maris...*

But he was grateful that it'd gone better than he'd dared hope.

Looking forward to getting Zarya home, Darling led the way to the war room where they'd left the others. He'd only gone about halfway when they met up with Nykyrian.

"We're ready to move forward," Darling told him.

Nykyrian didn't respond.

A shiver of dread washed over Darling. While the Andarion prince was usually somber, there was something about him different. Something more rigid than normal.

"What's wrong?" Darling asked.

Nykyrian sighed heavily. "The media is going wild again."

Darling let out a sound of utter disgust. Of course they were. "What did the League do now?"

"They..." Swallowing hard, Nykyrian hesitated, which was something he'd never done before.

That, in and of itself, scared the shit out of him. This was bad. *Real* bad.

His face emotionless, Nykyrian held his mobile out toward Darling. "The League has released a statement that while torturing one of their prisoners for information about the Resistance and you, the prisoner died during interrogation."

Darling's entire body seized up as he heard those words. *Please, please don't let it be who I think it is.* He wanted to look at the mobile, but he couldn't bring himself to do so.

Because in his heart, he already knew what he'd see and he couldn't face it.

"Who did they kill?" Drake asked.

Nykyrian's eyes turned dark. "I'm so sorry to be the one to tell you, Darling. But I didn't want you to find out from someone else."

"No," he breathed as his vision darkened. "It's not her."

Nykyrian winced. "I'm afraid it is. Zarya's dead."

25

Darling forced himself to look at Nykyrian's mobile. For a full minute, he couldn't breathe as he saw Zarya's battered, lifeless face and the cold, static writing around it that chronicled her last few hours of utter hell.

She'd told them nothing...

Even with their torture, which was plainly evident in the picture of her, she hadn't betrayed him or his friends. She could have destroyed them all and saved herself.

Or at least quickened her death.

She hadn't. To the very end, she'd been loyal to him...

Pain racked him in a way it never had before. His senses reeled as dizziness blurred his vision. It hurt so much and so deeply that he wasn't sure how he remained on his feet.

I failed her.

The one person in this world he should have protected above all others, had been brutalized and murdered by his enemies while he'd been powerless to find her and stop them.

In that one moment of soul-splintering agony, he had total clarity over what Zarya had gone through while she'd searched for Kere. No wonder she hadn't checked on him as a political prisoner under the care of her men. She'd been right. The fear and desperation were all consuming. That horrific need to find the one you loved while you imagined what was being done to them...

This awful, sickening sensation of knowing they were out there and you couldn't get to them while life went on. You still had to pay bills and attend to daily matters that seemed so trivial and inconsequential.

But they had to be done. The world didn't give a shit when you were aching and lost. When the one person you needed and loved most was no longer with you, it didn't affect them at all.

Only *your* world was shattered beyond repair.

And then the absolute, impotent anguish that came when you saw the confirmation of your worst fears...

He couldn't take his eyes off her battered face.

Damn you all!

This was so much worse than what they'd done to him. He would much rather be back in that room, having Pip feed him shit than to be here right now, knowing he'd never see Zarya again.

She's gone.

Forever...

Having lived solely for her, how could he go back to living without her? She had been the only light in his darkness. When he had been lost to a place so dismal not even Maris could pull him out, she alone had returned him to sanity and given him sunshine again.

And he'd wasted so much precious time with her letting his hurt stand between them.

If I could just have one more hour back...

He wouldn't squander it by holding past mistakes against her. Rather he would revel in the miracle that he'd had her at all. That somehow, against all odds, two lost and battered souls had found each other, and there for one moment in time, had managed to be happy together.

Why did I waste it?

Why?

Maris moved forward to hold him tight. "Breathe, baby. Just breathe."

Darling couldn't. Not while his soul screamed out in the bitterest agony he'd ever tasted. A thousand memories tore through him at once. He saw Zarya's eyes light and happy as she teased him late at night. Her face as she looked up at him with an adoration no one else had ever given him.

Not even Maris.

Anytime she glanced at him, there had been the most beautiful twitching of her lips as if she was trying not to smile. A joy in her gaze that had never failed to set him on fire.

And now the last image of her, the one that would haunt him forever, was of her bruised and bloodied. Of her amber eyes lifeless and empty...

Reality crashed over him and ripped him straight out of his body. He saw himself as if he were looking down on the small group. Drake's pale face was drawn, but vengeance glowed in his eyes. Ryn and Hauk stood behind Nykyrian wearing the same stoic expression Nykyrian held as they braced themselves for his reaction.

Maris stood behind him with one arm around his waist and the other wrapped around his shoulders. He had his forehead pressed against the back of Darling's head and he felt Maris's hot tears on his neck as his best friend trembled and wept from his own grief. It was a protective hug, the kind Darling had used with Drake and Lise when they were children and he'd wanted them to feel secure and safe in the midst of all hell busting loose.

But he didn't feel secure. And he had no right to feel safe. Not after he'd allowed the only woman he'd ever loved to leave his protection and be tortured to death.

The grief and misery inside was so great that it left him suddenly numb. It was as if his mind knew he couldn't handle the full magnitude of her loss. So it shielded him with a cloak of apathy.

He hadn't felt like this since the day his father had been buried and he'd realized nothing would ever be the same—that *he* would never be the same. The first time his life had shattered into a trillion jagged pieces that had lacerated every part of him, body and soul.

And he knew it wouldn't last. Sooner or later, his mind would drop the shield and all that pain would flood over him. Even sharper and deeper, until there was nothing left except a rage so foul it would challenge his sanity.

Zarya was dead.

It didn't seem possible. Yet there was no denying that photo. She was gone from him.

I'll never hear her voice again. Never wake up with her hand tangled in his hair.

Never again have her stick her cold feet on his back whenever she got in bed with him...

He would even miss the way she always stole food off his plate before he had a chance to taste it. Those things had made him snap at her. They'd made him crazy.

I would sell my soul to feel those icy feet shock my skin one more time...

How could the gods have done this to him? Had he not suffered enough in his wretched life? Was he not allowed one shred of happiness after all he'd been through?

Damn you all!

In that moment, he hated everyone and especially the gods who'd betrayed him. They weren't real. They weren't there. Or if they were, they didn't care. How could he have ever worshiped beings so callous?

How?

But most of all, he hated himself for his inability to locate Zarya in time to save her life. Hated himself for not being there for her when she'd left this existence.

How could he have failed her so completely?

There was no such thing as justice. Just as there was no such thing as compassion or decency. The universe was dark and it was cold. Life-sucking and demeaning.

Treacherous.

And he'd had enough of it.

Breaking away from Maris, he stormed down the hall, toward the landing bay.

"He took that better than I thought he would," Hauk said from behind Nykyrian.

But Maris knew the truth. "No, he didn't. He's going to his ship right now so that he can make a suicide run for my brother and the League."

Hauk started cursing in Andarion. "I would ask you to tell me he's not that stupid. But..." He looked at Syn and then Nykyrian. "We've been down this road before and I've seen the hell it leads to." He let out a disgusted sigh. "What happened to our calm, rational little buddy that we raised? You know? The guy who never reacted to anything until after he'd carefully thought it through?"

"He had the shit kicked out of him one time too many." A tic worked in Ryn's jaw. "This finally did him in."

"We've all been there," Nykyrian said under his breath.

Without another comment, Maris headed down the hall in the same direction as Darling. There was no way he was going to let Darling do this alone.

"Where are *you* going?" Drake called out after him.

Did he really have to explain? "He needs a wingman and point guard."

"Maris, wait!"

Had it been anyone other than Nykyrian who barked that order, he would have ignored them. But Maris had too much respect for the Andarion prince to blatantly disregard him.

"What?"

"Can you stand Darling down for about twenty minutes? Give us enough time to rally so that you two will have at least half a chance at surviving?"

That wasn't as easy as Nykyrian might think. In this current mood, Darling wouldn't be easy to talk sense into. Not that he faulted Darling for that.

The only person he knew who could stop Darling from this stupidity was lying in a League morgue.

Maris fought down his own tears. He'd grown to love her, too. While he'd never had a sister, he'd started calling her one. "I'll try."

Nykyrian nodded. "Good luck."

Yeah, he was going to need it.

Maris ran after Darling, hoping he could catch him before he launched. His heart was broken for him. But worse than that was the fact that he knew Darling would be dead before this day was out.

One way or another.

There was no way he'd come back here without Zarya. Maris could try to soothe him. But in the end, it wouldn't be enough. Nothing would ease the agony Darling held inside himself now. No amount of words. No amount of alcohol.

Nothing.

And the sad thing was, he knew he'd die with him. He understood what drove Darling more than he wanted to.

Without Darling in his life, he had no reason to live either. He'd already lost his entire family. Every friend he'd stupidly thought he had. Friends who'd tormented and mocked Darling for being something he wasn't while Maris had stood there and let them do it.

The guilt of his inaction would forever haunt him.

That won't be much longer now...

And he didn't mind at all. Zarya and Darling were the only ones who'd never judged him.

Darling, alone, had stood by him no matter what shit-storm ravaged him. He couldn't bear the thought of getting up in the morning and not seeing or at least speaking to Darling.

"Dar!" he called as he finally saw him in the landing bay.

Halfway to his ship, Darling froze at the sound of Maris's voice. Turning around, he frowned. Maris hated to run. He always had.

Yet he ran toward him as fast as he could.

"What are you doing, Mari?" he asked when Maris finally reached him.

Maris took a deep breath to slow his rapid breathing before he answered. "I'm going with."

Darling shook his head. It was bad enough he'd lost Zarya, he wasn't about to allow Maris to throw his life away, too. "No, you're not. You're staying here."

Defiance glared at him through those dark eyes. "Oh hell no, I'm not. And *you* can't stop me."

That was debatable, but he didn't want to fight with his best friend. He wanted to save his venom for the ones who deserved to die for their actions. "You don't understand, Mari."

"Yes, Darling, I do," he said emphatically. "I get it completely." His gaze steady and harsh, he put his hands on Darling's shoulders. "Through thick and thin, we're brothers to the bitter end. And if you're going to hell, buddy, I'm driving the bus."

Those sincere words touched him so deeply that they burned all the way to his soul. Finally, Darling felt the tears stinging his eyes. "I can't let you do this. I won't kill you, too."

"You didn't kill Zarya, and you have no choice." Maris pulled his arms away and pointed to the embroidery on the sleeve of his burgundy battlesuit. "Hello? Decorated war hero. I'm every bit as well trained as you are, and I trained longer. So move your skinny ass out of my way so that I can get to my ship and show you how it's done."

Darling didn't buy in to that arrogance for even a heartbeat. And he wasn't going to watch Maris die. Not today. "I'm serious, Maris. Stand down."

"So am I, Darling." Maris's gaze softened as he cupped Darling's face in his hands and forced him to look at him. "Don't you know that *you* are my Zarya? You always have been. I've been in love with you since the first day we met and you took a beating for me. Would you really ask me to watch you fly out of here, knowing you're going to die and do nothing about it? Really?"

Darling swallowed against the bitter lump in his throat. He'd always known how Maris felt about him. Just as he'd known that he was the reason why Maris had never been serious about anyone else. At times he'd taken advantage of that love and selfishly kept Maris with him when he shouldn't have. Kept him by his side instead of allowing Maris to move on and find someone else to dedicate his life to.

Still, Maris had stayed. Even though he knew that as close as they were, friendship was all they'd ever have.

A part of him hated what he'd selfishly done to Maris just so that he wouldn't be alone in his hell. So that he would have at least one person he could depend on without question or fail.

And he did love Maris. He did. But not like *that*. Not the way he loved Zarya.

Closing his eyes, Darling laid his hand over the one Maris had on his left cheek—the cheek that still bore the external scars that marred him soul deep. "The gods fucked us both, didn't they?"

Maris took his hand into both of his. "I don't think so. These last few years, I've been able to live with the only man I've ever loved, and I see him night and day." He gave him a teasing, lopsided grin. "Having sex with him once in a while would have been infinitely better, but I actually don't mind what we have. You own my heart, but I own a part of you no one else does. Not even Zarya."

It was true. Because they'd been through so much, had protected each other and been there when no one else had, they had a bond tighter than marriage and friendship.

And it was eternal. There was never any fear of betrayal or abandonment. Never any doubt about how far the other would go to protect or shelter the other. One call and they would walk through the fires of hell. Side by side.

How many people could say that about their friends and family?

Even now, Maris was with him.

To the bitter end.

Maris winked at him. "Now let's go avenge our lady and teach those bastards their manners."

Reality came crashing down again. So swift and brutal that for a full minute, he couldn't even catch his breath for it.

His soul screamed out again, railing against the gods who'd done this. But he wouldn't cry. Not now. Tears were weak and Zarya didn't deserve his weakness.

Zarya deserved only his utter best.

"I'm going to kill your brother, Maris."

"I know. And while a part of me still loves him, he's not the same brother I grew up with. I truly hate the assassin he's become and I'm so sorry he hurt you."

Darling squeezed his hand, then released it. "For Zarya," he breathed. He stepped to the right so that Maris could go around him and walk to his own fighter.

But Maris didn't move. "Nykyrian asked if you could wait twenty minutes for them to rally and go with us."

Honestly, he didn't want them to. He didn't want to endanger anyone else. Never mind his true friends, and especially not Maris. Unfortunately, he knew they were every bit as obstinate as he was. Nothing would deter them.

And if Maris wasn't with him, he'd never wait.

One is easily overtaken. Two can fight back.

But a group united is hard to destroy. Another adage his father had made him commit to memory.

"Twenty minutes. Then I launch."

Inclining his head, Maris relayed the message through the com-link in his suit. Darling turned to climb aboard his fighter while Maris went to his.

Once he was harnessed into his seat, he glanced over, then froze. It was so strange to watch Maris skillfully strap himself into his cockpit and systematically run the flight checks. While he and Maris had been friends all these years and had fought together in a couple of bar brawls, they'd never gone to war as a team.

Never once.

In his younger days, Maris had fought in the Phrixian Fighter Corps under Kyr's command.

And Darling had only fought with the Sentella and Resistance with Hauk as his usual wingman.

It was always so strange to him how life turned. Usually when you least expected it.

Never had he seen this one coming. And the fact that Maris was fighting with him against the brother he'd once protected...

Yeah, fate was a bitch with a wicked sense of humor.

571

And today we're all her punch line.

As Darling ran through his own checklist, he tried his best to not think about the first time Zarya had touched him. She'd been right here, in this very ship. If he closed his eyes, he could still see her with him in the darkness of space, feel her mouth on his body as she went down on him. It'd been the first time in his life that sex with someone else had given him pleasure. The first time anyone had made love to him…

I miss you so much…

How could I have let you die? Had he been the man she deserved, she would never have been in this situation. He should have run away with her when he had the chance.

To hell with Arturo and the empire and his duties.

She was the only thing that had really mattered. Why hadn't he taken better care of her?

He should have just grabbed her and run to live on some colony somewhere else. Screw duty. Screw honor. The gods knew, he had enough money even without his inheritance, they could have had an extremely comfortable life together.

For that shortsighted stupidity, he now bled internally.

"You all right?"

Maris's voice and his concern brought him back to what he was doing.

Darling pulled his helmet on so that he could respond. "All right would be a stretch. But I'm operable."

And he wanted League blood. Enough that it washed over and through him until he saw nothing but red…

Firing his engines, he put in his request for launch.

Let the slaughter commence…

Zarya hissed as Ture pried the blood-soaked hair off her face and his fingers brushed against the bruise on her forehead. After they'd dumped her back in the cell with him, he'd pulled her into his arms to hold her like she was a small child.

She hated that he was here because of her. Ture wasn't a soldier. He wasn't a fighter. He was an innocent cook who had no business here. She'd only brought him with her so that the Resistance would trust her again.

And while they didn't interrogate him daily like they did her, they hadn't spared him either. His handsome face was bruised and swelling from his beatings, and she suspected his nose was broken.

Still, he continued to watch over her and protect her as best he could.

"What did they do to you, this time?" he asked, his voice cracking.

Too weak to move, she listened to his heart beating beneath her ear. "They killed me."

His arms stiffened around her. "What?" he asked in disbelief.

She groaned as a sudden pain stabbed her body. "Obviously, they brought me back so that they could continue torturing me. I think I was only dead for a few minutes."

And the machine they'd used to resuscitate her felt like it'd broken every rib in her chest.

But at least she was alive. Pip hadn't been so fortunate. He'd died under their torture about an hour before she had, and when they'd gone to resuscitate him, his body had caught fire.

Panic seized her at the memory. His death had been both gruesome and excruciating. His screams would haunt her forever.

Don't think about it...

Gods, how had Darling stood months of this? Every part of her ached more than she would have thought possible. How could anyone be in this much pain and not die?

But at least she hadn't been raped. Thanks to Safir who'd

reminded them that even though she was an outlaw captured in Resistance headquarters, she was still an aristo. As such, by their own laws, they couldn't have her raped while in their custody.

How sad that they had to make what should be common decency a law. And sadder still was that such a law made them better than her Resistance brethren who hadn't been so kind to Darling.

When would the cruelty stop?

Ture winced as he carefully turned her face to survey the latest damage. "You have got to think of your baby, sweetie. Give them something—anything—so that they'll stop this before it's too late."

Tears stung her eyes. She feared that she'd already lost her baby. She'd been spotting earlier, before they'd pulled her out to interrogate her again. But there was nothing she could do now, not unless she told them she was pregnant and that was too big a risk, too. "I can't."

"You mean you won't."

She wouldn't argue that. No matter what, she would never hurt Darling. It didn't matter what they did to her. She would not betray him.

"He'll come for me soon. I know he will," she said with as much conviction as she could muster.

"You're such a fool, Zarya. How can you be so blind after everything you've seen? People just aren't that decent or reliable. They're not. We all want to believe in the magical hero who flies in at the last minute with his army and saves us from our enemies. But it doesn't happen in real life. Ever. People hurt you and they disappoint you, and there's nothing you can do about it. You have to take care of yourself first, and realize that when the rain comes, you're standing in it all alone."

She shook her head, then hissed at the pain it caused her.

"You're wrong, Ture. When someone really loves you, they don't give up on you. Ever." And she would never give up on Darling, nor had she stopped looking for Kere—not until she'd found him.

Ture leaned his cheek against her hair in a way that reminded her of how Darling held her. "I used to be like you. And when my life fell apart I saw the ugly truth of people. They don't care about anyone but themselves. There's no such thing as friendship. People only hang around when there's something in it for them."

She frowned at the bitterness in his tone. "What are you getting from my friendship? Other than beaten to a pulp and starved to illness?"

He brushed at her hair. "When we're not imprisoned, you make me laugh. And I missed not having a friend. You keep me from being lonely."

Still, she didn't believe his argument. "And when I called you, you came to me to do something dangerous. Why?"

"Because I'm stupid and loyal, even when I know other people wouldn't be that way for me. I learned a long time ago that I never get out of a relationship what I put into it."

She winced as he struck a bruise on her scalp. "You're not the only one who's loyal and decent, Ture. It's why I won't betray Darling. He wouldn't betray me and I know it. When someone really loves you, they find a way to get to you, even in the darkest night, against all odds. Through the worst nightmares, they are there, holding your hand. They're there to stand with you to the end. I don't just believe that. I know it."

Ture scoffed. "When I was a child, I believed that, too. I did. But my hero spit on me and walked out. I hope for your sake that yours doesn't."

"He won't."

Ture sighed. "But he's not here now…"

"He'll come…"

Ture kissed her forehead. "I hope so, honey. Just once in my life, I'd like to be wrong."

"So what's our plan?" Hauk asked as Darling adjusted his trajectory settings.

The link crackled before Nykyrian answered. "Keep Darling alive."

Darling rolled his eyes at Nykyrian's droll tone. "You two are aware of the fact that I am on this frequency, too, correct?"

"Of course we know, sugar," Jayne said. "It wouldn't be any fun to talk about you if you couldn't hear us. So anyone got some juicy Darling tidbits to share? If we push it, we can probably make his skin match his hair... C'mon, Mari, I know you have to have good dirt."

"I do, but... I'd rather keep it to myself. You never know when you're going to need blackmail material."

Jayne laughed over the link. "You suck."

Darling ignored them and returned to Hauk's original question. "The plan is to get the prisoners out and back to Caronese territory before we get killed."

Syn cleared his throat. "I don't mean to be the kick in the crotch, but you do know that this would have been easier had you given us enough time to pull specs and actually formulate a plan of attack."

Probably, but Darling hadn't been willing to wait. "By then, they could have killed another hostage. Or all of them."

No one argued that.

So Darling continued. "We have cursory plans of the prison's layout. Hauk and I will go in to distract the brunt of their forces, while the rest of you pull out my people."

"Uh, you're not going to make anything explode, are you?" Hauk asked.

Darling snorted. "One of these days, we've got to get you over your fear of explosives."

Except there wouldn't be a future for him. Not after this. Darling had no intention of coming back...

This would be his last fight with his friends.

He didn't want to think about them mourning him. He couldn't afford that.

Not now. This wasn't about love or family. It was about vengeance. Making the people who hurt Zarya pay...a life for a life.

Nothing else mattered.

None of them spoke much as they flew in under the League sensors, courtesy of Nykyrian's knowledge of their security procedures and equipment, Syn's hacking abilities—along with the fact that he, Jayne, Ryn, and Nero were four of the very few who'd escaped League prisons and lived, and the updates that Saf had sent to them. Darling had no idea why Maris's little brother was sticking his neck out for them, but he was grateful that whatever madness had infected Kyr hadn't traveled down to Safir.

Yet.

Once they were safely through the barrier, they docked in an area where the League patrols wouldn't be able to see or sense them. Something that was helped by the fact that there was only seven of them flying in first. They would take down the scanner system and alarms so that the prison wouldn't be able to call for help.

At least not until the Sentella had enough firepower and backup to make the League High Command think twice about attacking them.

The beauty about most League prisons, and this one in particular, was that they were outposts far removed from the bulk of the League's army or any largely populated planet. The thought being that if the inmates became too frisky and took control of it, the League could detonate whatever rock the prison was on and take out every prisoner. Yes, they'd lose a few staffers, too, but the League wasn't really worried about collateral damage of their own people since their prisons were staffed with their more problematic soldiers and older assassins who weren't mentally sound enough to be trusted with regular assignments and normal sentient populations.

The drawback for them on this mission was that the staffers were much crazier and more bloodthirsty than the inmates.

The League also kept their prisons remotely located to discourage escaping. If, by some miracle, a prisoner did make it out, in theory their sentries would be able to catch up to them before the escapees could disappear into a populated zone.

Caillen tucked his hands into his pockets as he joined Darling by his ship. "You know, this is a much nicer prison than mine was."

Darling shook his head at Caillen. "Yours wasn't a League prison."

"True. If I ever get locked up again, I'm going to put in a transfer request. Send my butt here."

"Yeah, it's official, Cai," Syn said as he joined them. "You're insane. Trust me, you'd much rather be in your baby jail than this place."

Ryn nodded in agreement. "I definitely concur. I don't ever want to be in a League prison again. Bad flashbacks attacking with a strobe like effect. I'm getting hives just from seeing the security grid."

Darling tried not to think about the fact that he was the reason Ryn had those nightmares.

Life was all about coming to terms with the mistakes made. Learning to live with them even when they cut soul deep.

Syn tsked at Ryn. "Be grateful they let you out. Me, Nero, and

Jayne had to find our own door. Believe me, I'd much rather be breaking in than breaking out."

"Oh yeah," Caillen laughed. "They find out you guys are here and they're liable to keep you. On second thought...What the hell are you doing here, Syn? You get locked up and I have to face the sister-beast. You know, she don't hit like no girl and since I'm her baby brother, she has no compunctions against beating my ass. And I know *you* know this, she strikes below the belt when she fights. I'd like to have a son someday and for once at least match if not outnumber the estrogen army in my home."

Syn arched a brow at his tirade. "Are you finished? Or do I need to sedate you?"

"I'm temporarily finished. However, if you get taken, kill me. I don't want to face Shahara."

Darling would take Caillen to task, but he well understood those sentiments. Shahara could be a hellcat when something set her off. He definitely didn't envy her brother those fights.

Nykyrian, Maris, and Hauk joined them and rounded out their number.

Even though Nero was still in agony with his migraine, he, Chayden, Drake, Fain, Jayne, and the others were on standby to come in and transport their people home as soon they brought down the prison's network.

Like the rest of his group, Darling didn't remove his helmet and he kept the voice distortion on as they quickly prepped for their assigned roles. Only a very small handful were privy to their identities. The rest of the Tavali and Sentella with them knew that Darling fought with them and made weapons for them, but none of them needed to know he was really Kere.

Not until he was dead.

Syn was the only one of them who'd never hidden his real

579

identity. The son of one of the most notorious serial killers and outlaws in history, he didn't care who knew his name or face. Not until he'd married Shahara and had a family to protect.

While Syn worked on hacking the prison's relays and feed, they checked in with their waiting ships to make sure they were ready to land as soon as the shields were down.

"So Nero," Hauk said into his link. "We're going to get out of this, right?"

"Not psychic. I can tell you what is, but not the outcome. Why can't you people get that through your heads?"

"Not people, human. I'm Andarion. Why can't you human's get that through *your* heads?"

Darling cleared his throat to get their attention. "Once Syn has their transmitters down, I'm going in, explosives blaring. I'll have them diving for cover. Let me know when you have the prisoners safe and I'll protect your exit."

Nyk inclined his head to him. "You got it."

Hauk grabbed extra blasters and tucked them into his holster, within easy reach. "I'm ready to cover you. Just don't lob one of your toys at me by mistake."

Darling clapped him on the back. "Don't worry, Dancer. By the time you see it coming, it'll be too late."

"Great...just great. Love your sense of humor." Hauk glanced at Nykyrian over his shoulder. "Why didn't one of us train him on how to use blasters?"

"He liked explosives better," Syn muttered as he typed furiously.

Maris grabbed an extra rifle. "I'll pull the back."

Darling shook his head. "I want you to stay behind. Hauk and I are a team. We've done this thousands of times."

"And I know every thought you have three seconds before you do. An extra gunner won't hurt."

He would argue, but he knew better. Maris always won their fights.

"All right," Syn said. "Feed is down. Sentella and Tavali, land the ships and Kere...it's your show now. Run it."

"Thanks." Darling gave a nod to Maris and Hauk. "Let's paint some walls with entrails."

But before Darling could leave, Nykyrian pulled him into a man hug. "May the gods walk beside you every step of the journey, little brother."

The meant a lot to him coming from the Andarion prince. Nyk had been an atheist who believed in nothing until Kiara had entered his life. For him to whisper a prayer for Darling...

It was special indeed.

One by one, the others did the same, and wished him well. It was something they'd never done before. Which made Darling wonder if they did it to try and keep him from killing himself or if they'd accepted the fact that he wasn't coming back and they wanted to say their last good-byes.

They kept him so long, that it gave Nero and Jayne time to land and join them.

As Darling turned to head for the prison's back entrance, he froze. There was a Kimmerian Corps uniform in with Nero's crew. It stood out as much as Maris's Phrixian battlesuit.

He frowned at the unknown soldier. What the hell was a Kimmerian doing here? They were a vicious breed of freelance assassins. Highly trained, they were known for their ruthless kills and merciless natures. Their uniforms were jet black, and like the Sentella's tinged with whatever color the blood of the wearer was so that it would camouflage them should they ever be wounded.

This one was red blooded.

"Can we help you?" Darling asked him.

"I'm here for you, brother. To the end and beyond."

Darling's jaw went slack as he recognized a voice he knew as well as his own. "Drakari? What the—"

"You're not the only one harboring secrets, Kere. One ass-whipping in a lifetime was enough for me. I won't ever go down like that again, and by the gods, you're not going down today. I won't let you."

Darling wanted to both hug and slap sense into his brother. Simultaneously. "We can't both go in there. You know that." If they both died, it would leave Caron without a governor.

But Drake wouldn't be swayed by logic. "Then we both better get out alive. I mean, c'mon, do you *really* think I should lead anyone anywhere besides the local pub?"

He did have a point with that.

Touched by his brother's loyalty, Darling reached out and cupped the back of Drake's helmet in his hand. He pulled him forward and hugged him close. Nipple to nipple—just to piss him off. "I love you, little brother. You die on me today, and so help me, I'll spend eternity kicking your ass."

"Ditto."

Darling released him and looked to Maris. "Keep him safe."

"I intend to keep you both safe."

And Darling was determined to see his people freed and then to blast this place to the real Kere's domain. After that, while his friends, family, allies, and people headed back to Caron, he was going to fly to the League command center and drive his assassin's blade straight through Kyr's chest cavity where his heart would be if the man had one.

But he didn't tell them that. They'd find out about it later, on the news.

Darling grabbed his backpack and headed for the rear entrance where there would be fewer guards. Thanks to Syn's magic, all their sensors and alarms were deactivated. None of them detected anything.

Not until Darling reached the door and set off an explosion so massive, it brought down the entire back fence and two guard towers.

Hauk made a "heh" sound as the explosion echoed all around them. But for the dampeners in their helmets, they'd be partially deaf from it. "I think you overrang the bell there, Kere. But just in case some of them are sound sleepers, shall I wake them?" He opened a volley of cover fire.

Darling started forward to set another explosive for the inner door that was also locked.

All of a sudden, something went sailing past his head to land in the prison's doorway. It beeped once, then blew the door wide open.

Cursing, Darling jerked around to see Drake pulling out a fresh round from a pocket on his leg and loading it into the launcher that was attached to his right wrist.

"You didn't really think you'd hogged *all* the chemistry and engineering genes, did you?" He locked his weapon and lowered his arm. "I managed to pick up a few things from those diagrams you left laying around the house."

Darling had a whole new respect for his brother's abilities. Drake was right. He wasn't a baby anymore and it was time Darling acknowledged that fact.

"All right. You win. You're an adult who can kick ass on his own. Now get behind me and cover Maris."

Maris laughed. "Face it, babe, you'll always be five years old to your brother. Now get back here with me before I spank you."

Drake returned to Maris's side. "I'm not afraid of that threat, Mari. My fear is that you'd do it and enjoy it."

"I would, but not for the reasons you think ... And only because a good spanking for you is a long time overdue."

"Incoming!" Darling snarled as a rocket came at them from somewhere inside the prison.

While Maris and Drake dove for cover, Darling returned the attack with one of his own.

Hauk moved around to Darling's front so that he could lead, and the two of them did what they did best.

They kicked ass, took names, and nailed that list to the foreheads of their enemies.

Moving forward as a single unit, they tore a hole through the prison big enough to drive a freighter through it. Nykyrian and the rest shouldn't have a bit of trouble getting in here and extracting the prisoners.

Smoke billowed around them as they went through the prison systematically taking out any threat to the others. Soldiers, assassins, androids, unmanned canons ... everything.

Because of the extreme heat, it interfered with the enhanced vision in their helms. Darling switched his optics as Syn's voice navigated him through the halls, toward the cells where his people were most likely being held.

"We're right behind you," Nykyrian said.

League soldiers poured out into the halls as alarms blared everywhere. One of their techs must have brought part of their system back online.

Ignoring the intense, piercing sound, Darling concentrated on confusing their enemies as much as he could.

He took a number of shots straight to his body from their blasters, but so far nothing had penetrated his armor. While those shots bruised and hurt, they didn't wound. And so long as those shots didn't wound, he could do major damage.

An assassin came out of the smoke on his right. Darling threw the explosive in his hand in the opposite direction, then tackled the assassin. They went for each other with everything they had.

Darling wrenched the man's arm and sent him to the ground at the same time Maris came in behind another assassin and cut his throat before the assassin could shoot Darling.

As Maris dropped back, Darling realized his friend was alone. "Where's Drake?"

"With Nero."

Good. Nero would make sure nothing happened to his brother.

As they blew through the first doors to the holding cells, Chayden cursed through the link in Darling's ear. "They've split the prisoners up. There are more in the basement and on the first, fifth, and eighth floors."

"We're heading to the basement," Darling told them. That would be the heaviest fortified area where they would most likely be keeping the gerents and Resistance leaders. And from down there, his explosives could do more structural damage.

It'd be easy to set the charges that would bring down the whole damn place.

This is for you, Zarya.

"Get everyone out," Darling told them.

"Trying to. Promise I'm not scratching my butt." Chayden's words were punctuated by blaster fire.

Darling didn't comment as they made it to the stairs and blasted open the door off its hinges. He listened to the others who were making good progress extracting his people and running them to the transports.

They were all taking heavy fire, but so far no fatalities and very few went down who couldn't get back up.

Completely calm, he lobbed three more charges down the stairs in front of them to handle anything that might be waiting as a surprise. They were bio-charges that wouldn't detonate anything inorganic such as the stairs they were using.

However, if you had flesh on your body...

You didn't want to be near them when they went off.

At the bottom of the stairs, they stepped over the remnants of several guards.

Darling pulled up short when he saw the holding cell area and realized how bad it was down here for those prisoners. Whoever was being held in those cells was extremely important to the League. All the assassins had fallen back to this area to protect it.

This was most likely where Zarya had died.

That knowledge almost sent him to his knees.

Suppressing his agony, Darling started to go forward, but Maris caught him and whirled him around, then pinned him to the wall.

Armor-piercing blasts flared and would have ripped him to shreds had Maris not acted.

But it wasn't until Darling moved that he realized Maris had been wounded.

Badly. At least a dozen rounds had hit him. Most didn't penetrate his armor, but three were definitely embedded in his body.

"I'm all right," Maris assured him in a strained tone. "Nothing major pierced...Except...my battlesuit." He stepped back to glance down at it and let out a sound of extreme anger. "Would you look at what those bastards did? They ruined it! Handmade, Phrixian silk. Do you know how hard this is to come by? And the blood is impossible to get out of it, especially after it's soaked in." He straightened up and Darling was sure he was glaring at him from underneath the helm that hid all his features. "And you wonder why I hate battle so much." He gestured down to his torn battlesuit. "You see!"

Darling laughed in spite of the danger. "You're insane, Mari."

"Ha! It doesn't matter how you feel so long as you look good while you feel it."

"We need to get you out of here."

Maris fisted his hand in the fabric at Darling's shoulder and held him by his side. "Not without you."

Darling growled at him. "You're such a stubborn bastard. I really hate you."

"I hate you, too..."

Wanting to strangle him, Darling moved forward, down the hallway, blasters out so that Maris could check the doors behind him. But just as he neared the end, he realized the mistake they'd made...

"Do you hear that?"

Zarya could barely understand Ture's words. Something kept buzzing and it wouldn't stop. "Hear what?"

A blast hit their door. At first she thought she imagined it. Until it struck again.

And again.

Could it be...?

You're dreaming. It's not real. Just a hallucination brought on by your fever and pain.

In her mind, she imagined Darling carrying her out of this nightmare like he'd done when she'd sprained her ankle in the kitchen. *I swear, if I get out of this alive, I will never leave the palace again.*

An instant later, the door lifted. Smoke billowed into the room, filling it instantly. She choked and coughed, trying to breathe around it.

Ture tightened his arms around her, holding her close as two League soldiers spilled into the room. Preoccupied with whatever was happening in the hallway, neither of them looked back at them.

"Grab the woman!" someone shouted from outside the cell. "We have to have her or we can't leave."

The two soldiers turned around.

Zarya's heart pounded as she tried to understand what was happening. Why they wanted to take her again. Aching to the point it hurt to breathe, she didn't move until they closed in on her—in their hurry, they'd forgotten to handcuff her.

Their mistake.

She reverted to her strict training. Grabbing the blaster from the first one, she used it to shoot his partner. Shrieking, the soldier went down.

Before she could move, the one she'd grabbed brought his fist down across her face. The room spun, nauseating her.

Ture lunged at him and slammed him back against the wall as more soldiers poured into the room.

Zarya fought as hard as she could, but she was injured and outnumbered. Still, she didn't let it daunt her.

There were more battle sounds out in the hallway.

A new group of soldiers rushed her and Ture. She leveled her blaster at them and pulled the trigger, only to discover it was out of charges.

Turning it around in her hand, she intended to use it as a blunt object against their heads.

But the men didn't make it. Before they could reach Ture and her, blasts struck them and sent them to the ground at their feet.

A second later, the smoke cleared enough to show another soldier coming inside to check on the League soldiers who'd fallen.

He'd barely stepped inside before he was attacked by three more League soldiers. With skills that defied description, he turned and caught the first one with a blow so hard, he shattered his attacker's nose. The next, he flipped and stabbed and when the third saw what awaited him in the bodies that were littered all over the room, he turned around and retreated.

The newcomer turned to face them.

He wasn't with the Sentella. Her heart sank as she saw the burgundy battlesuit with foreign markings she couldn't identify.

Unable to fight him, she prayed this was an ally and not another enemy out to do more damage to her and Ture.

Bleeding profusely from several wounds, he froze the instant he caught sight of her. Then he spoke in a language she didn't recognize.

Although... there was something vaguely familiar about it.

Where have I heard it before?

More blasts ricocheted in the hallway behind him.

In one smooth, impressive move, the soldier hit the floor, slid on his knees and spun around to shoot the three League guards who ran in behind him. He rolled over and came to a stop by her side.

"Zarya?"

Tears filled her eyes as she recognized that deep voice. "Maris?"

He nodded. "Can you walk?"

Before she could respond, the room was invaded by even more League soldiers.

Darling heard the mayday from Maris, but he couldn't get to the room where they had Maris pinned down. There were League soldiers everywhere now. All of them shooting.

Were they cloning the bastards in a back room somewhere?

Instead of their numbers decreasing, they seemed to be multiplying by the heartbeat. Like some mythic beast. Kill one and two emerged to take his place.

"Mari?" he called, needing to know his friend hadn't gone down.

No answer.

Darling checked for Maris's vitals on his bio scanner.

There weren't any. Nothing at all was registering. His heart stopped beating as cold panic consumed him. And his anger went to a place so fierce and foul that it screwed up his vision even more than the jerking did.

Letting out his battle cry, he charged the soldiers who had him cut off from Maris. All Darling could think about was getting to Mari before it was too late.

He flipped one assassin who came at him over his back and stabbed him through the throat. Turning, he took down another and then shot a third and a fourth.

As Darling came around the corner, he dropped a bead on the next target who was in the room where Maris had gone.

Then he froze in place.

No.

It couldn't be.

Blinking, he tried to make sense of what he saw. To understand something that couldn't be. Maris was in the room with a woman in his arms. A woman who wasn't supposed to be here...

"Zarya?" Darling breathed as his knees went weak.

Maris nodded.

"Darling?" The sound of her voice brought tears to his eyes.

Still, he couldn't fathom what he saw. Not until Maris handed her off to him. The warmth of her skin...

Her scent...

She was alive.

It wasn't a dream. It was real and she was here. With him. Not dead. Not missing...

Alive.

Her face was badly bruised and her features pale, but it didn't matter to him. She'd never looked more beautiful than she did right now.

Tears fell down his cheeks as he clutched her tight.

"I knew you'd come for me," she breathed, laying her hand against his helmet. "I knew it."

"She never once lost faith in you."

Darling looked past her to see the man Maris was now helping to stand upright. Like Zarya, he was filthy and bruised from repeated beatings.

The man licked his chapped lips before he spoke again. "I told her it wasn't feasible. That you'd never find us, but she was right. She said you'd promised her that you would bust hell itself open to get to her. And that you never lied." His legs buckled.

Maris caught him before he fell, then swept him up in his arms. "Don't worry. I'll get you to the medics as soon as I can," Maris assured him.

Darling started to remove his helmet so that he could kiss her, but Zarya stopped him.

"They can't know who you are, sweetie," she whispered. "It would be an act of war for the Caronese governor to attack a League facility."

She was right about that.

Still, with her in his arms, alive and breathing, nothing else mattered. Nothing at all. Everything around him faded until it was just the two of them.

He was so centered on absorbing every part of her that he forgot where he was, and what he was doing.

Something brought home an instant later when she reached down and grabbed his blaster, then shot over his shoulder. He turned to see a League soldier who'd had a clear shot at him. But for her, he'd have probably died just then.

Maris growled deep in his throat before he pulled back into the room. "They're coming in fast and furious." He set the man in his arms down.

Darling hated letting Zarya go, especially since he had her again. But he had no choice. Not if they were to make it out of here.

And he had no intention of dying today.

He set her on her feet, then swung around. "Let them bring it. You ready, Mari?"

"You know I hate fighting. But I think a little payback for my battlesuit might actually make me feel better for once."

"I know it'll do great things for me." Darling pulled a fully charged blaster off his holster and exchanged it for the one she'd shot. "Stay behind us."

Maris handed one to the man. "Do you know how to shoot?"

"Not straight... in more ways than one. But if I aim at their feet I can hopefully wound them until one of you finishes them off. And that way if I really miss, I won't kill an ally. You'll just limp a little."

Maris laughed. "Thanks for the consideration. I'm Maris, by the way, and I should probably warn you that it didn't go well for the last guy who wounded me."

"I'm Ture."

Darling tapped his link to call the others. "Hauk? You still evaccing civs?"

"Yeah. You pinned?"

"No. We're coming out of the last cell. I just didn't want you to shoot us by mistake. I know how caught up you get in a fight."

Hauk hissed. "Why are you bitching about that again? I only shot once and it was an accident caused by your premature exploding problem. Had you not startled me while I was changing our charges, it wouldn't have happened."

"Anyway," Darling said, ignoring his outburst, "there are four of us. Don't fire." He turned then to see Zarya's face before he plowed into the thick of the hallway battle.

Zarya paused as she watched Maris and Darling open a hole for them through the thick enemy fire. Fearless and skilled, they moved in total synchrony.

While she'd known Darling was exceptional, she now realized why Maris got so offended whenever she questioned his abilities. He was an incredible fighter in his own right. No wonder he was decorated.

She and Ture stayed behind them with her giving cover fire as Maris and Darling led them down the hall, then up the stairs. The stench of burning wires turned her stomach. But it was much better than the stale air of her cell.

They'd barely reached the upstairs landing when the entire building went dark. Darling and Maris fell back to cover her and Ture.

"They've reestablished their connection," Syn warned them through their headsets. "We need to tel-ass, folks, or we're going to lose our posteriors."

Darling swapped out his charges before they ran out of juice. "We're on our way."

As they rounded a corner, a group of assassins opened fire. Darling shielded her while Maris covered Ture. Making sure to keep himself between her and the volley, Darling returned their attack. "I could really use the tricom right now."

"Sorry. It was broken when I was taken."

"Figures." Darling cleared the assassins, then nodded to Maris. They started moving again.

Slowly, they made their way down the hall until they met up with Nemesis who was helping a large group of prisoners get to safety.

Zarya's panic welled up inside her as she remembered what had happened the last time Nemesis had been in a room with her.

He'd tossed her to Jayne.

"Is everyone out?" Darling asked the legendary killer.

Nemesis nodded. "The last group is coming down behind you."

Zarya gaped in disbelief. Even with the distortion added to disguise his voice, she recognized Nykyrian's syntax and tone.

Now there was a billion credits worth of knowledge. His was the most guarded identity of any Sentella member.

Now she understood why.

Just as her group joined theirs and she saw some of the people who'd been kidnapped with her, the walls around them flickered.

Kyr's face flashed, then enlarged to the size of the walls that worked as a transmission monitor.

Talk about creepy. She felt like she'd stumbled into a horror story.

And Kyr was furious over the attack. "Do you know who I am?"

Nykyrian snorted derisively. "We know. We just don't give a shit."

Curling his lip, Kyr raked him with a repugnant glare. "You have breached the sanctity of one of our prisons. Have you any idea the sentence you've brought down on your heads?"

Now it was Darling's turn to scoff. "Add it to the other twelve dozen death sentences we carry."

A tic started in Kyr's jaw. "I don't think you truly understand the magnitude of what you're doing. Return my prisoners to their cells or—"

"Fuck. You," Darling snarled, punctuating each word.

Kyr's nostrils flared while he did an amazing job of keeping his temper under control. "Those prisoners do not belong to you. They are League property. You have absolutely no right to them."

Before anyone realized what he was doing, Darling snatched his helmet off and threw it to the ground so hard, it bounced three feet high.

Kyr held the same shocked expression Zarya was pretty sure they all held. Every gerent and Resistance worker around her was rendered speechless and spellbound by Kere's real identity.

Fearless, Darling went straight up to the wall on the right and leveled a killing glare at Kyr. "The hell you say. They are *my* people, not yours. You sent your army into *my* territory and took not just my citizens, but *my* consort. How dare *you*!"

Kyr gave Zarya a look that said she hadn't bathed in a month or more. "She's *not* your consort."

Darling shook his head in denial. "She wears my ring and was officially bound to me when we were children—something sanctified and approved by *your* predecessor."

Zarya gasped at his unexpected disclosure. Was any of that true? She was desperate to know, but didn't dare interrupt them.

"By all laws," Darling continued, "she is my consort. And five minutes after I get her home, she will officially be my wife."

Kyr arched a daring brow. "So you're declaring war on us, then."

Zarya inwardly cringed as she realized what Darling had done. For her.

The moment he'd yanked his helmet off and allowed Kyr to know Kere's identity, he'd legally declared war on the League.

Now, there was no going back.

But Darling was nothing, if not a brilliant politician. "Interesting concept. I would say that *you* declared it on us when you marched your army into our empire and destroyed our property, then kidnapped our citizens. And now we're answering it. No one seizes my people. I don't care who you *think* you are."

"We were invited in by your own council who wanted you removed from power."

"Were you?" Darling asked with a hint of laughter in his voice. "That's not what I heard. In fact, I have the entire CDS who will swear they never asked for you to intervene. That you took it upon yourself to attack us."

"Do you really think they'll back you over me?"

Darling grinned evilly. "Since they declared me emperor, yeah, I do."

"You have no idea what you're unleashing right now, verikon."

Zarya wasn't sure what that word meant, or the language it belonged to, but from Darling's reaction, it was obvious he knew it well.

"And neither do you, ciratile. You *ever* try this shit again with me and mine, and I will rape and plunder the village, and burn the motherfucker to the ground..." He looked around at the bodies on the floor. "And as you've seen here today, there ain't nothing you bitches can do to stop me. Talk is cheap. Pain is free. And I'm peddling the shit out of it. So you come on and get some."

Kyr laughed as if he relished the thought. "War it is. Good luck, *Emperor.*" He sneered that title. "No one will *ever* support you in this. You're about to find out what happens to nations that fight alone."

Nykyrian jerked his helmet off and moved to stand beside Darling. "You would be wrong there, Zemen. Not only does he have the full backing of Nemesis and the Sentella, he has that of my people. From *both* sides. Human *and* Andarion."

"And you can add mine to it, too," Caillen said as he exposed his face. "The Exeterians fear nothing, and I'm pretty sure the Qillaqs will back us, too. After all, they love a good fight. The bigger, the bloodier, the better."

Fain, Ryn, and Chayden didn't expose their faces, but they stood shoulder to shoulder behind Darling. "The Tavali will always fight and back the Sentella, especially against the League."

Kyr took a full minute before he spoke again. "All of you will regret this."

Darling smirked. "The war is on. Can't wait for our first dance."

An instant later, the screens went dark.

"How rude!" Jayne tsked. "It's a good thing he's on the other side of the universe, otherwise, I'd have to hunt him down and school him."

Syn let out an evil laugh. "Yes, but not rude on his part." He held up his wrist computer. "I killed the feed. Five more seconds of looking at him and I'd have hurled." He turned his attention to Darling. "Remind me later that we really need to send you to anger management therapy."

Darling widened his eyes innocently at Syn as he pulled Zarya against him. "I have no idea what you're talking about, Rit. I'm all good."

"Yeah, but we're not," Hauk said. "We just got busted."

Fain draped an arm around Hauk's shoulders. "*We're* not busted, little brother. Only the morons who showed their faces." He passed a pointed stare to Nykyrian, Darling, Syn, and Caillen.

Caillen shrugged. "What the hell? I never liked feeling safe, anyway. That's for old women."

Jayne came down the stairs, holding Nero against her.

Darling rushed toward them. "What happened?"

"He protected me and got shot."

"I'll be fine," Nero said with a grimace.

"Thought you weren't psychic," Darling reminded him.

"I'm not. But I know my body and right now, my head really hates you, Dar." Nero winced in pain as he met Zarya's gaze. "Don't worry. You're both fine."

She burst into tears, then rushed to hug him in a way that made Darling jealous. "Thank you! I've been so scared."

Why was she hugging Nero over the fact that she and he were safe?

Nero patted her on the back, then stepped away. "Darling? You really should show her those papers you found."

Darling sighed. "I hate it when you do that."

"I know. Now I need to lie down for a few decades."

Hauk took over from Jayne and draped Nero's arm around his shoulders. "Let's all get out of here before reinforcements come. Kyr may be on the other side of the universe, but not all of his army is with him."

Darling agreed. They had a lot of civilians to take care of. The last thing they needed was to fight more League soldiers with them in the way.

While the others left, Darling walked slowly toward Zarya. She looked so tired and pale. But even with those ugly bruises marring her face, she was still the most beautiful woman he'd ever seen. "Are you all right, baby?"

She bit her lip. "Funny you should use that word...According to Nero, I'm pregnant."

For a full ten seconds, he couldn't breathe as those words sank in. And here he'd stupidly thought that Nero was talking about the two of them. "Are you sure?"

"Nero swears he's not wrong."

And he wouldn't be...

Zarya was pregnant.

Undefined emotions ripped through him all at once. Stark terror. Panic. But above all was a joy so profound it left him reeling.

He was going to be a father...

Have a baby.

And that thought brought a tidal wave of pain crashing down around him. "I saw a photo of you dead, Zarya. I thought I'd lost you." He couldn't keep his voice from cracking. "I came here only to avenge you, and to die. Now…" He placed his shaking hand over her stomach where his child was growing inside her. "Now you tell me that you're pregnant…why in the name of the gods did you leave the palace in that condition?"

She clutched his hand in both of hers and pressed it flat, wishing they could feel the baby move. But most of all, she wanted him to understand how much he meant to her. "Because you were in danger. I didn't want to lose *you*. Not after what I went through when I couldn't find you. I thought that if I went to the Resistance, I'd be able to talk sense into them. I had no idea they were under League surveillance, or that the League was planning an attack on them."

He wanted to choke her for that. But most of all, he wanted to kiss her and make love to her until neither one of them could walk. "I knew they were under surveillance, and that the League was going to attack them. If you'd only told me be—"

"You would have insisted on coming with me. And that wouldn't have gone over well with them. I had to go alone. I'm sorry."

"I hate it when you're right." But he was so grateful to have her back. Alive. Nothing else mattered. He brushed his hand over her bruised cheek. "Who hit you?"

"You killed him in the hallway."

"I wish I'd known who it was. I'd have made it hurt a lot more."

Zarya kissed his lips as joy tore through her. "You're being so reasonable about all of this that it scares me."

"I promise, I'm going to be mad later. Right now, I'm just so relieved to have you with me that you have a free pass to do anything you want."

She clutched him against her and inhaled the warm, masculine scent of his skin. "Thank you."

"For what?"

"Coming to get me. And I'm so incredibly sorry for everything that was done to you while you were in our custody. I know I've said it before, but it's never enough. And now, after all of this... I fully understand why you can never trust me. But I swear to you, on the life of everything I hold sacred, that I will never, ever, ever, ever leave you alone again. Not even if you beg me to."

He kissed her breathless. "You have nothing to apologize for, Zarya."

She knew better. "That's your relief still talking." She kissed the tip of his nose. "But that's okay. I still love you."

"And I love you." He scooped her up in his arms, and started down the hallway.

"What are you doing?"

"Attempting to sweep you off your feet. Is it working?"

She smiled at him. "Honey, you did that the minute I saw you in my cell."

"Good. 'Cause you stole my heart the first time you looked up at me."

"I stole it?"

He flashed a wicked grin. "Good point. I gave it to you. I just hope you learn to take better care of it than the rings I keep buying you."

EPILOGUE

Three months later

Zarya had her eyes closed as she sat on the cold marble floor with her long, maroon silk lace dress fanning out around her while she leaned back against Darling. Cradling her in his arms, he held a cool cloth to her forehead.

She groaned out loud in utter misery. "I can't believe this is how I'm spending my wedding...sick on the bathroom floor."

Nuzzling her cheek, he laughed softly in her ear. "Well, at least I have it all on video. The priest asking you to confirm your vows to me, and you instantly dashing off to throw up. Kind of apropos really, given *our* relationship. I'm so glad to know that the concept of being married to me makes you sick to your stomach."

"You're not funny."

He laid a tender kiss on her bare shoulder. "Sure I am. You'd laugh too if you hadn't just tossed up a vital organ or two."

Smiling in spite of her queasiness, she cupped his perfect cheek in her hand. How he could be so kind and find humor in this given the insult she'd inadvertently dealt him, was beyond her. But then that was why she loved him so much. "I'm so sorry, Darling."

"Don't be." He placed another kiss on her shoulder. "I'm quite happy right now. I have the best view in the palace, and I'm willing to sit here all day, holding you if you want."

She slid her gaze up to see him staring down her décolletage. The hunger in his eyes and the sudden sensation of him bulging against her hip set fire to her own blood. "You're so bad," she teased.

"Can't help it. I find you completely irresistible."

A light knock sounded on the door.

"Come in," Darling called.

It was Gera with Shahara, Desideria, Jayne, Maris, Ture, Sorche, and Lise. They came into the room to form a semicircle around them.

Could this day be any more embarrassing?

Maris passed a smug look at Ture. "I told you he wouldn't be angry at her."

Ture folded his arms over his chest. "I'm impressed he hasn't at least choked her. I don't think I could be so kind if you did that to me, Mari. So take note. I don't tolerate vomiting on me in the midst of a public event, especially when it's being videoed."

"Then I shall forever endeavor to confine all such drama to the washroom."

Zarya would laugh at his comment if she wasn't afraid it would unsettle her stomach again.

Kneeling beside her, Ture placed a kind hand to her brow. "How are you doing, sweetie?"

She tilted her head back to see the concern on Darling's face while he continued to hold her. "Darling needs a new pair of shoes, and I need my dignity repaired. Other than that, I'm totally miserable. I can't believe I did this at my wedding. I'm so humiliated."

Returning to stand over her, Ture bit his lip. "Look on the bright side, it's not really *your* dignity that should be bruised, hon.

Darling's the one who was left at the altar while you rushed off gagging...Great timing, by the way. The media is having a field day with it."

With a light laugh, Maris wrapped his arms around Ture's waist and rested his chin on Ture's shoulder. "Thank the gods, if we get married I don't have to worry about you having morning sickness in the middle of the ceremony."

Ture laid his hand over Maris's cheek. "Exactly. If I get sick, you definitely know you're the cause of it."

Shahara laughed. "Yeah, you both might want to be careful what you eat beforehand."

It still amazed Zarya how close Ture and Maris had become in such a short amount of time. Since both had been hurt badly in the past by others and given the depth of Maris's feelings toward Darling, they'd started off very slow after they'd returned home—just friends who hung out. But as of last week when Ture's brother had gone after Maris for the bounty on his head and Ture had chosen Maris's well-being over his brother's, they'd become inseparable.

She was so glad to see them both happy. They deserved to have someone love them who treated them with respect and deference.

Gera brought over a fresh cloth and switched it with the one Darling held against her forehead. "Would you like me to have the priest come in here to finish, my lady?"

"Oh goodness, no." Nothing would be worse than to have her vows broadcasted across the universe from the bathroom while she sat on the floor.

Not that they needed to take their vows. Technically, they were already married. As Darling had promised, he'd made her his wife the moment they returned to the palace.

He hadn't even given her time to clean up. The priest had literally met them at the door, ready to go, and they'd been married just inside the foyer.

One thing about her first baby, when he made a promise, he kept it.

But for her to be accepted as Darling's legal consort and for their child to be acknowledged as the legal Caronese heir, they needed a public ceremony before the gerents and people.

She drew a ragged breath. "I think I'll be all right. Let's try this again."

"Are you sure?" Darling's voice was filled with warm concern.

She nodded.

Carefully, he helped her to her feet.

Desideria handed her a small package that was wrapped in a lace kerchief. "It's lerin root. Place a small bit under your tongue and it'll help with the nausea."

"Are you sure?" She'd never heard of it before.

"Absolutely. My people have been using it for hundreds of years, and other than some minor brain damage, which can't really be linked to it, no one's suffered from using it. And I'm pretty sure the brain damage comes later in the child's life, like during training." She winked at Zarya.

Laughing, Zarya tried it while Desideria put a bit under her own tongue, too.

She arched a curious brow that caused Desideria to blush.

"Yes, there's a reason I just happen to have some on me."

Zarya beamed for her and Caillen. "Congratulations! I'm so happy for you."

"Thank you, and I pray this one is a boy. I'm not sure poor Caillen could handle being surrounded by any more women during holiday meals."

Zarya placed her hand over her stomach as she realized that her symptoms had all but vanished. Stunned, she widened her eyes. "It really does work. Thank you."

"You're welcome. I'll make sure and have Chayden bring you

more. I'm one of those women who has morning sickness from the moment of conception until birth. I hope you don't."

Her, too. She'd actually been lucky. This was her first bout of it. But what timing…

Sorche returned her small bouquet to her. "You sure you feel up to this?"

Zarya glanced at Darling and smiled. "Absolutely."

Maris kicked off his shoes, then scooted them toward Darling with his foot. "Change with me, hon. I'm not the one being broadcast all over the universe."

Darling stepped away from her to exchange his shoes with Maris. "Thanks."

"I would say anytime, but I hope we never have to do this again." Maris smiled at her. "I love you, dearest, but I don't want to wear your DNA."

"I'm so sorry."

Maris wrinkled his nose at her. "Don't be. We're all waiting for that little one to come out so we can spoil it unmercifully. I've always wanted to be an overindulgent aunt."

"Don't feel bad," Jayne said graciously. "I promise you, this isn't nearly as bad as my last pregnancy. I tossed all over my mother-in-law's prized sofa that's been in her family for three generations. I'm still banned from her house, and my baby's about to start school."

Zarya laughed.

While she and Jayne had gotten off to a bad start, she now counted the female assassin as one of her dearest friends.

Clapping her hands to get their attention, Gera took charge. "Emperor, we need you to leave now, and I'll have the ladies and gentlemen resume their places."

Zarya saw the hesitation in Darling's expression. She placed her hand on his cheek again. Goodness, he was so breathtaking in his royal uniform with those blue eyes gleaming at her. She hoped their baby had the same coloring as its father. "I'm fine, really. Desideria's root is working miracles."

"You know we won't let anything happen to her," Maris assured him.

Nodding, Darling took her hand and kissed it. "I'll be waiting." He made a formal bow, then reluctantly released her hand and left them.

Maris held his arm out to her. Since she had no male relatives left, he was doing her the honor of presenting her to Darling for the wedding.

Ture, Shahara, Lise, Desideria, and Sorche made up her wedding party. Kiara would have been here as well had she not gone into labor a few days ago. So both she and Nykyrian, and their entire brood, were attending via video uplinks.

Ture turned and frowned at her. "Oh give us a minute, please, Gera. I need to repair her makeup. We can't have her going out there with it smeared."

Gera gasped as she looked at her. "I can't believe I didn't notice."

When Gera started forward to help, Ture placed a kind hand on her arm. "I have it, hon. Get the others ready and we'll be right out. Mari? Can you run and get my bag out of our room? I have sealant in it that should keep her eyeliner from running again."

As soon as they were gone, Ture pulled a tissue out of his sleeve and dabbed it under her right eye. "Look up."

She did.

Ture quickly repaired her face, then smoothed her hair, and adjusted the small headdress that matched her maroon gown. Smiling in satisfaction, he straightened her official state necklace around her neck. "You are such a vision."

She didn't believe a word of it. Not for a minute, but she was grateful to him for his kindness.

"You're the best, sweetie." She straightened the ribbons on her bouquet. "Ture, do you mind if I ask you a personal question?"

"Not at all."

"Are you really happy here?" He'd never been the kind of person who suffered pomp or ceremony well. And those were two things that Maris seemed to adore and thrive on.

His eyes brightened with exuberance. "Oh, honey, how could you doubt it for even a second? I never thought I'd be in love like this. But Mari..."

He smiled a smile that lit up his entire face. "He's so funny and sweet. Considerate. And when he goes all military tough around me..." He shivered. "I now understand exactly what you meant when you talked about Darling. For the first time in my life, I honestly believe that Maris would walk through hell to keep me safe. I've never had that before, not once."

It was true. Like Maris, Ture had been abandoned by everyone he'd ever loved.

His lips quivered. "I can't thank you enough for introducing us."

Was that a euphemism or what?

"I can't believe you're thanking me for getting you imprisoned and tortured."

He shrugged nonchalantly. "Believe me when I say Maris is totally worth it."

"I'm so glad you feel that way." Returning his smile, she allowed him to take her outside to where the others waited.

He took the spray from Maris's hand and quickly applied it to her face, then he stepped away.

She paused a second to glance at every member of the small group around her. This was her family now...A strange motley bunch of tracers, pirates, aristos, and assassins. Yet they were the most decent beings in the universe and they were always here when she needed them.

Best of all, they cared. Truly and deeply about Darling and her. In all her life, she'd never imagined this as her reality.

And she wouldn't have it any other way.

Just as Gera started to organize the procession, the doors opened.

Zarya was floored as Darling's mother swept into the room with a grand flourish. Paying no attention to anyone else in the room, not even Lise, she planted herself in front of Zarya.

Her expression unreadable, Natale clutched at a small wooden box in her hands.

Please tell me that's not an explosive device of some sort...

With Darling's family, one could never tell.

"Have I missed the ceremony?"

"No, Momair," Lise answered in a suspicious tone from behind her. "It was interrupted."

Natale didn't ask how or why, she merely gave a curt nod. "Good. I was afraid I'd run out of time. Now leave us."

Without hesitation, Gera ushered the others out immediately. Except for Lise who moved to stand next to her mother. "Don't tarnish this for Darling, I beg you. He deserves to have one normal, happy memory. Please, let him have it."

She gave her daughter a withering glare. "Leave."

Lise sighed before she obeyed.

Zarya was torn between the urge to slap Darling's mother for all the things she'd put him through, and the one that wanted some answers about his past and why his mother had mistreated him when he'd done nothing to deserve it.

Lady Natale looked her up and down with that same emotionless gaze.

Zarya waited for Natale to judge her lacking.

And when his mother finally spoke, Zarya wasn't sure if it was a set down or what. "You're not showing yet. I'm sure that's a relief to you."

"Not really. I can't wait until my belly shows and I can feel the baby moving."

A sad light darkened her eyes. "It is one of the most miraculous experiences. That time when you know your child's safe and that no one can hurt it. When it's just the two of you, night and day. I used to talk to my babies all the time when I was pregnant. Dream about how they'd be once they arrived."

Her lips curled into a bittersweet smile. "They're never what you think they'll be. But that's not a bad thing. Every day they grow, they amaze you."

Clearing her throat, Natale opened her small box and stared at its contents. "I know I shouldn't be here. That neither you nor Darling wants me here, and I understand why. I almost didn't come, but..." Her eyes clouded over as if she'd lost herself to some distant memory.

"But what?" Zarya prompted when she didn't finish.

Tears glistened in Natale's eyes as she placed the box in Zarya's hand. "This belongs to Darling and I wanted him to have it from you. Don't tell him I was here, please. Like Lise said, he deserves one happy, unspoiled memory, and I don't want my presence to taint it."

This wasn't the selfish bitch she'd imagined Natale to be. Rather, she was a woman in extreme pain. One who did appear to care about her children.

So, why had she said such awful things to Darling?

"My lady, may I ask you something?"

Natale met Zarya's gaze levelly and sincerely. "I know what you're going to ask. I do love my son. Just as I love all my children.

But loving someone doesn't mean that you always want to be around them. Whenever Darling looks at me, I see his hatred for me and I can't stand it. He was always cold, even as an infant. He didn't want me to hold him, not even to feed him. I tried not to let it bother me, but it was hard. He was my first child and I'd made all these plans about how close we'd be. Darling would have none of it. And when his father died, it became worse. When they brought him home from school for the funeral preparations, he wouldn't even speak to me. When I met him at the door, he looked at me like he wished I was the one who'd died, and it killed something inside me. Something that has made me want to hurt him the same way he hurt me."

"My lady, I think you greatly misjudged him. When Darling is deeply hurt by anything, he draws within himself. It's not hatred. It's how he copes. But if you don't leave him alone, if you continue to stay with him, he will embrace you. It's not immediate. But I promise you, he loves you more than you know."

Natale squeezed her hand. "I'm glad he has you."

Unsure of how to respond, Zarya looked down at the box to find a man's wedding band inside. "I don't understand. What is this?"

"It's the royal governor's matrimonial seal that is presented to every governor by his first wife at their wedding. I took it off Drux's hand before Arturo could steal it, and...I've kept it safe for this day." Her hand visibly shaking, she wiped at her eyes. "Given Darling's declared homosexuality, I thought it would be Drake who wore it. But I'm glad to see it go to Darling."

Clearing her throat, Natale picked it up to show it to Zarya. "When Darling was little, his father would take it off and place it on his tiny finger before he made Darling recite his rules of conduct. I always waited for Darling to protest having to do it, but he was such a little man about it. All he wanted was to please his father and make him proud. He would clench his hand." Natale demonstrated it with her own fist. "And stand tall, then repeat all twenty flawlessly. When he was done, he'd take the ring off and stare at it in awe. And every time he gave it back to his father, he'd promise that one day he would be the best governor Caron ever had."

Her eyes filled with agony, Natale covered her mouth with her hand. "Unlike Drake and Lise, he actually remembers his father. The two of them were *so* close. Darling worshiped the ground he stood on." She swallowed and lowered her hand. "He's just like his father, you know? It's so hard to look at him sometimes when all I see is everything I've lost. He has Drux's voice and his bearing and mannerisms." She almost broke down into tears again, but somehow she caught herself. "Anyway, I should go now and leave you to him."

Zarya placed her hand on her arm. "Please, don't."

"You don't understand."

"I think, I do. Both of my parents are dead, and you're the only one Darling has. Please honor him by attending the ceremony. I know it would mean a lot to him to have you here. He does love you, my lady. He always has."

"And I do love him...It's just been so hard at times. But if you're sure..."

"I am."

Nodding, Natale squeezed her hand, then left.

Zarya wasn't sure if his mother had really stayed for the ceremony or not until they opened the doors to the chapel. Natale stood just a few feet away from Darling.

The moment her gaze met his, Zarya felt a rush of heat go through her. Even though they were married, she still trembled as the weight of her position hit her. After this, she would officially be the Grand Empress of Caron. One day, her child...*their* child would rule this empire.

It was terrifying to think of all that responsibility. It was hard enough to raise a child. Period. To raise one who was destined to lead a vast empire...

Darling was lucky she wasn't running for the door.

But as Maris walked her down the aisle and she saw Nero in the crowd, she relaxed. Nero had been right to tell Darling to show her the papers that Darling had found.

Even now after she'd seen them and read the files, she still didn't believe it.

The reason why Darling's father had brought him to her home that very first trip was so that her father could meet the boy he was betrothing her to.

They'd been destined for each other from the moment of her birth. It gave her chills every time she thought about that.

Nero's words haunted her. *"In all incarnations, except one, he would have always married you."*

And in that one exception, Darling had died as a teenager.

"You are the only woman he would have ever married, Zarya. Never doubt his loyalty or his love for you."

She curtsied to Maris before he handed her over to Darling.

Darling bowed formally and kissed her inner wrist. It was so scandalous an action that several gerents gasped. But she didn't care. Lacing his fingers with hers, Darling tucked her hand into the crook of his elbow and held it there while the people cheered for them.

Ever since their return, the Caronese people and gerents, and especially the Resistance and royal guard had embraced their emperor. They had declared him their pride. And referred to her as the heart of the people.

Her throat tight, she was so grateful that now the only ones they had to fight were the League. It wasn't an easy war, but it was much better than having to fight their own.

And when she placed his father's ring on his hand, Darling trembled.

"Where did you get this?" he whispered, clenching his fist just the way his mother had demonstrated.

She indicated Natale with a tilt of her head. "Your mother brought it for you. She wanted to make sure you had it for your wedding."

A shocked smile played at the edges of his mouth as he turned in his mother's direction and gave her a formal bow.

Natale dabbed at her eyes with her handkerchief as she wept silently.

Darling took Zarya's hand and returned her ring to her finger. "I expect it to stay there, this time."

"I will never again remove it. I promise."

Then to her complete surprise, he took her other hand and slid her mother's original wedding ring onto her finger—the one her father had been forced to sell for food.

Stunned, she gaped at something she'd never expected to see again. "Where did you find this?"

"I had Syn track it down since Pip lost your other one. It still has their initials and wedding date engraved inside the band…" He kissed her fingers. "I'm so sorry I lost the one you gave me. I know how much that ring meant to you."

Tears flowed down her cheeks. He'd lost his finger trying to protect it.

Before she could think better of it, she threw her arms around him and held him close while she wept on his shoulder.

"Um, Your Majesty," the priest cleared his throat, "we're not to that part of the ceremony yet."

Still, Darling held on to her and whispered in her ear with that deep, damaged voice that sent chills all over her body. "In all my life, I have only had one haven that sheltered me from my hell. One woman whose smile made me fly even after I'd hit the ground so hard that I didn't think I could ever stand again. There is nothing in this universe that could destroy me, except you, Zarya. You have taken a monster and made him human. My wounded soul was healed because of your smile. So long as I live and even beyond this life, I am and will always be ever yours."

Her tears fell even harder as she heard the sincerity behind those words.

"Ever yours" was what he'd engraved in the band of her wedding ring...

She tried to get a hold of herself, but it was impossible. "Gera and Ture are going to kill me for destroying all their hard work."

He gently wiped the tears from under her eyes. "Even with your makeup blurred, you are still the most beautiful woman I've ever seen."

"And you are the sexiest man who ever walked. Perfect in every way."

His smile widened. "I'm going to remind you of that later when you start fussing at me about all my annoying habits."

The priest cleared his throat again. "Majesties? Are we to finish?"

Darling winked at her. "What do you say, my lady? Are you ready to finalize this marriage?"

"Absolutely, my lord. And I look forward to many, many more years of scandalizing your gerents."

Do you love fiction with a supernatural twist?

Want the chance to hear news about your favourite authors (and the chance to win free books)?

Keri Arthur
S. G. Browne
P.C. Cast
Christine Feehan
Jacquelyn Frank
Thea Harrison
Larissa Ione
Darynda Jones
Sherrilyn Kenyon
Jackie Kessler
Jayne Ann Krentz and Jayne Castle
Martin Millar
Kat Richardson
J.R. Ward
David Wellington
Laura Wright

Then visit the Piatkus website and blog
www.piatkus.co.uk | www.piatkusbooks.net

And follow us on Facebook and Twitter
www.facebook.com/piatkusfiction | www.twitter.com/piatkusbooks

piatkus